I0634679

Time Never
Runs Back

Time Never Runs Back

A Novel

Nelson Martin

SUNSTONE
PRESS

SANTA FE

Sunstone books may be purchased for educational, business, or sales promotional use.
For information please write: Special Markets Department, Sunstone Press,
P.O. Box 2321, Santa Fe, New Mexico 87504-2321.

Cover painting by Sandra Martin
Book and Cover design › Vicki Ahl
Body typeface › Laurentian Std
Printed on acid-free paper
∞
eBook 978-1-61139-284-5

Library of Congress Cataloging-in-Publication Data

Martin, Nelson, 1938-
Time never runs back : a novel / By Nelson Martin.
    pages cm
    ISBN 978-0-86534-995-7 (softcover : alk. paper)
    I. Title.
    PS3613.A7836T56 2014
    813'.6--dc23

                        2014013931

WWW.SUNSTONEPRESS.COM
SUNSTONE PRESS / POST OFFICE BOX 2321 / SANTA FE, NM 87504-2321 /USA
(505) 988-4418 / ORDERS ONLY (800) 243-5644 / FAX (505) 988-1025

To the Memory of my father, Irvy "Abe" Martin, who taught me most of what I know that is important in life. He left this world almost twenty-five years ago, yet we share a smile most every day, even enjoy a visit from time to time.

A special thank you to Father Jack Vessels, SJ, a Catholic priest who recently came into this lifelong Protestant's life. Father Jack is a blessing to all he meets, whose bride is Life, who read my manuscript, and assisted me with Biblical references. The man is a true treasure.

And to Susan Mary Malone, Malone Editorial Services, the lady responsible for most of my ego bruises.

1

A busted-spring buckboard stood leaning on the far side of an *arboleda alamo*, its front spoke-wheels missing their iron rings, two mangy horses standing in their harness, near jaded from pulling their heavy load. The wood of the *alamo* was not much good for a cook stove, but the trunks and roots of the stately cottonwoods caught floating branches and limbs of fallen trees and mesquite during the annual flooding of the *Rio Grande*, making it a favorite spot for wood gatherers.

Seems Mother Nature's serenity has but one fault: it's easily shattered by man.

"No sirree, Rye, I ain't a'touchin' thet girl, much less beddin' her. Uglier'n a pile of fresh shit, 'n caint never say no words. Likely witched."

"Then by gawd, Seth, tie her up! Let's give us a try on her brother. I need me some bugger 'n I don't care if it's boy bugger or girl bugger. Let's get him!"

IB scampered away, but Rye yanked the rawhide lariat around his neck with such force that the boy fell on his backside. Seth wrapped a rope around Shelly Brom's waist, hurried back to IB, and was on him before he could scramble to his feet.

"I dibbies firsts this time, Rye. You got firsts on thet lil' gal last month."

IB screamed, "*Let my sister go.* Ya gotta let Shelly Brom go. She caint hurt you none 'n she's all I got. Let her—"

Rye backhanded him while Seth pulled at his britches. IB struggled, but the man's heavy frame pressed him to the loose gravel where the dry arroyo met the bottomland of the *Rio Grande* plain.

Shelly Brom untied the loosely wrapped hemp rope, backed up the arroyo, then turned and ran like a rabbit toward the Montgomery's dugout, her single pigtail streaming in the wind like yellow-gray straw. She found me and Coot milking the last of Papa's goats while he was out gathering strays.

She was frantic, tried to sign the cause of her grief, but we couldn't make sense of it though she made humping motions with her thin hips. Coot hugged her until she settled a might. "*Shhh*, Shelly Brom, calm down so we can understand. Is it IB?"

She nodded, pointing down the wagon road to the *Rio*. She signed: "Two men. Holding IB. Bad men."

Coot said, "Come on, Narlow. Grab up that grubax and let's see what's going on with IB."

IB and Shelly Brom were twins, the four of us having been born within six days of each other in March 1859. His thinker was on crooked while his sister bore a bubbled, purple birthmark that covered the entire right side of her face and neck. Mute as a buried anvil.

Shelly Brom could dern near outrun a cottontail on her stubby legs, so I had to move right along to keep her in sight. She stopped at the top of the last mesa, the copse of tall cottonwoods just past her at the bottom of the arroyo. I ran up, Coot trotting along behind. She pointed.

The men had pitched their camp on the nearside of the clearing, their loaded buckboard back a ways.

IB was stretched out on his stomach over a cottonwood log, trousers down, arms pulled tight, a lariat around his neck, all drawn taut by a huge man, while another was pleasuring himself at our friend's rear-end. They were laughing, hurrahing one another across the log.

Shelly Brom and I raced at them as the one pumping IB yelled out, "Hey, Rye, want some'a this?"

Rye shouted, "Watch out!" as I pounded down with the grubax on the man's skull with all the grit I could muster. The ax turned on the big man on the offside of the log, hit him a dozen times before he rolled in the gravel, a Navy revolver strapped to his waist. The ax kept pounding on him, beating his body, legs, arms. He turned to crawl away from the ax and its crazed bearer. I was witless with fright, scared shitless, awkward, clumsy as I scampered over the man covering IB at the log and their campfire, afraid the huge bastard would get to his feet before the ax could keep him down permanent-like. Coot was yelling, but the ax kept pounding at the man while he tried to crawl away, beating him as fast as the ax would swing in my hands. It found the nape of his neck, he slumped in a heap, but the ax kept whacking at his head, blood spurting with every lick.

Coot jerked me back. "Stop, Narlow. *Stop.* You'll kill him. *Look.* Look what you did to that big man's arm. You've broken it!"

I bent over, sucking for air, trembling.

How could I have broken his arm? It was big as a tree. I didn't break it, the ax broke it! The ax probed under the man's elbow. His lower arm appeared to be attached backassards, the bone of his upper arm torn through the skin, splintered, bleeding.

Coot said, "Dern it, Narlow, you should have waited for me to handle that big one. I'm more his size."

I leaned on my knees, quaking, took in a long breath, then tried to let it go but the air wouldn't pass. Wheezing, gazing at my lifelong friend, then at Shelly Brom. "Coot, I–I was afraid–afraid of him. Afraid this big one would get–get to his feet. More afraid that if he did, you'd yank this grubax out of my hand, hurt him–hurt him bad, kill both–both of them."

"Looks like you dern near got it done by yourself."

"Yeah, Coot, but they're still alive. If you'd'a been on the end of this ax handle, I couldn't have–couldn't have stopped you. You never quit. I couldn't–couldn't trust you."

The man on IB had not moved since the moment I hit him. Coot rolled him off of IB, lifted IB to his feet, cut the lariat off his neck. Shelly Brom pulled up IB's pants, snugged the rope at his waist, dusted him off, hugged her helpless brother.

Coot found a double-barrel shotgun in the boot of the buck board. "Here, Narlow, you'll likely need this to persuade these bastards to go on their way." He turned to our friend. "Come on, IB, let's go down to the *Rio*, do a little skinny-dippin' like we did when we were just little shavers. Clean ourselves up a bit. Want to?"

IB moaned his misery. "Y'all boys'll never like me no more. You seen what theys done to me. *You seen 'em!*" He slumped to the ground, his dapple-gray eyes gazing up, blinking at the bleak sky.

Coot said, "Is that so, IB? I didn't see anything. Narlow, you see anything? Shelly Brom?"

She shook her head, shrugged, signed that she hadn't seen anything.

I gazed at Coot, wondering what he and Shelly Brom were up to–then, "Oh, *yeah*. Nope, I didn't see a blessed thing, but it's sure warm to be the first day of the year. Other than that, I haven't been aware of or seen a blessed thing all this live-long day. Pretty dull round these parts."

Coot led IB by the arm, turned back at the edge of the clearing. "Narlow, you okay? Okay to leave you with these bastards? Territorial marshall's up in Socorro making his rounds, no lawman to turn them over to. Can't put them in your papa's care. He'd kill 'em, and that might cause him some grief. You'll let them go on their way, that right? I can depend on that?"

"Yeah–yeah, sure. You boys take your time. Won't be anyone here but me

9

and Shelly Brom when you get back. That is if I can ever get my air."

I stepped over the log and relieved the big man of an old Navy revolver at his belt, found a wooden bucket in the buckboard, and asked Shelly Brom to fetch me a pail of water from the *Rio* while I kicked life back in their campfire.

"Water 'em down good, Shelly Brom. Nap time's over. Besides, we have business with these gents."

The big man with the busted arm twitched, yelped. The one who had been on IB came around first, rolled over, sat, bewildered, tasted the blood streaming off his nose.

I said, "Pull your britches up. There's a lady among us."

He glanced at the shotgun, stretched out in the gravel, fumbled his britches back up, got himself more presentable. He never took his gaze off the hollow, black eyes of the double-barrel, his hand waving in front of him as if to move the barrel away.

"What's your name?" I asked.

Still waving his hand, he said, "Huh?"

"You heard me. What's your name, damn it?"

"Seth. Seth Byrne."

"Your friend's name is Rye. What's his surname?"

"His what?"

"His family name. His *last* name."

"Green. Rye Green."

"Your buckboard's loaded with sacks of flour and beans, a barrel of salt pork. Expensive stuff. Too much for the two of you. Steal it?"

"Aw hell no. What do you take us for, highwaymen? We's been down El Paso way. Sent down there by the wagon master of a bunch'a miners camped up north of Dona. We's headed for the far side of the Arizona territory. Got us a claim." He snickered. "Maybe strike it rich."

The man named Rye sat up, bolted to his feet, staggered, then slumped to the bloody ground, befuddled, screamed when his arm fell in his lap.

I sat on the log where I could keep an eye on both of them, swinging the shotgun back and forth between them.

Seth snickered. "Hey now, boy. Be careful with that thing. I done filed them triggers down pretty fine. Theys mighty techy, don'cha know. Holes in the ends of them barrels look like stove pipes. Mind pointing that thang away?" He snickered again.

"Don't snicker, you snake. It irritates me. Besides, this ain't a snickering matter. You're in a heap of trouble. Know that? Pretty deep pickle vat, I'd say." I kicked sand in his face. "You bastard! Treating my friend like that. A defenseless waif. Pick on someone who can defend himself, you bastard-of-a-turd!" I kicked at him again.

Rye's face was drawn up in pain like a sun-baked prune, but he snickered. "Aw, we was just funnin' thet boy. Caint you boys take a little tease?" He snickered again. "Dint mean no harm."

"Don't snicker. I already told your friend this ain't no snickering matter."

Seth grinned. "How old'r you, boy?"

"Can't see why that would interest you, might even hurt your feelings knowing you've been bested by a mere boy and a girl. But, if you gotta know, I'm fourteen. She and her brother's both fourteen as well. So's my friend with him."

He shook his head. "Damn, Rye. Jest shithead kids."

I kept the shotgun pointed at them with one hand, picked up a stick at the fire's edge and stirred it back to life. "If my papa was here, I believe he'd say it'd be right fitting to give you a spoon of your own medicine."

"Who's your papa, boy?" Seth asked. "Caint be much of a man if yor all he has to show for his loins."

"Abe Montgomery. My friend's daddy was Orville Boldt. Our granddaddies are Shelby Montgomery and Skinner Boldt. Still alive. Hell for stout. Piss on your liver raw, eat it raw. If you like, I'll fetch 'em for you. They'd be pleased to make your acquaintance."

Seth scoffed. "Never heard tell of any of them shitass skunks."

Rye struggled to his feet, cradling his useless arm. "The Montgomerys and the Boldts? I dang certain heard of them. Heard 'bout them at Shiloh, Injun wars 'n sech. Mean sumbiches. *Terrible* mean. Meaner'n them goddamn Comanches o'vr at San Antone my daddy tolt me 'bout what happened back in '38. Boy, me 'n Seth, we don' like to be no trouble to nobody. 'Specially you gentlemen and this here purty lady. Now, if you don't mind, we'll just be moseyin' on, that is if you don' mind, Mr. Montgomery."

"*Mr.* Montgomery? *Ha.* I wish my friend was here to hear that. But come to think of it, I do mind. Mind a lot. *Sit down.* Stay there until I tell you otherwise. Stand up again and I'll empty both barrels in your gut. Cut your worthless hide in two. And don't call me son, you lowlife. You've got a busted arm for your trouble. Something to remember us by, though you'll likely lose the use of it without a doctor to set it proper.

Right now, we're going to give your partner here a little remembrance as well. Something he'll bear in mind while bouncing down this rough old river road on the hard-rock board seat of that buckboard. When we get that done, you can go your way, explain your condition and circumstances to your wagon master. The territorial marshal'll be coming down this way in a month or two, we'll give him your names and descriptions, tell him where you're heading, what you were doing to our friend. Maybe he'll go after you, maybe he won't."

Seth said, "Well, thet's right kindly of you, Mr. Montgomery."

Rye felt around his waist with his one good hand. "Whur's my Navy? My daddy gimme that revolver—want it back!"

"What, this rusty old thing?" I said as I handed the revolver to Shelly Brom, told her to cock it, then stepped over to a nearby yucca and broke off a dry stalk, stabbed it deep in the coals. "Seth, stand up and drop your drawers and be quick about it."

He stood, but balked. "I ain't droppin' my drawers for no boy. No sirree!"

I shoved the double-barrel in his paunch. "You weren't bashful about dropping them when you had my friend draped over that log. Drop your drawers! If you don't, I'll send this young lady back home to fetch her pet porcupine, and we'll have you fornicating that pig before you can say turtle feathers. *Now, get on with it.* You can be on your way after you drop your drawers."

Shelly Brom brushed back her straw-yellow bangs, licked her lips, leveled the revolver square at his face with two rough, steady hands. I was scared to death and she was as cool as anchor ice.

Her jaw tightened, while Seth's tobacco-drooled jaw dropped. He loosened the rope at his waist, and his britches dropped to the gravel.

I tested the yucca stalk's flame, pointed with it. "Bend over that log and spread your cheeks."

Seth knelt in front of the log, then jumped to his feet. "I ain't gonna. Ain't gonna even if you kilt me."

"Get down there!"

Rye shouted, "Best do what he says, Seth, cuz them boys' menfolk'll do worser. Come after us like'a pack of wolves drawin' 'n quarterin' a rabbit. Bend over that goddamn log! Don't be a sissy 'bout it."

Seth stood trembling, shouted, "No, I ain't gonna," then bent over to pull up his britches. I nudged him with my boot and before he could get off the log, he was sporting a flaming yucca stalk poking out between the cheeks of his ass.

He lay in the gravel, moaning, sobbing. "You done took my man away from me. I'm ruint."

"*Get up*, you son-of-a-turd-sucking-bitch Your manhood is still with you, but if you two bastards don't get in that buckboard and get yourselves out of here pretty dern fast, our menfolk will dern sure relieve you of what little manhood you ever possessed."

2

Coot and I stayed close to the twins for a time, not wanting IB to dwell on it, get down on himself. Coot stayed closer than me as his mama's farm was right next to their place, and Papa's goat ranch was far across the valley in the high-desert country where the mountain gave way to steep mesas cut through by deep arroyos leading to the *Rio Grande*.

I never did get around to telling Papa about all that business. He was a kindly man, crystal, gray-blue-honest eyes, probably the best educated man in the Mesilla Valley. Read every book he got his hands on, the entire library owned by Old Man Simeon Hart. But Abe Montgomery was quick to rile about such goings-on, widely known never to leave a slight go unattended.

But, I was sorely tempted to talk to Papa about it, 'cause he'd help me work through it. I couldn't shake my actions with the grubax, the memory of Seth groveling in the gravel with a flaming yucca stalk waving in the breeze taunted me.

Why didn't I just let them go like Coot said? But what really took me to my knees was my fear that I was becoming just like my mama—mean, brutal, cruel as a polecat teasing a crippled lizard.

Coot kept telling me that JB would forget his torment, pointing out that he never remembered to even tie his shoes. But Papa says that time never runs back, his way of saying some things cannot be forgotten or forgiven.

Shelly Brom's disfigurement glowed the left side of her face, but with all the attention we showered on her and IB, she seemed to glow all over like a smoldering mesquite ember.

One evening at sunset, I told her that being around her was like being in the presence of a curtain of rain dancing across an empty barnyard, swirling in the light wind as if teased and guided along its path by God's hand. She pressed down her feed sack dress, glowing like that setting sun. Coot told me I'd best watch talk like that or I'd be soon hitched. But the girl was special, and Coot agreed.

Then one day, she was sitting by her ditch, stood, scrambled over to pick up a stone to hurl at a mourning dove, knocked him out of the sky with the flip of her wrist, stooped to retrieve it, obviously unaware that the back of her dress was spotted with blood.

Coot said, "Uh, Shelly Brom, the back of your dress, it . . . it's . . ." She twisted around, pulled at her dress, glanced down, became frantic, turned to bolt from our presence. Coot grabbed, cradled her. Her body shook, her silent sobs choking both Coot and me.

"It's all right, Shelly Brom. You're all right. All of this was probably brought on sudden-like by your grief and fear for IB. But in any case, there's nothing to be afraid of, nothing to be ashamed of. In fact, you know what, Shelly Brom?"

She gazed up in Coot's eyes, wiped her own with her stubby hand. "Shelly Brom, this means you're a woman. Shelly Brom, you're no longer a girl. You're a woman, a real *woman*."

I gazed at the two of them. How could Coot be so calm? Who taught him to be so kind, so caring, and compassionate to a girl who just experienced a life-changing event in every young girl's life without a grown woman to explain things to her? And, how in blazes did he know? I had no idea, but I was proud of him. More important, I was proud *for* my lifelong friend.

Shelly Brom and IB lived in a clapboard shack at the top of a sandhill overlooking the valley, willed solely to her by their mama. She died four years ago just before the twins turned ten. Some folks made motions of taking them in, but then I don't recall many pressing the issue, and Papa doubted the intentions of those few. Shelly Brom wouldn't have tolerated it anyway.

Their parents were Charlie and Ida Mae Crane. Charlie, the mister, got himself shot in a duel shortly before Mrs. Crane birthed the twins. Of course, that was before Coot and I came along as well, but we heard rumors, talk that Coot's daddy, Orville Boldt, might have been carrying on with Mrs. Crane. She was far from what might be described as a looker, fact is, she was an old crone, boot-ugly. Coot and I gave that notion scant credence.

The Crane Place was 200-acres, exact size as the Coot's mama's farm, with one exception: The Boldt farm was known as the best piece of ground in the valley, while the Crane holdings were 197-acres of sandhill, and a sprinkled three-acres of bottomland. That made not a scosh of never-mind to IB—"Two hundred acres is 200-acres."

IB's thinker was a bit off-plumb, but he had a wondrous manner with animals. They sensed his kindredship. Coot's daddy died when we were eight, but before that sad day, he'd taught IB to handle a team of sixteen-hand mules better that any man around. Whether it was pulling a plow, a drag, pulling stumps, or handling a fresno, neighboring farmers were quick to pay IB a quarter a day when they had a chore they needed doing, done right the first time.

IB loved those old black mules, and judging how they nuzzled him, and positioned themselves between him and strangers, you might conclude they returned his worship in kind.

Shelly Brom tended her three-acre garden and fed their stewpot with a daily cottontail she brought home with the slingshot she kept tied at her waist. Coot's daddy was also a renowned shot with that lowly, ancient leather device, the same contraption that David used to even things while slaying the giant.

Rumors about Orville Boldt and Ida Mae Crane began to die off before we were even near grown, but Coot's mama kept it going best she could, even forbade Coot to step foot on ground owned by a Crane. After his daddy died, Coot was her only hope, her only hand. Besides, Coot was never one to be bossed; he was a burly one, quick to box the ears of some idiot that broached the subject of a possible connection between the Boldts and the Cranes in his presence.

Coot was also truthful, faced life square-on—about everything but that. He said once, "Narlow, your papa always said we were joined at the hip at birth like a couple of Siamese twins he saw one time in a traveling road-show. Uncle Abe always smiles when he says we're like two peas in a pod. No, not blood brothers, but as close as two boys could ever be. And maybe you're just bigger'n me about things like this, but, I'll never be big enough to admit that IB and Shelly Brom are my kin. Never be man enough."

3

Papa limped up to the horse corral, climbed the pole fence, sat beside me, rubbing his thigh.

"Papa, your leg's not healing like I'd suspect. You always mend real fast."

"Not as young as I used to be, son. You'll learn soon enough about that." He grinned, his slate-gray eyes taking in his all-time favorite horse, Traveler, a six-year-old, dapple-gray gelding. "Come here, you jawsel-jawed buzzard bait. Traveler, tell me what's going on behind those bright, black eyes of yours. You're a smart one. Let's hear it. Whisper in my ear like you did when you were a spindly legged colt."

Papa raised him, named him in honor of General Robert E. Lee's own war horse that he rode throughout the Civil War.

Traveler's muzzle came up, his lips and whiskers caressing the side of Papa's face, whimpering a soft low nicker, almost a snicker, a whiney, an understanding known only to the two of them.

Papa nodded. "Uh-huh. *Really?* You don't say!" Then pulled back and waved the gelding off with his hat. "Aw, horse feathers, Traveler! That's the dangdest load of balderdash you ever came up with. Go on about your business, think up another lie to tell your only true friend."

He whinnied, hunched and gamboled off to the far side of the corral. Papa laughed.

"Papa, you said we had to fix the washout behind the barns and pens before leaving for the Black River next month. Only three weeks to go, and we've got the nannies to tend to as well. Too much work for me on the end of a shovel, and Fernando Valdes has to mind the main herd at Bishop's Cap. How are we going to move all that gravel back in place before we strike out?"

"I've been thinking on that. That old rusty fresno scoop pulled behind our mules can move more dirt and gravel in an afternoon than two men with shovels can get done in a month of Sundays. Suppose we could get Coot to come over and lend a hand?"

***

At sunup, I set off to fetch Coot west of the *Rio* and half-a-day's ride upstream. When I rode up, Coot was cutting wood for his mama's cook stove, his uncle Doyl busy hurrahing him, offering advice on proper wood-stacking techniques, claimed to be an expert in that regard. Uncle Doyl came to the Boldt farm not long after his brother, Orville died, Coot's daddy. His mission was not work related, nor did he have his sights set on his brother's widow. He was there for Coot. Without Uncle Doyl, Coot wouldn't hang around for long. Coot had a younger, lazy brother, Richard, and a demanding mother who blamed Coot for everything.

Uncle Doyl smiled when he saw me ride up. "Get yourself down off yor daddy's gray, boy. Set yourself down over here in the shade, help me instruct this shiftless friend of yors. Takes two able-bodied men to keep Coot on the straight and narrow."

Coot stuck his ax in the chopping block, shook his head, grinned, took off his hat, and wiped his brow with a bandana. I helped myself to a dipper of cool water, took a dipper to Coot, then plopped myself down beside Uncle Doyl.

"What brings you all the way over here from your papa's place, Narlow? Lost? Want to hire out helping Coot chop firewood?" He laughed, slapped me on the back. "You and your papa 'bout ready to head for the Black River next month? Hope so, cuz this work's 'bout got me beat down to my knees."

I grinned, exercising caution to keep from being dragged into one of his traps he sprung on us boys at every turn.

"Well, sir, about a month ago, the *arroyo* flooded a good one out back of Papa's horse pens and barns, cut the bank within five-feet of the fence. Papa says we just gotta fix it before taking off for the Black River next month. Then Papa up and bruised his leg three days ago, and he's still limping around pretty bad. Papa thought maybe between his two big mules and his fresno scoop, Coot and me, that we could take care of that chore in less than a day's time."

Uncle Doyl laughed. "Yeah, I reckon your papa and four stout mules like the four of you could get that chore done all right. I can stay around here and watch Coot's woodpile, while he lends your papa a hand, lazy as Coot be, that is."

Coot promised to leave the next morning, long before sunup.

As I turned Traveler to head back home, Uncle Doyl hollered out, "Hey, Narlow, tell your papa that I have a message for him."

I stopped, swiveled in the saddle. "What's that, Uncle Doyl?"

"Tell him that Doyl Boldt says, 'Abe Martin, me 'n Coot will be waiting at the crossing above La Mesa, mules packed to the sky, four jugs of my special, home-grown sour mash riding safe and secure. Be there early of a morning, sixteenth of next month. All y'all don't be late, ya hear me, boy?"

***

Coot didn't show by noon, so I rode out looking for him, see if he needed help. Less than an hour out, I spied him crossing the *Rio* at Sloan Crossing. He rode up, his trousers burned off halfway to his knees, his boots showing blister spots as well.

"Sorry I'm late. Old Man Gillett was burning weeds in his ditch and it got away from him. Wind came up from the west, spread that fire clear across our dry grass pasture like a cyclone. By the time Uncle Doyl and I got it stomped out, that fire was within fifty feet of our hay barn."

"Well, looks like that crazy, ill-tempered old buzzard owes you a pair of boots and some new britches."

"Yeah, Narlow, I'll let you collect that dollar from that ornery old tightwad."

"No, I'll pass. Grouchy old toot. That's why all three of his friends call him, *Grunion*."

When we rode into Papa's corrals, he said, "Well, Coot, I see Narlow found you all right."

"Yes, sir, Uncle Abe, he found me all right. You'll have to forgive me. Didn't mean to be here so late in the day."

"Well, son, by the looks of your boots and britches, looks like you've been walking in Nebuchadnezzar's furnace. Been walking in fire, have you, boy?" Papa waved off his question, turned and headed for the barn to hitch-up his mules, a pair he'd had since they were just long-eared shavers. We watched him walk away, limping pretty bad.

"Dang, Narlow, you told me that Uncle Abe hurt his leg, but it looks like he hurt it pretty bad, judging by his limp."

"Oh, he's already a bunch better. Yesterday, he could hardly get around without a walking stick."

We helped Papa harness Jeff and Jiggs, a mirrored pair of sixteen-hand, ten-year-old mules, then Papa backed them up to the fresno.

"Narlow, you ride up here on Jeff. Coot, you're bigger, you handle the fresno, and I'll try to help you best I can. Be careful of that handle, don't hold it between your legs, or we'll be calling you, Miss Cooty. If that scoop hits a hitch-rock and you don't have your wits about you, eyes gawking around at the moon, the handle of that fresno will sail you right up on the back of old Jiggs."

After a near mishap or two, Coot got pretty good on the handle of that testy old fresno. By nightfall, we had the flood damage repaired to Papa's satisfaction.

"Come on, boys. Soon as we curry-down these mules, set some grain and hay before them, I'll see what Narlow's mama has to offer two starving boys."

Papa always said we could eat a cow if a big enough man was around to hold her head. Mama only showed herself one time that whole afternoon. Caught her peeking past the goat skin that served as a door to our dugout. Never a howdy to Coot, not even a pail of water. That was plenty all right with me. If she wasn't giving me the silent treatment, she was calling me a son-of-a-bitch, "a no-count half-breed, just like your no-count half-breed father."

Mama was a strange one. A man might think she as also not too bright, but that man best not sell her too short. But I often wondered that if her son was a s.o.b., what did that make her? Why didn't she think that through? And, yes, Papa was a half-breed—half white, half Chiricahua Apache. And yes, I was a half-breed, but if that was my bloodline, how could that be if mama was not also a half-breed? Which she was—half white, half Comanche. Whole passel of half-breeds living around that dugout, tending upwards of 4,000 goats.

Papa brought out a pot of venison stew along with the necessary hardware, a quart jar of canned peaches under his arm. We ate while Papa hurrahed Coot unmercifully.

"Well, Shadrach, you going to tell me how you got your britches burned and scorched? How you got your boots near burned off your feet? Your mama's liable to tan your hide."

Coot grinned. "Shadrach? How so, Uncle Abe?"

"You telling me that you don't remember in the Book of Daniel, and Nebuchadnezzar had Shadrach and two of his cohorts thrown in a fiery furnace, and they walked right out of that inferno? You don't recall that?" Papa laughed. "Shadrach fits you just fine. Your uncle Doyl will like that real fine. Can't wait to tell him next month."

✳✳✳

Coot bedded down with me in the hayloft. I took up the habit of claiming it as my personal sleeping quarters, started that when Mama took a horse quirt to me late one evening as I was finishing up my chores in the milking shed. I was twelve, back then. Papa was off with Fernando Valdez at the time. I tried to keep it pushed way back in my dark place. I wanted to tell Coot about it, but lately, every time I told him I had something serious to tell him, he'd laugh, ask if I was taking piano lessons.

✳✳✳

Before sunup the next morning, Coot threw my blanket at me, asked if I was looking forward to our annual trip up to the Black River.

"Mercy, yes! A steady diet of my mother's silence wears on me. If something ever happened to Papa, I'd be gone in a flash, leave with Fernando Valdez, go wherever he lead me. I don't know what's eating on her, what I ever did to her—besides being born, that is."

He kicked the straw at his feet. "Aw, Narlow, you dwell too much on stuff like that. I think all women are crazy. My mother's not near as mean as your mama, but I do all the work around our place. *Every* drop of it, while my little brother never lifts a finger. Mama says, 'Richard's too little to work all day at the end of a shovel.' When I remind her that I've been cleaning water ditches since I was six, and Richard's now fourteen, she ignores me, says, 'Lil' Richard's special.' Sometimes I'd sure like to bust Special Lil' Richard's head and—"

"Now look who's dwelling on whose stuff."

4

Early Manhood Y Hombres del Campo
Northwest of the Pass April 16, 1875

Yes, it was April 1875. I'm not usually that certain about dates, but Coot and I'd just turned sixteen. Turning sixteen is important for any man, and I can only suppose it's important for the ladies as well, but I've no experience in that regard. My little sister, Mary Jewell died of *viruela* long before she could even dream of being that old. I didn't even know the nature of *viruela* until last fall when I heard a neighbor lady explain it being the same as smallpox.

Coot and I hadn't a clue what the balance of 1875 had in store for us—important, life-turning events of great proportions for two boys. Events that grab and hold tight as pine sap stuck to your underarm curl if you're not careful while napping under a big ol' oozing tree. We were tender and tough, bristling with the spirit of youth minus wisdom's anchor. Coot always lorded it over me that he was older, he got the start on me by six days to be exact. But when we grew older, I got even, called him the Old Man.

For as long as I could remember, Coot and I, my papa, Coot's Uncle Doyl, and Coot's daddy before he died, had trailed on horseback northwest out of The Pass, heading for our annual hunting trip in the White Mountains on the eastern edge of the Arizona Territory. We followed the menfolk up there every year, generally be gone a shade over two months. It was serious business as our families depended on the hunt for their year's supply of meat. Leastways that's what Coot and I were led to believe. Papa had over 2,000 prime goats on his 9,000-acre dry, high-desert ranch, land he leased from Old Man Zach White. If we had so many goats, why did Papa go on an annual meat hunt? Three good reasons come to mind: One, Papa's goats were for selling, not for our table except on special occasion, though my mama never observed any; two, those nanny goats gave lots of rich milk, and the *asadero* cheese we made from clabbered goat's milk sold for a premium in El Paso; but the third, and *by far* the most important reason Papa took off for two months out of every year, was my mama. *That* was reason enough for any sane man. Some folks said Mama might be a couple of bubbles off plumb, but mean or crazy, it's hard to tell the difference when one was subjected to a daily dose of that woman's cruel ways. Papa's two-month reprieve would put a broad smile on his face wide enough that you could drive a team of horses through. That grin, and his iron-stout will, had to see him through 'til next spring.

We could count on long hard days in the saddle, but for two strong boys, it was all fun and challenge, a chance to prove our grit, our mettle. Over the years, we got to where we could do as much work as the menfolk, took a lot of pride in that. While we were still a long way from our prime, we were strong as Longhorn bulls. Coot had shot up like a tall ol' cornstalk, and everyone just assumed he would be six-feet-five like his daddy. But Coot's cornstalk had already cropped off a shade less than six-feet. Lately, I had taken up where Coot left off, and I was as tall as Papa at six-two, but not near as stout, a fact I knew without testing the point.

Our destination was the confluence of the Black River and Pacheta Creek, a gurgling, clear-running little stream. The difficult trip on horseback took us upward of eight days, the weather having more than a little to say about our pace. After crossing the Frisco River's gentle headwaters, we passed through meadows ten miles wide, forty long, a God-given tread of green. Meadows of unending grasses of all varieties, smells, and tastes, tall dandelions peeking their bright yellow heads through the grasses, while tucked below, strawberry blossoms hiding their white.

We approached Rattlesnake Point from the northeast, trying to gauge our arrival at the Point with enough daylight to allow us to tiptoe the horses and mules down the steep, narrow trail before dark. Spring nights on the Point would always bring heavy frost, frozen water in our canteens. You could just about see forever from that high promontory.

One time Coot and I were resting our horses before going down the trail to the river. Far below, a mated pair of Mexican eagles, flying golden, playing, darting, daring, catching an updraft, sailing them high above. They reached out to each other, locked talons, falling in a love swirl, a gyrating wheel, talons loosening, parting at the last moment, glided apart, swooped in a high arc above us.

Papa was sitting his horse behind us. "Boys, you just witnessed a rare ritual of play I have only witnessed once before in my entire life. Mighty special."

The narrow trail off Rattlesnake Point went through a crack in a rock ledge that fell off fifty-feet near straight down, then gentled out its slope along a foot-wide hogback ridge to the meadow where the Black River ran, its flow flashed between the pines and oaks. From the top of Rattlesnake Point, you could make out a line shack, old beat-up, rusted-tin roof, lonely, forlorn. It housed our meat-drying racks, Uncle Doyl's prized dutch ovens, ropes, and other gear that we left behind last season. The sight of that line shack would invariably bring wet to my eyes. I'd bite my lip, look away from the men so they wouldn't see. Every year I'd promise myself not to let it affect me so, and every year I'd do the same silly thing, asking myself, why Lord? Why does that dad-gum line shack strike me down to my knees?

The line shack's only company was the Black River and Pacheta Creek flowing close by. The Black didn't flow deep at all, but dark, in places so smooth little flaws of wind-whipped patches of still water stirred into fleets of ripples. The forest was a vigorous mottle of trees, a true "coat of many colors," mostly Ponderosa pine towering above a sprinkling of maples, and aspens, fluttering yellow-lime, heavy oak groves along the riverbank. The meadow, shape of a serving dish, would come to life during our early spring visits, grasses lying under a veiled profusion of flowers, red, yellow, blue, purple, and fragrances, heady, pungent, sweet as hay. In wet years, all manner of ferns grew in the deep shadows of the tall pines, like a thick, green comforter. It seemed a shame to ride our horses and mules through that blanket of lush, as the animals stomped the ferns flat to the ground, and every dad-gum year Coot would catch me fretting over those ferns. He'd grin and call out, "Quit worrying about those ferns, Narlow. They'll grow back in a day or two, and you'll never know we passed this way." But I knew, no doubt the ferns knew of our approach, our passing, our lack of respect for their private rest.

The Black River formed an S-curve above our camp, flowing north to south at our headquarters area to the line shack, on past to Pacheta Creek. At that point, the river made a sharp turn to the east for 200-yards. There it met a sheer granite cliff, tremendous, unforgiving, that turned the flow back north for a wandering mile, then began its meander to the west past Bear Wallow Creek for a hundred miles, eventually catching up with the Salt River.

It was a special place, visited by no white men, only an occasional Apache, of whom we had no fear in this remote mark. The People had known our fathers, our grandfathers for nearly a half-century, knowing them to be truthful men who admired the Apache, their ways. Our only visitor was a tall, lanky Apache named Many Fast Feet Two Sticks. No other visitors came to our camp.

Like most places in the west, Rattlesnake Point and the meadow below was named with a purpose in mind. Rattlers in the usual places waited along game trails for an unwary meal to pass by, most often at the river's edge. The area seemed to be a perfect nursery for the little varmints, a mottled gray-black, the shape and texture of a pine twig. Rattlesnakes during daylight were not much concern to us. It was the town folks who were bitten, while a nighttime encounter with a serpentine of its ilk was a peril to all. Those rattlers were joined by a cautious list of other cold-blooded creatures, black widows, scorpions, centipedes, as well as the common honeybee and wasp.

One day, Coot and I had seen several rattlers before the sun was an hour high. I asked, "Coot, you ever wonder why all poisonous critters are cold-blooded, the kind of animal that relies on the sun for its warmth?"

"No."

I asked, "You've never once wondered about that? You're telling me that you didn't know that?"

He said, "I know it, but I've never wondered about it, and that's what you asked me."

I asked, "I wonder why that is so?"

Coot replied, "I've noticed that a considerable number of the two-legged, warm-blooded variety have ice sickles in their veins, but I've never wondered about that either."

I started, "I wonder . . ."

He grinned. "You wonder too much."

That night we bedded down. "Hey, Coot, listen to the wind whinny through those big ol' pines. I heard it said that every tree has a voice that speaks when the wind passes by. It sure seems to me that pine trees have the most to say by the rush

23

of wind through their high boughs. And they have stories and centuries of secrets to tell. But, you gotta be real quiet and listen close."

"Well, then, I reckon we'll never hear those centuries of secrets."

"You know, Coot, you don't know near as much as you credit yourself with."

"Yeah? Like what?'

"Well, like you don't know that . . . that . . . that birds ain't got a belly button."

"Heck, I know that." He rolled over, propped up his head on his burly fist. "Everybody knows that."

"I don't think so, and I sure never heard you say it."

We hunted every other day, using the off-day to rest our horses and mules while we prepared our kill for the long trip back to the Pass. We jerked thousands of pounds of elk, deer, and bear meat. The jerked meat was much lighter to haul, while retaining its flavor, richness, its nutrients. We cut it in thin strips, hung them on our racks to dry for a couple of days in the sun and the smoke of our fire, making a tasty pemmican from ground jerky, suet, berries, and a smidgen of honey. Papa saw to it that nothing went to waste. He was never a man to pick many nits, but he was a certain nit-picker when it came to Nature's bounty, her gifts.

Once Papa, armed only with a barrel stave, took on two men for shooting a hummingbird—blew that hummer to smithereens with a double-barrel shotgun, they did. Papa boxed those men's ears good, making me fearful he'd do 'em in. I imagine that prospect entered their heads as well, and they had to be real proud that Papa couldn't get his hands on a grub-ax handle with hefty-more authority than the barrel stave he whipped them with.

Through puffed, bleeding lips, one of them said, "Mister, we were just funnin'."

The men's humor was lost on Papa. He often said, "God put His animals under our care. He invites us to use what we need, but we will not waste nor abuse them."

Papa was lank, knotty, tough as a mesquite rail, hands that never witnessed gloves, the self-confidence of an iron wagon bar. We boys may have had occasion to be overly proud of our ever-increasing knowledge and wisdom, but we were ever-mindful that compared to Papa, we were yet as the sun is to two faraway stars.

Coot's uncle Doyl, now he was a sight. Everything about Uncle Doyl was grin and fun, the leanest, lankiest man I ever saw. He was straight as a wagon tongue, long as a wagon track, a man dedicated to teasing us boys without mercy. Like one day, Coot and me were skinny-dippin' in the Black River on a hot afternoon. We were just little tadpole-boys back then. That cold water would make you suck up your belly and catch your breath, even if you just stuck a toe in its chill.

Uncle Doyl hollered out over the roar of the water, "You boys don't seem to be too worried about those turtles—you boys are sure brave. Yep, mighty brave—mighty brave little tykes."

Coot and I dog-paddled over to the riverbank, trying to splash him, but he was always too quick for us. "Why do you think we're so brave, Uncle Doyl? There ain't no turtles in this river. This water's too cold for turtles, you know that, Uncle Doyl—ain't nuthin' in this water to be a'scairt of."

His eyebrows arched. "Oh, you just think there's no turtles under that water, but they're there, sure as I'm standing on this rock ledge. Thing about those particular turtles is you never know they're there until they sneak up on you. They're little buggers, but they just happen to be snappin' turtles—you best watch 'em real close-like, that's my recommendation."

We laughed. "Aw, Uncle Doyl, you beat all. You're just funnin' us. We ain't a'scairt of 'em. Why don't you ever come in and go skinny-dippin' with us, Uncle Doyl? Bet you're scairt to death of those mean old turtles, ain't you, Uncle Doyl?"

He jerked up straight. "Dern tootin' I'm sceered of them snappin' turtles. Why, when I was a boy, me and this other boy, Henry Hawkins, we went skinny-dippin' in this very river, and there were turtles all over the place. They were hiding in that dark water just like they are this very minute—probably these here turtles' grandpas and grandmas. Anyway, we'd been swimm'n for just a bit, when of a sudden, little Henry, he lets out a yelp you could hear five miles upstream.

Uncle Doyle laughed, pointed downstream. "He stood up in the river just over yonder and run back a'shore over there by that willer yonder, holding real tight to his private parts as he run a'shore. I followed him to see what was the matter with my little friend, and do you know that one of them snappin' turtles had snapped on to little Henry's prune, grabbed a'holt, just a'danglin' there. Had a devil of a time getting that turtle to turn loose of poor Henry's prune—dang near bit it plumb off."

Coot and I grabbed our prunes, high-tailed it out of there *right now*. Took us a number of years before we gathered up enough nerve to do any serious skinny-dippin' in that river again.

Uncle Doyl laughed at just about anything. "Life is too short to be taken too seriously." Then he'd say, "Never, never, never say you're sorry." He considered an apology a sign of weakness. Don't do anything you'll be sorry for or ashamed of. If you do, live with it as just being part of you. Look it square in the eye, confess it, if it requires confessing, but never apologize. Apologies wouldn't be fitt'n. Coot adopted that credo. "Sorry" was a word I never heard him say.

Our headquarters centered on an ancient oak that had fallen at least a century ago. Papa said that oak was lying right there the first time he came here as a boy in 1822. The ground stayed damp under the cover of heavy pines, shielding the ancient oak from the summer sun, the winter months covering it under snow and ice. That big old tree saved us from many a soaking rain, that's a certain. We used canvas tarpaulins to cover the oak's heavy limbs, scraps of elk and buffalo hides still draped, dangling from those dark limbs that our very own granddaddies used so long ago. That fallen oak was about the most wondrous thing in the whole world to Coot and me. When we were kids, we were convinced that old tree was the heavy bones and bleached skin of Kipling's *Elephints haulin' teak, In the sludgy, squdgy creek*.

Every morning, long before sunup, I was up, kicking life back into the coals we banked up in the fire pit the night before. Early mornings were always special, maybe because Papa was always quoting a little ditty, "The breeze at dawn has secrets to tell you. Don't go back to sleep, you cannot afford it." While I wasn't certain the early breeze ever told me its secrets, I was always up early to hear them should they take a notion to whisper in my ready ear. While still in my covers, I'd think, there's something happening out there, something to see. Curiosity always got the best of me.

Uncle Doyl was always up before sunup himself, and when Uncle Doyl was up, everybody was up. Papa was always awake hours before sunup, but he enjoyed lying there in his covers, thinking, dreaming. Uncle Doyl climbed out of his bedroll, put on his boots, stood, stretched, and came over to the fire. Before he even sat down, he'd pick up a stick and chunk it at Coot. "Get outta them covers, boy. Come on, let's see 'em, Coot—both hands out of the covers. Come on, let go of yourself and get up here, boy." He'd chunk a stick at Papa. "Come on, Abe—come on over here 'n sit yourself. Got something bother'n me 'n need your recommendation."

I started the coffee and warmed the leftovers from last night's supper for our breakfast. Papa said I made the best coffee in our outfit because I made it while I listened to the wind. "Or parting it," Coot would say off to the side. I'd pour Papa and Uncle Doyl a scalding hot cup of coffee, and as surely as I'd hand Uncle Doyl his cup, he'd laugh and say, "Narlow, yo'r papa's right about most things, especially yo'r coffee, mainly cuz it ain't timid. I swear this stuff'd float a horseshoe."

After a gallon of coffee, Papa and Uncle Doyl would saunter down to the Pacheta to shave. Cleanliness never played second fiddle to those men, whatever the inconvenience. Coot started joining the ritual last spring. I sported only a few sprigs of sparse blonde whiskers, but I had to admit Coot had a full black beard when he was just fifteen.

The four of us hunted and worked well together, all trying to see who could kill the most game that day, who could skin-out an elk the fastest without the help of others. We'd take a noon break to rest a bit and eat, Papa relishing that time to read, most times not even coming back to camp to eat. He'd sit his big, gray horse, Traveler, or lie down by the river, and read whichever book he brought along. Papa was with the General, but never talked about that grisly horror of the War. Sometimes I'd wander off to find Papa, wondering what he was doing, what manner of thoughts would be going through his mind. I'd never disturb him, contenting myself to just sit and watch Papa from a distance, wondering about that great man, wondering if I'd ever measure up to his equal.

Soon the noon break was over, Uncle Doyl would say, "Narlow, wrap up a chunk of that venison in a cloth, and I'll take it out to your papa. He's thin enough, don't need to be missing his feed."

Around the evening campfire, the men would talk about the old days, back when it was rough. Comparing 1875 in the west, and the 1820s of their boyhood, the only difference we could identify is they didn't have sulfur matches in their youth. But matches cost money, far from a necessity, so we didn't have the convenience of matches either. Coot and I had to admit we'd never even seen a sulfur match.

Coot and I fed the fire, dreaming, listening half-heartedly to stories we had heard scores of times. We'd sit on a stump, lean over and try to ease one off without Papa catching us. He didn't cotton much to boys or men that broke wind in company. If he caught us at it, he'd chastise our lack of manners. Uncle Doyl would say, "Aw hell, Abe, they're just being boys. Life's too short to be worryin' 'bout such things." Papa had no budge when it came to manners, disapproving of swearing as well. "Cuss words are the adjectives of fools." If he really got wound up over the issue, or someone foolishly challenged him about profanity, he would quote Byron, "As he knew not what to say, he swore." Papa had a way of having the last say, as it was difficult to argue stark truth, and the volumes he stored under his old, sweaty hat.

Coot would nudge me and whisper, "Listen to them old farts. Why, to listen to them, it used to snow in the middle of July in the Chihuahua Desert."

I always defended our menfolk. "They ain't old farts, Coot. You shouldn't a'oughta talk about your elders that a'way."

"Well, they are old farts. I call a fart a fart."

"Well, if you're so tough, why don't you call them old farts to their faces?"

"'Cause I don't like to hurt old men's feelings, that's why."

"Yeah, sure, or maybe you don't want Uncle Doyl tannin' your backside."

Most of the boys we grew up with didn't think much of books and literature, even less of those who read the stuff. To their way of thinking, reading was for girls and sissies. Papa always encouraged us to read what was proper for us, what we enjoyed. Papa said he read somewhere that while a learned man was deciding which book his son should read, another boy had read both. Lots of times, we'd be sitting around the campfire fighting the urge to get in the warmth of our bedrolls, afraid we'd miss something. Coot or I would look over at the other and quote a line from Hawthorne's *Hiawatha*. "By the shores of Getche Gumee. By the shining Big-Sea-Water, Stood the wigwam of Nokomis. Daughter of the Moon. Nokomis." I asked Papa about the shores of Getche Gumee, because I never heard of a lake with that strange name. Papa explained that while he was not certain, he thought it was the Indian name for Lake Superior.

Often as not, Coot would start out from Tennyson's *Charge of the Light Brigade*. We both liked that poem, visualizing every line. Coot knew it by heart, but I could follow along, and we'd take turns calling out the next line. We could visualize the *Cossack and Russian, Reel'd from the saber stroke. Shattered and sunder'd.* Most times, Coot would start out, not at the beginning, but somewhere down those several lines, thinking he'd trick me. But I stayed my ground with him.

"Forward the Light Brigade," Coot quoted, grinning an evil grin, teeth and eyes sparkling mischief, dark as a raven's wing in the fire light, the reflections of Cossack and Russian reeling in his shadowy eyes.

I'd counter, "Was there a man dismay'd?", and on and on we'd go through all those fifty-odd lines:

Not tho' the soldier knew
Some one had blunder'd.
Theirs not to make reply,
Theirs not to reason why,
Theirs but to do and die
Into the valley of Death
Rode the Six Hundred

Papa and Uncle Doyl would sit amused, curious to see if one of us would stumble, and need a boost back on the lines. When we finished, they'd clap, let out a hoot. Coot didn't embarrass easy, but for some reason the men's approval seemed to discomfit him greatly. Me too, but oh how I enjoyed their applause. It was like we had our own stage and audience, and sometimes I'd stand, grinning, bowing. and scraping until Coot chunked a rock or stomped on my toe.

One time when we had just finished trying to trick one another with the poem and Uncle Doyl asked, "You boys know the history of that poem, do you?"

Coot looked at me.

I shrugged. "No sir, Uncle Doyl, we just like it. Tell us."

Uncle Doyl said, "Well, as you know better than me, it was written by Alfred, Lord Tennyson. I've always like the style of that name, think I'll change my name to Doyl, Lord Boldt. Anyway, Alfred got himself named poet laureate for the entire British kingdom. He wrote that poem as a memorial to a British Cavalry unit in honor of their bravery in the Crimean War. That was just before you tykes were born."

Coot asked, "How do you know all that stuff, Uncle Doyl?"

He'd grin wide. "Oh, I've read a bunch in my day. I just talk ignorant, I reckon."

5

It was unusually cloudy, sultry, and hot. Coot and I were spending more time than usual tending the fires to dry the meat. We'd rather be mounted, off scouting out a herd of elk.

Papa yelled out, "You boys take a break and cool off. Take a dip if you're a mind to. I'll watch your fire."

We raced out of the smoke to the river's edge. I stripped off my heavy shirt, running into the knee-high water. I soaked my shirt, using it to wipe off the sweat and grime of the oak fires.

After a water fight, Coot said, "Come on, just a couple of more hours and we can call it a day. Guess we better haul another oak log back to the fire."

The cold water from my shirt and the swift breeze combined to cooling me off to a chill as I walked shivering back to camp.

Papa was mending a mule harness and glanced up when we walked up. "What are all those goose bumps, Narlow?" he asked. "I thought you boys were hot."

Coot said, "Uncle Abe, that water's as cold as if it came off an iceberg."

Papa grabbed my elbow. "Hey, Narlow, what's that on your hip? Scrape yourself on a river rock?"

I turned, trying to twist far enough around to see what he was talking about. "I don't know, Papa—doesn't hurt. Sure is red though."

"Turn around, let me see that, son." He looked at the red mark and said, "Well, I'll be dad-gum. Narlow, you know what I think that is? When you were born, and up until you were a couple of years old, you had a birthmark on your forehead. Your mama and I took you across the river to Mexico to see Dr. Garcia, the only doctor around back then. He said it was nothing to be concerned about, that it would eventually disappear. He called it a *pichete*—birthmark. Later, it just sorta climbed into your hairline and disappeared. Dern if this red mark doesn't look just like it. Your mama always said it looked like a red mushroom. It embarrassed her, thought you were witched. She'd hide you anytime a neighbor came by."

Coot laughed and came over. "A red mushroom on Narlow's backside? Let me see that. Well, looky there, Narlow—know what they say about growing mushrooms and what you're supposed to feed them. That one's getting a fresh supply everyday. I don't blame your mama one bit for being embarrassed."

Papa shushed him. "It doesn't bother you at all, son?"

"No, sir. I didn't even know it was there until just now. It does sorta look like a mushroom, doesn't it?"

"No, Narlow, it doesn't look *sorta* like a mushroom," Coot chimed in, "it looks *exactly* like a red-hot mushroom."

Papa added, "We called those things toadstools when I was your age. Friend of mine died of eating mushrooms. If you tangle with the wrong variety, it'll poison your liver, kill you quick. It's probably nothing, son, but we better keep an eye on it just the same."

Uncle Doyl jealously guarded our limited supply of dried apples, and on Sunday mornings he'd bake us an apple cobbler in one of his big iron ovens. He took better care of his cast iron ovens than the concern he showed his wife, who died in childbirth twenty years ago. The baby was born still, leaving Uncle Doyl wifeless, without a baby, all in one long lonesome night. Since he didn't have any kids of his own, he made do with Coot and me. He'd make sure his heavy ovens were good and dry with a little oil applied to their warm surfaces before setting them aside. While he cooked up a real larapin' apple cobbler, we kicked around camp on Sunday mornings, repaired our gear, and checked the horses' and mules' feet and shoes. On Sunday afternoons, we'd all spread out on horseback and scout for herds that we'd stalk the next day.

We used the dutch ovens most every day. We'd sit around cutting up a fresh elk or deer backstrap, a couple of spuds if we had any, a whole bunch of greens like dandelion leaves, and a little plant that had a thumb-sized, potato-like root we called tater-spuds. All manner of edibles grew in the meadow and along the banks of the Black and Pacheta. Uncle Doyl would cover the stew with a thick layer of hot chili powder, we'd shovel in plenty of hot oak coals in a shallow pit, lower the oven and shovel coals in on top of the lid and around the sides of the oven. We'd stomp dirt over it with our boots to seal it up tight so not a whisper of smoke and heat escaped. That hefty, bodacious stew would have all day to succulate in those hot coals, allowing the ingredients to mix and mingle.

Come evening, we'd dig up the warm oven. The stew was always hot, cooked just right, never undercooked, never mushy from overcooking, the meat falling apart in big moist chunks. That always amazed me, but then Coot said I stayed amazed and full of wonderment. Coot and I would serve ourselves a couple of healthy helpings of stew, while Papa and Uncle Doyl would stoke their briars, and have themselves a shot or two from the several bottles of sour mash or *mezcal* they packed in for their evening socials. *Take the edge off the day*, they'd say. We ate, they drank, jawed, and hurrahed each other and us boys. Coot and I had a great time, learning real young to leave our feelings at the edge of the firelight as you would an unwelcome guest. Teasing was tantamount, a part of growing up that toughened the young mind and spirit.

Every fourth day, Many Fast Feet Two Sticks came down the narrow trail on the ridge spine, with a red bandanna, sometimes a piece of red-dyed rope tied around his brow, or his favorite headgear, a black stovepipe hat. Tall, reddish-brown as old polished boots. Glory, that man walked fast. His stride was only matched by the biggest feet I ever witnessed. Those moccasin-clad feet were so long you'd watch each step hit the ground and swear his feet never moved. He had the strange habit of using two walking sticks that made his stride even more powerful. His seven-foot-long sticks were stout, making it possible for him to glide over the roughest terrain. Papa said that his name in Apache was *Dalaago Dahale Bikee Naki Tsik*, and Coot and I were sure glad we could call him by his English name. He was a head taller than Papa and me, and lank. Uncle Doyl was the only one in our camp who stretched up as high as our guest, and wearing that black stovepipe hat, Many Fast Feet Two Sticks about reached up as lofty as a pine tree. His eyes were like black agate, face, a chiseled slab of burnt granite grained with a half-breed plank of oak and mesquite, his nose, long and curved as a hay hook, hair, black as a raven's wing, straight, stout as an elk's breastplate, yet caught the wind like fine corn silk. His hands seemed to stretch clear up to his elbows that appeared as knobby and rough as the end of a grubax. Everyone called him Two Sticks—everyone but himself, preferring his entire name.

Over the past couple of years, Two Sticks often told Papa, "Abe Montgomery, you boy Narlow has Power. He can talk to our god, Ussen."

Last week, he asked, "Narlow Montgomery, you no see Many Fast Feet Two Sticks, you no hear Many Fast Feet Two Sticks, but know when I come over the rimrock, start down the trail. How you know I come over rimrock, Narlow Montgomery?"

"Sir, I was not aware you came over the rimrock—that is, I mean, sir, I don't *think* I knew you came over the rimrock," I answered as truthfully as I could without seeming to doubt his always solemn word.

"Trail hidden from camp, many trees, rocks. Many Fast Feet Two Sticks peer through rocks on way down trail. Always Narlow Montgomery's eyes look at me, but cannot see me behind rocks. How you know where Many Fast Feet Two Sticks is if you not have Power?"

Trapped. "I don't know, sir."

Four days later, here came Two Sticks, dressed in buckskin as usual, coming down the trail with his walking sticks, gliding across the meadow, leading a stout red mule by a thick hemp rope, the other end tied around his own waist. Two Sticks had a Sharps rifle thrown over his shoulder on a leather strap, a staghorn knife at his waist that was long enough to be just as easily called a sword. He tied his mule to a sapling far from camp, and walked on up at his ground-eating stroll. At the edge of our camp he'd say, "*Mulo* stink. Smell like ass skunk." He wore a small piece of mirror on a string around his neck. He used it as a signaling device back when he was with Papa and Coot's daddy, scouting for the army. He was not ashamed of scouting for the Pale Eyes, though most of them never kept their word. He scouted because he was convinced that the Pale Eyes would kill them all if they did not agree to stay on the reservations. The red bandanna symbolized the scout. Two Sticks seemed never to look directly at any of us. Papa said all Apaches did that as it was their way. He may not have met our eyes, but there was never any doubt in our young minds that he knew what we were thinking, what we did yesterday, what we ate, maybe even what we dreamed two nights ago.

Papa asked, "Narlow, aren't you going to offer Two Sticks some coffee and honey?"

"Yes, sir, I sure will do that, sir. Yes, sir. *Right now.*" I jumped up from my hunkered position at the fire, over-corrected my lunge to get to my feet, and fell back in the dirt on my rear end. I stood again, embarrassed, and stumbled through the campfire, kicking a live coal right between Two Stick's moccasined feet. Did it take a whole bull elk hide to make those moccasins? Two Sticks did not move, though that big orange-hot coal was leaning, smoldering against his leather-clad big toe. I stumbled over, reached down between his feet, and flicked the coal back to the fire, the strong, acid odor of burning leather burning my nostrils. I jerked upright for the third time in ten seconds, meeting Two Sticks gaze dead-on, the one time in all those years that our eyes ever met. His eyes were sharp, black, mirroring, gathering images that were unseen by the white man's.

Then Two Sticks did a wondrous and simple thing. As I stood before him with our gazes locked, he reached out to my canvas shirt, and took its one remaining brass button between his bronze fingers. His long, heavy knife with a staghorn handle appeared in his hand from nowhere, deftly cutting the button loose, and stuck it in his "possibles" pouch. In the same movement, he flipped the elkhorn knife in his hand, holding it by its bright blade, offering his prize to me. Knowing his offer was much more valuable than my dull brass button, I didn't know how to react.

"Knife sharp," he said. "We trade. Brass button mine. Knife yours."

I hesitated, glanced over at Papa who was sitting there smiling. He gave me a faint nod, so I reached slowly for the knife and took it.

"Look-ee, Narlow Montgomery. Look-ee," he said, laughing, "I have shiny brass button. You stuck with old knife I steal from dead Navajo."

"Yes, sir, me stuck." I was about to bust, admiring that beautiful long sharp blade, a two-inch spike guarding the staghorn handle. Though mesmerized with its balance and heft, the thought flew through my mind, where's Coot's.

"The coffee for Two Sticks," I heard Papa say, his voice, far away.

Entranced, I heard myself whisper, "Huh?" still standing in front of our guest, feeling the cold, unforgiving edge of the knife.

"Narlow, the coffee and honey for Two Sticks."

"Oh, yes, sir. Right now," and dern if I didn't step back in the middle of the campfire, and would have upset the coffeepot had Coot not been so quick.

"Sit down before you stab yourself with that knife." Coot poured a tin cup full of hot coffee, and took it and a wooden jar of honey to Two Sticks. The Apache held the cup and poured in the thick honey until coffee spilled out over the edge. He stuck his middle finger into the blistering-hot brew, stirred while the honey melted, licked his finger, and drank the scalding hot liquid down in two gulps without a blink.

Two Sticks rose. *"Enjuh,"* his voice from the depths of a rocky well. The word raced through my mind, and though I knew *enjuh* is Apache for good, I always assumed he approved of the coffee and honey. Previous visits should have told me that it was his way of bidding his hosts farewell.

✳✳✳

The menfolk called off the hunt at mid-afternoon. We had gotten behind on the mules' feet and shoes, and Papa had no patience for neglect. Coot finished up on our pet mule, started to fetch the next one in line, stopped in mid-step, turned back to me. "Okay, what is it, Narlow? What's eating on you?"

"Nothing. Nothing at all. Just don't feel like talking, that's all."

"Don't feel like talking, huh? In all the years I've known you, you've never been quiet for one full minute that I recall. It's that new knife of yours that's got your tongue in a knot, isn't it?"

"Naw—well, yeah, I reckon it is," I said pulling the long knife from it's scabbard, "and you'd do me a real favor if you'd just take it as a present from me. Here, take it. Besides, you're a bunch better with a knife than I could ever hope to be."

"You beat all, Narlow Montgomery. Two Sticks came into camp this morning and swapped his knife for your brass button, and here you are trying to give it away. I say you're feeling guilty about it because he didn't give me one."

"Well, no matter. Here, take it."

"Narlow, if you don't put that knife back in that scabbard and put a smile on your face, and start talking sense, I've a good mind to kick your butt." He turned and headed for the next mule.

I picked up a rock and chunked him in the butt. He turned back and ran at me. I ducked under a mule and took off running. I tried not to laugh as I could never laugh and run. It was not going to be one bit funny when he caught me.

He tackled me and we went down in a heap. He pummeled me for a good five minutes, and in spite of goodly number of whelps, I could not stop laughing. He got

34

me in a headlock and rubbed my head raw with his knuckles. "Say you're sorry for acting like a little girl and I'll stop."

"I'm sorry."

"You're sorry, what?"

"I'm sorry for acting like a girl."

"Say you're sorry for acting like a little freckle-face girl with pigtails."

I caught my breath. "I'm sorry my best friend looks like a girl with freckles and pigtails," laughing myself sick.

The next morning Coot sat on the ground, feeling around in his knapsack. He looked up. "Where'd that old compass get off to? It was in this sack yesterday. You don't have my compass do you?"

"*Your* compass? When did *our* compass become *your* compass?"

He stopped, his arm stuck in the sack up to his armpit. He pulled out a piece of soft deerskin wrapped around something long and heavy. I watched as he folded the leather away, and there in his hands was a long knife with a staghorn handle, the pure unmistakable identical twin of the one Two Sticks had traded with me.

"Where did this come from? How did Two Sticks sneak this in here? And when?" Coot asked, turning to the menfolk who just smiled.

I laughed. "Well, Coot, I reckon Two Sticks was afraid my little freckle-face, pigtailed *amigo* would throw a fit if he didn't get one exactly like mine." When, and how, Two Sticks sneaked that knife into Coot's knapsack was a mystery. And we never did find that old compass.

As certain as a calendar, three mornings later, Two Sticks came for coffee and honey, and Coot proudly displayed the knife and the sheath he made to carry it on his belt. He tried to thank Two Sticks for the knife. The old Apache ignored him.

As I was serving his coffee and honey, Papa said, "Narlow, why don't you tell Two Sticks about your run-in with that grizzly yesterday?"

"Well, Papa, I could do that all right, but I have to admit I was napping through most of it. Coot saw it a whole lot better than I did. Get him to tell that story, Papa."

He turned to Coot. "Okay, son, tell Two Sticks about that mama grizzly you and Narlow ran into. He'd enjoy that story."

"Yes, sir, I will." He slapped his hat against his leg, circled the campfire, mustering up the courage and words to make a long speech in front of his elders. He turned and sat cross-legged on the ground in front of Two Sticks.

"Sir, Many Fast Feet Two Sticks, sir, me and Narlow were hunting elk up on the rim. We stopped when the sun was high to eat our noon meal. We left our horses staked out on good grass, and climbed up on a high ledge and ate our tortillas and jerky. After we ate, Narlow stretched out on a rock ledge below me, trying to get in the shade so he could take his usual nap. He was lying on his back, his head to the wind, hat over his face. I climbed out on the ledge above him, started chunking little pieces of wood at him to pester him, keep him from his nap. But the wind was blowing so high out of the west, the chips just blew away. I rolled over and reached for a heavier stick, or a pebble to chunk at him. When I turned back to him, there was a *full grown* mama grizzly with her neck all stretched out. I swear her head and snout were every bit of three feet long. And sir, she was pawing at Narlow's hat, and had her neck stretched *way* out, licking the salt off his hatband. I started to jump up and go get my rifle, but I was afraid I'd spook the grizzly, and she'd eat Narlow plumb up before I could get back. I never felt so helpless in all my born days. I thought about jumping off my perch and try knocking her off the ledge, but I was right above her, and knew that me jumping on her would be like spitting a paper wad at a boulder. I know that grizzly didn't smell us because the wind was strong and steady from the west, the direction she came from. She just happened on us. The bear kept licking Narlow's salty hatband, every once-in-a-bit, she'd stop her licking, snap at her hindquarters, kicking her right-hind leg out real mad-like, like maybe a bee was biting on her. She reminded me of a mare kicking at a wolf that was after her colt. In a minute, Narlow yelled, 'Cut it out, Coot,' thinking it was me funning with him. All the while, that mama grizzly was taking turns licking Narlow's hat, and kicking at whatever was pestering her rear-end. Then Narlow said, 'Jeez-amighty, Coot, you smell like you've been eating bear scat.' Hearing Narlow's voice, the bear pulled back for half-a-second then she *really* snapped and kicked at her rear-end. She eased back up to Narlow with her neck way out, and got pretty frisky licking the salt off Narlow's hatband—dang tongue on that gal was a foot long. Finally, she knocked his hat off his head, slobber drooling down on Narlow's forehead. Narlow glanced up and saw the underside of the jaws and neck of that grizzly. He jumped to his feet like he was blown out of a volcano. I never saw a man or animal move so fast in all my life. He was up with his new knife in hand, ready for a fight. Then the grizzly stood up on her hind feet. I remember thinking, 'So long, Narlow.' But the grizzly didn't do anything, and thank god, Narlow didn't run, even when she snapped down at her rear end again and kicked her leg back. I thought Narlow would bolt sure enough. They both just stood on that narrow ledge, gazing at each other, not more than five-feet apart, they were. She was *big*. So big, she made Narlow look like a rag doll, him standing there with that long knife in his hand that looked like a pin-knife compared to her claws. Then the grizzly stood on her back legs, and threw up both front paws above her head. I remember saying, 'Oh shit'—oh, beg your pardon, Uncle Abe. Anyway she started swaying back and forth, then dern if it didn't look like she was dancing, waving at Narlow, standing on that narrow ledge. Pretty soon Narlow did the same thing, putting both hands above his head, waving, swaying just like that grizzly lady. In a bit, that she-grizzly went back down on her all fours. I figured she'd charge him sure enough. She wheeled around, snapping at her backside, kicking a mighty kick, then lumbered on off just as pretty as you please. But Two Sticks, sir, the strangest thing about this whole story is that Narlow was dreaming when that grizzly showed up. The way he described it, I believe you would probably call it a vision. Narlow told me he had a vision of a sun-red mushroom that grew from the size of a pea to the size of a horse, screaming like a woman in severe pain, seemed to be warning him of something or other. That's when the grizzly knocked his hat off. I sure thought that was mighty strange. Don't you, sir?"

Two Sticks looked Coot square in the eye, studying him, and then at me for a long while. Then he turned to Papa. "Apache not kill bear unless bear attacks. Apache kill bear, no eat bear unless the People starve."

Two Sticks again fell quiet, then continued, "Abe Montgomery, many years I tell you these boys know Mother Earth like their own mother. They are like Apache boys. You tell me long ago about the dugout where you live. Narlow Montgomery live like Apache boy. His feet tread on earth when he goes to pallet at night, awakes in morning, greets day. He push aside goat-skin cover of dugout to see sun rise—he does not push open wooded door. Narlow Montgomery knows no wooden floors, walls, wooden roof above him. He always with the Mother Earth. Ussen never loses grip on Narlow. You grandfathers, Shelby Montgomery and Skinner Boldt, they save Apache princesses, Little Flower, from scalp hunters long ago. Her father, Smoking Wolf, he tell all Apache you fathers friend of Apache, all Apache honor you fathers—honor Abe Montgomery. Honor Doyl Boldt, brother Orville. You teach boys Apache ways. I see my own eyes, Narlow Montgomery and Coot Boldt run long way with mouth full of water. Learn to run with mouth closed like Apache warrior, like Apache boy. Ussen use vermilion mushroom to warn him of danger of bear. I tell you, Abe Montgomery, Narlow Montgomery special. Has Power. He has much Apache blood. Papa Abe Montgomery—you mama Chiricahua Apache. Narlow's mama—she half Comanche. Narlow Montgomery have much Indian blood. Much Apache—much Comanche."

"You are right, my old friend," Papa said. "Maybe Narlow's bloodline does have something to do with the Power you are certain he has. My Pale Eye grand-mama was a Louisiana swamp medicine-woman healer, and like you said, Narlow's mama is half Comanche, half Celtic from Badennoch. Those folks, far across the big water, believe in witches and medicine. Maybe you are right about Narlow."

Two Sticks studied me for a long minute then rose. "I will talk to medicineman, Na-Tu-Che-Puy, tell him about red mushroom warn Narlow about mama-grizzly. *Enjuh.*"

The next morning, I said, "Papa, wasn't Two Sticks here just yesterday?"

"Yes, he's not due back for three more days. Why, son?" He followed my gaze up the trail to the rimrock. The four of us sat waiting to see if I was right. In a bit, Two Sticks came around the boulder, striding across the meadow to our camp.

Uncle Doyl laughed. "Well kiss my ass and call me Charlie. How'd you know he was comin' down here this morning, boy?"

Papa only said, "Well, I'll be jiggered." That's about as close to cussing as Papa ever got. "Two Sticks may be right about you, Narlow. Maybe you *can* see through rocks."

Papa stepped to the edge of our camp, greeting his Apache friend. "Welcome, Two Sticks. Something must be troubling my friend. You are three days early, and you forgot your red mule."

Papa offered Two Sticks our best stump, motioned to me to fetch him some coffee. There was none, and as I went to start another batch, Two Sticks motioned me away.

"No. Coffee hurt *estomago* when drink much. Abe Montgomery, I tell medicineman, Na-Tu-Che-Puy about Narlow Montgomery dancing with bear, about red mushroom Narlow Montgomery see in vision as he sleep on rock. Na-Tu-Che-Puy ask me questions I cannot answer."

"Well, Two Sticks, you ask the questions and Narlow will give you straight answers to anything you want to know."

"Na-Tu-Che-Puy asks if Narlow Montgomery see red mushroom before grizzly, or this first time?"

Papa turned to me. "Narlow?"

"Yes, sir—I reckon."

"You reckon, son, or is this the first time?"

I was stuck. I had indeed experienced the vision one other time. But that experience hurt mightily.

"Papa, I can't talk about that. It wouldn't be fair—to you—to somebody else. I just can't talk about that."

"What is it, son? These men are your friends, your kin."

"Papa, I just can't. I reckon you'd likely want to kill me since I didn't tell you when it happened."

"Son?"

Now I was really in a pickle. My answer wasn't fair to the only person I would never do dirt without dying first. "Papa, I'll tell you, but I can't tell the whole world about it."

I bolted out of camp, Papa right on my heels.

Pacheta Creek gurgled as it rippled past, recalling the memory of that blasted flaming-red mushroom, its warning that would forever change any regard for Mama. Now Papa was going to learn firsthand why I quit calling her Mama, and would forevermore call her Mother when I was talking to her. I thought of everything I could come up with, but there was never any weasel room with Papa. But, I had to tell him, but it was ugly. I turned.

"Papa, it's a god-awful story, but a few years ago when you and Fernando Valdez were out tending the goats, I was sitting out in the dark, just resting, waiting for the moon to rise. Mama came up behind me real quiet-like, asked me what I was doing out there in the dark. I told her I was waiting for the moon dawn."

"Moon Dawn?" Papa asked, a frown on a face that never frowned. "I told you about her, but that was long after what you're telling me now. Had you heard about her before I told you about your mama's childhood?"

"No, sir, I knew nothing about all that. All I said was I was waiting for the moon to rise, and just used the words moon dawn instead. I didn't mean anything by it."

"Then what happened, son?"

I hemmed and hawed, but finally the story fell out of my mouth for the first time in those four years, tasting like a mouthful of acid. Telling him of the brutality of his wife, my mother. A most unmanly thing to do. Telling Papa that the call of the bull elk came like two bobcats caterwauling at night in the fork of a mesquite, a crying woman, the scream just like the night my little sister died. Anguish, anger shadowed by grief showed on Papa's face when I recounted that night when Mama hit me across the shoulders and neck as I sat on my milking stool, tending to the last goat for the night. I didn't tell Papa, but I wanted my own mother dead.

Papa and I stood peering at each other, studying the other, quiet-like, as though the gurgle of the creek was the only sound in the universe.

Then Papa spoke. "I never knew that, son, but I believe I remember when that happened. That was some time ago. Three or four years ago as I recall."

"Yes, sir, when I was twelve years old."

"Son, I didn't know what happened when I came home from tending the goats with Fernando Valdez, but I knew something real wrong had happened in my absence between you and your mother. I asked her what happened, she just shrugged, 'I don't know what's eating that boy, but I'm certain he'll cook up a good story to make his mother look bad.' I guess that explains the bandages she had on her hands and wrists that day. Well, son, I never asked you because I knew you'd never tell me. I guess I was right about that. You never said a word about it until just now. I know it hurt deep to talk about it."

Papa grabbed me by my shoulders. "Holding your tongue took courage. In a day or two, we'll get off by ourselves and I'll tell you about your mama's childhood. But for now, just remember your mama is half-breed Comanche, was raised rough by a full-bloodied, meaner-than-an-acre-of-rattlers Comanche woman by the name of Moon Dawn, and a worthless no-count white man." He smiled. "Come on, son. Let's go talk to Two Sticks. I'll handle it for you."

We went back to the camp and sat down. Coot only glanced at me for the briefest second, a glinting shadow of a question in his dark eyes, one he and I never had cause to have before.

Papa began, "Many Fast Feet Two Sticks, Narlow has had a previous occasion to witness the power of the red mushroom. Please forgive me and my son, but the story Narlow just told me stings his brave heart. The pain is too much to tell. It is about his mama. You may tell Na-Tu-Che-Puy that Narlow has had one previous visit from the red mushroom, and it warned him of a grave danger."

Two Sticks smiled directly at me, came over, put his hand on my shoulder. "There are things that a brave heart can say to few in this life. I will tell Na-Tu-Che-Puy that red mushroom visit you one time before."

He went on, "Na-Tu-Che-Puy asked me, I could not answer. He asked if Narlow Montgomery knew who was in kicking bear. Apache believe dead relative that not live pure life, live in bear before go to Happy Place. A man with Power will see in bear's eyes who in bear. Medicine man want to know. Who did you see in bear's eyes, Narlow Montgomery?"

40

Again I hemmed and hawed, glancing around our camp for something, or somebody to take me out of my misery. Four sets of friendly eyes gazed back at me, waiting for my answer. I picked up a stick, stirred the fire, stood, turned to walk off, came back to the fire. "Jeez-amighty."

"Narlow, tell Two Sticks who you saw in the grizzly's eyes. It's okay, son. Whoever it is, let's hear it. Was it your mama you saw in the bear's eyes?"

If I didn't answer his question then and there, I'd likely lose my tongue and forget how to speak forevermore.

"No Papa, it wasn't Mama." I turned to Uncle Doyl, then to Two Sticks. "Sir, I saw—I saw Uncle Doyl in that grizzly's eyes."

Uncle Doyl guffawed. "By golly, Narlow, I do believe you're touched in the head, boy." He slapped me on the back. "Boy, you'n Coot are about the two best boys God ever put on this good earth, and by God-for-certain, you're the two best things that ever happened to Doyl Boldt. If you seen me in that grizzly, then I'm right proud to wear her fur coat. And I reckon it could be said that your uncle Doyl hasn't exactly lived a pure life, just like Two Sticks said."

"Medicineman, Na-Tu-Che-Puy teach Narlow Montgomery how make medicine—how pray to our god Ussen. I take Narlow Montgomery to Na-Tu-Che-Puy, live with Many Fast Feet Two Sticks. Okay, Abe Montgomery?"

Now it was Papa's turn to be stuck. He knew what to say, but didn't know how to put it in words that would not offend his old friend. "Two Sticks, I must admit to you that Narlow knew you were coming down the trail this morning, long before any of us could see you coming. But we are leaving this place in a few suns, and we will come back here next spring like we do every year. You bring Na-Tu-Che-Puy here to visit us, and the two of you can study Narlow together. If Na-Tu-Che-Puy agrees that Narlow has Power, then you can take Narlow and Coot with you to study the way of Apache."

Two Stick's furrowed brow above dark eyes gazed at me for a minute, then Coot. "*Enjuh.*"

6

Two weeks later, we were busy cleaning up camp for next spring, storing some of our gear in the line shack. Ready or not, time to go home was nigh. It was mid-day, hot, and we just about had our mules packed up, ready to head out.

Papa said, "Well, boys, this will be the last time you'll be able to cool your-selves off for awhile. Better take advantage of the opportunity and take a dip before we get started."

Coot was off his horse and halfway to the river before you could shake a stick, stripping off his clothes as he ran toward the inviting cold water. I laughed out loud, watching that silly turd. Being splayfooted and knock-kneed combined to make his white butt do a funny dance as he ran to the river. "Coot, you *mojon*," I called out.

"*Narlow*," Papa scolded me.

"Oh, I'm sorry, Papa." I apologized for using my favorite Mexican word on my friend. But Coot was, in fact, a turd in any language.

Papa said, "Aren't you going to join him, son? That cold water looks mighty tempting. Go on and join him."

"Naw, I'll help you and Uncle Doyl store this tarpaulin, then I'll take a dip."

"Oh, we can handle that little chore. Go on. It's hot, and frankly, son, your aroma is a little ripe this morning. I don't want to follow you up that trail with you smelling like you're sitting on a polecat. We'll be ready to go in about an hour."

Papa sat his big gray horse, gazing at me, his steel-blue eyes forever sparkling, always reflecting his magnificent mixture of laughter and mischief. I would never forget that moment down there on the Black. Sitting my horse, returning Papa's gaze, the question crossed my mind as to why Mama despised him so, me as well. Papa was a good man. A kindly, strong, learned man. Mama mistook his gentle ways for weakness. It struck me for the first time, that Mama resented him being the man of the family, secretly coveting his position.

I shinnied off my horse, out of my clothes, and raced for that cold water.

"Hey, Narlow," Papa yelled out.

I stopped in mid-step, turned back to him.

"Don't forget to wash your privates, son."

That always embarrassed me. I laughed, waved, and took off for the river, hit-ting the water, running full out. Coot and me skinneyed around and had ourselves a bodacious water and boulder fight. We'd feel around on the bottom of that shallow, fast-moving stream, find a big slippery boulder, lift it heavy overhead, and chunk it as close to the other as we dared. A mountain of water belched up, covering us with cold spray. The strong current often took us off our feet and we had to fight to regain a foothold on the rocky river bottom. After awhile, we were tuckered out, out of breath, a long way downstream. We climbed out onto a rock ledge called Pricilla's Perch. We didn't know why it was so named, but made up all kinds of nasty stories that explained it to our satisfaction.

Coot asked, "Do you think you have Power like Two Sticks says you do?"

"Power? Nope, don't think so. Do you?"

"Well, Narlow, you are pretty strange sometimes, you know. You can see further than any white man I ever knew, next to your Papa, that is. I have to admit, you saw, or knew, or *something*, that Two Sticks was on his way to our camp the other morning. But other than that, I never have noticed anything very special about you like Two Sticks claims—other than you dancing with that grizzly the other day. *Whew*. That still gives me the chills."

"Oh, I don't know so much about that. Actually a lot of folks think I'm pretty special. Why, I remember just last—"

"Pretty special my butt, Narlow Montgomery. Come on, we'd best get our shriveled-up prunes out of the sun, and get on back. Men'll be looking for us. Time to head on home—ready or not."

We crossed the river and raced back to camp, Coot running as fast as he could, "one-handed," the other busy keeping his balls from banging against each other. He always won those races, though I was a bunch swifter, could never run and laugh at the same time. Most times, I'd fall down laughing myself to tears.

When we trotted back into camp all we found was the ancient oak and empty headquarters—no Papa, no Uncle Doyl, no horses, no mules, no panniers. Only our boots and britches sitting on a stump. We looked down toward the line shack, figuring they decided to fill their canteens at Pacheta Creek before leaving. Nothing there except their trail leading up the hill toward Rattlesnake Point.

"What the hey, Coot?" was all I could utter.

"I don't know, but something tells me those assholes are pulling more than a little of Uncle Doyl's horseplay on us."

"Now Coot, don't you be calling Papa names, 'cause—"

"You'll be callin' your papa worse than that if my suspicions are true. Check the shack while I take a look at their trail."

I stepped around to the front of the shack. A piece of rough, brown paper was folded over, stuffed in a crack in the door with our names penciled on the outside of the fold.

"Hey, looky here," I called out around the side of the shack and unfolded the paper. There in Papa's strong, self-educated hand were these few words I read aloud:

Greetings, boys. Welcome to Manhood.
Prepare yourselves to become Hombres del Campo—
Men of the Outdoors.
Here's my 10-gauge shotgun and Uncle Doyl's 44-40.
You'll find some line and fishhooks in the shack. Don't
be shooting at rocks and such. There's just enough
ammunition to get you back home safe and sound.
Don't tarry, now. Your mamas will have plenty of chores
waiting for you.
See you back at the Pass,
Papa

Coot and I saw it in the other's eyes. No, this was not a prank. We were 250-miles from home, afoot, and the menfolk had vamoosed with our bedrolls, all the grub, and every horse and mule in the outfit. We put on our britches and boots as fast as we could, not wasting time putting on our shirts. We took off at a dead run up the mountain and didn't stop until a half-hour later when we topped off at Rattlesnake Point. We tried tracking them, but they had turned loose the eight pack-mules and our two horses, and had run them around in circles in the soft dirt. This rodeo took us about a mile on north where the circling stopped, and their trail went in a dozen different directions at once—all the horses and all the mules, including my twenty-year-old mule named for my dear, dead sister, Mary Jewell.

"*You bastards!*" Coot yelled, not knowing which way to yell.

I didn't correct Coot this time as his assessment seemed to be closing in on the mark. We stumbled back down the trail, dejected, out of sorts as two boys could be, wondering what we were going to do, why they were pulling this prank on us.

"Hell, they even took Mary Jewell with them," Coot said. "Bastards."

"Jeez-amighty, how do they figure I can walk all the way back to the Pass in these old worn-out boots with one heel dangling off to the side? Guess you'll have to carry me, huh *amigo?*"

"Yeah, right. You wait right here 'til I get back and carry your skinny ass all the way back to the Pass. Wait right here, now."

Hadn't we worked hard, done more than half the chores, and why did they wait until the work was all done, and why didn't they pull this when we first got up here months ago? "Because, *numb-skull*," we shouted at each other, "they waited until the work was all done." We talked about why they had taken our carbines and left us the heavy 44-40 and a monstrously heavy, double-barrel, 10-gauge shotgun. "Because, you *mojon*, our saddle carbines are light and easy to carry 250-miles. Ever think of that?"

We took stock. We each had two knives apiece—our old worn-out varieties, and our new Two Sticks' prizes. We had rope, fishhooks, and line, some old rusted tin cans, along with odds and ends, discarded cooking utensils. We had twenty-five shells for the 10-gauge, and twenty rounds of 44-40. Enough to get us by, if we didn't find trouble. They left not one scrap of the jerky or pemmican that we had worked so hard to make.

Coot leaned his head over like he was making room for the devil on his shoulder, grinned, hefted the shotgun shells and 44-40 rounds. "Guess we won't be shooting many rocks after all. The worst about all this is they left us afoot. Know what they say about that: 'A man without a horse is no man at all.' Guess that's what they're telling us—that we'll be men when we get ourselves out of this."

Rain started slow, then pelted down. We dragged a tarpaulin out of the line shack and tarped it back over the fallen oak at our campsite, listened to the ticking of rain on the tarp for an hour.

We decided to fish for our supper, reflect on our plight before starting the long trek home. A light drizzle fell as we fished the rest of the day. Papa always said trout played during a rain, not as cautious as usual, bite at anything. Don't know so much about that, but before long we both had heavy stringers of trout tied to our knife belts. We sat around a hot oak-fed fire, baked fish after fish, head, guts and all, wrapped in watercress that we plastered on with a thick layer of clay.

"Why do you reckon they ran off like that?" I asked. "What are they trying to prove by running off? And what's all that 'Welcome to Manhood' stuff about anyway? What did he call it? *Hombres del Campo?*"

"I don't suppose *they* have anything to prove. It's *us* that's going to doing the proving. What do you think we oughta do?"

"Now, Coot Boldt, dern it, don't make no-never-mind what I think. Knowing you, you've already go this whole thing figured out, know exactly what we have to do all planned out in detail."

He scowled. "Because I want to hear what you think, damn it. Check my thinking. How do you see this little trip working out? Let's hear it."

"Well, I reckon there's but two ways out of this box canyon. We can take the easy way, follow the Black River on down west to the flats, circle around south, then home, but we heard Two Sticks telling Papa and Uncle Doyl just the other morning about the Apaches kicking up a ruckus down there in the Arizona territory. Or, I suppose, we could climb back out on Rattlesnake Point, backtrack the way we always come in, down to the Frisco River, except we turn south to Silver City instead of staying southeast like we usually do. We might get us a couple of horses at the village where old Ft. West used to be, work off the price of two horses, borrow or steel a couple if we have to. Maybe pick up an ore wagon train at Silver City that's headed for the El Paso smelter. That'd sure beat walking all the way back home, that's a certain. Reckon we can make it back, Coot?"

"Shit yes, we'll make it all right. Probably make it to Silver City in what? Maybe six or seven days, depending on the weather and stopping to skin out a doe and cooking her up. Speaking of cooking, let's cook up the rest of this mess of fish to take with us. That should last us through tomorrow and maybe the next, if you don't eat it all."

We roasted several more trout and jostled each other about being city-boy-dudes with nothing to ride but our worn-out boots.

"Say, Narlow, do you think Two Sticks was in on this *Hombres del Campo* crap? Him giving us these knives and all, I mean."

I nodded, threw a rock at the fire. "Makes sense to me. I bet that's why he mentioned the Indian ruckus over in Arizona. He knows we soak up everything our menfolk talk about. Seems too coincidental otherwise." I stood and turned to head for the line shack.

"Where you going?"

"I'm going to get us a couple of those big lard cans in the shack. Those and some rope should make us a couple of canteens for water."

I brought back the cans, a length of rope, a rotten old saddlebag to carry our limited exigencies, and two worn, but serviceable *sarapes*, to keep the sun off our backs, and the frost off our paunches. I also brought along a tin of acorns that somehow escaped the squirrels. The acorns were dry and wormy on the top but passable underneath. Papa told me that Apache warriors could get by on a handful of acorns a day. Leather straps would serve as slings for my shotgun and Coot's rifle.

We climbed out of the box canyon up to Rattlesnake Point before sunup, headed northeast, crossed Mule Creek, then kept east into the rising sun. On the morning of the third day, we were moving south, nary a thing on our minds but our bellies. I was all set to shoot us a turkey, a band-tailed pigeon, a badger, or heck, a skunk or a skinny lizard with the 10-gauge. Coot spent his time poking around trying to scare up a mule deer with the 44-40. At mid-day we found a big live oak to rest under and talk about the wild game we didn't have to eat, each blaming the other for more appetite than game to please our growling innards. But we were far from discouraged, as we were determined to see this through and make the most of it. We spent our time figuring how to get even with Papa and Uncle Doyl. We just had to keep our heads and eat whatever we found that wouldn't fight back if we swallowed it whole.

I said, "I haven't said anything about this 'cause—aw, nothing."

"You haven't said anything about what?"

"Nothing. Forget it."

"No, now Narlow, damn it. I'm not letting you off that easy. Spit it out."

"Well, it's just a feeling more than anything, but I've had the unmistakable notion that somebody's spying on us. Had that feeling since we started out this morning."

"Some*body* or some*thing*?

"A man. But I've glanced over my shoulder so often I've got a crick in my neck. I confess I haven't seen a thing, but we're being followed."

"Think it's your papa and Uncle Doyl?"

"No, it's not the menfolk, but somebody is sure trailing us."

"Well, then, maybe it's a ghost or a hobgoblin or maybe it's a—"

"That's why I didn't want to tell you 'cause you'd just fun me."

"Aw, hell, don't be so thin-skinned," he said. "Tell you what—let's climb that hill over to the west there, take a long look around. Maybe we'll catch a glimpse of whoever, or whatever you're so all-fired certain is following us. Maybe get a glimpse of Silver City smoke or something, that'll tell us we're headed in the right direction. We're still two or three days out of Silver City, but maybe we'll see something from up there."

We started out, our sights set on the top of the tall hill, still savoring the meal we just finished in our heads and empty guts. I kept my gaze peeled to our back trail. I stumbled, jerked upright. Something cold came over me.

"Coot, *stop*. Let's go back. I don't want to go any further. Something about this hill is not right. Come on—let's go on further south."

"Oh, crap, come on. It's just a little further to the top, and we can get our bearings from up there."

"I'm seeing that dang mushroom again."

"Rub some shit on it. *Come on*."

7

All the livelong day, the sand had blown a tyrant out of the west, the grit gumming up our ears to where I wasn't certain I heard the howl any more. But, we were soon glad it was blowing, and promised ourselves we would never cuss the wind again. Coot was in the lead as we approached the top of the grassy knoll. He stopped dead in his tracks, turning his head slowly, putting his finger to his lips. His dark eyes, dead-bone-cold. He peered through the heavy brush, moving his head slowly to the right to get a better view. He studied whatever he was studying for a bit, then started backing up, signaling with his hands for me to back down the hill.

We stepped behind an alligator juniper grove, and he whispered, "We damn near walked into an Apache camp. I suppose the wind kept them from hearing us. I think they were busy trying to get a fire started in this gale. Just squaws, their babies, little ones—no men or grown boys that I saw. We'd best get our young asses out of here, and be damn quick about it."

"I tried to warn you that I didn't like this hill, but you just had to—"

"Don't waste time blabbering about that right now. What do you think we should do?"

"Well, Papa always talked about the Mimbres River over there to the east. It runs along the foothills of the Mimbres Mountains. I think that's the Mimbres range there in the distance—that blue line yonder. What do you say we head for it? There should be trees and brush along the river. We need to get out of this open country."

Coot took off at a ground-eating lope, heading for the dark mountain range that shown hazy in the distance. He asked over his shoulder, "Do you know with any certainty that the Mimbres River runs north and south? Did your papa ever mention that?"

I chewed my lip, then caught up beside him. "Yes, I know that for certain. Papa says all rivers, east of the Divide, generally run north to south, or at least that's their druthers. Rivers to the west of the Divide, run east to west and southwest. The Mimbres is one of those exceptions to the rule, because it is just west of the Divide. It runs due south to beyond the end of the Mimbres Mountains, then heads toward the *Floridas* mountains, but peters out and goes underground before the flow gets that far south."

"Good. By the time we get to the Mimbres River, daylight will be about gone, then we'll walk upstream for a couple of hours, stop, figure out what to do next."

"Why upstream?" I asked. "Remember upstream is north. We want to go south, downstream."

He said over his shoulder, "Because, if the menfolk of that band of Apaches comes back, finds our tracks and follows us, we want to go where they ain't."

"So, why north?"

"When they discover we were that close to their camp, first thing those Apaches will do is backtrack us and determine we were coming from the north. It follows that we were wanting to go south. They'll track us to the Mimbres, may try to pick up our track north and south, but probably only south."

For the next five hours I kept one eye looking back, never spotting anything, though I still had a strong feeling we were being tailed. Two miles from the tree line to the east we guessed was the Mimbres River, I stopped. "I saw something back there."

We squinted into the low sun. Nothing. "Are you sure you saw something?"

"Yeah, I'm certain all right. But I'm not certain what. I saw something move way back there past those near hills, in those middle hills—those purple, lavender hills, there below that far blue mountain line."

He squinted into the haze, frowned. "Let's get to the river. You may have just seen ravens. You know how they dip and dive, and at a great distance they look and seem to be a man on horseback. Keep a sharp eye out."

We took a long drink of ice water out of the shallow Mimbres just after sunset.

"Your papa calls this trickle a river? Hell, even you can pee a bigger stream than this. But, for whatever good it will do us, let's stay in the middle of it, and walk upstream as long as the light holds. Then we'll stop, rest a spell until the moon comes up."

Sloshing upstream, Coot was in the lead. "We've been way too slack and lackadaisical. We've been going straight south for too many days, too many miles. We need to change it up. If you're right about someone following us, we need to make tracking us a little more difficult than just trailing along behind us. Besides, I don't want to tempt that band of Apaches back there. What do you think?"

"Oh, I'm perfectly willing to just tag along behind you and do what you've already decided we're going to do. So what have you decided?"

"I haven't decided a *damn thing*," Coot snapped over his shoulder. "I asked you a question, so let's have it."

"Well, I agree with you that our trail heading south day after day is not a good idea. We can't head back west, going north wouldn't be getting us any closer to home, so that leaves east. I'm guessing, but I'd say we were within seventy miles of Silver City back when we came on Apaches. Now we're twenty-five miles or so east of there. I remember seeing a town named Chloride on Papa's map. It's just east of the Divide, northeast of here. Papa says it's a mining town and the mine is still producing a little silver and—"

"How do you remember all that?" Coot asked. "Are you sure you know where we are? You *can't* know where we are. There's no way you can be any less lost than I am, and I am dead-ass certain *lost*."

I shrugged. "Papa's got maps of all this country. He calls them grid maps, have little squares all over them, each square being one mile on a side. He took old maps your daddy and Uncle Doyl and he had made, some he borrowed off of mountain men, and drew the squares in himself. He found that most of the maps had been drawn pretty true. Papa and I used to play a game, still do come to think of it. While we're sitting around a campfire tending our goats, we'd both study one of his maps for exactly ten minutes. Then we'd take turns asking the other where a town or settlement or the top of a mountain is located, how many miles it is from that point to, say the *Rio Grande*, or the Mexican border. The Divide was shown as a dotted line on those maps, and that dotted line starts at the Mexican border and wanders all the way up the western third of the New Mexico Territory until it crosses into Colorado near the *Rio Chamita*. Knowing the location of the Divide is mighty helpful. The *Rio Grande* meanders right up through the middle of the Territory. Papa boxed my ears at that game for a long time. Finally, I figured it out. There were twenty-eight squares, or miles, across a map, east to west, and forty-two squares, north to south. When I got that in my head, I started holding my own, then I beat him several times in a row. Papa grinned over the campfire. 'Well, son, you finally figured it out, didn't you?' Often, we'd play that game way into the night, and whoever won a game, got a rock, and at the end of the evening we'd count up our rocks to see who—"

"Okay, okay, Narlow, I believe you, I believe you."

We kept to the middle of the river in the pitch dark for a couple of hours, sloshing along in the numbing snow-melt stream until I danged near took the top of my head off on a cottonwood limb growing low over the river. Dern tree limb was not successful in knocking me clear out, but it sure put me flat on my backside in the chilly melt water.

"Well, that's what you get for being so damn tall," Coot said as he helped me up, retrieving my hat and soaking shotgun. "This tree limb is just what we need. We don't need to be tracking-up the banks of this river. Here, sling my rifle over your shoulder, boost me up on this limb."

I handed Coot my gear and the 44-40, then boosted myself up on the limb beside him. That cottonwood limb was about as comfortable as a corncob, but sitting felt good.

"Narlow, how long do you figure it will take us to walk to the fair city of Chloride?"

"Depends on how far it is," I said and dodged a big fist that would have put me back in the Mimbres.

"No shit—*really*? How far is to Chloride do you figure, dumb-shit?"

"Coot, listen to you. It's getting where you can't say a full sentence without using a cuss word. Your language smells and tastes like a copper peso. It's abrasive, sound like a muleskinner."

"Don't be Sunday-schoolin' me just now." He bristled. "Not now."

"Well anyway, back to your question. It's not far as the Stellar jay flies, but the last time I checked, you haven't sprouted wings. And, if the foul language you're using is any judge, you'll never sprout any. I'd say two hard days would get us there. You know, Coot, I've been thinking about those Indians back there. Papa says Apaches can tell a whole bunch from sign. Like how old a man is, how big. Whether he's carrying something, which side of his body he's carrying the load. Whether the ones he's following are men, or women with babies, or maybe old folks. If they can read sign that well, maybe they'll just figure we're a couple of harmless boys and go on about their business."

51

"Yeah, two harmless boys that are already bigger than most men, that we are carrying a heavy shotgun and a rifle."

We sat still and listened and rested the best we could, but I kept hearing or feeling things that made me uneasy. "Feel that, Coot? Hear that?"

"Feel what? Hear what?"

"That."

"That *what*?"

"You didn't feel that?"

"No, all I feel is the bark of this cottonwood tree up my ass. Feel what?"

"A man. Back there—downstream. Downstream where we came from."

We listened for over an hour, only the shallow river gurgling below our perch broke the silence. A thin, lazy layer of clouds shielded the moon, as the river glistened below us.

"Narlow, I think you're taking that medicineman stuff too seriously. Come on, let's go. watch your noggin."

We eased off the limb back into the river and started upstream. Up-river a ways, we found a slippery rock ledge, and used it and the rocky terrain to get a mile east of the river before we set out in earnest, taking no more time or care to cover our tracks. The wind was stiff at our backs that would soon hide our passing.

Coot led the way as he complained my long legs covered too much ground when I was in the lead. On three occasions I stopped him. "I think something's following us."

"Now it's a some*thing* and not a some*body*, huh?"

"I don't rightly know if it's a man or an animal, maybe both, but I think it's an animal. I won't lie to you 'cause I'm not certain I actually heard anything. It's more of a feeling than actual sounds or voices." We listened in the dim light, heard nothing but the stiff wind swirling in the *pinons*, and the mated, squawking ground-owls we had disturbed back a ways.

When I stopped him the third time, his irritation sparked. "Horse shit. Don't bother me again unless you actually see or hear something. Let's make tracks."

We turned to go on, but I stopped. Coot it, and turned back to me for the fourth time. "Now what, damn it?"

"Notice that?"

"What?"

"The wind stopped like someone shut a barn door. I bet we're in for a dilly of a storm pretty soon."

"Shit, you'll be beating on a tom-tom the next thing you know, doing the medicineman-two-step-trot and praying to Ussen. Come on, damn it, let's move."

As we stumbled along in the dark, I spent more time and attention looking over my shoulder than where we were going, relying on Coot to keep us in a straight line to the east. I hurried up beside him. "Do you remember two summers ago up there at *Brazito* when we came on those two wagons full of dead people?"

"Yeah, so what?"

"Well, I've thought about it, especially late at night. We came up on those two burning wagons with blood still oozing out of those people, oozing out of bullet holes, and holes with the feathers sticking out where arrows went clean through their bodies. Remember that one blond-bearded man who was the only one scalped? Papa said the Apache must have taken his scalp for a special ceremony, because they generally don't take scalps. Papa guessed those Apaches knew who we were, us being the grandsons of Shelby Montgomery and Skinner Boldt, so they didn't bother us. Coot, that was the very first time you and I ever buried anybody, you know that? The *very first time.*"

"Well, whoopty-do."

Just before daybreak, we stopped and hid in a cedar thicket. In spite of my sore feet, I didn't want to stop. Though dead-certain we were being followed, I was tuckered, and dozed off. Hours later, I came out of my snooze.

Coot was walking toward me, the sun burning full in his bronze face. "I backtracked better'n two miles. You limp turd, Narlow, nobody was following us last night. But remind me to take heed the next time you have one of your 'feelings.' We weren't being followed by Apaches last night, but a damn big mountain lion sure as hell was trailing our young asses. I found your boot track that was more than covered, side to side by the biggest damn cat print you ever laid eyes on. You didn't hear that cat, 'cause cats don't make a damn bit of noise. *Nobody* hears a mountain lion—not even a medicineman. How the hell did you know that cat was following us?"

"Well, like I said last night, it wasn't so much that I actually *heard* anything, I just sensed it, felt it. Felt it on the back of my neck—made my hair crawl and stand on end. You didn't see any sign of a man following us? Just a mountain lion?"

He reared back, then thrust his face up close. "No sign of a man, *just* a mountain lion, you say? Hell, I'd rather tangle with the entire Apache Nation than one damn mountain lion. But I'll tell you this, Narlow Montgomery—I have a feeling myself, and that feeling tells me that you and I will see a lot of this country in the years ahead. I'll take care of the planning and ciphering, you're in charge of looking, telling time, and feeling in this outfit. And if you find Chloride, and I'm beginning to think you will, then I'm making you chief geographist as well as Chief Medicine-man."

If those Apaches had bothered to track us, we would have been easy pickin's. We were out of the pine country, sitting in a cedar thicket. The cedars and junipers offered good hiding places, but were becoming evermore sparse. Our numerous footprints showed themselves in the pink, gravel soil, that led right up to our hiding place. We were hungry, but all we shared for breakfast was a yawn. We dozed, dreamed of the smells and tastes of fried eggs, ham, a dipper of grits ladled with all the butter those grits could soak up. Biscuits browning with butter and sorghum 'lases—biscuits browning with butter 'n honey—biscuits browning with . . . boys our age have just enough sufferable brain energy to adequately cover two subjects—their next meal and their prunes.

About mid-afternoon, I was snoozing peaceful in my cedar roost, when all of a sudden, *BOOM!* Coot let off a round from Uncle Doyl's 44-40 right next to my ear.

"What the . . ." I yelled out. My sleepy eyes focused on Coot, grinning as usual when he thought he was real funny and had pulled a prank. I jumped down from the cedar. "What are you grinning about, you low-life sack of dog shit? That's not a damn bit funny, you shithead."

He laughed. "Well now, Narlow. Look who has taken up the adjectives of the muleskinner. Dog shit, damn, shithead, all in the space of two sentences. Naughty, naughty, I'm gonna tell. Anyway, it's not what has gotten into me, it's what's *fixin'* to get into my belly. Forgive me for disturbing your afternoon slumber, Rip Van Winkle, but look over there at what I fetched-up for our supper."

"Coot, you shot some rancher's little calf."

"Yep, reckon I did. Been watching that little feller for more than an hour. Tried to catch the little shit, but he wouldn't be caught, so I shot him before he ran off to somebody else's table. I reckon that little doggie done lost his mama." That calf was as fat as a tick behind a dog's ear. We carved off every scrap of meat from his bones, and saved the paunch for a water jug. By sundown we had him butchered-out, every scrap of meat roasted. We ate all we could hold, then wrapped the leftovers in the hide we had scraped clean.

Coot said, "I thought you said we were in for a storm just because the wind stopped. Wrong again, huh?"

"That lightning and heavy cloud north of here doesn't look like I was wrong."

Bushed and full, still we talked and kept the small fire going until the half moon came up. I told Coot about what went through my head when Papa was encouraging me to take a dip back at the Black River—about my mother and the question I had about her hating Papa and me so much. Coot listened quietly, poking the fire with a cedar limb. I quit talking, wondering if he was even listening. He sat, slowly doodling the fire. Maybe I angered him talking bad about my mama. We razzed each other all the time, but somehow sensed the other's serious thoughts and respected those moments and the other's privacy. Why had I chosen this particular time to bring up the painful subject of Mama's way?

After a while Coot asked, "Remember that time last winter when you mentioned you were having trouble with your mama?"

"Yeah, I've always have had trouble with her, especially when Papa's away."

"When you told me that, I told you that I thought maybe our mamas were cut out of the same bolt of cloth." He paused, threw the stick in the fire. "I was wrong about that, and want to set that straight between us. My mama's had a pretty long hard row to hoe since Daddy died."

"You were eight years old, weren't you?"

"Yep, eight years old. When Uncle Doyl came to tell me Daddy was gone, the first thing that went through my head was, 'Why couldn't I go with him,' and I told Uncle Doyl as much. Why would Daddy leave me? I tried to understand it, but could not. Uncle Doyl stayed close for a long time, we talked a bunch. Then damned if their other brother, Uncle Kermit, didn't die of the same damn thing. They seemed just to up and die for no good reason. I hate that damn farm, and every miserable crop we ever got off it since Daddy died. Mama's brother Charles came out to take over the farm. The bastard had never seen a real working farm. Came all the way from Georgia, convinced Mama to take the farm out of production and plant those goddamn pecan trees on every stinkin' acre of the place. Pecan trees take seven years or better to produce, but we shut the whole damn 200 acres down all at one time. Uncle Charles promised Mama he'd make her rich, so she borrowed $16,000 to bring 8,000 little piss-ant, pecan seedlings all the way from Macon, Georgia. Well, you remember what happened to those trees, just like I predicted. Yep, the big flood of '69 floated every blasted one of those saplings clear down to the Gulf of Mexico. We almost lost the farm over his brainstorm. But one good thing came from that flood—Uncle Charles headed back to Georgia, and Mama's never heard hide 'ner hair from him since. And, speaking of worthless, my little brother, Richard, fits that description. That turd never hit a lick in his stinkin' life. Mama always took his side, says things like, 'He's too little to work out in the fields in that god-awful heat.' Hell, the bastard's a head taller than me, but little Richard's too damn little to shit by himself."

"Hot-dang, Coot! You mention Richard, and every time I think of him, I remember that time Richard and his two tough Mexican *amigos* were going to take that big ol' watermelon away from us. We'd been saving that fifty-pounder for just the exact ripeness of the moment. Dern, it was a big 'un. We knew they were going to gang-up on us, so we took off with that watermelon, and locked ourselves in your mama's smokehouse. Richard was banging on that creaky old door, and I just knew it would fall off its leather hinges. We got in there, dark as four feet of dirt. You were busy, up to something, but I couldn't figure it out. In a minute, my eyes got used to the dark, I could see that you had cut the top off that watermelon, and you were peeing in it. Then you hollered out, 'Hey Richard, you don't want this watermelon, 'cause Narlow done poured salt all over it, and you don't like salt on your melon. So you and your *amigos* can go suck a turd.' Richard yelled back, 'We don't care how much salt is on it. We'll eat the whole damn thing, salt, seeds, rind and all.' Then Coot, you yelled back, 'Okay then, if you want it so bad, here it is,' and you unlatched the door and handed it out to him. Those turdheads got to fighting over that watermelon, seeing who could eat the most. And, Coot, do you remember what I did while those idiots were out there eating that peed-on watermelon?"

"Yeah," he squealed, "you peed in your own damn pants."

"Dern, Coot, you can sure make me laugh."

We didn't get back on the subject of our mamas that night, and I was glad for it. We had talked about everything under the sun, as boys do, but boys don't like to hear bad things about their mamas, even true stuff. I was just coming to grips with the notion that my mama may not be the pure white linen and lace that mamas are supposed to be. My own bad thoughts, words about Mama, grated like brittle chalk on my soul. Shamed me.

8

I awoke at first light. Sore, feet swollen double, in no mood to "listen to the breeze whisper its secrets." I twisted off the remaining boot heel that had flopped with my every step the day before, chunked it at my traveling companion. "Hey, Coot, wake up. A fly's trying to mate-up with your lip. Sun'll be up soon, and I'd just as lief be in Chloride than out here in the open."

The wind had picked up around four in the morning, now blowing high, pushing us along at our backs. Late in the day, we were dog-tired. The howling wind turned, beating us in the face, then shifted out of the north. The temperature dropped like a rock. The wind was carrying more blinding dust than air, blocking out the ruby-dot, hollow sun. In early afternoon, the dust had cleared just a bit, and I glanced up.

I tapped Coot on the shoulder, pointing up at the bleak sun that was partially shielded by thin clouds, a broad ring circling it in the gray-blue sky. "A ring around the sun foretells wet weather, probably a fierce flood. And this wind's coming out of every direction at once. That heavy black cloud to the north is packing a lot of water, heading our way."

"What the hell's a ring around the sun got to do with anything?"

"Papa's Pale Eye mama was a Louisiana swamp medicine-woman. She knew weather better than anybody, prophesied that a ring around the sun was a certain sign that an unstoppable downpour was on the way. Papa read somewhere that the ring is formed by ice crystals. I suppose they're formed when foul weather's coming. We're in for it, Coot, and that's a certain."

"Floods in Louisiana are always a certain—not out here in this dry desert."

We blew into Chloride like a couple of tumbling tumbleweeds just at sundown. As we walked between the first rows of shacks, the miners were coming up out of the mine, heading to their shacks after another fifteen hours of dirt and drudgery. They'd fix supper, if they had the fixin's, then lay down to rest their backs with nothing to fill their dreams but more dirt and drudgery with the rising sun.

The mine foreman, a tall, rawboned, slouch-hat man, dirty, black as the mine he just stepped out of, gave us the once-over. "Say now, what we got us here? Say boy, you shor' do look familiar," he said to Coot. "Ain't you Orville Boldt's boy? Ye look just like him. Ain't near as tall as Orville, but the spitting image of him if'n I ever see'd it." He stood like Gibraltar, giving Coot the eye.

"Yes, sir, Orville Boldt was my daddy. I'm Edwin Boldt, but my friends call me Coot."

"Coot, huh? That's a right strange name to hang on a feller."

"Yes, sir, I reckon that's so."

"You shor' do favor yor daddy. Say, what do ye mean he *was* yor daddy, boy? Orville pass, son?"

"Yes, sir, he up 'n died on us eight years ago come August," Coot replied as he turned up the charm, beat-up hat in hand.

The old man's face softened, winced. "Sorry about yor daddy. He was a good 'un. I never hear't that he passed. What you boys doin' out in this here country afoot, noways? Lose your hosses? Get yourselves bucked off?" He laughed, making good-natured sport of us two boys standing there grinning.

"No, sir, we didn't get bucked off. My uncle Doyl and Narlow's papa—this here's Narlow—his papa and Uncle Doyl, they ran off, left us up on the Black River. Want us to prove our manhood or some such business."

Coot paused, smiled, honey dripping off every syllable. "Say mister, could we make the borree of a couple of those horses over yonder? We sure can promise to have 'em back to you in good shape in just a couple of weeks."

The man crossed his arms. "Manhood, huh? Sounds to me that your menfolks are trying to teach their young'uns something or other. Don't believe I'd cotton to no interfering if'n you was my boys. No, there'll be no hoss lendin' around here. No sir-ree. Tell you what though—you boys are welcome to come on down to my shack for your supper, such as 'tis. My lil' woman'll have something or other to offer ye, I reckon."

He turned to me, offering me his big dirty black paw. "Name's Horace Applebaum, what's yor'n?"

"Sir, my name's Narlow Montgomery, and I'm right pleased to make your acquaintance."

"Montgomery? Onct knew'd a man name'a Abe Montgomery."

"Yes, sir, that's my papa." I felt chesty and straighter.

"Well, I swan. I knew'd Abe Montgomery when me 'n the missus first came out here back in '42 from Kentucky. Your pa done be the bestest feller I ever knowd. Helped me out a bunch, I'm here to tell you. You boys can stay as long as you like, stay a year if'n you like. But let me tell ye a'gin and right up front. There'll be no hosses for ye."

We ate well that night, that's a certain. Mrs. Applebaum was some good cook, but I never heard her utter a single word. I thought maybe she couldn't talk, maybe she didn't have a tongue. But she gave us the warmest, darlingest smile I ever saw when her mister introduced her, and that same smile flashed across her face when we praised her supper and green-grape cobbler she set before us.

Coot and I bedded down on the plank floor, yellow wiggles escaped through the cracks of the cook stove danced their way across the black ceiling. We no more than had time to get dreamy when it came up a storm that beat all Coot and I ever heard or witnessed. Lightning, claps of thunder so dang close you couldn't even count half-way to one, white sheets of light flashing blue on the walls of the shack. Around midnight, Mr. Applebaum got up, lit a lantern, and stepped out on the porch. Coot and I followed him out.

"There's no need for you young'uns getting soaked. I jest need to look out after my mare. I 'spect she'll foal tonight."

After a spell, he came back in. "Now boys, I want to tell you something, so hear me good now. If'n this rain keeps it up like this here, ye won't be a'goin' no wheres for quite a spell. That ol' Cuchillo Crik'll be forty feet deep and a quarter mile wide purty dern quick now. All y'alls got to cross that crik right here, or back-track fifty miles to get around that granite wall to the southeast over yonree. Yep, y'all boys'll likely be eating another helpin' of Mrs. Applebaum's green-grape cobbler again after supper tonight."

Mr. Applebaum allowed as how back home in Kentucky, folks would call a storm like this "nervous weather." The rain pounded the tin roof, the thunder continued to shake the clapboard shack, great flashes spattered the bare walls. I couldn't sleep and guessed that Coot was awake as well.

"You're thinking about something, Coot. What are you scheming?"

"Nothing, I'm ciphering. Tell you in the morning."

"You're not scheming, but you're ciphering. I say your conniving something. What is it?"

He didn't answer, soon breathing heavy.

Mrs. Applebaum was up around four, stoked her stove, and added a few more sticks of cedar kindling. Cedar smoke has a warm, snoozy feeling about it. She roasted green coffee beans, ground them up in her *metate,* set the coffee to boil. She fed her mister three hen eggs and a slab of ham, toasted him a sweet *bolillo*, wrapped some leftovers in a checkered tablecloth for her man's noon meal down in the mine.

As he opened the door to leave, he turned to us sitting up on our pallets on the floor. "See ye boys this evening. You're right welcome to stay as long as you like."

Coot replied, "Thank you, Mr. Applebaum, but we won't be taking any further advantage of your hospitality. We do thank you kindly, sir."

"Best think on that, son. This here storm's not near done yet. That crik'll be techy as a teased rattler by now." He turned. 'Bye, Hon," and went out the door into the dark and rain, heading for more of the same, the dark, dank hole.

Mrs. Applebaum turned without a word, slowly, quietly closed the door behind her as she went back to their bedroom. I don't know why I noticed, but that was the only door inside their clapboard house. That, and the one to the outside were the only doors in the place. I lay there wondering why I would notice that. Strange. Maybe because we only had one outside opening to our dugout back home, covered by two goat hides sewn together, and an old holey wool blanket that separated my flour sack pallet from Papa's and Mama's slat bed.

Coot sat up. "You going home with me, or do you want to stick around here by yourself and eat another helping of Mrs. Applebaum's green-grape cobbler tonight?"

"Go *home*? You heard Mr. Applebaum. It rained hard all night, and he said the Cuchillo Creek would be forty feet deep and a quarter-mile wide. You're not thinking about backtracking are you?"

"No, we're not backtracking. I've been thinking—if this storm's got us holed up, this same storm's likely got your papa and Uncle Doyl holed up as well. Mainly because of those bug-eyed mules. You know how they act up when it's lightning and thundering. Know what we're going to do, Narlow? We're going to beat our wise-ass menfolk back to the Pass, that's what we're going to do, and use this flood to do just that."

"We're going to do *what*? You're as daffy as a cow swallowing peach seeds."

"Yep, sure as the dickens. We're going to build us a raft and float her down the *Cuchillo* to the *Rio Grande*, then on south to the Pass and home. We've seen that river flood dozens of times, and that muddy old river's got some speed to her when she's at full flood and—"

"Yeah, Coot, she's got some speed all right. And when she's flooding, she's also pretty dern testy, meaner'n my mama. And did you ever think that folks get drowned pretty dern *dead* in that brown, boiling water? Remember seeing all those stinking, bloated bodies a year ago last March? Out there in the middle of the river, men, women—*little kids*—all bobbing along like putrefied fish bait? You want your belly all swelled-up like a pumpkin, a turkey-buzzard using you for a skiff while he's picking at your gizzard?"

He threw back his blanket. "Aw hell, we're not going to drown or get eaten up by a damn buzzard. We'll be on a raft, safe and sound, dry as talc. I've got it all worked out. Come on. By the time we get down to the Cuchillo, it'll be light enough to start gathering logs. We'll borrow some rope from Mr. Applebaum."

Arguing was useless. Coot's mind was made up—we were going to float that boiling creek to the *Rio Grande*, and by-golly-bum, we were going to beat the men-folk back home, come hell or high water. We had plenty of at least one of the two, likely both.

It was still drizzling, but the eastern sky showed signs of pink and blue on the cloud tops. It was breaking up. We borrowed a long length of sturdy hemp rope and an ax from the barn.

Coot poked his head in the doorway of a shed on the north side of the barn. "Well, looky here. Looky what we got here—canned peaches. And looky what's up here on the top shelf. Tin cans marked 'Meat.' Let's take a couple of tins of meat and a jar of peaches. Mrs. Applebaum won't mind."

"Well, I don't know. Ain't that stealing?"

"Not exactly—well, maybe in the strict sense of the word it might be stealing, but when you're considering your belly, it's no time to get too strict on the particulars. Let's go."

Coot carried the peaches and tins of meat and I toted the rope and ax. We were almost out of the yard when I told Coot to go on. I thought we owed the Applebaums an explanation or apology and maybe both. I sneaked back into Mrs. Applebaum's kitchen, used her pen and ink, and wrote her a note:

Dear Mrs. Applebaum:
We hope you and your mister don't think
we stole your peaches and meat, because we are just
borrowing them. We also borrowed some rope and
an ax. We'll bring the ax back and send money for
the rope and peaches and meat we borrowed.
We sure hope you don't think we're highway
men that don't appreciate your hospitality,
because we're not and we do.
Narlow Montgomery
P.S.: We sure did like your larapin' good
green-grape cobbler.

I re-read the letter. Something was just not right about it, but as Coot said, it was no time for particulars. I replaced the pen and ink and hurried back out to the shed, leaving the letter hanging on a shelf under a jar of peaches. Mrs. Applebaum would find it in due time.

When I got to the Cuchillo, Coot was wrestling a log out of the water that was lodged in the rocks. Mr. Applebaum hadn't lied. The brown rage of water stretched across in front of me.

"Coot, this is just plumb *nuts, crazy*. Look at that water move. It may be only 200-yards wide, but that creek is moving faster than a race horse. Jeez-amighty, we might as well shoot each other and get it over real quick-like. And speaking of horses, look out there in the middle where the water is rooster-tailing. Isn't that a dead horse out there, bobbing along like a bloated barn?"

Coot stopped, glancing toward the creek. "Yeah, so? Come on, damn it. Help me with this log."

"You don't believe in omens?"

"Shut up and pull. Grab a root and growl."

The mere thought of getting on a raft and floating that creek-of-certain-casualty had me backing up like a mule climbing a ladder. But there was no use arguing. We lashed six logs together, a cross piece at each end. I had to admit she looked pretty dern stable. We cut two long slender saplings to serve as boat poles to keep us from crashing into the side of the granite wall that loomed high in the dark, dreary, downstream dawn.

"Narlow, let's tie our guns and gear down with some twine. Unravel a length of that rope there. We want the twine to be just strong enough to hold our guns and gear in place, but weak enough to break easy if we think we're going to lose the raft."

We leveraged the raft into an eddy out of the swift current and Coot jumped on board.

"Coot, *the ax*," I said, and took off with the ax at a dead run for the house. Coot yelled for me to come back but I ignored him.

As I ran back to the Applebaum's place, that stark, cold feeling was again running down the back of my neck. I stopped dead in my tracks, looked around. Nothing, but this time the feeling was sharp, focused, would not be ignored. Smoke. The odor of smoke from an oak fire filled the air, but there was only cedar around Chloride. I ran on. After replacing Mr. Applebaum's ax, I hurried back out of the yard.

A voice called out, "Ye boys take a care in that crik. She's mighty treacherous, ye must know. She'll get ye if'n you're not right cerful now."

The voice startled me so that I couldn't get my bearings. There she was standing on the porch—Mrs. Applebaum, dressed in the same feed-sack dress, a flowery bonnet on her head, looking down at me. The same warm smile on her sweet, honest face. I realized what my brain could not gather—those were the first words I ever heard that dear lady speak.

I gathered my wits, jerked my hat off my head. "Oh, yes, ma'am, Mrs. Applebaum—and we really did like your larapin' good green-grape cobbler."

Her quiet smile turned to a giggle. "I'd a never a'know'd it, Narlow Montgomery. I'd a never a'know'd it. Now ye boys take a care 'bout yourselves in that crik, ya hear? My mister showed me a ring around the sun the other evening, said he'd never seen that so late of a day, saying that never happened 'cept at noon, said he was a'certain there'd be a storm, something about the Bible. All y'all boys be cerful of that crik, ya hear?"

She knew what we were up to and she had already read the letter. But she couldn't read . . . could she?

"Yes, ma'am. We sure will do that, ma'am"

I ran back to within fifty yards of Coot and the raft. That same ice cold feeling I'd had since we left the Black River came over me. Now overpowering. A man, *that* man was watching us. Close at hand.

I stopped and looked back, thinking my feeling was just my knowing Mrs. Applebaum was watching me run back to the raft. She had vanished from the porch. I glimpsed all around. Nothing. Just cold bustling wind and water, the overpowering acrid smell of burning oak, the acid stench of smoldering leather swirling over me. A whirling blast of wind and rain blinded me. I wiped my eyes again, another gust caught me. I turned back to the raft.

There he stood, out of nowhere. All six-foot-five of him, Two Sticks standing at the edge of the creek between Coot and the raft. Standing cross-armed, unmoveable as the high granite wall looming up behind him.

"*No good!*" Two Sticks yelled at me over the pounding roar of the water.

I had too much respect for the man to yell back to him. I ran on up to him. "What is no good, Many Fast Feet Two Sticks?"

"Water no good, Narlow Montgomery. You drown. Coot Boldt drown dead. You go dead. Wait two days. Water go. You stay. I stay."

"Many Fast Feet Two Sticks, you are a true and good friend. Thank you, my friend, for following me and Coot, but we will be all right. We'll be okay."

"Narlow Montgomery, you have great power. Power does not speak to you now of this danger?"

"No sir, Many Fast Feet Two Sticks, sir, the power does not speak to me."

"Water no good. You dead. You wait. You stay. I stay. You no stay, I *make* you stay."

In time, Coot and I had him convinced that we knew what we were doing. Coot made up a story that we had built and used many rafts on the Big River. That seemed to satisfy him for a bit, but then again he told us to wait and stood between us and the raft, presenting a formidable barrier—an obstacle the two of us were ill-equipped to overcome if we were of a young notion to give it a try.

Two Sticks turned to me. "Narlow Montgomery, how you know I follow you these many suns? I saw you stop. You stop many times—many times over many suns. You turn, look. No one ever see Many Fast Feet Two Sticks. No man ever hear me. You no see me. You no hear me. You no see, hear big cat—no man see, no hear *ndolkah*, big cat. Coot Boldt find track of *ndolkah*. If you not have Power like I say, Narlow Montgomery, how you know?"

"I do not know, sir. I never saw you or that cat with my eyes. I did not hear you or the cat with my ears, but I knew a man, and sometimes an animal was following us."

He turned to Coot, pointing to his own eyes and ears. "Narlow Montgomery sees with no eyes, hears with no ears. He is your eyes, your ears. He warns you, Coot Boldt. Narlow Montgomery has good magic. Power. Believe him. Ussen protects Narlow Montgomery. Ussen is with Narlow Montgomery."

Coot reached out to Two Sticks' chest where our old broken compass dangled on a leather thong. Coot touched it, licked his lips, glanced at my old brass button sewn on the lapel of Two Sticks' coat. Coot touched the compass, then smiled up at Two Sticks. A faint wisp of a smile traced Two Sticks' raw brown face.

Coot said, "Friend, we are the sons of Orville Boldt and Abe Montgomery. We are now men. Papa Abe Montgomery must have told you it is so."

Two Sticks' chiseled face and lips never moved, even when he spoke. "Yes, Abe Montgomery, he tell me. Go. Go in the hand of Ussen. *Enjuh*."

We jumped on the raft and pushed off, waved to the solemn man who had followed us so very far, so many days, so many suns. Two Sticks stood motionless on the shore, certain with fear that was the last time he'd ever see us alive. I turned to Coot, started to shout Mrs. Applebaum's warning about the ring around the sun, but couldn't recall what she said about the Bible. He wouldn't listen anyway.

We learned soon enough that our raft was stout enough for our purpose, but she was far too heavy and waterlogged for us to control with our poles. Like all well-bred women and swift horses, she had a mind and temper of her own. Within minutes, the south fork of the Cuchillo merged with the larger *Cuchillo Negro Creek*. We rode the crest of eighty-feet of water, more than 400-yards wide, crashing, boiling, the brown water arching like a coffee-red rooster tail.

The raft jolted hard into the granite wall. I crashed forward on my knees. Coot didn't see the wall coming as the raft rushed along backward. The first I knew he had fallen overboard was when he bobbed to the surface. He grabbed my pole. I strained against the current to pull him to the raft. He scrambled aboard. Rattlesnakes also slithered along with us in the torrent, wanting permission to board. We discouraged them, slapping at them with our poles.

The dark outline of the mountains of *Fra Cristobal* to the northeast and the *Caballo* Mountains to the south of them were coming up faster than either of us could have imagined. The *Rio Grande* flowed swollen southerly along the western base of those mountains.

Coot called out, "That can't be the *Fra Cristobal* Mountains up there. I thought you said it was twenty-five miles to the *Rio Grande*. How long have we been on this raft?"

"Forty-five minutes or so. Maybe less, but if you don't believe our speed, pick out a rock on the shore and keep your eye on it and see how fast it disappears. You never rode a horse that fast, my friend."

We started slowing down as the *Cuchillo Negro* flowed into the much larger swollen river. The *Rio* had spread out the better part of a mile, but the *Cuchillo* had enough force in her to push us into the main flow of the river. We began to turn, heading south in the soapy brown current.

"Let's see if we can get over to the far bank without a wreck," Coot said. "We've got to figure out how we can make some other arrangements to control this raft."

We lashed a forked upright pole to one end of the raft, fitted a steering paddle into the fork, and secured it in the crook of the pole, making a crude but serviceable rudder. On the other end at one corner of the raft, we did the same, but here we fitted the fork with a long paddle we whittled from our raft pole. We pushed off again and soon were back in mid-stream of the boil. We had leverage on our side now, and learned to control the raft within tolerable limits.

A couple of hours before sundown, the cliffs of *Cerro Roblado*, and the brown, rock, and sand *Sierra de la Dona Ana* mountains east of Dona came into view. Those mountains meant just thirty-five miles to home. We turned a lazy, long curve, and in the distance the peaks of the Organs loomed, framed by the blighted-blue sky. Tomorrow would be a hot one.

Coot said, "What do you say we head to shore over there by that black lava flow? There's a stand of trees around that bend, likely be plenty of firewood."

"I thought you were in a hurry to get on home before Papa and Uncle Doyl showed up? Bet we could be home before nightfall. Don't you want to go on?"

"Naw, I've had all of this raft I want for one day. Besides, I'm in no hurry to get home."

We gathered wood, built a fire, and dried our clothes. We had our tins of meat and canned peaches, and decided to make that do for our supper. The peaches were good and sweet, making the canned meat passable.

"Coot, can you believe Two Sticks followed us all that way?"

"I figure he knew we'd be all right as long as we were near his people, but he probably was not so certain if we came across a band of renegades that didn't know our menfolks."

"What about Two Sticks taking your compass when he left your knife in your sack? And swappin' me for that old brass button. Papa says it's not mannerly to give a man a knife, because if he cuts himself with it, you're to blame. You have to get something in exchange—a penny or an apple." I grinned. "Even an old brass button."

"Did you see that embarrassed half-smile on Two Sticks' face when I glanced at your brass button sewn on his coat, and touched that old broken compass hanging from his neck? I almost laughed out loud." Coot drank the remaining peach juice down in four big gulps, winked, belched, and said, "*Enjuh,*" in a deep, rattling voice that sounded just like Two Sticks. I sure wanted some of that peach juice, but all I could do was laugh.

We kept the fire going late into the evening.

"I've been thinking, Narlow, thinking about home. About *not* going home to be more specific. We must have beaten your papa and Uncle Doyl back down here. For all we know, they're probably stuck back up there on the Frisco River. If I go home, it'll just be me and my mama and her darling little Richard. Mama will ask me a thousand questions—'Where's Uncle Doyl? Where's Abe Montgomery? What do you mean they ran off and left you?' That farm's no fun with Daddy gone, and without Uncle Doyl around, I'd be a sitting duck for a target."

"You don't see me crying 'cause you insisted on stopping for the night. Jeez-amighty, Coot, let me tell you what's waiting for me at home. A mama that calls me a half-breed son-of-a-bitch right to my face. That's the only bad word Papa will allow her to use in front of me, and she's got a thick, well-used dictionary of swear words. Papa will let her do her name calling, he'll agree with her, then say, 'Yep, that boy is a certain son-of-a-bitch.' '*See?*' she'll scream, 'you finally agree with me that he's a worthless son-of-a-bitch, just like his father.' Papa will say, 'Now hold on there, woman. You can call Narlow a son-of-a-bitch 'til the cows come home, but don't you dare use that name referring to me or my mother.'"

"Our mamas may be sisters for all we know," Coot said. "My mama often tells me 'I hope you have a dozen boys just exactly like you, the meanest bastard in the valley.' But Mama's heart is in the right place, she's just carrying a heavy burden without Daddy around. And if the truth were known, I guess I'd have to admit that I'm a hard-ass, stubborn mule at times."

Often times Coot or I would bring up something or other, and we'd say, 'I was just thinking about that myself.' We were friendly to other Mesilla Valley boys. Had a lot of fun with them fishing, foot racing, chunking, skipping rocks, and such, but we never talked about much unless it was just the two of us. Coot told me he read somewhere that no more than two people can have a meaningful conversation, the sincere, searching sort of talk. When there are more than two, there is no merging of the souls as they converse.

Coot's eyes lit up like a bull's-eye coal-oil lantern. "By god, that settles it. *We're not going home.* Let's float on past El Paso and go on down the river a ways. I hear there's a Texas town named Tornillo about sixty or seventy miles past El Paso and a Mexican town across the *Rio* named Guadalupe Bravo. We passed this *Hombres del Campo* test by a country mile. Let's go on down to Mexico, get us a jug of *mezcal.* Your papa's goats and that damned farm and Uncle Doyl can just go cut fish bait."

We grinned, letting the idea sink in for a bit, feeling pretty big in our britches. We were admiring the devil we saw dancing in our eyes in the firelight.

"*Let's do it.* And Coot, you know what else let's do? Let's leave a note in Papa's harness barn for him and Uncle Doyl. We'll say we waited, but soon tired of waiting for two, slow, old codgers."

We laughed, hurrahed at our menfolk's expense.

67

"Reckon we could get IB to bring us down some clothes?" I asked. "My knees are getting blistered through the holes in my britches, and the cheeks of your butt are showing. When we get to Canutillo, you go find IB, and I'll run over to our place and leave that note. I'd give a pretty penny to be there and see the looks on the menfolk's faces when they find out we beat them home."

We took off at first light, full of nothing but last night's sweet peach juice, sour tinned meat, and youthful vinegar. The river had gone down, not to its usual trickle, but it was receding fast. Within two hours we were close to home. Coot steered the raft over to the gristmill on my side of the river. That old mill marked the exact halfway point between our places. We knew that because we stepped it off one time. I jumped off the raft, and Coot muscled it over to his side of the river.

The wind was picking up, blowing caliche sand around in a whirlwind. When I got within a hundred yards of my folks' place, I started sneaking from one mesquite mound to the other. Out back, Mama was bent over a cauldron of boiling water, rendering fat for soap. Having trouble keeping the fire going in the wind, shoveling dirt around the base of the cauldron on the windward side. I crept around to the harness shed, and slipped through the squeaking hinged door, the stench of billy goat piss hit me in the face. My old dog Butch winded me, came barking and gleefully screaming with joy at the sight and smell of me, about to jump through himself. I squeaked open the door, he jumped through the opening, and I loved on him enough to quiet him down.

I looked through Papa's leather working tools and found a piece of brown wrapping paper. With a stub of a lead pencil, I scribbled out a note for Papa and Uncle Doyl:

Dear Old Folks and greetings ~
We waited and worried for you
a week, maybe two weeks,
but gave up on you knowing how
slow and old you are.
We figured you would be along in due
time like old folks do.
We have taken up the ways of the sea
and should reach the Gulf of Mexico by fall.
Don't worry yourselves about us Men
as we're not the worrying kind.

68

The Men of the Sea of Manhood and
Hombres del Campo
Coot Boldt & Narlow Montgomery
P.S. Mr. and Mrs. Horace Applebaum send
their kindest regards.

I stabbed the note on a nail where Papa kept his important papers and receipts for goat meat and milk sales, the first place he'd look when he got home. I peaked through a crack in the shed door and caught a glimpse of Mama hurrying into our dugout. She stopped, looked around, then seemed to glare right at me, sulfur strong in the dust of the shed. Mama never looked at me, or anything else for that matter. Her manner of seeing, of looking, was a glare. Maybe she was the innocent victim of the gimlet eye. She ducked her head under the goatskin, and stepped into the dugout.

I took off at a dead run, Butch hot on my heels. I stopped, tried to talk him into staying home, but for the life of me, I couldn't. He'd been separated from his best *amigo* for over two months, and that was plenty.

Coot and IB Crane, were poling the raft across to my side of the *Rio Grande*, a meal sack stuffed with clothes lying on the deck of the raft. None of the other boys would have anything to do with IB. The older boys teased him unmercifully, saying he only had one boot in the stirrup and only one rein tied to the tail of his burro. We didn't know what that really meant until a year or so ago. Fact was, Coot and I used to tease IB ourselves, but not any more. Ever since IB's run-in with Rye Green and Seth Byrne, we let no one bother IB and Shelly Brom. Coot put an end to boys taunting, teasing IB, boxed the ears of boy who said that our friend was dumber'n'a wound-down clock.

Before the raft nudged the river bank, IB commenced to scold me. "Now, Nar-low Mont-gomery, I done tolt Coot you boys is gonna make your mamas madder'n a passel a wet hens, and I don't mind telling you there'll be hell a'plenty to pay when you boys get back from your little funning down at Torniller."

Coot hopped back on the raft, whistling Butch on board. "All aboard that's going aboard."

I jumped on and we were soon in midstream.

Coot called out, "Hey IB, just tell them you didn't see us—we weren't here."

"But, I seen you, Coot. Seen Nar-low as well . . ."

"Jeez-amighty," I said. "Poor ol' IB will likely up and die over this one. He'll have this story so screwed up in his head he's likely to worry himself to an early grave."

"Yeah, I know it. Bless his heart. He makes me so damn mad I could choke him, but my daddy always wanted me to be good and gentle with IB. Uncle Doyl said IB was slow because he was conceived in the devil's bed, whatever the hell that means."

We watched as IB disappeared behind a cane break, having left him on the wrong side of the Rio.

9

Twelve miles down-river we approached El Paso, Texas and El Paso, Chihuahua on the Mexican side. Both were no bigger than the other villages we passed, but they shared more than their name—political clout. Adobe villages, with adobe-sounding names—Ysleta, Zaragosa, San Elizario. Ysleta holds the record as the oldest town in the entire state of Texas. Everybody learned in school where a bunch of folks landed on North America's east coast at a place called Plymouth Rock in the year 1620. Yankees seemed to think that was a long time ago, but considering that the Spaniards under *Don* Juan de Onate stepped across the *Rio Grande* right over there twenty-two-years earlier in 1598, the "Plymouth Rockers" were just Johnny-come-latelys. Another Spaniard, Cabeza de Vaca, came through here in 1535, eighty-five years before those step-so-lightly buckle-shoed gentlemen landed in New England.

Every village we passed was flooded, mud everywhere, their fields slopped with mud but renewed with rich soil from the mountains far to the north in southern Colorado and northern far reaches New Mexico. Men, women, and children were making what repairs they could to their homes, outbuildings, and corrals. They called out, "*Adios,*" waved their greetings, happy with life with little care about the flood and the destruction it brought them and their meager crops. Though their adobe homes were reduced to heaps and puddles of chocolate pudding, these happy, brave folks were not discouraged a twit. They'd get by. *Adios*—Go with God—the same God that brought this flood and ruin down around their shoulders.

We were floating by some pretty fair country now, with high grama grass and sage, making good quail cover. We saw covey after covey of Gambles on the Mexican side. About the time we thought that covey of quail would be the last big one, we'd spy an even bigger covey, all fat and sassy as a bunch of barnyard hens.

"Narlow, you suppose your papa's 10-gauge could gather us in a gaggle of those quail for our supper? I bet I could eat a baker's dozen at one sittin'."

"You *mojon*, quail don't gaggle. Geese gaggle, quail covey. But, I bet you can't eat as many as this old side-by-side can gather up for you to peel and cook for our supper."

I thought about Papa scolding me for calling Coot a *mojon*, but the word sounded so rich and so much more genteel than "turd." Quickly mastering the adjectives of the muleskinner, I made a mental note to watch my mouth when I got back home so Papa wouldn't remind me with a generous helping of lye soap.

"Steer over a little closer to the bank," I said. "I'll shoot, Butch will retrieve." We soon had eight plump quail for our supper. We skinned and gutted the birds and roasted them on a stick over a hot mesquite fire. The mesquite served up all the flavoring required, we ate 'til we just about popped. We gave Butch a bird that I had blown to smithereens along with our scraps. That night we lay out on our *sarapes* looking up at a clear, moonless sky. The air was cool and brisk off the river, keeping the mosquitoes at bay. We had out-foxed our elder foxes. We had full bellies. Life was good. And, best of all, we were men.

I rolled over toward Coot. "Jeez-amighty, look up yonder at that blue-black sky, will you? Reminds me one time Papa read a line of poetry that went: 'The largess of the stars is mine.' He asked me whether the poet was speaking for a prince or a pauper. I told Papa that I supposed it would be a prince. How could a pauper own so many stars? Papa told me to rethink on it, and I reckon I will. There must be upwards of sixteen-million of them. Reckon if we started counting them all, and tallied them up real careful-like, star by star, and when we got all through counting, and were extra special certain we counted them all, reach up, shut our fists upon each star so we don't double-count, do you reckon there would be an even or odd number of stars? Ever wonder about that?" Coot made no comment.

"Well, you're probably wondering what I decided about the largess of the stars, aren't you? And, I bet you're counting them right now, wondering whether there's an even or odd number of stars, huh?" Coot chunked a rock at me so I'd shut up.

71

But I took no offense. Me and Coot were like Rumi's "mouse and frog," Coot laughing, saying that old Persian must have had me in mind as the mouse, what with all the chatter he says I do. We were open, telling each other stories, sharing dreams and secrets, empty of fear or suspicion of the other. Important things stayed just between us. I *knew* he was over there trying to close his eyes, counting stars in spite of himself, considering the largess of the stars. By golly, I'd stick with my *amigo*, even if his count turned out odd. That's what friends are for, I figured—to stick together on important stuff. But then I had to remember that a cow gathers more beauty from a rainbow than Coot ever could.

We pushed off before dawn, the muddy *Rio* reflecting blue and orange.

Coot called out, "That must be Tornillo up there on the left. 'Torniller' as IB calls it. That'd be Guadalupe Bravo on the Mexican side."

As we approached the brushy Tornillo side, a dapper Mexican man and a little girl appeared out of nowhere. A slight-built man in his late twenties, dressed immaculately, even formally to be out here by this muddy old river. His red Prince Albert coat was worn, but neatly pressed, a black top-hat perched on his handsome head, his tight, black britches tucked into shinny, tall black boots.

"*Buenos dias, hombres*," he said, gesturing with his hands for me to throw the raft's tie-rope to him. "Here, sir, let me have that rope and I shall pull you to shore." His English was flawless. His presence spoke for itself, needing no introduction nor acknowledgment. His little blue-eyed blonde lass eagerly chased after him, shiny as a bright new *peso*.

"I am Rodolfo Bustamante de Enriquez, *a sus ordenes*," he said. He turned to the little girl pulling at his trousers. He knelt and picked her up, pecked her on her cheek. "And permit me to present *mi hija*, Sarina." She could have stepped right out of a picture storybook.

"Howdy-do, *Senor* Bustamante, I'm Coot Boldt and this here's Narlow Montgomery," Coot said, shuffling his boots in the damp sand.

I scuffed Coot aside in an attempt to polish over our rough appearance. "*Senor* Bustamante, it is a distinct pleasure meeting you and Sarina. It is our pleasure to be so honored with your kind reception. I, sir, am Narlow Montgomery, and my companion here is Coot Boldt. We, sir, are at your service."

Coot stood grinning at me.

Rodolfo Bustamante insisted we join him at his home, a beautiful *hacienda* off the square in Tornillo. We tried to back off, to decline, but he insisted, saying that it was not often that he had an opportunity to entertain guests. He ordered hot water for our bath, and clean clothes for us. I laughed when Coot came out after his bath in his white garb, his black hair, wet and curly, shaggy as a buffalo's hump. We dined on the most delicate corn tortillas I ever wrapped a tonsil around, with frijoles, grilled green onions and green chili, and choice pieces of *cabrito*. Rodolfo saw to it that we got all the soft, delicate meat under the horns.

Coot and I spent nearly a month with Rodolfo Bustamante. He enjoyed our company, and it was a pleasure to entertain him and Sarina. One evening, he told us how he came to lose his wife. She had been killed by a stray bullet during a feud between Mexican and Texas ranchers. The Mexicans found unbranded cows south of the *Rio Grande,* and had no plans to give them up without a fight. That was three years ago, and while it still pained Rodolfo, he held no grudge.

Butch was a favorite with Sarina and the children of Tornillo. There were no other dogs as a hydrophobia epidemic in late spring required destroying every last one of them to protect the villagers and their livestock. We swam and played with Sarina, taught her to fish with the hooks and line we brought along from the line shack. She caught a catfish one evening that weighed nearly seventy pounds. That old lunker far outweighed Sarina, and, yes, Coot took most of the fight from her hands, but she dragged him up on dry ground with no assistance.

Late one afternoon, a rider came through Tornillo while Coot and I were out hunting deer in the hills along the *Rio.* The rider was posting reward offers for information regarding the whereabouts of Narlow Montgomery and Coot Boldt, $500 in gold. The reward offer was signed *Abe Montgomery.* Rodolfo knew the rider, and while not letting on to that we were so close at hand, he pressed him for any information he might have. The rider told Rodolfo that Abe Montgomery and Doyl Boldt had been caught in a flood, that most of their horses and mules had drowned, lost all of their equipment. Abe Montgomery made it out with his horse and two others that he was leading at the time. The flash flood caught Doyl Boldt, swept away in a thirty-foot high wall of water. Believed to be dead.

Coot's eyes and voice grew hollow as the noon sun. "Narlow—the grizzly—your kicking and dancing with that mama-grizzly. Uncle Doyl."

I said to Rodolfo, "But that information has to be nearly a month old." That statement spoke volumes. If Uncle Doyl had been found alive since then, the rider would know it.

Coot took the news without a blink, but his dark eyes glistened. He stood like a pillar of salt as Rodolfo recounted the rider's story. I didn't know what to say. Uncle

Doyl was as much my uncle as he was Coot's, but it was different—he lived with him and his mama for Coot's sake, all he had.

"Coot, I guess we better get on home."

"We'll talk about going home tomorrow. Right now, I don't want to talk about anything." He walked out of Rodolfo's *hacienda*, heading down river.

I heard Coot come in around midnight, heard him rummaging around. After a bit, I dozed off, got up around four—he was gone. He had changed into his clothes, leaving the britches and shirt Rodolfo had loaned him folded on a chair. He left a note telling Rodolfo that he had borrowed a horse and saddle, and would return them both when he had time to work through all this. He closed by telling me to go on home, and that he would come on in dreckly. His tracks headed northeast and I figured I knew where he was going. Coot had no heart to go home. Without Uncle Doyl there, he might never go back.

"Well, Rodolfo," I said, "I guess it's my turn to do some horse borrowing myself."

10

I rode through Papa's pasture gate long hours after dark. Butch had left me a mile back, and I knew he was headed for the river for a long drink and a cool soak. We had traveled fast all day and half the night with no rest. The wind was a rage of grit and sand, but Papa was still out back at his forge, great showers of orange sparks leaping into the night. I was reminded that Two Sticks often referred to Papa as *Pesh-Chidin*, the Apache's belief that a man working iron at a forge possessed the Spirit of Iron, a witch. His blacksmith area was carved into a low caliche rise on the south and west, the north walled with gray wooden slats, open on the east. I rode behind our dugout and into the horse corral close to the caliche rise.

Papa came over as I was unsaddling Rodolfo's dun. "I guess you know about Uncle Doyl, son?" he asked, a heavy hand on my shoulder.

"Yes, sir. A rider came through Tornillo yesterday afternoon. Coot took off sometime during the night. I woke this morning to find him gone, left a note telling me to go on home."

Papa wouldn't say much about Uncle Doyl, fact is, he could barely speak about what happened. They were caught on a spit of land next to the sheer wall of Monticello Canyon on the Alamosa River, a flash flood swept Uncle Doyl and his horse and all six of the mules away in a torrent of water. My mule, Mary Jewell, was one of them.

Papa yelled over the wind, "I'm awfully sorry about your Mary Jewell. She was a good old mule. I feel right bad about her, know how much she meant to you." He picked up my saddle and motioned for me to follow him back under his blacksmith lean-to and out of the wind.

"Aw Papa, don't grieve yourself about Mary Jewell. I'm just happy to see you and to know you're okay."

In the low light of his forge, Papa's eyes showed puffy with grief, his square shoulders slumped as though weighted by his anvil. As I was rubbing down Rodolfo's dun, Mama came running through the corral and right up to us in the low light of the forge, cussing a blue streak, calling me a lazy no-good. I winced when she called me a worthless half-breed son-of-a-bitch for running off down the river with Coot to get out of work. Her eyes and face dark as the inside of a tar barrel.

I turned so I couldn't witness that sight, taste the god-awful evil pouring out of her copper-lined insides, her breath like rancid coal oil. Papa tried to shush her, but her pent-up venom would not be denied. He stiffened, eyes so dark yet ablaze, I feared he'd quiet her.

I brushed by her, not looking her way. "Hello, son. Welcome home, son. Sorry about your mule, son. It's good to have you back home safe and sound, son."

Mama let me be after that. Maybe Papa had something to do with her silence. I was glad for the relief. But Coot's mama was there to take up the slack. Bright and early every morning, she came over in her buggy, looking for her "no-good" son, screaming at me to tell her where Coot was hiding.

"Doesn't he know he has a farm to work? Does he think I can do it all by *myself*?" She never once asked if Coot was all right and never a word about any sorrow for losing Uncle Doyl. That old gal sure had hard bark on her. Mrs. Boldt was not as coarse as my mama, but plenty rough enough.

Two weeks later, Papa asked me when I planned on returning Rodolfo Bustamante's horse, go find Coot, bring him on home. I tried to tell him that Coot wouldn't be in Tornillo, and, if it had been Papa instead of Uncle Doyl who drowned, that I wouldn't be there either. I told him I figured I knew where I'd find him. Papa saddled Traveler for me, packed a mule with provisions. I left at first light, trailing the mule and Rodolfo's mare.

Just as I predicted, Coot was not in Tornillo. Wasn't there, and hadn't been. After supper, Sarina climbed up in my lap, sweet as a bee-kissed honeysuckle blossom. She was still for awhile, then asked, "Uncle Narlow, do you think you can find my Coot?"

"Why sure, honey, I'll find Coot for you."

She began to cry and beg, "Well, Uncle Narlow, someday I'm going to marry Coot, and I don't want anything bad to happen to him. Please bring him back, Uncle Narlow, *please*." Her sad blue eyes glistened. "Uncle Narlow, my Coot told me you are half Indian and have magic and power that other boys don't have. Will your magic and power help you find him?"

"I'll do a war dance tonight before I go to bed, Sarina. My magic and power will sweep me up and take me right to Coot before you even wake up in the morning. I'll find him, sweetheart. Promise."

Before sun, I was saddled up and ready to go. Rodolfo helped me pack my mule. I swung up and settled into the saddle and handed Rodolfo a small, heavy pouch. "Rodolfo, here's $500 in gold dust from Papa. He wants you to give it to that rider that came through passing out the reward offer."

"It will be an honor, *amigo*. Truly an honor. That is very noble of your papa. The rider passes through here every month with the mail. I will see that he gets it, I assure you."

"Rodolfo, I know it's not necessary to thank you for all you have done for me and Coot, but you have our thanks anyway. If I'm not home in three or four weeks, Papa will come looking for me. If he does, tell him I headed up into the New Mexico territory to a cabin in the Sacramento Mountains—a cabin Coot's daddy built over twenty-five years ago. It's located near a spring west of the Penasco River, down in James Canyon. Papa knows the place."

Rodolfo had one warning for me. I could feel the dread in his dark eyes when he said, "Narlow, go due north out of Tornillo. Stay far west of the saltflats at Guadalupe Peak. Many Mexicans have been killed there for taking small amounts of salt, many have been murdered. Their ancestors have been using those salt flats for centuries, and they are looking for revenge. A lone *norte americano* would be an easy target for their hate."

I cut due north for the Hueco Mountains that straddles the New Mexico-Texas line. After passing the boulders of the Huecos and skirting the salt flats, I turned northeast across the barren Tularosa Basin for the Sacramentos, a high, green-whiskered mesa in the far distance. I camped at the base of the mountain, and was back in the saddle well before sunup. High on the steep, rocky mesa of the Sacramentos, deep forests of Ponderosa pine shaded the trail, and the cool was a blessing. By early afternoon of the following day, I eased Traveler into a wide valley, and crossed the high mountain range that tops out over 9,500-feet, overlooking James Canyon.

Sure enough, from Coot's daddy's lodge, a thin blue curl of lazy smoke drifted from the rock chimney. Coot was by the corral fence, working at something. I let out the high-lonesome, triumphant scree of a hawk. After a bit I screed again, and he raised his arm, long knife flashing. He'd be dressing out a mule deer, and I was sure ready for my share. On the steep ride down to the cabin, I tried to count the days since we learned about Uncle Doyl's passing. Must be seventeen.

Coot was out back dressing out a young spike he had tacked to the log corral. I reined in and sat watching him work the sword-like knife.

Without turning around he said, "Your papa must have bumped his head on a rock during that flood he got caught in. That might explain why he'd let the likes of you ride off on Traveler. Narlow, you're just like these silly-ass Stellar jays around here—you sound more like a hawk than a hawk, but like a Stellar jay, you just can't resist screeing again. A hawk rarely repeats itself—unlike some I know."

He turned, grinned up at me. "About time you showed up. What kept you, shithead? Light down and tell me what's happenin'."

"Jeez-amighty, Coot, why didn't you shoot a *real* small deer while you were at it? Reckon that little spike will have enough backstrap on him for two hungry boys? If not, I dibbies."

Our gazes locked. He started to speak, grinned, wiped the blood on his knife against a fence post, then leaned his head over, grinned, and went back to his chore. Coot had a way with a knife. Two Sticks' gift was sharp, heavy-stout, and Coot used it to cut tender venison and tough tendons with ease, broke, separated bones with a flick of his thick wrist. We didn't talk about anything in particular. I just let him lead me where the talk would go between us, but I did tell him about little Sarina and her wedding plans for him. He got a big kick out of that. Took the edge off.

Coot hadn't shaved, and when he went without a razor, he always reminded me of a buffalo, but now with his shaggy hair and beard, he could have gotten real amorous with the prize heifer of the herd.

"You're not standing close enough to your razor, Coot. Never thought I'd see the day you didn't shave."

"Don't have the equipment. Tried shaving with Two Sticks' knife—it's sharp enough but I'd bleed to death without a mirror."

I reached back in my saddlebag and tossed him a sack of lye soap and shaving gear and mirror Papa sent for him. "Boy-howdy, if Papa and Uncle Doyl saw that beard, why they'd wrestle you down and—Aw, Jeez-amighty, Coot. I didn't mean to bring up Uncle Doyl. You've gotta forgive me."

"Let it pass. I'm having a hard time remembering, even *believing*, that Uncle Doyl's dead myself. Anyway, how's Uncle Abe doin'?"

"Oh, not too perky."

"I didn't expect he would be. Knowing him, he probably blames himself for Uncle Doyl drowning."

"How'd you know that?"

"Oh, I just know Abe Montgomery, how he thinks. I'd likely feel the same if something like that happened to you. But, we'll never know will we, Narlow? I'll likely die young like my daddy and his brothers, but you, hell you'll likely live forever, won't you?"

"Yeah, I reckon I will, just about anyway."

"I admit I've spent a lot of time up here on this mountain thinking about Mr. Bones. Death seems to about have me covered up. It occurred to me that when a favorite person like Uncle Doyl passes, we shed an ocean of tears over it, but what are we crying about? Why are we *really* sad? Because Uncle Doyl didn't have twenty or thirty more years to live? No, it's not *his* losing the years that grieves us, it's the years we'll miss having him around, all the fun *we'll* miss. When I figured that out, most of my grief passed. The dead are dead, and I reckon the rest of us will trail along in due time."

"Well, by golly, Coot, look who's getting philosophical in his old age. You sound just like me. You'll be counting those even-numbered stars if you're not careful. But I guess you're right about that. Papa was telling me about Uncle Doyl's dying, and recommended you and I shouldn't spend too much time trying to figure out the 'why' of it. Papa says death does not need a reason. Borning and dying are just part of life—two extremes of life, they're just on opposite ends. Death just is."

I told Coot my mama didn't have much to say when I got home, and that I supposed Papa had threatened her like he sometimes does when she ought to hold her tongue. Coot laughed when I told him his mama came by every morning to take up the slack. Coot shaved, we stoked the fire in the rock fireplace, and roasted our backstrap. He got quiet and I knew he was thinking about some way to bring up another sore subject. We both seemed to always get quiet before bringing up tender topics.

"Narlow, I—I've been thinking about your mother—mine too. It's awful to hear about your mama, and you know I mean no disrespect by bringing this up."

He was quiet again for a minute, then continued, "When Daddy died and Uncle Charles showed up and planted all those damn pecan trees, I thought Mama might be crazy. I know now Mama had a lot of weight on her shoulders, and she just made a mistake by following her slick brother's advice. But what you said about your mama, Narlow, that's different, my friend. Do you reckon your mama's just plumb crazy?"

I thought about telling him about the time she beat me with the horse quirt, but those words could find no vent. This was more about Coot than me.

"No," I said, "I used to think Mama was crazy, but her older half-brother, Howard, told Papa once that Mama was always like this, even when she was a little girl. Not crazy, just meaner'n hell, and I can sure vouch for that. Mama's side has a pretty good sprinkling of Comanche blood, and Uncle Howard says those Comanches are the meanest Indians in the country. Says Apaches can't hold a candle to them when they get riled, and they're right easy to peeve. Just like my mama."

He turned to face me, his gaze dropped, stood a moment, then said, "Let me ask you a question, Narlow. You don't have to answer it if you don't want to, but do you like your mama? I don't mean love her, do you *like* her?"

"Funny you ask that question. On my birthday this very year, Mama came up behind me and called my name. The wind was strong, so strong I barely heard her. I turned, thinking, *hoping*, she was going to wish me a happy birthday. Instead she asked, 'Why don't you like me?' All I could think to say was, 'Huh?' but she kept at me, insisting on an answer. I was stumped. How do you answer a question like that from your own mama? *Especially* when it's as obvious as your thumb in your nose. The wind was blowing so hard, I suppose she thought I couldn't hear her. She got right up in my face, yelled the same dern-fool question again, over and over, 'Why don't you like me, you son-of-a-bitch? Why don't you like me? Why don't you like me, you worthless bastard?' the odor of acid-soaked garlic strong in the air. I hemmed and hawed, wanting to ask her why she didn't just wish me a happy birthday, and not ask me that god-awful question. I kicked the dirt, stuttered, mumbled, and braced against the wind. No, I couldn't tell her I liked her then, and

I won't say I ever liked her, but I sure felt sorry for her. When I wouldn't answer her, she turned and walked off, yelling over her shoulder, 'I thought so, you half-breed son-of-a-bitch.' You tell me, Coot, but liking or loving a mean person like that is hard to do—even your own mother."

I sucked in a gallon of air, bucked myself up. "Coot, I never said this before to no man, but I have a hollow spot in my chest, like a bit of my heart is frozen solid as an icicle. But, shoot, here we are talking about whether I like my mother, and it just struck me that I have never heard her say she loves me. But then, I don't recall telling her that I love her either. I guess we're square on that score. I don't know if the word 'love' is even in Mama's vocabulary. I'd kill for her, Coot, put myself between her and any danger *whatever*. But that doesn't mean I have to like her—does it?"

He stabbed his knife in the dirt, cleaned its edge on his boot. "Derned if I know, Narlow, derned if I know. My mama and her 'little Richard' and that damn farm make me so damn mad I could spit nails, but her heart's right. She just plays favorites, blames me every time Richard gets in trouble. I'm sorry to bring this up, Narlow, but I had to get this straight with you about my mama. She's all right."

"Well, I'm glad for you, glad it's settled in your mind." I stirred the fire and started to say something I needed to say, but the words caught in my throat.

Coot caught my eye, but his gaze flashed back to the fire.

I had to say it. "Coot, I need to tell you something. It's eating on me, and I need to let it out before it eats me up and drives me nuts."

"You mean nuttier, don't you?" he asked with a grin, his black eyes now warm.

"Remember back at the Black River when Two Sticks asked me if my mushroom had ever warned me of danger before that kicking mama grizzly came on us? Remember? I hemmed and hawed, and finally I told Papa that I just couldn't tell the whole world since I had never mentioned it to him. Remember, I stalked out of camp?"

"Sure I do—wondered about that, but I'd never ask. I figured you'd tell me if you ever was of a mind to."

"Well, this hurts to recall, and the words taste like iodine on my tongue. I can taste the bitter before I even say the words, but I just *have* to tell you. It wouldn't be fair to our friendship, our brotherhood if I held back."

"Aw, Narlow, forget it. You and me are tight as a roll of barbed wire."

"I know, but I'm going to tell you just the same."

I stood, threw another pine log on the fire, plopped down on the plank floor in front of Coot. "This goes back to when I was twelve years old. Papa and Fernando Valdez were up on the mountain near Bishop's Cap, tending goats. Mama and I were there by ourselves, except for fifty-five nanny goats Papa had left for me to milk twice a day. Seems like I've been milking goats even before I was born."

"Yeah, Narlow, milking those goats gives you the only grip I can't overpower. I can put all our friends on their knees in a hand-squeezing contest, but you can dang near put me on the ground. I really have to suck it up to keep you from besting me."

I went on. "The night this happened, I was sitting on a caliche rise just east of our dugout, Butch by my side. It was early, not quite dark, the moon still hiding behind the mountain. Mama came up behind me—"

I stood, kicked a dirt clod. "Coot, that's not fair to Mama. First I have to tell you what Papa told me about the way she was raised. She lead a tough life as a girl. Papa told me about her upbringing, about her unbelievably cruel mother named, Moon Dawn. I can still hear Papa's kind, soothing voice when he talked about those days. He said, 'Narlow, I think it's time you know something about your mama, how she was reared. Maybe it will help you deal with her unloving ways. Your Mama's mama was a full-bloodied Comanche. Her Indian name was *Tlẽ'gona'ai Hayolkaalyu*, Moon Dawn. They lived in the mountainous region of the Sierra Madres in northwest Mexico, the roughest, most unforgiving country in the hemisphere. Hardly any Comanches were down there at the time, mostly Apaches and local Indians, but Moon Dawn and her two daughters were living with a no-count white man. Moon Dawn caged your mama in a stout salt cedar box, strung her out on the limb of a gnarly tree, high over a cliff by a leather thong above the valley floor. Moon Dawn warned her yet-tender-fifteen-years-old daughter to be quiet, to be still, or the slender thong would break, that she would die on the rocks far below. After five days, no food, no water, blistering July heat, her little sister pulled her back from the precipice, cut the cage's rawhide bindings. When Moon Dawn found the empty cage, she became enraged, repeatedly stabbed the younger sister until your mama hit her own mother at the base of her skull with a war club, scattered her brains all over that rock shelf.'

"Well, Coot, when Papa finished, I thanked him for telling me, now I could understand why she's so dern blessed mean. Papa thinks that going without water in that inferno may have cooked her brain a might, maybe even damaged her mind beyond repair. He said that a full-grown, stout man can handle just so much abuse, go without food and water for just so long, then with the passage of just a single minute more, destruction is done. Her mind was damaged. Her soul as well, if she ever possessed one.

"Papa said that her Pale Eyes father was a shabby, lice-infested creature, that he had seen him once over in El Paso, Chihuahua about fifteen years ago. He wanted a handout, demanded to see his daughter. Papa gave him a single *peso*, told him there'd be no more, warned him to leave his wife alone. Anyway, after Moon Dawn's death, their worthless father took the sisters to Ciudad Chihuahua, sold them for a burlap-wrapped jug of cheap mezcal. The man who bought them was a lawyer from El Paso, Texas, took them home with him, thought about putting them in an orphanage. But changed his mind, decided to raise them as his own, adopted the girls. The younger sister died suddenly. That made the lawyer suspicious of the older sister, that would be my mama, but there was no doctor around at the time to determine the cause of her death. Papa knew the lawyer as he did chores for him in partial payment for law lessons he gave Papa in his spare time."

Coot said, "I guess that's why Uncle Abe knows so much about the law, that and reading everything he comes across."

"That explains it all right. Anyway, the lawyer was suspicious about Mama and the dead sister, but Papa felt sorry for Mama, convinced the lawyer she was innocent. About that time, Mama was agreeable to marrying Papa. She detested living in the lawyer's house, something she called the House of the Bad Pale Eye. Papa and Mama finally agreed on living in the dugout."

I slumped to the ground beside Coot. "Like I started to say before, one night I was sitting out on the edge of the *arroyo* outback, and Mama came up behind me, silent as a flea lighting on a newborn kid's ear. Even Butch didn't stir until she spoke. Mama growled her growling shrill, her voice always the same with me, 'I called you for your supper over an hour ago, but you needn't worry yourself none about that—I slopped the hogs early. What the hell are you doin' out here anyways?' I told her, 'Oh, nothing, Mama. I'm just tired. Thought I'd watch the moon dawn.'

"She swung at me, knocked my hat off, screamed, 'What the hell do you mean, watch the 'moon dawn'? Where did you hear that from? Who told you about her? Your goddamn father tell you that? He did, *didn't he*? *Answer me*, you goddamn son-of-a-bitch.'

"I didn't know what had riled her. 'Where did I hear *what* from, Mama?' I asked. 'I swear I don't know what you mean.'

"'Your goddamn father told you all about Moon Dawn, didn't he? *Didn't he*?

Answer me, goddamn it to hell. Who told you about her? Answer me or I'll beat the tar out of your heartless foul soul.'

"'Moon Dawn?' Mama, I don't know anyone named Moon Dawn. I just said I was waiting for the moon to daw—'

"'You're a damn liar. The moon *don't dawn*, the damn *sun dawns*, you half-breed bastard. Tell me who told you about Moon Dawn. *Right now.*'

"I knew there'd be trouble if I didn't get away from her. I took off running, her vile words chasing me down the *arroyo* to the *Rio*. Racing after me like devils that had taken on scorpion wings. But that wasn't the worst of it."

I stood, leaned against the fireplace, my hands stuffed in my pockets, sighed. "Well, Coot, the very next evening, I was sitting on my milk stool in the milking shed. It was late, but the full moon coming through the slats of the shed gave off enough light for my milking. I remember that I had just three more nannies to milk. I brought in another nanny, poured a half-cup of grain in the milk stall's trough, started milking her. I was tired, sleepy. I leaned my head against the nanny's warm, soft, velvet-fuzz bag, breathing in its honest cleanliness, bathed by her tongue, feeling the rhythm of the foamy white stream from her tits hissing into the half-full bucket. Dreaming, I became aware that there was suddenly more light on the wall of the shed in front of me. A purple mushroom showed itself. I heard the cry of a little girl, like the night my little sister, Mary Jewell, passed from smallpox. I just figured the cry and flash of a nonsensical thing like a purple mushroom was because I was groggy, dreaming. I nuzzled the velvety bag, inhaled its innocence, its cleanliness. The mushroom got bigger, brighter, more purple, garish-like. I shook my head. Heard a whir. Something stung me, *hard*, hard across my shoulders. I turned to see Mama standing over me, a lantern held above her head in one hand, a horse quirt in the other. Before I could stand or hoist my arm to fend her off, she swung again, hitting me across the neck, biting me all around my throat. I jumped to my feet. Grabbed the wrist that held the quirt. She swung the lantern down at my head. I ducked, grabbed her other wrist. I stood squeezing her wrists. Holding them above her head, one still gripping the quirt, the other grasping the lantern."

I slumped to the floor, legs straight out, leaned against the shack wall, as Coot jumped to his feet. "Damn, Narlow, that's god-awful."

I looked up at Coot. "Of a sudden, her face took on the yellow glow of the lantern, began to turn pink, then purple, and her head and face were now in the hand where the lantern was. Like I wasn't squeezing her wrist, but her neck. I squeezed hard, harder, *harder*, with all the might I could muster. Her face turned deeper red. I thought it was because I was squeezing her neck. I was squeezing so hard it made my fists, both our whole bodies shake. Until that moment, I don't recall ever wanting to hurt anything or anybody. But there I was, wanting to hurt *this* somebody *real* bad – my own mother. I squeezed harder, like I was sitting on my milk stool, milking a nanny, trying to get her to give me that last drop of milk. My hands kept squeezing, wanting her to feel real pain, to bleed. I admit I wanted her dead. My own mother—I wanted my own mother *dead*, but I—"

"Narlow, you don't have to—"

"I kept squeezing, shaking us both. Then the boards of the milk shed began to rattle, the ground quaked, an eerie purple light all around. Mama looked about, aware of the ground quaking. The purple light and mushroom subsided.

"I let go of her wrists, and grabbed the lantern and quirt away from her. I asked, 'Why? Mother, why? Why did you—'

"'Because *I can*. I'm your *mother,* goddamn you. And you know about Moon Dawn, and you lied about it.' We stood looking at each other. She saw it in my eyes—there would never be any more whipping—for *any* reason, good reason or *no* reason. She was powerless. For the first time in her life, she was weak. She stood rubbing life back into her hands and wrists. Again she screamed, '*You half-breed son-of-a-bitch*. You should be *real* proud of yourself. I wish I was a man 'cause I'd whip your goddamn ass right where you stand. You oughta be ashamed, picking on a poor defenseless woman. Your *own mother*, damn you. You're no damn good. You're just like your goddamn father, and you'll grow up to be just like him—*weak*, a worthless son-of-a-bitch.'

"I started to speak. But, what was there to say? I looked deep in her evil, black, swimming eyes that I swear spewed a copper stench. All I heard, saw, smelled, felt, was hate, deceit."

I stood, squared around to Coot. "When Papa followed me out of our camp that day back on the Black River, at first I just could not tell him. I told him I felt it would be breaking a sacred trust. Papa asked me if someone wronged me, and I confessed someone had. 'But, Papa, it won't happen again, I *promise.*'

"Papa turned to go back to camp and he said, 'It dwells on me heavy that somebody wronged my son and that I will never—'

"Coot, I could not let him finish that sentence. 'Papa, *wait*. I'll tell you.' And I told him what happened. I doubt Papa will ever mention that to Mama. He'll set her straight about me, but he won't bring that up. After I finished, he said he would handle it with Two Sticks.

"While we were still up there on the Black, Papa told me something kinda strange. I've thought on it, but not certain I fully understand it. Even now. Papa said he read where some Englishman wrote, 'If you strike a child, take care that you strike it in anger, even at the risk of maiming it for life. A blow in cold blood neither can nor should be forgiven.' Mama's blows with that horse quirt were no-doubt in cold blood, but then she does everything with a good measure of ice. I'm not certain I'll ever forgive her.

"I've had over four years to think on what happened that night. I guess I understand it as well as something like that can be understood. But there's one thing I haven't been able to get a handle on—I still refer to her as Mama when I'm talking about her to you or Papa, but to her face, I call her 'Mother.' She is my mother—nothing I can do about that, but she sure as hell isn't my mama. And, no, Coot, I would have never told you that story, because it pains me so much to think about it, much less talk about it. But I had to explain why I stalked out of camp that day. I still remember the questioning look on your face as I walked past you. If I hadn't told you, you would always question it, wonder where you stood with me."

Coot smiled, looking me square in the eye. "You need to ease off on yourself, and terrapin yourself along for a spell. I understand, but that makes it all the more strange."

"Strange? What's strange?"

"Remember that storybook my little sister had when we were little tykes? The one with a picture of a cow dancing on a rainbow? To me, you've always been that cow, a'dancing around on a rainbow. You've always been easy to be around, a naturally happy boy, and in my mind's eye, I often see you dancing on a rainbow. Kinda strange how you can have a mother like that, yet always a smile plastered on your face."

"I'll tell you something else that's strange, Coot. Real strange. Mama never mentioned that god-awful night, not one time—except once. A couple of days later, she said, 'Narlow, about the other night.' She stopped, I thought she was going to apologize, but that was not to be. She went on, 'Did I just dream it, or did the ground seem to shake, the milk shed rattle, purple all around?' I made no reply, only returning her burning, burrowing gaze. She stood strong, then her shoulders slackened, she backed away, a faint hint of fear in her squinted eyes, then she turned and scurried back in the dugout. Since that day, I've often caught her looking at me that same way. I don't know what it means, but she's got plenty of Comanche in her, superstitious. Probably something in her gut tells her that I'm not to be trusted, to be careful of me, that I have it in me to do her harm."

"Narlow, she's scared of you, thinks you may just be meaner'n she is. And I suspect you are."

I sighed, winced as his words took root. "That's not easy to hear, but my true friend, I'm afraid you're right about that. A few days after I told Papa about Mama hitting me with the horse quirt, he came up behind me while I was tending the smoke fire. 'Son, I'm worried about you dwelling on your mama—it's not good for you, not at all healthy. A boy's respect for his mother is about the most sacred, most important thing he has in this world. A line in Milton haunts me, worries me for your sake. He wrote, *Never can true reconciliation grow where wounds of deadly hate have pierced so deep.* I'm not asking you to forgive your mama, and I can appreciate your hurt, but for the sake of your future, for the family you'll have one of these days, you must work at somehow reconciling with her. If you don't, it will sour you, make you unable to love a woman, respect her.'

"Coot, I've never read Milton, but I've dwelt on that line and believe I grasp it's meaning. For the life of me, I can't find a crack in Milton's thinking. I just don't know. Don't want to disappoint Papa, but I just don't know. Heaven help me if I'm never man enough. I just hope God doesn't damn me if I fail."

"God will never damn you for that, so just rest easy on that score." After a while, he asked, "Well I guess your papa thinks we're real *Hombres del Campo* now, doesn't he?"

"Yeah, we passed their manhood test all right. Say, Coot, what do you think that was really all about? That Manhood and *Hombres del Campo* stuff. Do you know what that was really all about?" I was standing by the rock fireplace, my arm resting on the mantle.

He looked up, his face dark as saddle leather framed by a glory of raven hair, eyes glistening like black diamonds. "Yeah," he said. "I reckon I do. But I'd like you to verify it for us—if you're a mind to."

"Well, all right. Papa and I didn't say two words about it when I got home from Tornillo. He did say that Two Sticks knew they were going to leave us up there on the Black. He asked Papa and Uncle Doyl if it was okay if he gave us those knives—something to have to remember the occasion about becoming grown men. I told him about Two Sticks following us all the way to Chloride. That didn't surprise him one bit.

"Anyway, I think Papa and Uncle Doyl loved us about as much as two men can love two wild-assed boys like us. Remember Uncle Doyl saying we weren't born, we were foaled? And if I ever saw two men that loved life and pure freedom, it's gotta be Abe Montgomery and Doyl Boldt—and, of course, your daddy before he died. They see those same qualities in us, but they were much too manly to attempt to communicate what they see in us. So they showed us, tested us, gave us our rein. They believed in us, and had the courage to put us on our own out there in the wild.

"And Coot, you know what? Uncle Doyl's probably up there in heaven smilin' down on us right this very minute, just a'whittlin', a'spittin', and a'grinnin', telling tall stories like he always did, and you know what else—"

Coot shot out of that cabin like fodder out of a cannon, blurting out something or other about tending to the horses.

11

We saddled up and headed east down James Canyon before sun. We brought the venison we cooked up the night before, and some jerky Coot had smoked when he first arrived at the hunting camp. Behind Coot's saddle were two bamboo fly rods in an old stiff leather case his daddy had purchased on a steer-buying trip to San Antonio the year he died. How that man loved to fly fish. It was a treat to watch that hell-for-stout, tall man fishing, dreaming of the day we would be old enough to handle that long rod like a bandleader's baton, watching the light dance on the line, far, far out on the water, trout rising to his hand-fashioned fly.

We had no need of a pack mule on this little trip, but Coot said if I thought anything of that cussed dang mule, I'd best trail him along. Grizzly sign was abundant, and if I left the mule in the corral, he'd likely be grizzly scat before we got back. I told Coot that it'd be a decidedly good idea to bring the mule along for company and intelligent conversation, he being far better than my alternative. Coot's answer was typical: "You and that mule are pretty close kin, aren't you?"

We had determined to spend a few days fishing the Penasco River. We overtook an old-timer pushing a burro up the trail, man by the name of John Winklejohn. Said he'd been prospecting these mountains since back in '32. He styled it the

"Penny-ass-co." The Penasco's one of those high mountain rivers that cuts through heavy, rich soil, bound together by deep grass and watercress. Only a foot deep, and a man can step over it in most places. Colder'n the 'proverbial,' loaded with trout that Coot's daddy called *Rio Grande* cutthroats.

Coot baited his hook with moths and all manner of flying bugs, catching them in mid-flight with a quick cupped hand that rarely missed. On occasion, I'd whip a bug off my arm, but mostly I relied on black woolly worms I found in the damp earth under a shady spot or wiggling over a rock.

We fished, napped, reminisced. About men things, us being men and all, like whether we'd be goat ranchers or cattle ranchers. Or, maybe the biggest, richest farmers in the entire Mesilla Valley, but we'd have a passel of farmhands so we wouldn't have to get our own hands dirty *ever again.* We'd be gentlemen farm-ers—yes-siree, gentlemen farmers. We weren't sure whether we'd farm or ranch, maybe both. One thing was certain—we'd never be sheep ranchers. *Hated bunch of no-counts, them sheep ranchers,* we'd heard all of our lives. Want a fight? Just call a man a sheepherder, or a lamb-licker, and you'll likely get all the fight you crave, then some. I didn't see much difference between a sheep and a goat, and Papa had over 4,000 of the critters. But I kept that finely tuned observation to myself.

Sometimes I thought Coot and I had been together for all time, not just all of our sixteen years, but for centuries—maybe longer. Possibly ferocious Vikings who sailed the seas, fought Romans, the garlic hoards of Baghdad. I asked Coot if he ever thought or dreamed anything like that. He just said I was nuts, as full of shit as a Christmas turkey. *How full of shit could a Christmas turkey be?* I asked. Coot scuffed my ear to shut up my wondering. But other than his non-dreaming ways, we talked about anything and everything.

We promised honesty in all our discussions about important subjects. Truth was a natural trait that we inherited from our fathers. Papa told me when I was just a pup, "Narlow, always tell the truth, and if you don't lie to me, I'll never whip you or lay a hand on you. You've got my word on that." And, I sure took him up on that promise. Papa was a big, rough, stout man, someone I *never* wanted to tangle with. Oh, sometimes I'd get in trouble at school, or like one time when I got caught stealing peaches off a neighbor's tree and had to return them to their owner, stuffed in my sweat-soaked shirt on a hot summer afternoon, those fuzzy varmints about to drive me nuts. Then there's the time Papa came real close to breaking his promise not to whip me, *real* close, but Papa kept his word. He was trying to teach me to tell time with his big wind-up Big Ben. I just couldn't get it. Why, when the big hand is on 9, and the little hand is on four, how could that be a quarter 'til 4? I could sorta see how it could be 9 'til 4, but not a quarter to 4—a quarter is twenty-five. Yes, sir, I was mighty afraid I was going to have to remind Papa of his solemn promise. Almost drove that good man to whipping me and taking up the adjectives of the muleskinner, all in the space of one lazy Sunday afternoon.

Papa allowed no looseness in talk. He required Coot and me to call everything by its proper name, never allowing us to call an object a "thing." If we did, the whole lot came to a halt, and he'd just wait until we came up with the proper descriptive word. He pardoned no blunder of speech, reminding us that Nature pardons no errors, abhors a vacuum, that water freezes punctually at thirty-two-degrees, boils with equal precision at 212-degrees. Coot and I were so close it was almost like we were under the same skin. Papa said we reminded him of a set of Siamese Twins that he saw one time in a traveling freak show in San Antonio. The Siamese Twins were joined at the hip, least that's what Papa said. I thought he was funnin' us about babies being joined at the hip, but then I read about it once.

Coot did have one obsession that made him almost human. That fixation was death. He would spend many late hours sitting by his daddy's grave that was on a little knoll out back of the Boldt place. Coot made a wrought-iron fence that enclosed the spot where his daddy and Uncle Kermit were buried. One time, a traveling parson told Coot that his daddy was not in that hole in the ground, "Your daddy is in heaven." Coot told that preacher he knew *exactly* where his daddy was. He had put him in that hole, and piled up big rocks to keep the wolves and coyotes from digging him up and eating him. Coot could feel his daddy was close when he sat out there in the dark, and sometimes he would talk to him. Coot told his mama, "Don't tell me Daddy's not here. I can feel him, hear him." Then, when Coot was just eleven, his baby sister died, and that about broke what was left of Coot's heart. Coot dug her grave next to his daddy, carried her fevered body inside the pretty, black, iron fence, buried her deep, patted the moist soil that would hold her for all-time.

We were quiet—*deafening*. I blurted out, "Remember when Uncle Doyl would say that his horse was faster than a stripped-ass ape? I wonder if he ever actually saw a stripped-ass ape?"

"I wonder," Coot said, teasing. He sighed. "Oh, Uncle Doyl, Uncle Doyl—bless him, please Lord, bless him. What a man. He promised me he'd stay on the farm as long as I stayed around. He'd say, 'Coot, don't you worry yourself none about your old uncle Doyl. I'll be right here for you as long as you stay with your mama, but you see, boy, I'm a yondering man, I'll just mosey on down the road, find home where I hang my hat that night.' Uncle Abe and Uncle Doyl have been my daddy. I'd have never gone to school, if it weren't for them. Mama made me quit when Daddy died—said I had to work the fields—but those two men kicked up such a fuss she gave in, and I got to go back to school."

Coot and I talked about our similarities and differences, and he recalled, "It's just like your concern about Mrs. Applebaum. You were so damned worried that—"

"By the way, Coot, you owe me a dollar. Half of what I sent her."

"A *dollar*? You sent Mrs. Applebaum two dollars for a jar of peaches and two tins of meat?"

"And forty feet of rope, don't forget. Yep, shore did, *amigo,* and I bet right about now she's telling Mr. Applebaum what fine, upstanding young gentlemen they had as guests, who dived into two helpings of her green-grape cobbler."

"See there, Narlow? I'd'a paid those folks back someday, but things like that weigh on your fragile conscience to where you can't even breathe. Anyway, as I was saying about those folks back in Chloride, you went to the trouble of returning their ax and writing her a letter assuring her that our intentions were so admirable. Me, shoot, I just assume folks know me for what I am, and if they think I stole something, that's *their* cross to tote. I don't have time to nursemaid folks the way you do."

Yep, Coot and I talked about everything under the sun up there on that high meadow, fishing the Penny-ass-co. But I skirted one subject for four full days and nights. I should have brought it up when I first rode in like Papa advised me to do. But then, the subject could no longer be avoided, things got taut, uneasy, quiet between us as we sat close to our campfire, a stiff cold breeze at our backs.

Without warning, he stood, threw a rock into the dark. "Now, Narlow, don't get on my ass about going home. I'm not going back to that farm, and I'll tell you why. First off, I don't like that damn place since Daddy died, and *much* less, now that Uncle Doyl's gone. Second place, I don't want to take orders from Mama. She's so damn smart, knows so much about farming, she can just farm it with her favorite little boy, Richard. Little Lord Fauntleroy bastard! And that brings up the *third* reason I'm not going back, and that's shithead Richard Boldt. I've got to tell you, I've got it in me to kill that bastard. He didn't like Uncle Doyl, and Uncle Doyl couldn't tolerate him. If that dog turd said one damn word disfavoring Uncle Doyl, I'd kill him in his tracks. So don't talk to me about going back, 'cause *I ain't goin'.*"

He was wound up tighter'a wadded-up javalina. I stoked the fire, threw on another couple of pieces of cedar, acted busy, not wanting to rile him about a sore subject. After a while, he repeated himself, for all I know, he may not have even been talking to me. "I *ain't* goin'."

"Coot, I don't recall saying anything at all about going home. You brought it up, I didn't."

"Yeah, but you've been thinking about it every damn minute since you rode in the other day, how you could best bring up the subject."

"Well, you're right about that, I reckon, and I sure don't blame you one bit. I don't look forward to going home either, but let me tell you what Papa said when I was packing up to come looking for you. I should have told you this straight out, but I didn't know how to bring it up, how you'd take it and all. Coot, Uncle Doyl had a little over $5,000 in gold—"

"*Five-thousand dollars* in gold? Five-thousand simoleans? Hell, Narlow that's a *fortune*. The man never even bought himself a new hat that I ever knew about."

"Yeah, Coot, and listen to the rest of this, 'cause, *amigo*, you're a rich man. Papa has been stashing that gold for Uncle Doyl all these years, and you're the only one even close to a son Uncle Doyl ever had. Papa says that gold is yours, says Uncle Doyl would want you to have it, and Papa knows you won't waste it. You'll take care of it, put it to good use. And listen to this. Papa's sending me off to the university in Austin come fall, and thinks you oughta go with me. Put Uncle Doyl's gold to work and all."

Coot gave me a big, wide grin. "University? You and me at the university? Maybe IB is right about you smoking those funny little Mexican cigarettes. The university in Austin?"

"Yes. Papa thinks we're too smart not to get some formal education. He says we're sometimes too smart for our britches, but he gives us credit for having something besides ear wax in our heads. He wants me to—"

"The university—"

"Yeah, Coot. And Papa wants me to study the law because of my gift for gab. By golly, I reckon I will. He thinks you should try your hand at engineering. You're real good with your hands and all, and you can figure out anything mechanical and—"

"Your papa wants us to go to the university in Austin?" His eyes brightened, danced, his face glowed, completely taken aback for the first time that I ever witnessed.

Well, somehow or other that idea slowly took hold in Coot's head. Over the next couple of days we'd be fishing, I'd hear him off downstream a ways say, "Uncle Abe wants us to go off to the university," then laugh.

He leaned his casting rod against a rock and came over. "Narlow, we can't go off to the university. Your papa promised Two Sticks that we'd be back up on the Black River next spring, and you and me would go off with Two Sticks and his medicineman—what's his name? Oh, yeah, Na-Tu-Che-Puy. Uncle Abe can't break his word for us."

"I reminded Papa of that promise, and he said that sometimes a man has to go back on his word when life deals the unexpected. Uncle Doyl's passing has changed our lives forever, and Papa says a man has to live life, play the hand he's dealt. He said he'll either go back up to the Black by himself next spring, or send word to Two Sticks. When he hears about Uncle Doyl, he'll understand."

"Uncle Abe will *never* go back up to the Black River alone, not without Uncle Doyl."

Over the hours and days, the idea of our going off to the university soaked in, and the question began to take the form of a statement, *We are going to go to the university. We're going to go to the university in Austin.*

The last night at the Penasco after supper, Coot scraped off his plate. "Narlow, tell me something. How in the blazing hell does your papa think we can ever get in to that university? If we were to go to Austin, that is, how would we even get past the front door? There must be some qualifications to get in a university, isn't there? A test, credentials, *something*. Hell, we only went to three years of grade school down at Frontera in a one-room shack before the school closed down, and those were only half-years at that. That's not exactly a stepping stone to a state university, you know."

"You're right, and I told Papa that same thing. But Papa's been talking to Judge Murdock and the Judge thinks we're already better educated than boys that have gone to formal schools all the way up through the grades. Even to preparation schools back East. We know our multiplication tables up to twenty times twenty. Judge Murdock says he never heard of such a thing. Says most boys and girls can go up to ten times ten, a few up to twelve times twelve. We know the Pythagorean Theorem. I can work it out on paper, but you can do it in your dern fool head. *And,* you understand what it means. *And,* Coot, remember you researched Mr. Pythagoras and found that his theorem had been known by every rope-stretching surveyor on the Nile, 2,000-years *before* Pythagoras? We've read about every book that's made it this far west, every dern book in Simeon Hart's library, and that's the biggest library between Dallas and San Francisco. You've got a memory that's stouter'n a baited bear trap. Once you've got a handle on a subject, *nothing* loosens your grip. And, Papa's not exactly uneducated, and he says—"

"No, he sure's hell not. Uncle Doyl told me your papa studied the law by correspondence. Through some university up in Chicago. What kind of brain does it take to master the law through the mail? It takes *months* to get a letter through to Chicago, if at all, or *ever*."

"That's my point, Coot. You've just *got* to believe and trust, *hope* in your heart that Papa's right. That we can not only get in that university, but we can make the grades to boot, maybe even graduate. Papa says it's your sure ticket off that farm."

We rode back up to the fishing lodge and packed our gear. Coot trailed me and my mule out of there, following me back up the long canyon to the western summit of the Sacramentos. Ever once in awhile, he'd laugh, call out, "Narlow, you and me are going to the university. I can just hear IB Crane saying, 'Who'da thunk it?'"

After a while he yelled out, "Damn it to hell, Narlow, we're just preening our own prunes thinking we've got what it takes to get in that university."

"We'll see, *companero*, we'll see." I laughed over my shoulder. I got to thinking about us going all the way to Austin to that college. When Coot had brought up our limited formal schooling, it reminded me of the one-room school we attended down at Frontera, six miles south of our place. Teacher-man by the name of Wales Pembrooke really got under my skin one day when I was ten years old. Right there in front of all my classmates, he accused me of smelling like a billy goat. I was sitting on the back row, recall the pretty little girls upfront, turning in their desks, smiling, their eyes telegraphing their support, their friendship. Pretty lasses they were, Hanna Rae Rosenberg, Mia Helene Honeycomb, Emily Ann Weatherwater. Mr. Pembrooke made me *real* mad, and if I'd been as big as I was now, I would have invited that gentleman outside. I told Papa about that, and he thought Mr. Pembrooke might have a point, suggested I best clean up and change clothes after my milking chores every morning before heading off to school.

***

As it turned out, the Boldt farm wouldn't have nary a crop to gather come fall. A hailstorm in late July, with walnut-sized stones, beat every last cotton, corn, tobacco, and watermelon plant clear to the ground, and peeled off the gray slate roof from their house. Coot thought the sight of that awful mess was about the prettiest spectacle he ever saw. Coot's mama blamed him for the loss, but that didn't bother Coot a bit. He had learned to accept and ignore her silly notions. No, Coot didn't kill his brother Richard either. That brainchild went even further east than Austin, to a little isolated east Texas town in the middle of the Big Thicket to a place called Huntsville, the home of the state penitentiary. Seems Richard and his two Mexican *amigos* decided to do a little "highway mining." That sparkling threesome held up a stagecoach east of El Paso on the Butterfield Trail, which just happened to be transporting three Texas Rangers who had ventured out from Austin to settle the El Paso Salt War. Little brother would be the guest of the Blue Bonnet State, making horsehair bridles for fifteen-years-to-life, depending on good behavior.

Coot grinned when he heard the verdict. "Thank God Almighty—that means life."

12

Papa and I spent most of August tending goats without the able services of Fernando Valdez. He'd returned to Mexico to see his family, a visit he had not made in over ten years.

Papa grinned. "Son, if we don't find Fernando's fifty-odd goats before he gets back, you're going to be in a lot of trouble with that man."

"*Me?*" I asked, laughing. "I didn't lose Fernando's goats. You know, Papa, we've looked just about everywhere there is to look on your 9000 acres without a sign of them. Suppose something got 'em? Maybe ate 'em?"

"I suspect you're right there. That old crippled mountain lion must be back in this country. Probably has a cub or two with her. Let's head for Red Mesa, and if we don't find 'em up there, I suppose we'll just have to give it up."

Though camping in the hot, dry desert was rough going, we were free from Mama's constant haranguing. Quiet is a blessing. Our only irritation was the constant high wind and dust, which was uncommon for late August.

We spurred our mounts up the steep face of the red rock mesa, and as we topped out, we were heading straight into the wind. What greeted our sun-and-wind-blasted eyes was more of a blur than real. That old mama lion was right there on top of that mesa, nursing two cubs. With the first sight of us, she was gone in a flash, two cubs in hot pursuit. As Papa pulled his carbine from its scabbard, he spurred Traveler, tried to head her off before she made it to the downhill side of the mesa. That old gal may have been old and crippled, but faster'n quicksilver.

"Well, son, by the looks of all the bones and scraps of fur and skin around here, I'd say we solved the mysterious disappearance of those fifty goats. That ledge over there is probably that lion's den. I'm beat—let's make camp and take a load off."

Next morning, while sitting around the fire drinking the last of our coffee, Papa asked, "Well, son, ready to head on back home? You'll be heading for Austin in less than two weeks, you know."

"Gee, Papa, being with you and your goats sure doesn't put me in much mood to be going off to school, but the longer I put it off, the harder it's going to—"

I jumped to my feet, my head turned up and around as I caught a familiar odor carried by the westerly breeze. "Smell that, Papa?"

"Smell what?"

"Burning oak and leather—elk leather—moccasin leather."

"No, I don't smell anything. What do you mean, moccasin leather?"

"Two Sticks. I don't know where he is, but he's close."

"Narlow, you know that Two Sticks is dang near 300-miles from—"

"No sir. Two Sticks is right over there across the valley," I said, pointing west. "He's right *there*, where the sandhills meet the valley floor. He's there."

"Son, it's over six miles down to the *Rio Grande* from here, and another four miles to the sandhills. That's ten miles. Even you can't see that far."

"I can't see him, but he's there all right. And he's walking south toward our dugout. He's striding heavy, brings news—bad news."

"Narlow, I haven't said anything about it, but you've been dreaming a lot the past several nights, like you're having nightmares. On one occasion you yelled out to me to 'run from the purple.' I suppose you were dreaming about your mushroom. You haven't spoken of medicinemen, or the Power that Two Sticks is so certain you possess in quite a spell. But you're certain he's down there, huh?"

"Yes, sir. Sure as you're sitting on that red rock. *Certain*. Dead certain, Papa."

"Well, if that's the case, we best make tracks for home before Two Sticks gets there. Your mama will put a hole through that Indian if she gets a bead on him. She may be half Indian herself, but she hates Apaches worse than anybody I ever saw."

I thought, *Yes, Papa, and you're half Apache.*

We rode into the corral. No sign of Two Sticks.

"What do you think, Narlow? Think he's had time to walk this far?"

"Yes, sir, I do. He's here. He's waiting for us up North Arroyo."

We rode up the *arroyo*, and hadn't gone more than a half-mile when a fist-sized rock rolled across in front of us. We looked in the direction the rock came from, and there he was—squatting on his haunches, gazing right at us.

Papa breathed. "Well, I'll be jiggered." He raised his hand and called out, "Welcome, Many Fast Feet Two Sticks, *mi amigo*."

"*Hola*, Abe Montgomery. *Hola*, Narlow Montgomery."

"Two Sticks, what are you doing here?" Papa asked. "You walked all the way from your reservation? Over 300 miles? The agent in charge of your reservation will not be happy to learn you left."

"Many Fast Feet Two Sticks worry about many things. Abe Montgomery, not worry about agent who cheats us out of our rations. Yes, I walk here. I walk to talk to you, Abe Montgomery. Talk to Narlow Montgomery. I get your letter—my son, Iron Chain, he read it to me. Many Fast Feet Two Sticks bad sorry Doyl Boldt die. Doyl Boldt friend. Narlow Montgomery see Doyl Boldt in kicking grizzly. You remember, Abe Montgomery?"

He walked up. "Now I bring bad sorry news. Medicineman Na-Tu-Che-Puy. He sick bad. Na-Tu-Che-Puy say he die before next summer come. He have vision. Vision of Narlow Montgomery's purple mushroom. Mushroom tell him Mother Earth soon die too. Many purple mushrooms kill Mother Earth. Na-Tu-Che-Puy want Narlow Montgomery come now. Learn Power. Maybe Narlow Montgomery save Mother Earth." He stood with his arms across his chest, waiting for Papa's answer.

"Two Sticks, I am sad to learn of Na-Tu-Che-Puy's ill health. But I do not see how Narlow can be of any help to him. He is going far to the rising sun to go to school, to the university in Austin, Texas. He leaves in only twelve suns. When he finishes his schooling, he will go to your reservation to learn Power. It would not be just to ask him to go with you now."

"Abe Montgomery, how you know Many Fast Feet Two Sticks in this *arroyo*? Many Fast Feet Two Sticks never see you home in past. How you know Many Fast Feet Two Sticks sit here waiting for you? You and Narlow Montgomery take ride in heat of day?"

"No, I must confess to you that Narlow and I were far up on that mountain." He pointed. "There, in that red part of the mountain. Narlow told me this morning that Two Sticks was near by. We came here and found you here. Just as he said."

"I take Narlow Montgomery to Na-Tu-Che-Puy now. He learn Power from great medicineman. Then he go to school in Texas."

96

Papa sat his horse, mulling over how he could tell his old friend that the white man does not believe in Power. Yet, he just witnessed his own son make a wild prediction that came true before his very eyes. He was speechless.

He turned to me. "Narlow, you are a grown man now. If you want to go with Two Sticks, I'll not stop you. What do you say, son?"

Now I was on the hot seat. I hesitated, not knowing how to best say what I needed to convey to this great man. "Many Fast Feet Two Sticks, sir, my papa is the best man I ever knew. He wants me to go to the university. He has saved much gold so that I can go there. I cannot go against his wishes. Please tell Na-Tu-Che-Puy that I am sorry."

Two Sticks came around to the offside of my horse. "Narlow Montgomery, you papa good man. You good boy to do what he say."

He turned to leave, then stopped, smiled at Papa. *"Enjuh."*

13

Coot didn't go to Austin with me that September. He went north to the new university in Boulder, Colorado. Coot's aunt Beulah lived in Boulder, and insisted that Coot come up there and live with her free. He would have his own private room, and could devote all of his time to his studies. Coot's mama never knew about Uncle Doyl's gold. Papa told Coot that his mama might think that Uncle Doyl may have come to that much gold by other than honorable means, might even claim it for herself. Papa couldn't think of anything else, so he told Mrs. Boldt that he was paying for Coot's schooling, that Coot could pay him back over the years. News of that got back to Mama, and she promptly threw a wall-eyed fit. Accused Papa of bedding down with Coot's mama, bunch of crap like that. I heard Papa and Mama arguing late one night, and I believe he came real close to separating her head from her ass over that accusation. Forever the suspicious sort, thinking everyone was gawking at her, talking bad about her.

The night before Coot left for the University of Colorado, I had supper at their place, stayed over. The next morning, I was helping him saddle his mare and pack-mule for the long journey north to Boulder. I felt guilty, uneasy, wanting to talk to him but I could not force the words. Coot was in the saddle before I could get it out.

I handed him the lead to the mule.

"Narlow, this is about the hardest thing I ever did in my life. We've been close, you and me. I'll miss you, friend."

I reached up to shake his hand. "Coot, wait a minute—I just have to tell you something." I looked up at him in the gray dawn and stuttered, "Coot, I—I—"

"I know how you feel, Narlow. Let me hear from you from time-to-time. See you soon. *Adios*." He reigned the sorrel around and went out through the gate, his mule braying like a stuck pig.

Two days later, it was time I boarded the Butterfield stage for Austin. I was on my horse, holding Traveler's reins, waiting for Papa to come out of our dugout. I could hear him and Mama arguing. Papa was not happy with her, and, as usual, I was the cause.

He came out, his slate-gray eyes ablaze. "Go in and say goodbye to your mama. She doesn't want to go all the way to El Paso. Says she has a bellyache."

"Aw, Papa, that's all right. I'll be back in a few years." My words rang hollow as a tin barrel, their meaning taking hold. "Come on, Papa—we don't want to miss that stage. I've never been on a stagecoach, and sure don't want to miss my first opportunity."

Papa was standing between my horse and Traveler, fidgeting with his saddle. He turned, looked up at me. "Son, don't you want to take a minute to say goodbye to your mama?"

"Papa, I know how much this hurts you. But my going in there would only make things worse. No offense, Papa, but in your gut, you know that's true. Let's just go."

Papa had bought my ticket all the way to Austin the week before. When we rode up behind the coach, the other passengers were stashing their luggage in the boot. The one lady-passenger was already in her forward-facing seat.

A stagehand on top of the coach hollered down, "Toss her up, son. I'll rope her down real tight-like for you."

I threw my duffel up, turned to Papa, who was tying Traveler's lead rope to the rear of the stage.

"What are you doing, Papa? I can't take Traveler with me."

"Why not, son? You'll be the envy of all your fellow students with a horse like Traveler. I'd be right proud for you to take him."

"My old horse June Bug will suit me just fine, Papa. I'd never forgive myself if something happened to him. And besides, I'll need a horse, but I sure won't be needing a horse as fine as Traveler where I'm going."

"Well, son, you never know about things like that, and besides," Papa said with a wink, "I've already promised Traveler that he was going on a trip. I try not to disappoint an animal like this fine gray mount. He's stout, dependable, and I want you on him when you need him. Best get aboard, son."

"Gee, Papa, I don't know what to say."

"You're all set, Narlow. You've got $500 in gold tied under your shirt, a fine horse and saddle, and a ticket off my goat farm that will soon have you a long way down the road you have decided to travel."

"Gosh, Papa, I just have to tell you something. I need to tell you that—"

"And here's something you can call your own, son." He handed me a small canvas bag.

"What is it, Papa?"

"Open it later. Best get in and take your seat before this stage is half-way out of town." He stuck out his hand.

I took it. We stood smiling at each other. A mist forming at the outside corner of my eyes. I knew I'd lose that fight. "Goodbye, Papa. I'll try to make you proud." I jumped in the coach, looked out the window, and there sat Butch, looking up at his master, smiling as smart dogs do, tail a'wagging.

I jumped back down, squatted, gave him a hug. "You mind your manners, Butch, and help Papa and Fernando Valdez." I jumped back to my seat.

The driver gave a whistle, cracked his whip, the team of six horses lunged into the harness, and the coach followed the team down Overland Street heading east out of El Paso. The coach and six passengers would be in Austin in five or six days depending on the weather and luck getting through Comanche country.

I settled back, then remembered the canvas bag Papa gave me. I reached down between my feet and opened the sack. Inside was something wrapped in a fine kidskin. I pealed the skin back and there in my hand was Papa's Bible.

The lady passenger wore a dark green dress, with a gold-colored hat that sat at an angle on her forehead. "That is a fine present your father gave you, young man. I know you deserve the gift, and trust you will take excellent care of it, and never part from it."

"Oh, yes, ma'am—I mean, no ma'am. I mean..."

The men in the stage all hurrahed me, and told stories of Bibles that had been in their families down through the years.

99

By mid-afternoon, the stagecoach slowed, the drive hollered out, "Hueco Station. You folks have time to stretch your legs."

I asked the driver how far we had come from El Paso. "I reckon this station is right about sixty miles east of El Paso. We're making pretty dern good time."

I climbed up on top of the stage, untied my duffel, and tossed it down.

"Where you think you're goin', son?" the driver asked. "You got a ticket all the way to Austin, and that's another 550-miles yonder way."

"Oh, no, sir, this is as far as I go, sir. Guess my papa made a mistake when he bought my ticket." I tossed my bag behind Traveler's saddle, untied his lead, tightened the cinch, and mounted up.

"Now son, this ain't real friendly territory. You ought'na be goin' off by you'sef like this. Comanches roamin' southeast of here 'bouts."

"It's all right, mister. We have a place just south of here. I'm real familiar with the country. Thank you for your help."

I turned Traveler south toward the *Rio Grande*, topped a hill, stopped, stared back at the coach. It too was topping a hill, and soon went over the other side, dust boiling after it. I turned Traveler. That's when I noticed Papa had forgotten to take his 44-40 repeater out of the scabbard. Or, had he? I reached around and opened the saddlebag. What I found answered my question. There was everything a man could need in that saddlebag, but not the sort of equipment a student of law would require in Austin. There were two boxes of 44-40 shells, a press and lead for making more cartridges, gun powder, twine, needles and thread, Papa's prize leather repair kit, a new pair of elk leggings, and moccasins that had an unmistakable Abe Montgomery look and feel about them, a bound journal with no entries, ink, and several quill pens. There was a bag of jerky and a bag of pemmican. Those two bags really made me suspicious.

At the bottom of the saddlebag was a note:

Narlow ~
I hope you find your schooling to your liking and
that you never quit learning. I don't believe you will,
as you have a turn to learning and wonder.
I have always been proud of you, never prouder than I am
at this moment. Your Mama shares my pride.
May you have mellow moons and happy skies.
Let us hear from you by and by,
Papa

100

I was struck numb. Papa knew what I was up to, but how?

By sunset Traveler and I were overlooking the border village of Tornillo and Rodolfo Bustamante's *hacienda*. The pink of the sunset shown on the white of his hacienda, turning it the prettiest blush I ever witnessed. I decided to camp, think things through. Did Papa know what I was up to, where I was headed? I read Papa's letter a dozen times trying to determine that with some certainty, but the words did not reveal the answer. The jerky and pemmican told me more than Papa's letter. A terminal case of remorse settled in on me and my campfire. I felt bad-guilty. My braggadocios new adult-self suddenly became little Miss Self-Doubt. *You need to try to catch that stage before it gets too far ahead of you.* I picked up the saddle blanket and threw it on Traveler's back.

"Aw, shoot, Traveler. I don't know what to do, but I just gotta do what I gotta do."

Traveler turned and looked at me with a wondering eye that a smart horse can give you from time-to-time. I chewed on the jerky, and began writing a letter to Papa. The warm fire put me in a dreamy mood. My letter rambled. I awoke as the eastern sky was showing its own shade of blush. I tore up the letter. Nothing I could say in a letter that Papa didn't already know. He understood. Guilt was eating at me for not telling Coot. Right or wrong, do or die, I was committed. I mounted up and rode on down to Rodolfo's place. He and Sarina would be up and around by now. Maybe there'd be a fresh batch of warm tortillas waiting on the table, some butter, coffee, fresh cream.

Rodolfo Bustamante pressed me to stay over a few days, but his main reason was to dissuade me from heading west. "You should go east to Austin, not west. Take advantage of this wonderful opportunity to earn a college degree. Your papa is right. You will make a fine lawyer."

I did my best to tell Rodolfo about the mushroom, but getting that story over to someone takes a great deal of time, and a lot of belief from the listener. I heard myself mouthing those senseless words, realizing how strange they must sound to Rodolfo. I asked him to honor my wishes, and we spoke no more about it.

Sarina wanted to know where "her Coot" was, and why he wasn't with me. I tried to explain that he had gone far north to the snow country of Colorado, that he was going to get a college education.

"But my Coot is already smart, Uncle Narlow," she repeated often. No amount of explanation seemed to make any impression.

In late afternoon, I saddled up. "Rodolfo, the next time you're in El Paso getting supplies, will you do me a big favor?"

"Anything at all, Narlow. Tell me and it will be done."

"I want you to deliver this pouch of gold to Papa. The last time I gave you a pouch of gold it was for the line rider that told you about our uncle Doyl. That gold was from Papa, this pouch of gold is for him. He gave it to me for my books and keep. We spent a good part of this summer digging it out of his little gold mine on Anthony's Nose, but I won't be needing it. I suspect your visit and your news will not come as a surprise to him, but if you will, please have your conversation with just Papa. Mama will have more questions and accusations than you'll have time or information to supply. Papa would want it that way. Tell him that if he's a mind to that I would enjoy a visit with him at our headquarters on the Black River. I will be waiting for him mid-April."

That night I camped just downriver of El Paso. Traveler and I were on the trail again before dawn. I stayed off the usual trail north of town and kept to the sandhills far west of the *Rio*. The further north we traveled, and the closer we got to the river ford that led east to Papa's goat ranch, the more determined Traveler was to go home, but he behaved himself. He was trained by the best.

14

It's a four days ride to the confluence of the San Francisco and Tularosa rivers. When we were headed for the Black River on our hunting trips, we always tried to camp at that convergence. Cold water to quench our thirst, giant mountain cottonwood trees with cavernous shade, succulent grass for the animals. The next morning, Traveler and I rounded a rock outcropping. Upriver about a mile, there appeared to be a man on horseback. At that distance, the mounted horseman appeared as a speck, but I had the notion he was looking right at me. I lifted the 44-40, and let it drop back into its hard leather scabbard. Papa always did that when he thought he might have need for it. I kept Traveler to the eastern shore, and in a few minutes, I was within 400-yards of the mounted man, but the trees and brush along the river kept me from getting a clear view of him. Again I lifted and dropped the repeater.

The river made a wide turn, sweeping around to the east, back to the west, then north. It was always shallow during the fall and winter, so I cut across the oxbow, making my way again on the east side. A stand of mountain cottonwoods blocked my view, but when I came around, there sat a sight I was ill-prepared to see.

"*Coot.* What in blazes are *you* doing here?"

"Same thing you're doing."

"You're supposed to be in Boulder, Colorado by now. Little off course, aren't you? Get yourself lost without me showing you the trail?"

"Your papa might say the same thing about you. Your stagecoach must have pulled into Austin two days ago, and you're already tardy for your first class."

We sat our horses, grinning at each other.

"Where do you think you're going?" I asked. "Nobody ever said you could be a medicineman, did they?"

"No, you're the only one around here that's brainless enough to think he has what it takes to become a medicineman. One idiot in an outfit is plenty. But I'd say your papa might be a little touched to be lending Traveler to a scalawag like you. Besides, Two Sticks invited me right along with you—remember that?"

"Yeah, I suppose, but he was just being polite. What about the university in Boulder?"

"What about the university in Austin?"

We sat grinning at each other. Coot looked Traveler over. "Steal him?"

"Steal who?"

"Traveler—stole him from your papa, didn't you?"

"No, I didn't steal him, but I have to agree with you about Papa. When he tied Traveler's lead rope to the back of that stagecoach, the thought crossed my mind that he had gone daft."

"Well, chief medicineman, are we going to sit around here all day, analyzing your poor papa, or are we going to pay a surprise visit on Two Sticks?"

Coot turned his horse and led his mule up the trail.

"How'd you know I wasn't going to Austin?"

"You got quiet—*real* quiet. Quiet is a subject you're real shallow in. I knew something was eating on you, because you're always jabberin' about something—wondering why a hawk landed on a particular limb instead of a better limb you had picked out for him. That sorta nonsense. I figured you were up to something.

I ciphered on it, figuring this was what you were up to. I was right, as usual." He turned in his saddle. "Wasn't I?"

"Yeah, I suppose you were, but what about your aunt Beulah? She'll be worried to death if you don't show up in Boulder."

"Don't worry about Aunt Beulah. She'll be all right."

Heavy black clouds got us to thinking about shelter as we came into view of Diego de Luna's holdings. Coot pointed to a dilapidated barn. The storm hit as we rode through the barn's high doors.

I brushed back the floor straw and built a small fire in the dirt, while Coot unpacked his mule and rubbed down the animals. Remorse settled in around me in that cold, dark barn.

"Coot, do you think we'll regret this—giving up an opportunity to go to college and all?"

"Naw, there's plenty of time to get educated, besides, neither one of us is the dullest knife in the drawer. Oftentimes you remind me of a box of hair, but I figure if you stick close to me some of my spare smart will rub off on you."

"Yeah, you're sharp all right. Sharp as an ax left out in wet weather to rust in the morning sun."

"Well, Narlow, ol' *amigo* of mine, you asked me a question, and I'll tell you how I feel about going off to that university up north. We know that the west is going to change and change plenty fast. Railroad'll be coming soon, and that will be the dead-ass end of the west. Uncle Abe's already assured us of that, and I believe him. Before this country is settled, I want to see it all. I want to rub it in my chest, pack it in my eyes, stuff it in my ears, so I won't forget a damn thing. Spending a year or two up there with Two Sticks is something I am ill-prepared to pass up."

"How do you suppose we're going to find Two Sticks?" I asked. "We know he's on a reservation, but where? I always figured he was on the San Carlos Reservation. Is there another one?"

"Hell yes, there's bunches of them. If you were half as smart as you think, and priding yourself with map reading and all, looks to me like you'd know that."

"If Two Sticks is not on the San Carlos, then where is he?"

"I don't know for certain, but he always came over the ridge, and down the same trail we always traveled."

"So?"

"So it just so happens that the Black River is the dividing line between the San Carlos and the White Mountain Reservation."

"So?"

Coot squatted by the fire, brushed back the straw, and with stick in hand, drew a curving line in the dirt. "Do you remember an old Apache named Charley One Stab who shows up now and again? Well, he came by our place just a week before I left home. I asked him about the San Carlos Reservation and exactly where it was, how big. Charley One Stab drew me a map in the dirt like this. The first thing he drew in the dirt was a long swooping line. He said, 'That Black River. San Carlos Reservation here,' and he stuck his stick in the dirt south of the river. I asked him if he had ever heard of Pacheta Creek. He said he knew of it. He drew it coming down from the northeast to the Black River. I asked him what the land is called where Pacheta Creek comes down to the Black. He said, 'Indian reservation—called White Mountain. Much more better than San Carlos. Sickness, much people go hungry. Much people die, but at San Carlos *all* people sick. *All* people hungry. *All* people go die they stay there.'

"I asked him if he knew an Apache medicineman by the name of Na-Tu-Che-Puy. He thought he had heard of him but wasn't certain. I asked him if he knew an old army scout by the name of Many Fast Feet Two Sticks. Charlie One Stab said that all Apache know Many Fast Feet Two Sticks, known as a lead scout for the Blue Coats. He said that the agent cannot keep neither Two Sticks or Charley One Stab on the reservation and quit trying long ago.

"I asked him if Two Sticks lived on the San Carlos. He stabbed his stick in the ground where the Pacheta Creek was drawn in the dirt, and scratched the stick to the north. Ft. Apache. The hub of the White Mountain Reservation."

"Well, I guess that settles that," I said. "Maybe I'm glad you tagged along after all. Did Charlie One Stab give you any idea of how to find Two Sticks? And what happens if the army finds a couple of white boys wandering around and living on an Indian reservation? What then?"

"He says there's never many soldiers on duty at any one time. Only when there's trouble, or when a bunch of warriors break out. Then there's plenty of soldiers and hell to pay, from half rations to quarter rations. Both the San Carlos and the White Mountain reservations are big. Charley One Stab said it takes a man on a good horse two full days to go from one end to the other. They're not fenced or patrolled. The agent counts heads once a month and sends his monthly report off to Washington. His count is always twice as high as the actual count. That way he can pad his books and sell off more salt and bacon to his white-man cronies. Once a month, everybody shows up at the Issue House for their rations. Charley One

Stab says the rations are poor—salt that is half caliche dust—a quarter of a beef that is likely to be rancid, enough beef to feed two is divided among eight, sometimes as many as ten or twelve people. They're starving, making them susceptible to disease and diarrhea. Some of the men have rifles they've stashed, but pitiful-few cartridges. You and I have rifles and a lot of ammunition. That'll make us real popular with those people. Charlie One Stab believes Two Sticks calls home at the foothills of a mountain the Pale Eyes call Baldy—that's where the Pacheta Creek starts. We'll find him all right."

It took us four days to get in the vicinity of Ft. Apache. We were guessing where the headquarters of the reservation would be, but we kept within five miles of the Black River to feel pretty certain that the small stream we crossed at noon was the Pacheta Creek. We followed it northeast, camping at dark, mounted before sun. By mid-morning we rode over a steep ridge, and there far below us were scores of lodges with many Apaches milling around. Must be the reservation headquarters. A high rock outcropping furnished enough shade to get us out of the sun, hiding us and our animals. We could see for miles around, figuring our next move would be evident from our high perch.

Every hour or so, a man on horseback would ride by, generally from the west. We decided to make our way toward that direction in hopes that we might stumble onto Two Sticks, or a friendly looking face that we could approach to make our inquiry. The afternoon came and went. Now and again, a man would return to his lodge with a small bundle of firewood tied to his poor pony.

"Well medicineman, what do you think?" Coot asked. "Do we show ourselves or do we spend the winter up here on this rocky ledge?"

"I don't know. Papa always told us to seek and we would find. Well, we seeked and we guess we've found, but what do we do with it?"

"Let's ride south a ways and make camp. Tomorrow we can come back up here and take another look and decide our next move."

We returned to the rock outcropping at sunup. Soon men were milling around just like the day before.

Coot asked, "What do you say we stake out our animals in that canebrake over there? We can get closer if we're not mounted."

We made our way down to the trail and climbed a lone tall sycamore and hid in a high fork. About the time we got settled down in our high lookout, Coot nudged me and pointed down to a tall boy who was walking along the trail. I judged him to be about our age, though taller than Coot and me. As he walked below, I pulled out my Barlow and let it fall. I wanted the knife to fall close to the boy to get his attention, but it soon became apparent my aim was too good. The knife fell straight for the top of the boy's bare head. *Thunk*.

"Damn, Narlow. Your knife sounded like it hit a ripe watermelon, and that boy went down in a heap. What the hell did you do that for?"

"I didn't aim to hit him, just get his attention."

"You're going to have more than his attention when he wakes up—*if* he wakes up." The boy was lying face down and didn't move.

"Come on," Coot said. "Let's get down there before he gets up and starts looking for somebody's ass to kick."

We scurried down the sycamore and ran over to the boy, dark red pooling in the dirt. I said, "This is going to be one mad Apache when he wakes up."

"He'll wake up soon enough, and I think I'll hold you for him and let him get even."

"Think we better sit on him so he can't get the best of us or run off for help?"

"Naw, let's just sit down here in front of him. I expect he'll wake up here dreckly. He'll push up on his elbows, and be looking right at us."

The boy stirred. He cradled his head in his hands, his elbows on the ground. He rubbed his head, looked at the blood on his hand, looked around, then our eyes locked. He jumped up in a flash and we did the same. He made a questioning move-ment as if to ask why we had hit him. Coot and I knew only a few words of Apache, two of them were *enjuh* and *dencho*—good and bad, and those didn't fit what we needed to get across right now.

Although Apaches don't hand sign much, Two Sticks had shown us how to sign his name with our hands. My hands went up and made the three quick signs Two Sticks had taught us.

The boy looked at me, shrugged. Coot signed the name again. The boy hit his chest with a closed fist, grunting something.

I signed Two Sticks's name again. The boy again hit his chest, proudly grunted the same thing, and wiped the narrow streak of blood running down his nose. We were at an impasse. Three boys with no way of communicating with one another but with grunts and sheepish grins.

The boy asked me in a heavy tongue, " Coot—Coot Boldt?"

"No," I said, shaking my head.

He made a motion as if he were going to charge me.

"*No,*" I shouted, pointing at Coot, "me no Coot Boldt, me Narlow Montgomery. *He* Coot Boldt."

He stopped, a smile sweeping over his bloody face. "Me," he said lifting his foot, slammed his fist into his other palm. I shrugged. He again lifted his moccasin-clad foot, and with his clenched fist, hit his ankle a stiff blow.

"You Iron Chain?" Coot asked. "You son of Many Fast Feet Two Sticks?"

The boy grinned wide and proud, nodding. He pointed to the top of his head, then the thin streak of blood dripping off his nose. *What about this?* he seemed to ask.

I stepped up to him, lifted my chin, and pointed to it. "Hit me right there, Iron Chain, then we'll be square."

He stood looking at me.

Coot stepped over and made a swinging motion at me with his fist, pointed at my chin. "Hit him, Iron Chain. Right there—*hard.*"

Iron Chain laughed, shook his head, then motioned for us to climb back up the sycamore, pointed to himself, then in the direction of the lodges.

Iron Chain was gone for a long time, the sun almost chest high when Two Sticks strolled through a stand of dead salt cedars, Iron Chain trotting along at his side. They stopped, Iron Chain pointed up to where we were hiding.

Many Fast Feet Two Sticks came on, still trying to get a glimpse of us. He stopped, smiling up at us. "You come, Narlow Montgomery. You come, Coot Boldt. Welcome. You come with Indian Moon. That good. Many Fast Feet Two Sticks happy—proud. This my son, Iron Chain. You make blood with him but he welcome you. Come, I will take you to Na-Tu-Che-Puy's lodge. Medicineman will be happy to see Narlow Montgomery. Happy to see Coot Boldt. Teach much. Abe Montgomery be proud. Uncle Doyl spirit happy."

We scurried down from our perch and caught up with Two Sticks who had started toward the lodges.

"Many Fast Feet Two Sticks, sir. I just had to come to your village. The mushroom has taken over my head. I had to come, and Coot wanted to come too."

Strange. Two Sticks had not questioned my coming or what Papa thought of it. We would soon learn that Apaches wonder very little about what needs no explanation. Nor do they waste time trying to sort out trivial matters.

Na-Tu-Che-Puy was sitting in the shade of a stick-woven arbor, resting on a fine elk skin when we walked up to his lodge. Two Sticks motioned for Iron Chain, Coot, and me to stop. Then he went on up to the thin man. His coarse hair was the color of pounded silver, in a single braid that fell to his waist. It was hotter than Hades, yet he sat there cool as a mountain trout. Two Sticks turned to us, motioned for us to kneel, then squatted in front of the medicineman. Iron Chain motioned with his eyes for us to take off our hats. We quickly doffed them and held them across our chests.

Na-Tu-Che-Puy was not happy that Two Sticks had brought us to him, as it appeared our friend was getting an old-fashioned chewing out. But Two Sticks persisted. We heard him say our names, our father's and grandfather's names, to remind the old medicineman who we were. He peered around Two Sticks, giving us the once-over. His frowning scowl blazed a hole between our eyes.

They talked for a long time. Two Sticks turned to us and said, "Na-Tu-Che-Puy say Narlow Montgomery and Coot Boldt first learn Apache's ways. Na-Tu-Che-Puy want to see mushroom. Stand and show him."

I stepped forward, peeled my trousers down, and turned my hip toward the medicineman. He studied the mark, touched it, and spoke to Two Sticks.

"Na-Tu-Che-Puy want to know if you have brother or sister with bad mark like that on your hip. Ever touch someone with bad mark?"

"No, I don't think—wait. There is a girl we know. She has a bad mark on her face. Purple, but not small like my mushroom. And, her mark is not rough like mine, but smooth, kinda bubbly. It covers one side of her face and neck. I don't recall ever touching her bad mark, but maybe I did by accident. I just don't know. She and her brother are twins. He does not think real good. He is slow."

Na-Tu studied me for a long while. "These twins. What are their names? Do you live close to them?"

"There names are Shelly Brom and IB Crane. They do not live close. They live a half-day's ride from where my parents live in their dugout."

"The girl with the bad face. Is she slow like her brother?"

"No, sir. I would say she's a real smart girl. Can't read or write, that I know of anyway. But her thinking is quick. *Real* quick."

"Tell me about their eyes. Do they have the same color on their eyes?"

"No, sir. Shelly Brom's eyes are blue, clear as the morning sky. Brother IB's are faded, more yellow than anything else."

"We call twins by the name, *naki gozlii*. Twins share the same spirit. When one dies, the other loses much of their spirit. They become lost without their *naki gozlii*."

Two Sticks made a long speech to the medicineman, then stood. "*Enjuh.*"

He turned to me. "I tell Na-Tu-Che-Puy story of you and bear once over. He say mushroom is as I say, believe Many Fast Feet Two Sticks. He say you must learn much Apache ways before he teach you Power. Come. I show you. *Come*." He led us back past the place where we first saw Iron Chain.

He stopped at a barren place. Only a few dead salt cedars graced the area.

"Narlow, you stand. Stand here. Coot stand there. Face that way. Not turn. Not talk. Say no words. Not sit on Mother Earth. Not lie down. Not put knee on ground. Not drink water offered you. Do nothing. You stand. No talk. I return in three suns." He turned and Iron Chain followed his father past the clearing.

"Two Sticks—*wait*. Our animals. Papa's horse, Traveler. He's hobbled in a canebrake south of here."

Two Sticks only raised his arm, and Iron Chain took off running to the south.

Until that moment, I don't believe I'd been still or stood in one spot for more than one minute in my entire life. I had eaten when the mood hit me, regularly slugged down gallons of cool water and goat's milk. I could outrun a herd of goats, but was soon to learn that doing nothing, and going nowhere, is a much tougher challenge to a boy than heading off a lion-stampeded bunch of nannies. We were standing back to back, no more than three feet apart in a clearing with the late summer sun beating down.

I commenced to sweat. The sun made its way across the sky, then began showing itself through the low branches of the stand of dead salt cedars. Sweat soon turned to a chill, the chill turned cold, numbing, teeth-rattling. I promised myself that tomorrow I would not hold the warming sun in disdain, forever relishing its warm.

By the time the eastern sky showed rosy, I was fighting the urge to walk. To take just one step. *Who would know?* My every muscle, joint, and bone screamed for the release that movement would bring. I fought the urge to turn around to see if Coot was still standing behind me. I couldn't hear him breathing. Maybe he slipped off. Time crept by. I busied myself tracking time by the shadows of the dead cedars, wagering with myself when a particular cedar's shadow would swing around to the base of a tree on the other side of the clearing. When my shadow was the shortest, it pointed to a cedar in front of me. Due north. I'd see if the north star shows itself above that cedar. That was the first of many silent conversations I would have before my three days would grind by.

I tried to meditate. Apaches meditated, spending much time praying. My meditations failed me. Cussing this fine state of affairs, I imagined what my dormitory room in Austin would look like. Would it have hardwood floors or stamped earth like our dugout? Would there be a pot-bellied, coal-burning stove like the catalogue picture, or a fire pit like our dugout? I bet the cook was a real nice lady, and I'd be her favorite, sneaking me an extra slice of cherry pie, a treat I had never experienced but one that now obsessed my being.

By late afternoon, nagging dreams of sleep took over my thoughts. Food and water became less important. If I could just kneel down. I wouldn't have to lie down—just kneel down, put my chin on my knee for a bit. No one would know. I found myself slumping. I fought the urge to let go. *No*, don't kneel. Just turn around to see if Coot was still there. *No.* I fought off everything that ever made sense to me.

The night and next day melded into one. I could not remember if I had been standing there for an hour or a month. By nightfall, I rebelled against my own will. There were two of me: One who wanted to honor my commitment to Two Sticks, the other who scoffed at the idea of standing for two more full days and nights without sleep, food, or water. And for what? For the honor and recognition of a red man imprisoned on a godforsaken reservation set aside for him by his white masters? *You are not that stupid!*

Dawn. I tried to convince myself that I only had this day and night and a part of the next day, and it would all be over. The morning of the first dawn, I had drawn a line in the dirt with my boot. But after that first dawn I had no recollection. Had I drawn another line? Had I drawn the line at dawn or dusk? I dragged my boot through it.

Late in the afternoon of that second full day, cold gathered around me. Clouds gathered. Thunder rolled, lightning burst. I wanted to scream, *Rain. Soon it will rain. Water will be mine!* And the rain came, raining hard late into the night. The first big, cold drops hit. I raised my head to drink what would fall in my open mouth. Two Sticks' words leaped above the thunder: *You not drink water offered you.* I wanted to lift my head, taste the cool wet. *But wait.* Maybe Ussen was offering the water to test me. The water began running past my feet, forming a muddy creek. But the murky water looked good. Again I lifted my head to drink. *No!* I fought the urge to relieve myself, to pee, but the gurgling of the water overcame me. Dark yellow puddled out the bottom of my britches. The rain stopped as if a giant umbrella had been opened. I looked up and whispered to myself, *Ussen sir, I didn't mean to scream at you, sir.* No doubt about it—I was going nuts.

Dawn came, gray, pink, and black streaks pointing to the sun that would soon be hollow overhead. I doubted my legs would hold me up for the few remaining

111

hours left. My three days would have run their course, but Two Sticks would find me lying in the mud.

By mid-day, I was convinced this was not my third day, but my second day. I dreamed that I had been sleeping, that my three days had only begun. I was confused, tired, thirsty. Food had no appeal to me, only water, sleep. My tongue, swollen, feeling like an overripe tuna. A tuna that had fallen from a prickly pear, swollen, oozing its purple juice, piss-ants devouring it, then wrinkling in the hot sun.

I thought I was talking to myself. I couldn't decide. I couldn't think. My mind was numb, numb as my feet and legs. I became aware of my legs, they started trembling. I looked down at them and fought the urge to scream at my legs. *Stop shaking, damn it.* I thought that was pretty funny and started laughing. *Shut up, Narlow. You're talking to yourself again.*

"You sit, Narlow Montgomery."

I fought it. I wanted to yell, *What? No. I cannot sit. Two Sticks told me to stand here, and by god I will stand until he says my three days are up.*

Someone was shaking me. I glanced up and saw an old broken compass dangling on a rawhide cord. Behind it was a shiny brass button sewn to heavy cloth. I reached up, took the compass in my hand, looked up at the bronze face of Two Sticks, and smiled. I jumped back.

"Welcome, Many Fast Feet Two Sticks, sir. I'll fetch you some hot coffee and honey, sir."

Coot's water-craved voice graveled. "Sir, you'll have to forgive Narlow. Sometimes he's a little touched."

15

The Apache language was difficult at first, but we mastered a few basic words, then our grasp of their tongue seemed to snowball. Numbers, however, came much slower as their counting system was difficult, especially for me.

Standing for three days and nights without rest, food, or water proved to be only a minor test of a young warriors' mettle. But those three days were more like hell than anything I ever read in *The Revelation*. Truth was paramount to the Apache. Those who stretched even a minor point were shunned, sent to the women to gather wood and fetch water. Tests of strength, speed, endurance, of running many miles with a lengthy, memorized message to a teammate waiting on a far hill, were important drills. We memorized countless messages, running untold miles until we got it right.

In the old days, the young boys would be invited by a sponsoring warrior to go with him on raids. Once he performed to the warrior's satisfaction, he would become a warrior in his own right. Apaches at our reservation had plenty of enemies, but now they were the "guests" of their enemies, and anyone participating in a raid would be shot. We played serious games that practiced killing our enemies—age-old unfriendly Indian tribes, but mainly the Pale Eyes.

A great challenge among us would-be warriors was to find a wasp nest. We carefully planned our strategy, circled around behind our enemy, and charged in from all directions, knocking the nest to the ground, swatting the wasps with willow whips, killing them all, taking many injuries ourselves. None yelped in pain. We wore the red welts with pride. My arms and hands swelled near double, and I ran a fever for days. My allergies were not mirrored by Coot, and only a few of my fellow warrior trainees.

Iron Chain and Coot and I were fast friends, together constantly. We enjoyed the devil we caught in the other's eye, and went on many night raids against fellow students, serving up much misery. When Na-Tu-Che-Puy's nephew, Sly Fox, came to White Mountain from the Mescalero Reservation, he was quickly accepted by us. Almost as tall as Iron Chain, but stouter like Coot and me. A handsome boy who's only apparent failing was poor eyesight. He had been fitted with eye spectacles back east, at a place called Carlisle Industrial School. Sly Foot told us about his short time at Carlisle, describing the school buildings as a deserted cavalry post in Pennsylvania, known as Carlisle Barracks. He told of how he came to be chosen to go to Carlisle, chosen by a tall man who came to the reservation looking for prospective students. He was dressed in a black shiny suit and bow tie, a tall stovepipe hat such as Two Sticks wore, stern, a keen edge of pre-eminence showing for all to see. Sly Fox was sent off to Carlisle. Shortly after his arrival, the schoolmaster accused Sly Fox of cheating, which he denied, but was whipped with a cane and sent home in disgrace.

The four of us were faster and stronger than the others, and could hold our own with any six of the other boys. While none of the boys ever taunted us for being Pale Eyes, they each had their turn at testing us. When we passed their every test, they appreciated us, accepted us as equals. My years of milking Papa's nannies gave me a powerful grip that even full-grown warriors could not best. They called me, *Ndoh Kigan,* Tight Hand. Coot was just naturally strong as a bear. A stout bond grew between Iron Chain, Sly Fox, Coot, and me. While we were in our training, no one spoke to us, or even acknowledged our presence. We were tested daily, every waking moment. We hauled great piles of firewood, endless buckets of water. We never spoke unless spoken to, never sat, ate, drank, slept, barely breathing without permission.

We'd been with the Apaches for almost four months—moons—yet the Indian agent did not yet know of our presence. Since we were not officially there, we were not being issued rations, eating at the expense of the others.

"Young Believer," a voice said behind me.

I dropped my load of firewood, turned with my long-knife in hand.

Na-Tu-Che-Puy stood before me. "Your reactions are good, Young Believer."

"Young Believer?"

"It is not to be your Apache name, but it is what I will call you until I name you."

We stood five feet apart. I had only seen him at a distance since Two Sticks took me to his lodge.

"Young Believer, I have many visions in my long life. Many visions. Now, only one vision. The vision many times I see. I cannot explain your mushroom, or how your Power warns Young Believer of danger. I have tried, but the answer escapes me. Maybe you can explain Na-Tu-Che-Puy's vision. It is always your vision that comes to me in my dreams. Your vision and that of the mushroom. In my first dream, only one mushroom. Then two mushrooms, bigger than the greatest mountain on Mother Earth. Now my vision has hundreds of mushrooms. Hundreds of hundreds of mushrooms. No one can count them all. Mother Earth cries out in my vision. My wife, Can See Far, she says I cry out in my slumber, 'I am Mother Earth.' The mushrooms of the Pale Eyes covers my body. They belch fire out of my body, the dark red of my blood flows. I die. Young Believer, I cannot explain my vision, or why Mother Earth fears your mushroom. Mother Earth fears nothing. Your mushroom has great Power. Can you explain my vision?"

"No, great Medicineman, I cannot," I said to this great man whom all revered. "My vision is only one mushroom. My people call the color 'purple.' Dark, dirty-red as dry, caked blood."

"That is the color of my mushrooms. Young Believer, you are grandson of Shelby Montgomery, son of Abe Montgomery. Great men. I am sad that I have not welcomed you to my lodge, but I fear your mushroom. I do not understand it, do not like your mushroom. That is why I go slow with you. Do you understand, Young Believer?"

"Yes, great Medicineman, I understand. My papa tells me I am guilty of off-putting, but he is patient with my failing, says what you say about going slow. You do not understand this thing, which makes you afraid of it, making you not like it. It is true what my papa says—off-put, as he calls it. When faced with that, he encourages me to take it on. To do it. Doing it allows Nature to explain it to me, to see there is nothing to fear, nothing to dislike in all of Nature—in all of Mother Earth. Maybe great Na-Tu-Che-Puy off-put like Abe Montgomery tells Young Believer."

Na-Tu-Che-Puy rarely smiled, but when he did, it was slow, seemed to be crawling through his jaw bones, looking for release. "All Apache know your papa. Your papa a wise man. I will remember what he teaches you, Young Believer. I will think on it much." He turned and sauntered away like the mist in a hollow.

Two Sticks came to me two hours after sundown. "I have told Na-Tu-Che-Puy that you have passed every test you have been given. You have learned much. You learn Apache words, Apache ways. You not know all, but much. Come with me—Na-Tu-Che-Puy will accept your visit. Time you live there."

"What about Coot? If I live with Na-Tu-Che-Puy, can Coot live there as well?"

"No. Coot stay with me and Iron Chain. Coot my son."

"Many Fast Feet Two Sticks, I am doubtful that I am ready for this great medicineman. I may fail to learn what he has to teach me."

His head jerked around. "You *not* fail. Never say that word. It is bad. It is time you had a name. Our people will welcome you when Na-Tu-Che-Puy gives you a name. Coot need name. I will think on a name. Na-Tu-Che-Puy is slow to accept people. He watches, he learns. With the People he is slow. With outsiders he is slow like sap from dead tree. It is time I press him to take you. I know how that is to be done."

Na-Tu-Che-Puy was sitting on his fine elk hide in front of his lodge, rolling tobacco in an oak leaf. Two Sticks approached the medicineman.

"Great medicineman, I bring you this young brave. He grandson of Shelby Montgomery, son of Abe Montgomery, friend for all time of all Apache. He has passed all tests, often better than Apache boys. This warrior strong, swift, truthful. I am proud of him. I will take him into my lodge as my own son. He will be part of my family."

Na-Tu-Che-Puy motioned for Two Sticks to sit before him. As Two Sticks sat, he motioned for me to kneel behind him. Na-Tu-Che-Puy lit his *cigarro* with a live coal brought to him by his wife, Can See Far. He puffed until the *cigarro* was burning to his satisfaction, then handed it to Two Sticks. Two Sticks puffed, blew smoke to the four winds, smiled at the medicineman, and returned the *cigarro*.

Na-Tu-Che-Puy scoffed. "I do not need anyone to remind me of the legend of Shelby Montgomery and Skinner Boldt. I know of their sons, Abe Montgomery and Orville Boldt. You are a great warrior—great scout, but no medicineman." He sat smoking, studying Two Sticks. "You have not named this boy?"

"No, great medicineman. I ask your permission to welcome him to my lodge. I will name him."

The medicineman studied Two Sticks, smoke curling from his lips. "Leave the boy here with me. Tomorrow, I will take him to the agent. It is there that I will give him his name."

Two Sticks stood. *"Enjuh."* He turned and walked past me, the faintest smile on his long, bronze face.

Na-Tu-Che-Puy stood and went inside his lodge.

Can See Far came out with a heavy buffalo robe. "You sleep here on ground under this robe—you stay warm. Na-Tu-Che-Puy say he is not afraid of your mushroom."

That was the first time I had ever touched a buffalo robe. It was heavy, warm, as she promised.

Pink was showing in the eastern sky when Na-Tu-Che-Puy came out of his lodge, walked to the top of the knoll, and stopped. He turned, called back asking me if I was going with him. We fell in with other families, making their way to the Issue House at the base of a high hill, a part of the agent's headquarters where the people received their rations. Everyone in the line motioned for Na-Tu-Che-Puy to step to the head of the line. He waved them off. Coot was with Two Sticks and Iron Chain. Coot winked at me, and did his little girlie blinking, his black eyebrows dancing. I laughed. Na-Tu-Che-Puy asked me what was funny. I pointed at Coot, but he straightened up as soon as the medicineman glanced his way.

A smile fought for release on Na-Tu-Che-Puy's cragged face. "I like your story about dancing with mama bear that kicks. Tell me that story while we wait."

I finished the story just as the top half-door opened to the Issue House. The agent stuck his head out. "Any of you red skunks hungry?" The big, sweaty man wiped his brow, laughing at his sour joke.

The head of each family made his mark, and was issued a quarter of a poor cow, a portion of salt, coffee, and flour. When Na-Tu-Che-Puy and I approached the window, he poked his head in and said in Apache, "This is my son who has come from Mexico. I want to make the mark on your ledger so that he can receive his rations."

The agent did not look up from his ledger, a great insult to any Apache, especially one as honored as Na-Tu-Che-Puy. The agent sat with his side to us, acting as if he had not heard.

Na-Tu repeated in Apache, "I am Na-Tu-Che-Puy and I—"

"Speak English, *goddamn it*. This is the United States of goddamn-America, you red son-of-a-bitch. We speak English here, not that guttural, grunting goddamn Apache crap. And I know who you are, damn it. Just a minute and you can register him. Out of Mexico my lily-white ass."

"When I look at you all I see is ass," Na-Tu-Che-Puy said softly in English.

"What'd ya say, chief?"

"I say I will wait patiently here in the grass."

After a bit, the agent stood and brought a heavy ledger to the window, threw it on the sill. "I haven't seen much of you lately, chief medicineman. Where ya' been?"

Na-Tu-Che-Puy stood silent.

"Write this boy's name and age on this line," the agent said, grinning a snaggletooth smile.

"You know I cannot write in your book."

"Well, maybe this boy can write his own name. He looks like a smart enough injun," he said, giving me the once-over. "He's sure not as dark as most of you heathens, chief. Your boy, huh? You must'a mounted a white woman to produce a lad like this one, a big 'un at that."

"He is the son of my wife, Can See Far. She is full-blooded Warm Springs Apache. I am full-blooded Chiricahua Apache. This boy is full-blooded Apache. You want to register him, or do you want him to leave the reservation so you will have an excuse to kill another Apache?"

"Best watch your tongue, old man."

The agent turned to me. "What's your name, boy?"

I said nothing.

The agent's brown hair, splotches missing, scurvy, or a mule kick, greasy, uncombed. The gold watch chain on his vest led to a watchless fob, tell-tale signs of copper shining through the fake gold. An agent of the US government.

Na-Tu-Che-Puy spoke up. "He speaks none of your tongue—only Apache, some Mexican."

The agent swung the big ledger around, grabbed up the quill. "All right, chief, what's this boy's name—the one you claim is your son. What's his name?"

"His name is . . . his name is Young . . . " Na-Tu-Che-Puy hesitated, looked back at me. "In your tongue his name is Kicking Bear."

"Kicking Bear, huh? Well, ain't that just real nice. Crazy bastard, huh? How'd he get a name like that? I'd like to see that big injun boy try to kick a bear's ass. Does chief Kicking Bear know he better behave himself here on my reservation? Does he know who I am? Does the bastard know what I'll do to him if he gives me any back-talk?"

"He knows the agent. Agent Harold Drue. He knows of you."

"He knows *what*?"

"He knows he must behave. He knows what you do to bad Apache."

Agent Drue wrote my new name in his ledger, and turned the book. "Is that the way you spell your name, injun boy?"

I made no answer, and fought to hide my contempt for this foul man. The thought flew through my mind of what Papa did to the two men who killed that hummingbird. I had to fight a smile, imagining what Papa would do to this *mojon* of a man.

"Chief Medicineman, best learn this injun boy some manners, or I'll have his hide. Understand that, injun boy?" He whirled the ledger back around. "How old is this injun boy, chief?"

"Kicking Bear sixteen winters."

The agent stuck the sharp end of the quill on the end of the old medicineman's nose. "*Sixteen*? He's the stoutest damn sixteen-year-old I ever seen, and injuns grow damn few giants. You right certain about that, chief, him bein' sixteen and all?"

Na-Tu-Che-Puy pushed the quill aside. "I know. I was there the night he came from his mother."

"From her red ass you mean," he said, and took the ledger back to his desk. He returned to the window with the rations for Na-Tu-Che-Puy.

"The rations for Kicking Bear?" Na-Tu-Che-Puy asked.

118

"Next time. I gotta get authorization for any new injuns that come in," he said, and slammed the door shut.

On the way back to his lodge, Na-Tu-Che-Puy reached up and touched my shoulder. "Kicking Bear, you like your new name?"

"I like it just fine, Na-Tu-Che-Puy—just fine. And I'm sorry for the way the agent talked to you, the way he treated you and all. Made me want to try him on."

"My son, you are Apache while you are on this reservation. You will learn that you do not have any rights except to do as you are told. You became angry at the agent. Your anger showed, that is not good. You must learn to control your anger. If you do not, your anger will control you. It will shame you."

"My papa warns me about my anger."

"Come. We have much to speak of. Much to teach. Much to learn."

16

Six Weeks Later

Two Sticks told us that a tribal meeting would be held the following night, that there would be a feast afterward. One problem—ten days remained before the monthly rations would be distributed, and there was pitiful little food the people could put together to call it a feast.

"You have rifles. Fine horses, pack mule. You will take my red mule. Go east behind Tall Mountain—plenty deer—plenty elk. We have big feast. The people will be happy for many days. Sly Fox and Iron Chain will show you."

I asked, "Many Fast Feet Two Sticks, may I ask you a question?"

"Yes. What do you want to know?"

"Your people are starving, their flesh hangs in loose folds off their bones. With all that game, why don't you send out hunting parties to feed them? The agent's rations are mighty paltry."

"We have few old rifles, but fewer cartridges. The agent believes we turned in all of our rifles. We are forbidden to have one rifle, one cartridge. We take great care keep them from the agent, so we hunt not so often. Good time to hunt, fill our bellies." He smiled. "Agent not here. He go his home bury his mama, go two, maybe three moons. His men drink much whiskey, stay drunk."

It was good to be out on a meat hunt again with Coot. The weather was cool during the day, cold at night, with heavy frost in the morning. We hadn't gone thirty miles when we came across a sizable elk herd, then over the next rise we spooked up a herd of mule deer. We staked out the mules and started hunting. The four of us shared our two rifles, never missing a shot. Soon we had two elk and three deer down—far more than any two mules could carry, much less one. After we butchered our kill and hung the quarters on the low cedars, we sat roasting slices of elk, thinking through our problem. We'd pack the mules, Coot's horse, and Iron Chain's stout pony, build a travois for the excess and ride double on Traveler and Sly Fox's pony.

The People welcomed us when they saw we had plenty of meat for everyone. Soon the fires were reduced to coals, and great slabs of elk and venison were laid out for roasting. The mixture of cedar smoke, sage, and roasting meat filled the air, putting bright smiles on those hungry people's broad, handsome faces. The choice backstrap and sweet meats were put aside for the enjoyment of the elders.

Across the fire pit, Coot and Two Sticks were laughing and pointing at me. I knew Coot was telling lies. He was trying to convince Two Sticks that he had killed all the game, that my rifle kicked so much that I was afraid to shoot it. I doubt Two Sticks put much stock in his fibs, but he sure enjoyed Coot's mischief.

The feast was a grand affair. After everyone had their fill, the elders sat in a circle near the fire, the women and children crowding around behind them. There would be dancing, many stories of the old days, the old ways. Stories and legends the young ones would be expected to know and repeat verbatim as part of their passages to adulthood. The fire was fed late into the night, many songs, chants, and dancing continued.

One of the old men asked Many Fast Feet Two Sticks why Coot was so named. He confessed that he did not know, and asked Coot why he was named for a duck-like bird that seldom flies, and scoots across the top of the water.

Two Sticks asked, "Is it because you run fast on water, or are you a swift swimmer?"

Coot laughed. "No, I have trouble enough running on dry land, difficult for me to stay afloat in a horse trough."

Two Sticks reported his answer back to the elders, and again he came back to Coot. "The elders want to know how you have name like mud chicken. They ask you to come before them and tell that story.'"

Two Sticks escorted Coot within the circle of elders. He turned to Two Sticks and said, "My father, I do not have the words in Apache to tell this story, and even if I did, Narlow can tell the story much better. If the elders do not mind a funny story, they should call Narlow, I mean Kicking Bear, before them and ask him to tell the story to you in English and you, Many Fast Feet Two Sticks, can translate it for the elders."

Two Sticks turned to me. "Kicking Bear, come in the circle of elders. You tell story of your friend Coot and how he get that name. You speak in your tongue—I tell your story to elders, the people."

I turned solemnly to the elders and began, "When Edwin and I—"

"What Edd-ween?" Two Sticks asked.

"Edwin—Edwin is Coot's real name, sir."

He turned back to the elders, pointed at Coot. "Edd-ween." I never heard so much laughter. Maybe Edwin was similar to some Apache word. The laughter died down, Two Sticks turned to me, wiped his eyes, motioned for me to continue.

"When Edwin and I had just turned seven years old, Edwin sneaked his daddy's shotgun and game bag out of the house. We decided to go duck hunting along the banks of the *Rio* Grande. We sneaked along the river's edge and Edwin shot the running ducks one after another. The big shotgun kicked like a mule, but he would not let me shoot it, telling me that I was much better at wading out in the river to retrieve the birds. Pretty quick, we had that game bag filled to the brim, and we started back to Edwin's home. We hadn't gone far when we were met by his daddy and Uncle Doyl, driving a wagon behind a team of mules.

"His daddy called out, 'Edwin, what do you have there in my game bag, son?'

"Edwin answered, 'This here game bag is full of ducks. Shoot fire, Daddy, these ducks are easy to shoot, 'cept this ol' shotgun sure does kick hard.'

"Edwin's daddy got down from the wagon and said, 'Well Edwin, let's see your ducks—dump 'em out here on the dirt so we can take a look at them, son.'

"Edwin handed me the shotgun, turned the game bag upside down, and the dead birds piled up at his feet.

"Uncle Doyl congratulated Edwin and praised his marksmanship. He asked, 'Well Edwin, that's mighty good marksmanship, mighty dern good. But tell me, Edwin, how high in the sky were these birds when you shot 'em?'

"Edwin puffed up like a banty rooster. 'Oh, Uncle Doyl, they didn't fly, they just fluttered, flapped their wings, and ran across the water. They were plumb easy to shoot.'

"Edwin's daddy said, 'Well, pack up your birds and let's get on home, you too, Narlow. You boys deserve to make a feast out of those birds. I bet you boys can eat a whole bird apiece.'

"We jumped on the back of the wagon and we went back to the Boldt's place. Uncle Oliver pulled the team around to the back of the barn and said, 'You boys pick out four of the plumpest birds you have there – two for each of you, and pluck 'em real good. We'll build you a hot mesquite fire, and we can sit around here and watch you roast them up real golden brown.'

"Edwin asked, 'But Daddy, what about you and Mama and Uncle Doyl? Don't you want to eat some of our ducks?'

"'Oh no, son—those birds are yours and Narlow's. *Nobody's* going to eat not *even one* of them, isn't that right, Uncle Doyl?'

"Uncle Doyl grinned like he was going to bust wide open. 'I guarantee you there's not a man alive that would eat one of these ducks. Why Oliver, I'd starve plumb to death before I'd eat one of these boy's ducks.'

"Me and Edwin should have smelled a rat but we were as proud as a pup with a bone to be aware of anything but our ducks."

I paused so Two Sticks could catch up with his translation.

He turned to me. "What you mean, smell rat?"

"I mean we should have known something was not right since the men re-fused to eat our ducks."

Two Sticks repeated that and again there was a great shout of laughter.

"Edwin and I started plucking four plump ducks, we plucked for two hours, and Uncle Doyl said, 'You know what, boys? I do believe you fellers have more feath-ers on you than your kill. I say they're ready for roasting, what do you say, Oliver? Don't you think those pinfeathers will burn off in that hot mesquite fire?'

"'I believe you're right, Doyl. Okay boys, here's a couple of sharp pointed sticks for you—slide those birds on 'em and get to roasting. You must be mighty hungry after all that work.'

"'Yes, sir, Daddy. Yes, sir Uncle Doyl.'

"Me and Edwin commenced to cooking those fat ol' birds up, then Edwin said, 'Daddy, we forgot to gut these ducks.'

"His daddy replied, 'Oh, don't worry yourself none about that. Fact is, me and your Uncle Doyl never gut a plump duck. That just adds to the flavor.'

"Pretty soon those birds were golden brown, juices squirting out, and you could imagine the guts in those ducks were succulatin' around in there, making the meat tender and juicy. Pretty quick the juices were squirting out on the cook fire, pretty near spittin' sparks."

The People howled at Two Sticks words.

"Edwin's daddy declared, 'Looks like your feast is ready, boys. Sit yourselves down there on the ground near the fire. Eat your fill.'

"Edwin and I grinned across the fire, and helped each other get a bird apiece off our roasting sticks. We bit into what we thought would be the most succulent duck meat we ever ate, chewed off a big hunk, sat back, started munching on a mouthful of turd that tasted like swamp bottom. We gagged, looked at each other across the fire, both wondering what we were going to do with the hunk of dirt that was growing in our mouths. We spit out our prime roast duck, wondering what in the world could have gone wrong, continued to spit trying to rid ourselves of the swamp-bottom taste.

"Edwin's daddy asked, 'What's wrong, boys?'

"'Don't taste too good, Daddy.'

"'Know why, son?'

"'No, sir.'

"'Because, son, what you filled my game bag with was not ducks. Close, but not ducks. What you shot was a bevy of coots.'

"'Not ducks?'

With that Coot and the elders and the people howled with laughter.

I stood there expressionless. When one of the elders saw me standing there with nothing on my face but the light of the fire, he doubled-over, pointing up at me. My lack of expression caught them as real funny. The laughter died down, I repeated the line again, "Edwin asked, 'Not ducks?'" and again everyone laughed.

"'No son, not ducks—coots. Plain ol' mud coots.' Edwin's daddy squatted down in front of us. 'Now boys, let this be a lesson for you. You're big enough to go hunting on your own, but you sneaked my shotgun out of the house without permission. No harm done and all is forgiven, so forget it.'

"Uncle Doyl said, 'You know what, boys? Me and Oliver were always taught by our daddy to look for the silver lining, and by-golly-bum I do believe this is Edwin's finest hour. Son, you never did like being named for your mama's brother, so from now on, I will never call you Edwin *ever again*—from now on it's Coot Boldt.'

"And that's how my friend, Edwin came to be know as Coot."

Solemn—then smiles—then another burst of laughter.

Two Sticks made a long speech and concluded it by declaring, "Many Fast

Feet Two Sticks have name for new son, Coot Boldt. He be known to all Apache as *Ha'akehe Nal'eeli*—Running Duck."

From that night on, every time there was gathering of the people or a feast, Two Sticks would call on Running Duck to tell another story. He'd stand before the elders, think on it, then say, "Many Fast Feet, sir, I want Kicking Bear to step forward and tell the story about the time our little friend IB Crane came over to my daddy's farm with a three-legged scorpion tied by a string to his shirt and was sitting on IB's shoulder."

We had scores of stories, and the people loved them. Even after Coot or I could have told those tales in the Apache tongue, they preferred the old way, with Coot standing before them declaring the story to be told, me telling it with a straight face, and Two Sticks repeating the story in Apache.

***

Na-Tu-Che-Puy said, "Two Sticks believes you have much Power. He says you can see through rocks. He says you can hear a mountain lion creeping along far away in the night. He says it is true, and believes you have great Power. Two Sticks speaks the truth. Do you think you have great Power, Kicking Bear?"

"Sir, I have never claimed to have Power. My papa says I can see a long way off. It seems to me that much of what Two Sticks believes as my power is just coincidence, chance, not Power. I am always truthful with you, and must tell you that the real reason we came to you and your people was curiosity, for adventure. We wanted to see the West before it is no longer, before the great locomotives come to your world. Papa says it will change your world forever. Sometimes I know things that I cannot explain, but they are minor things and not very important. Yes, it is true that long before the others knew, I was always aware when Two Sticks came over the rim, walked behind boulders, then appeared strolling down the trail to our campsite, dragging his red mule behind him."

"Two Sticks tells me about you dancing with mama bear on a high rock ledge. He says you saw your uncle Doyl in the bear. Soon he died. Can you tell me how you explain that if you do not have Power, Kicking Bear?"

"I do not know, my father. Maybe I'm lucky—*sha its'ig*. Just another coincidence, I suppose. I should tell you that when Coot and I learned that he died, we recalled my vision. His gaze at me was different, like he believed my Power. It scared me."

Na-Tu shook his head, combed a thin hand through his silver braid. "I must tell you, Kicking Bear—I still do not understand your mushroom. Perhaps if I see this mushroom again, I will know. You show me this mushroom when you first come here. Tell me how you get your Power, and tell me how your mushroom warns you when you are in danger. Show me this mushroom one more time."

I peeled down my breechcloth, and turned to show the purple mark on my hip.

"It is like Two Sticks say—it is like a mushroom that grows in a place on the earth that is wet. But it is not like a mushroom I eat. The color is not a good color. What do you call this color?"

"Purple—we call it purple."

"Purple. Ugly word for ugly color." He examined the purple mark a long time. "Kicking Bear, you have this mushroom on your hip all of your life?"

"No sir, or I mean, yes, sir, or actually, sir, I am not certain. Papa says I had it when I came to this earth, when I was a baby. It was here on my forehead. My mother thought it was ugly, a bad sign, a sign of *diablo*. She hid me when neighbors came by, and wouldn't let anyone see me until it receded into my hairline. Papa says that was when I was about two years old, two winters."

"The mushroom warns you when danger is near?"

"Well, I guess. I reckon it does, and I suppose it told me that Two Sticks came to our dugout to bring me here, or when Two Sticks was coming down the trail to our hunting headquarters. I haven't had many reasons for it to warn me of any danger since I am seldom in real danger."

"When did mushroom first warn you? You remember the first time?"

"Yes, sir, I do."

"Tell me that time."

"The memory is painful, sir. I would rather not speak of it."

"Tell me about that first time. Miss no details. Your words are safe with me. I must know all."

I recounted the night when I was twelve years old and Mama took a horse quirt to me late one night in Papa's milk shed. Na-Tu-Che-Puy stopped me several times as I told the story to be certain he understood.

He sat gazing at me. "The mushroom has much Power. That is a powerful story. Bad story. Two Sticks says your mama half-breed—half Comanche. Many Comanche women mean like *tiish bitseghal*—like rattlesnake. Mad, not crazy *Mean.* Your mama not crazy—*mean.* You mama not dead, but you must never speak of it again. It must die within you."

He studied me for several minutes, smiled, motioned for me to sit close by his side.

"Kicking Bear, I believe you have much Power. It is time for you to see what I carry in my medicine bag. If you are to become a medicineman, you must own a medicine bag of your own." He opened the leather bag and began by pulling out chips of pine wood, burned on their edges. "I took them from a tree that had been struck by a bolt from the sky. *Hada'didla'.*"

"Lightning?"

"Yes, I believe that is the word."

"You see the chips are not only charred, they are yellowed by the lightning. These chips have much Power. I keep them with me. This small bundle tied with rawhide is the inner bark of *t'iis*, you call it cottonwood tree. It has many purposes when I treat burns." He held his palm up, filling it with a handful of cattail blossoms, patches of dried skunk weed, fetishes, then produced from the medicine bag a small leather pouch. "This is *hoddentin*. It contains the pollen of the tule. We call it *teel*. All warriors carry their own small bag of *hoddentin*. You see them greet the morning sun, blow a pinch of *hoddentin* to the dawn." He produced a twist of tobacco. "Warriors chew this when no water to drink, no food to eat." He picked up a small pouch, offered it to me to smell it.

"Smells nice. What is it?"

"Sweet pine needles and crushed flowers stuffed in punk from *t'iis*. Women sew it in little bags, keep them in their belongings. When it looses its odor, they open it, burn it as incense."

He laid out roots, bark, the ear of a wolf, charms, herbs, and dried plants, then began replacing the items in his medicine bag.

He hefted the bag of *hoddentin* and smiled. "Pale Eye has much trouble believing in my medicine. Ask the Blue Coat sergeant at our reservation. He not admit it in the presence of the agent, but he a believer. One night, he sent for me. His wife dying, medical doctor could do nothing to save her. When I go to the sergeant's quarters, doctor drunk, passed out on a chair, the male nurse became angry, ordered me leave. The sergeant remove all nonbelievers from his lodging. I asked him remove his wife's clothes. He did so. She was not aware, breathing low, hot to my hand. I applied the yellow powder of the *hoddentin*. First to her forehead, in her mouth, form of a cross on her breast, circle of yellow around her hairy patch of womanhood, on the head of sleeping doctor, open his mouth, place the powder on his tongue, the sergeant's forehead and mouth, to my own head and mouth. I

126

danced and chanted until dawn. The woman stir, open her eyes, smile at her husband. The sergeant, he look at me, his eyes wide. He said, 'She has not moved in four days.' His gaze go to his wife, she reach out her hand, he took it, turn to me and asked, 'What does this mean.' I tell him I believe it meant his wife would live, but he must believe."

Na-Tu chuckled. "He say he believed, take my hand, tell me he believe. I believe he does. Every moon, he bring a slab of goat cheese to my wife."

I spent the rest of the winter with Na-Tu-Che-Puy and Can See Far. We were together from early dawn until well after dark. He taught me much about Power and much of his language. He was curious about English, and I taught him more than he was able to teach me of Apache. I told him he was smart, but he smiled and said, "I have a better teacher."

17

On a blustery-cold winter night, Can See Far was roasting pinons on her small warming fire in our lodge, the smoke drifting through a hole in the roof.

A voice called out, "Oh great medicineman, Na-Tu-Che-Puy. I come to your lodge for help. My wife will die if you do not come with me."

I went out with Na-Tu-Che-Puy to talk to the man. He was from a guarded camp of Apaches at Ft. Tularosa over in the New Mexico territory. The man promised to have Na-Tu-Che-Puy back in twenty suns.

He agreed to go, then turned to me. "Can See Far and I go. You cannot go to Ft. Tularosa. Captain there mean man. He learn about you, he kill you. Do not worry as Ussen is always with us." They left that night.

The next morning Coot and Iron Chain and Sly Fox rode up, leading Traveler and four other horses.

"Come, young medicineman," Coot said. "We're going for a little ride."

"Where do you think you're going?"

Sly Fox spoke up. "I want to visit my grandmother. She is at the Mescalero Reservation. We will be back before we are missed."

"The Mescalero Reservation?" I asked. "Na-Tu-Che-Puy told me that is where Little Flower and Flower That Grows live. But don't you know that it is over 250-miles to the east? We'll be seen. We'll be caught, and you know what the Blue Coats do to young warriors caught off their reservations. They'll shoot us on sight. You are crazy—all of you. Sly Fox, you and Iron Chain have been listening to this loco Running Duck again. He's going to get you in trouble. Na-Tu-Che-Puy will not be happy with us."

Iron Chain's pony stamped. "Kicking Bear *gonaihgo indaa.* Kicking Bear worries when there is no worry. The agent and the Blue Coats think we all stay on the reservation like they command. They cannot watch us all. They do not know how. It takes Apache to track Apache—Apache to watch Apache. You stay here, Kicking Bear. It will be safe for you here. We will spend one day with Sly Fox's grandmother, then we will return in eight suns."

"*Eight* suns? Five hundred miles in eight suns—seven suns, counting the day you will be with his grandmother. I don't—"

Sly Fox tossed me Traveler's reins. "In half-a-day's ride, we'll be at the base of the *Sierra de Mimbres.* We have spare horses and will rest them often. We will show Kicking Bear how to get all a horse has to give. If the young Pale Eye must rest, we will stop for you."

I smiled up at him. "Running Duck and I have ridden many miles with you and Iron Chain. Yes, we have learned much from you. Now, my friend, perhaps you will learn from us. How to chase young goats up and down rocky ledges, and steep arroyos. How to stay mounted while holding a baby goat under each arm."

The three of them sat their horses smiling down at me. I jumped on Traveler's back, and we were off with a whoop.

We rode out of the White Mountains, riding hard, skirted the Mogollon Rim and the Mimbres Mountains by crossing the vast Plains of San Agustin, through the pass between the Gallinas and San Mateos ranges, crossing the *Rio Grande* below the mining town of Socorro. We rode like the wind, across the northern tip of *Jornada del Muerto*, the San Andres, the *Malpais*, the Tularosa Basin. At that point we were at the base of the 12,000-foot Sierra Blanca, the northernmost point of the Mescalero Reservation.

We were young, tough, and our animals were up to the test. While Sly Fox and Iron Chain had their visit, Coot and I searched the reservation for Little Flower and her family. We wanted to meet this woman our granddaddies had saved from that band of scalpers back in 1833. We wanted to see the look on her face when she met the grandsons of her rescuers, grandsons who were studying to be Apache warriors.

We found an old woman who said she knew Little Flower and her family. She told us that Long Tongue, Flower That Grows, and her mother had broken out of the reservation and were going to the Sierra Madres in Mexico to join Geronimo.

Many weeks later, Na-Tu-Che-Puy said, "We will go to Sacred Mountain far to the rising sun. We will gather herbs, roots, clay for powerful medicine. You have much to learn. Running Duck, Iron Chain, and Sly Fox will come with us. Can See Far will come. She knows much about the herbs and roots that we will gather."

I was not certain of the date of the month, but was fairly certain my seventeenth birthday had just passed. It was now early April. I aimed to make good on my promise to meet Papa at the confluence of the Black River and Pacheta Creek. I reminded Na-Tu-Che-Puy of that promise, and told him I wanted Running Duck to go with me.

"Kicking Bear, you may have much Apache blood from your father, much Comanche blood from your mother, but you worry the same as all Pale Eyes. You must have faith if you want to learn Power. You will meet your father as promised. Come, my son—we must prepare for our journey. Go and tell Running Duck, Iron Chain, and Sly Fox to prepare to leave before tomorrow's sun."

It took us four days to reach the base of Sacred Mountain, a high desert peak we had seen on the second day of our ride to Mescalero. We had followed almost the exact route as the trip Coot, Iron Chain, Sly Fox, and I had made earlier. The four of us had to guard our talk, as Na-Tu-Che-Puy did not know of that journey.

When the egg-shaped mountain first came into view, I said, "Na-Tu-Che-Puy, I believe your Sacred Mountain is the mountain the Pale Eye calls Salinas Peak."

Na-Tu-Che-Puy stopped his pony, a smile on his cragged face. "How do you know that, Kicking Bear? Your mushroom tell you?"

"Oh, no sir. I just know generally where we are from studying my papa's maps. Sacred Mountain is the only egg-shaped mountain near here."

We skirted the base of the peak and came to a place where Na-Tu-Che-Puy pointed out a free-flowing spring, cautioning us not to allow the horses to drink. He said that though the water was only slightly salty to the taste, it would loosen our bowels and those of our animals to an extreme.

He looked at Iron Chain. "When you made this trip only one moon ago, did you have trouble finding water here, my son?"

Iron Chain's eyes brightened. "Oh, no. We found a large spring to the north and—" He grimaced, looked at us for help.

We shrugged and shook our heads.

Na-Tu-Che-Puy led us over a mile away from the base of the mountain, explaining that there was a good spring where we could camp nearby.

Na-Tu-Che-Puy sat his pony. "Apache does not camp close to water, as our ponies would spoil it. Animals of the desert will not come to water if we are close. If enemies come, they will go to water first. We camp close to water, they find us plenty quick. Better if we camp long way from spring."

He gazed across the open plain. "There are many plants here that I use. The wild mint you see there by that boulder. It makes a nice tea, good for stomach pain. The tall yarrow grows in this high place. It is good to stop bleeding. If the wound is cruel, a stalk placed in there, set ablaze. It is painful, but a warrior chooses pain over death. Sagebrush grows over much of our land, good for bad stomach, diarrhea. When a man comes to me for his bruises, or those of his wife or children, there is nothing better than that skunk cabbage you see growing in the shade of that tree. If it is not handy, I use charred honeysuckle vine, or the pitch from a pinion pine. Ussen gives us all we need, my sons."

After we made camp, Na-Tu-Che-Puy looked across our small fire. "Iron Chain, my son, your father Many Fast Feet Two Sticks is troubled. He asks me to explain to you why he scouted for the Blue Coats long ago. He thinks maybe so you are ashamed of him. Is that so, my son?"

"Na-Tu-Che-Puy, I am not ashamed. I have many questions why, but I know my father is an honorable man. He must have had his reasons for scouting for the Blue Coats."

"My son, in the old days the Blue Coats came to our people to help them find their enemies who were also our enemies. In those early days, it was a great honor to be chosen as a scout. Only the greatest warriors were chosen. Many Fast Feet Two Sticks always chosen first. It was good for them to be free of this thing called reservation, our prison. The scouts were given a rifle, ammunition, and paid eight pieces of silver every moon. They were admired, envied. Then the cavalry started to use the scouts against our own people. The cavalry officer reminded them of grave consequences of desertion. Cavalry men would shoot deserters with no questions. No trial of the Pale Eyes. Just shoot deserters. At first, the scouts were proud of the red head-cord they wore, but once the scouts were used against their own people, the red cord became the red badge of servitude. Your father was not ashamed to scout for the cavalry. He told me it is better that he find our people who break out of reservation, and bring them back. If he did not, the cavalry would kill many of our people, *all* of our people. He was wise. He was right. Be proud of your father. Many Fast Feet Two Sticks still wears the red cord. No one is brave enough to deny him that. Not so long ago, he walked in rough country, men on horses killed their animals in pursuit of your father. They never caught him. He is a strong man. Never doubt his strength. We will never speak of this again, Iron Chain. You must promise me you will not think it again."

He pulled on his clay pipe, tamped the loose tobacco. "Tomorrow, I show you how to gather herbs and roots and the white clay we need to make powerful medicine. Come. We will pray until the rose lights the eastern hills. We will pray to Ussen to show us the best herbs and roots and clay."

We had ridden hard for four days, and we were in strong need of rest. I felt like I could sleep for a week. Na-Tu-Che-Puy and Can See Far were old folks, but neither showed any sign of requiring rest. He did not remind me of a man who would not make it through the summer, as Two Sticks had told me and Papa back there in North Arroyo. I smiled. I would never accuse that great man of lying, just rearranging the facts to have his way with the Pale Eye.

The six of us prayed until dawn, mounted up and rode to the top of the peak. I recalled from studying Papa's maps that Salinas Peak was around 9,000 feet. At our noon meal, I attempted to explain to Iron Chain and Sly Fox the meaning of altitude as it relates to sea level, failing miserably.

Coot explained, "My friends, Kicking Bear is loco. All his friends, his *aashchos* know he is crazy when he talks about 9,000 feet being stacked up one on top of the other. Forgive my friend, for he is loco."

Sly Fox laughed. "Yes, all Apache know Kicking Bear is loco. Our perch here on top of Sacred Mountain is much higher than the valley floor below us. That says all there is to say."

The view from the height of that peak was a show of far-off peaks, deep valleys, basins that set the mountains off with their colors of soft green, purple, and brown. We spent the day gathering herbs and digging for roots of certain plants. Na-Tu-Che-Puy and Can See Far handled the herbs and roots reverently, naming each of them. We wrapped them in soft doeskin, securing them behind the saddles of our ponies. He explained the uses of the herbs and plants – slices of prickly pear leaves were applied to wounds, cooked and used as a poultice. The root of *o-chin-ah* was chewed then smeared on sores. *I-zeho-chi-ne* was black medicine, pounded, mixed with water, applied to injuries. *Me-tci-da-il-tco* called "narrow medicine," and was used on sores and small wounds. *Chil-check* was from the chaparral and greasewood, used for arthritis and bruises. Osha root, found on high mountains, was used for headaches. Its tea slackened harsh colds and coughs.

The medicineman laughed. "One time, we had this poor man, his name *Enjady,* he had a wound on his neck. He could not breathe through his nose, he breathed through this hole in his neck. I burned stickers off prickly pear leaves, made a poultice, covering the hole in his neck. Pretty quick the sore healed, and he could breathe through his nose. *Enjady* was happy with me. Very happy."

We spent another night praying until the early sun showed itself again on the stark canyon walls of Sacred Mountain. By late afternoon we had all the herbs and roots Na-Tu-Che-Puy required.

He stood. "Now, my sons, come with me behind this bad spring water where we will dig for white clay. The clay is moist and we will put it in this woven pot that is sealed with pine resin. It must stay moist, or lose Power." He announced we were through with our tasks and congratulated us on being excellent assistants, even finding a rare brown clay on our own.

I sighed. "Father, I am very happy you are pleased because I am sorely in need of a good night's sleep."

"Why, Kicking Bear? Have you forgotten you are in a hurry to return to our lodge? You and Running Duck must prepare to meet your papa on the Black River." The old Apache helped Can See Far mount her pony, mounted his own, and turned toward the setting sun.

On the first evening of our return trip, Na-Tu-Che-Puy asked, "When do you plan to meet your father on Black River, Kicking Bear?"

"I sent word that if it pleased him, I would wait for him at the Black River in the month of April. My papa and our grandfathers have gone there for many springs. We went with my friend Running Duck and his Uncle Doyl before he was killed last summer."

"You say April—this thing you call April. Why is it named so, and how do you know when April comes?"

"I read in a book that April came from Latin or the Greek. It means to open, but I do not recall what is supposed to be opened."

Na-Tu-Che-Puy smiled, waved his clay pipe in a circle. "Perhaps the opening of leaf buds and flower buds."

"That's right. That is *exactly* what it means. I remember now, but how did you know that, my father?"

"My son, when you learned that buds of trees and buds of flowers come after the snow and before the heat of the summer, did you read that in your book?"

"No, sir."

"Neither did I, my son."

He frowned, sucked on his pipe. "This month you call April—what does it do?"

"We have what we call a calendar that we hang on a wall. I saw one on the agent's wall, but it is many years old. It has symbols printed on paper—twelve sheets of paper, one for each one of the Apache's moons. When I say I will meet Papa in mid-April, I mean I will meet him there fifteen days after the start of the month. Like you would say fifteen suns after the full moon. It is sort of the same thing."

"If it is the same thing, Kicking Bear, why don't you say fifteen suns after the full moon?"

I started to try to explain, but Na-Tu-Che-Puy smiled and explained his own question. "Because that is the way of the Pale Eyes. They live their lives as a hunk of pretty iron they call a clock tells them to live, not as their spirits tells them. What does the clock made from a hunk of cold iron do? The Pale Eye listens to the ticking of the clock that tells them when to rise in the morning, when to eat their food, when to go to their bed, when to have babies, when to die. The Pale Eyes are known for complaining about never enough time. They will never learn what a great Indian chief to the north told them long ago, that they have all the time they have, nothing more, nothing less."

He rolled a *cigarro*. Can See Far lit it for him. "Kicking Bear, you have no calendar, so how do you know when it will be time for you to meet your papa at the Black River?"

"I have spent my life much like an Apache boy lives his life. Outside, where he loves and appreciates Mother Earth, the stars, moon, and sun above. My papa teaches me to be mindful of what is going on around me, to watch the length of shadows when the sun is high. To know that when that shadow is short, that summer is here, when it is long that winter is here. I was aware of the date we call December 21, four moons ago when my shadow was long, and everyday since then, my shadow has been shorter. Not much, but shorter. Spring and fall months are just as predictable, and though I cannot tell you the date on the Pale Eye's calendar without looking at it like my papa can, I can tell you within three or four days. If the agent had a current calendar on the Issue House wall, I believe it would tell me that today is April 10. It has been many moons since Running Duck and I came to you. Many moons since we have seen the calendar of the Pale Eyes, but I believe it is April 10."

"It seems Kicking Bear has much to teach his teacher. Then, my son, if it is only five suns until the day you chose to meet your papa, we must part when we cross the river you call the San Francisco. You and Running Duck go to meet your papa, we will go to our lodge, and wait for you to return."

He hesitated. "You will not make me wait for long? You will return, Kicking Bear?"

"Yes, my father, my chief, I will return, and you will not wait long. We will meet with Papa for four or five suns, then I will return to our lodge, and some of Can See Far's good cooking."

We were all quiet for awhile. I stoked the fire, gazed over at this great and gentle man. "Na-Tu-Che-Puy, may I ask you a question, sir?"

"Yes, my son, what is it you wish to know?"

"When Many Fast Feet Two Sticks came to our dugout, and my papa and I met him at North Arroyo last fall, he said you were very ill. He told us that you had a vision, that it was important for me to come to your lodge soon, as your vision told you that you would not live through the summer. Tell me, Father, was that your vision, or a story you and Many Fast Feet Two Sticks made up to get Kicking Bear to come to your lodge?"

His dark eyes danced. "Kicking Bear, you will never make a good Apache. Never be a good medicineman—never learn much about Power." He grinned, studied the fire, drew on his *cigarro*. "Kicking Bear asks too many questions for a young warrior. Too many questions for a tired old medicineman to answer."

"Yes, sir, but you know what else, my chief?"

"What?"

"You and Can See Far are stronger than Iron Chain, Sly Fox, Running Duck, and me. You can go long without sleep or food or water. I believe I will live to be over one-hundred years old, but you know what, sir?"

"What, my son?"

"You will be there to pray to Ussen, and say nice words when you put Kicking Bear in the ground."

It was late in the second day of our return trip. Na-Tu-Che-Puy pointed to the west. "The black mesa there in distance. That is *Mesa de Contadero*. The Great River flows on the other side. We will camp there. Apache knows this spot for all time. In the old days, Mexican people used the narrow pass to count their beeves for many winters—hundred, hundred winters. Good place to camp."

The mesa, a flat-topped black lava flow, stopped at the *Rio Grande's* edge, forcing the river to the west, and around it. The mesa was over a mile long and rough. We had been riding through deep sugar-sand, creeping along. I figured it would take us two hours to reach the base. We pushed our mounts on.

A mile from the mesa, I stopped. The shrill of a bull elk's bugling-whistle filled the air, mixed with the cry of a woman's wail. The sound had no source, no direction. Like a dream you try hard to remember, but the harder you try, the further the memory escapes. Then a large mushroom appeared over the southern end of the mesa.

"Running Duck. *Coot.* That damn mushroom is after me again. Something bad is up ahead there."

Coot was with Iron Chain, leading us through a salt cedar grove. I turned and spurred my pony, yelling to Na-Tu-Che-Puy to stop.

He turned as I rode up. "What is it, my son?"

"My mushroom warns me. My mushroom has the voice of a bull elk bugling and the cry of a woman wailing. The sky is full of the sound, but comes from no where."

"What does the mushroom warn?"

"Men—many men on horseback. *There,* crossing Great River on the south end of *Mesa de Contadero.*"

"You have not spoken of the bull elk or cry of a woman. Why did you not tell me?"

"It has never happened in the past, my chief. I do not know."

"Who are these men? Does the mushroom tell you who these men are? Enemies?"

"I am not certain, my father. Only that they are not Blue Coats—not Apaches. I fear they are thieves, murderers, no-good Pale Eyes, Mexicans, half-breeds."

"*Comancheros!*"

"Yes, my father—*comancheros!* They are headed this way. We must hide. There is no time to ride to the protection of the mesa."

Na-Tu-Che-Puy turned to the others and barked, "Run your ponies to the mesa. When *comancheros* show themselves, turn and go north around the mesa to the Great River. Cross there and go upstream. You will lose them when the sun sets. Kicking Bear, stay with me and Can See Far."

The three turned their ponies and rode off. Na-Tu turned to me and motioned for me to lead them out of the way of the advancing *comancheros*. The Apache training and Na-Tu-Che-Puy's plan made quick sense for our escape. I turned south. We loped off toward a low jagged hill that could offer concealment and shelter for the night. A mile later, we approached a sharp rise. I motioned for Na-Tu-Che-Puy and Can See Far to stay put. I jumped off my pony and crawled up the rise until I could look back along our trail. Napoleon could not have devised a strategy any quicker or more certain than Na-Tu-Che-Puy's plan.

The boiling dust of our companion's ponies were beating a trail to the north around the black mesa, followed by a the large dust cloud of their pursuers. The *comancheros* had not split up—no one was following us.

We kept to the deep arroyos that led to the *Rio Grande*, and soon found a place to cross the river at a ford. We waited until dark to cross. By noon the following day, we approached the *Mimbres* mountains, and soon enough Coot, Sly Fox, and Iron Chain joined us. They had crossed the river north of *Contadero*, rode two miles, then swam their ponies back across the river after brushing away all sign of reentering the stream. They hid their ponies behind a knoll, watching the *comancheros* approach. A band of fifty-six men crossed the river, and followed the boys' trail north. When the trail disappeared, they seemed to talk it over, then moved on to the north, leading more than a score of horses carrying men and women, all tied to their horses. They were mainly Pale Eyes with a sprinkling of Mexicans, all showing signs of abuse by their captors.

Na-Tu-Che-Puy motioned for me to follow him out of the camp. He asked me to explain how the mushroom had warned me of the *comancheros*, and about the mournful noise I heard just before the mushroom appeared.

"It is not my way—not the Pale Eye's way—to believe in Power or visions. We call it witchcraft. We only believe what we see for ourselves, things we can touch with our hands, smell, taste, hear. It is hard for me to accept my vision, even harder to explain it to you. When I first had a vision, I told no one—not even Papa or Running Duck. But I learned to believe the vision, the mushroom, in spite of my doubts and disbelief. I don't know if it is the mushroom that speaks to me, or makes the sound of the bugling elk, as it has no mouth to speak. The vision comes to me not in words, but the knowledge of the vision is given to me. It is something I can not ignore, as it commands me. And I should tell you that the voice of the mushroom first reminded me of my sister's crying the night she died."

"Your sister, she died? When did she die and why? What was your sister's name?"

"Her name was Mary Jewell—"

"Mary Uul?"

"Yes, Mary Jewell. She died many years ago, when she was only three years old—she died of *viruela*. I learned later that *viruela* is what we call smallpox."

"Mary Uul was your sister. Visions come to our people with Power when they ask Ussen to help them, to direct them, to tell them if enemies are near, help them cure coughing and bad gunshot wounds. Our great chief Victorio's sister, Lozen, is a great woman warrior. She prays to Ussen in a certain way. Ussen tells Lozen if enemies are near. She has great medicine, but she must ask Ussen for He is silent unless she asks. But you tell me you do not ask Ussen, that your warning comes to you like the wind, with no effort, like watching a moth drawn to a campfire. Maybe your Power is not from Ussen. Maybe your Power comes from your dead sister, Mary Uul. I will think on it."

Late the afternoon of the second day, we rounded a high ridge. Far below, the San Francisco River flowed between the deep green of groves of mountain cottonwood. Na-Tu-Che-Puy reined his pony and slid to the ground. I dropped down, he came to me, embraced me long and hard. I could feel the bones and muscles in his back, the thought passing my mind that he was like hugging an ocotillo with just the tips of the barbs clipped. Strong, taut, unconquerable.

"This is where we part, my son. Can See Far will prepare a feast for your return. Our people will look forward to Kicking Bear and Running Duck return. You will tell us many strange tales from your truthful lips. You will not disappoint our people. You and Running Duck will return to us soon, my son?"

"Nothing can keep us from returning to you, my father. We will see you in five or six suns. That is our promise to you."

I mounted up. "Come on Running Duck, let's get going. We've got a long ride ahead of us."

"Naw, you go on along. You and your papa need a visit—a *private* visit. I'll see you when you get back. Tell Uncle Abe I said howdy."

"Aw come on, Coot. Papa will want to see you as bad as me. Come on, let's go."

"Nope. Not going."

I turned my pony and headed west.

18

I sat on Uncle Doyl's all-time favorite stump. He liked it, "'Cause I can sit here and watch the wind whip up all those swirling, little ripples as it glides over that old dark river." Then he'd say, "I reckon the Apaches watched those ripples a hundred centuries before us, that's what I reckon." I hadn't thought of Uncle Doyl much since I went to the reservation. I jumped to my feet. "You should be ashamed!" That tall, wagon-tongue of a man meant so much to Coot and me. I looked out over the river as the water chased a warm breeze and could almost make out Uncle Doyl skipping a flat rock at the ripples.

Uncle Doyl was such an affable man, to him hear say it, he was, "searching life, looking for that four leaf clover."

Why did Coot refuse to come with me to meet Papa? I couldn't make any sense out of it. Coot was a burly boy, just turned seventeen, black hair and curly black eyelashes. I recalled the day he mimicked a school girl he caught giving me the eye. He'd blink those heavy dark lashes, wink, close his eyes, hold his head down low, open his eyes again, blink a couple of times while sucking in a breath of air for effect, raise his head to the side, and say, "Oh, Narlow, I declare, you are the handsomest boy in the whole world."

Voices and sounds, images and flavors of those many trips to this mystic place swirled around me at that old campsite. Coot belching, *"Enjuh,"* mimicking Two Sticks. Uncle Doyl telling a yarn as he made up a Sunday morning apple pie in his iron oven. Papa reminding us of our manners. Horses snorting on the picket. Mules braying, the smell of damp earth and horse dung; new grass and flowers...

"Huh? Papa!" *Papa—mounted and leading a packhorse just dropped off the top of the trail at Rattlesnake Point.*

I glanced down at my loin cloth, felt my shoulder-length hair, wondered what Papa would think of his son. I was the same boy, I told myself, but that was only partially true. So much had happened since the spring before. So many things would never be the same. I sat up straight. Papa would be following my pony's tracks down here, likely assume that I was not mounted on Traveler because something bad had happened to that fine animal. How would he understand that I rode a bony

Apache pony when I had Traveler? Papa would have to understand that Na-Tu had not allowed me to ride that grand animal until I proved my manhood. My loincloth, knife belt, moccasins on my feet were all I wore. I hoped Papa's surprise would not be too disappointing.

I stood and waved at the tall boulder at the top of the bend in the trail just before Papa appeared, mounted, leading a packhorse. He was several hundred yards away, but I took off at a dead run to meet him. As I approached, he stepped down, and met my embrace. Papa was never comfortable about men hugging or touching each other, but this time the mood held him.

"Let me look at you, son. Good lord, I do believe you've grown a foot, brown as a bronze juniper."

"Traveler is just fine, Papa," I blurted out, realized my outburst, and hugged him again. "I'm sorry, Papa, but I'm so proud to see you I'm about to bust. You look just the same, Papa. Just the same."

"Well, I could say the same for you, son, but that would be a mighty stretch of the truth, now wouldn't it?" he said, looking at me and my scanty outfit. "You're a fine specimen of a man, Narlow Montgomery." His wonderful slate-blue eyes glistening.

"Aw Papa, you sound just like Two Sticks, calling me Narlow Montgomery like that."

We walked down to our camp, both too full to speak. My eyes formed a lake that I could barely see through. We sat around the fire, filling each other in on what was going on. Papa said my old dog Butch was ornery as ever, that Fernando Valdez threatened to return to Mexico when Papa told him about me going to an Apache Indian reservation to learn to be a medicineman.

"Coot's with me. Did you know that, Papa?"

"I supposed he was. His aunt Beulah wrote me asking after him. She and Coot's mama don't see eye-to-eye on much. I wrote her back, told her that Coot's plans had changed, that I'd let her know more about him when I saw him. I figured he'd come down here with you today."

"At the last minute he backed out, telling me that you and I would need a private conversation, or some such nonsense."

Papa smiled, dabbled at the fire. "I don't suppose Coot is over the loss of Uncle Doyl. Coot's lost all the menfolk on his daddy's side of the family—his daddy and both uncles, all dead before they were fifty years old. I've always considered Coot as your brother."

"Coot feels the same way, Papa. I know he does, but he can be a stubborn cuss."

For hours I told Papa about my training, which had not included much about being a medicineman or learning much about Power. Papa concluded that was the Apache's way of making certain that I could be trusted. I told him the story of Na-Tu-Che-Puy naming me Kicking Bear at the spur of the moment at the agent's Issue House. He thought that was a right fitting name, and he really got a kick out of Coot's new name, Running Duck.

"I tell you, Papa, the Apache know how to train their boys to become warriors, and they're tougher than iron by the time they're grown. They can endure *anything*, they *never* flinch, and they're all just like Coot—they *never* quit."

"That sure makes me proud of what you boys are about. You are experiencing something that no white man will ever experience or witness. In the old days, I have seen warriors outrun horses in rough country, and the very next day, that same bunch of warriors were up and gone, the horses, lame for days. I've seen Two Sticks do that for days on end. I'm proud of your decision to go to Two Sticks and Na-Tu-Che-Puy."

"I've sure missed you, Papa. It's strange, but the thing I've missed the most about you is your smile and sparkling blue eyes. You're real special. And Papa, everyone on the reservation knows about you, and I bet I've told the story about our granddaddies saving Little Flower from those scalpers a hundred times. The People couldn't hear that story enough if I told them every day. They believe what our granddaddies did for them was a gift from Ussen."

Papa reached behind him, handed me a long package wrapped in oil cloth. "And speaking of gifts, here's a little something that will make you and Coot heroes with the ladies back on the reservation."

I unwrapped it – a bolt of bright red cloth.

He said, "Vermilion – the Apache's favorite color. The brighter the better."

Thank you, Papa, and as Uncle Doyl would say, 'That's right thoughty of you.' Na-Tu-Che-Puy tells me that I have taught him more than he's taught me. It's pretty hard to best that man. Just like you, Papa. And Papa, speaking of gifts, here's a little something for you." I handed him the journal he had packed for me when I caught the stagecoach to Austin. "I filled that journal plumb to the brim, Papa—not an empty line remaining. There's a lot of stories in there that I imagine you'll enjoy reading. When you have the time, that is."

"Oh, I'll have the time real soon, son. Thank you, and you can be assured I'll take good care of it. One of these days you'll want your sons and daughters to have this—to read their daddy's journal."

"Aw Papa, I'm not going to have any children, get married, and all that stuff. Shoot, I'm scared to death of girls. How would I ever be a father?"

He chuckled. "Oh, you'll figure it out. The Lord has mysterious ways of helping a young man to figure out things such as that. He has Mother Nature, and a pretty gal's smile will explain things to you, my boy."

"Papa, do me a big favor. Turn to the page I folded over. I want you to read the part about our Apache concealment training. Read that, Papa. I'm kinda proud of that story."

Papa opened the journal. "Mid-February 1876—This morning before sunup, the elders came for us, and we ran behind their ponies for many miles. By mid-morning we found ourselves out on an open plain, with only large clumps of grass scattered around, no trees, bushes, just a few scattered yuccas. Far off to the south, the elders spied a herd of antelope. They dismounted, and hid their horses in a low area of the plain. Each of the elders took two of us boys, each group loped off, spanning out in the direction of the herd. For the next hour, we were on our hands and knees, on our bellies, getting as close to the herd as possible. Our elder, Standing Elk, tore off the corner of his red bandana, and tied it to a yucca stalk. He told me and the boy with me, Lukey No-No, to hide ourselves well—*very well*. Standing Elk checked to make certain we were hidden to his satisfaction. He waved the stick with the red cloth above him, back and forth, then stuck it in the earth. I watched him take up tufts of grass, place them on his body, then sprinkled just two handfuls of sand over himself in a certain way, disappearing before my very eyes. In just a bit, I could hear the soft treading of four antelope, sniffing their curiosity at the red cloth on the yucca. Standing Elk reached up with his knife, and slashed the throat of a large buck. The others shied away a few steps, but came right back to the red cloth. Lukey No-No was hidden on the far side of Standing Elk. I saw his knife come slowly out of nowhere, and the antelope standing almost on top of him slumped to the ground. The other two antelope only scooted away, hesitated, then came back over me. I reached up less than a foot with Two Sticks' long knife, and cut the throat of the doe. The other young doe stood stamping her front foot at the doe I just killed, but she showed no fright. I thought, *If she would come just one step closer*. The herd panicked and ran off. We shouldered our prizes, and joined the other groups of elders and boys who gathered and counted the kill. Sixteen antelope. Our group's count of three was the most of any group, but every group got at least one of the animals. It won't surprise Papa when I tell him that Coot got two nice-sized bucks. Dern it's hard to best that boy. We dressed out the antelope and carried them back to the reservation, arriving just before dark. Plenty of fresh meat for all the People. The elders said it was good, like the old days when the people shared. I have never been prouder to be alive as I am this day."

Papa closed the journal. "Son, that's about the most profound story I've ever read. Ol' Coot got two, huh? I have to admit I sure do miss that boy."

Papa said he'd been keeping an eye on IB and Shelly Brom for us, knowing we'd want to know they weren't going without. "Son, Shelly is a pure-dee mystery to me, something I can't quite put my finger on, but she's special somehow." He grinned, his slate-gray eyes glistened. "Like—like, I swear that girl could sing like the Bells of Saint Mary's, but that poor child's bell has no clapper. I read somewhere that the saddest of songs is sadder still than the silent song of a stillborn child. The girl somehow reminds me of your little sister, Mary Jewell. Sure miss her sweet innocence. Surely, I do, but I know God holds her in the palm of his hand."

"Papa, what you said about Shelly Brom is about the nicest thing I've ever heard said about another human being. You sure have a way with words. You're a blessing, Papa."

The stars came out bright. We had our supper and hinted around about getting into the warm blankets Papa had brought.

He said, "Well, we've talked about everything under the sun today—what else? Oh, and your mama is fine, son. Just fine."

I hadn't even asked about my own mother and it embarrassed me. I'm supposed to be a man, but I act like a spoiled town boy. "Oh, I'm sorry, Papa. I should have asked about her."

His gaze shot up to a bright star. He sat for a moment. Even when sad, his slate-blue eyes shown bright as marigold at the sun's edge. "Don't worry yourself, son. Your mama doesn't worry about anything, not even much about herself. I wish I could say she sends her love, but she still thinks you are in Austin going to college. She was about as warm as a hen laying eggs in a pail of cold water when she came to grips about you going 600-miles away to Austin just to go to school. She preached at me about always wanting to go to school herself. Here I was spending all that money for nothing. That woman is a case, I am here to guarantee you, Narlow."

The next morning we awoke early. I had just returned from the Pacheta Creek to fetch a bucket of water. Papa gathered an armload of oak, squatted down, poking the fire back to life. I set the bucket of water on a stump, got down on my all-fours beside him, and blew on a warm ember to help get the fire going. I smelled burning leather, and oak. I first thought it was just the campfire. It was this same campfire, but not *this* fire. What I smelled was a fire nearly a year old.

I jumped to my feet. "*Papa.*"

"What is it, son?"

"It's nothing, Papa. Sorry to shout at you like that. It's just that ol' mushroom-medicineman stuff acting up again." I smiled. "But, you might like to know that Two Sticks and Coot just came over the rimrock on horseback. What do you reckon they're up to?"

In a minute, they appeared around the boulder at the top of the trail, the sun just coming up at their backs. Two Sticks handed Coot what looked like a leather pouch, pointing down to us. He raised his arm in a salute, and Papa returned his greeting. Coot turned his horse, starting down the trail toward us. The tall man with the red bandanna started back up the trail.

Coot rode into camp, slid off his pony, wearing nothing but a loincloth and a sheepish smile. A look I had never seen on him. He strolled up to Papa, stuck out his hand. "Howdy, Uncle Abe—sure good to see you, sir."

"Mighty fine seeing you, my son. I understand it's Running Duck now."

"Yes, sir, it's about as good as Coot, I reckon. Either one of them suits me a lot better than the one I was born with."

I asked, "What made you change your mind about coming down here?"

"I'll tell you later," Coot answered with a hint of that sheepish look returning to his brown face shining in the early light. He turned to Papa. "Uncle Abe, when Narlow and I showed up at the reservation, I gave Two Sticks this $5,000 in gold to safekeep for me. He gave it back to me just now, saying I should give it to you. So here it is, sir."

Papa hefted the tote. "Well, I'd say it hasn't lost half an ounce. I'll safe-keep it for you, but the gold is yours. It'll be there when you're ready for it."

We told stories for another hour, munched jerky, and drank a gallon of coffee. Coot and I hadn't had coffee for many months, and it was good. Papa stood. "You boys excuse me, but while it's on my mind, I need to tack a shoe on my pack mule. Cussed old fool. I swear she kicks her shoes off just to spite me."

I turned to Coot. "You going to tell me what changed your mind about coming down here to meet Papa?"

"Yeah, I'll tell you. That tall gentleman with the stovepipe hat changed my mind. After we left you at the Frisco River, we showed up at his lodge. He asked where you were. I told him that you had gone to meet your papa. He asked why I hadn't gone with you, and I told him that Abe Montgomery is Kicking Bear's daddy, that I didn't want to impose. I tried to explain, but that tall Apache just got madder. 'Abe Montgomery you daddy now. Uncle Doyl dead. You daddy dead. You go to Black River see you daddy Abe Montgomery.' I tried to talk him out of it, but he dug his heels in, black eyes flashing a storm. Took me by the arm, walked me back to my pony, grabbed me by the nape of my neck with one hand, my knife belt with the other, lifted me off the ground, and tossed me on the back of that pony like a two-pound rag doll. 'You big boy, but just boy. When you and Kicking Bear go on Cuchillo Creek on raft, I *let* you go. Bad water, but Many Fast Feet Two Sticks let you go. Think of manhood training you men plan for you. Want you be *Hombres del Campo*. I could stop you from that raft, just like I sit you on you pony this day. Papa Abe tell me long ago you and Kicking Bear were brothers joined at hip like he had seen one time ago. You go to Papa Abe Montgomery. Many Fast Feet Two Sticks go with you, make *sure* you go see Papa Abe Montgomery.' That was one mad Apache, smoke coming out of his black eyes, steam out of his wide ears. And here we came, just like he said, and here I am, just like he said. You and I, and two more just like us, couldn't handle that man when he gets riled."

I laughed. "Well, I knew something was up when you rode up this morning. You had the most sheepish look on your face. Something I've never seen on you before."

"Two Sticks has a way of strapping the sheep on a man, *boy*, as he reminded me. Sheepish fits me just fine when it comes to doing *exactly* what Two Sticks says."

We stayed with Papa three more days. Leaving him at the top of trail was the hardest thing we ever did. "Uncle Abe, why don't you come with us? You'd be real welcome at the reservation. They'd sure like to meet the son of Shelby Montgomery. Come on. Go with us."

"No, that wouldn't be fitting. You boys go on back like you promised. But I tell you what I'll do. I don't know how much longer you boys plan on staying with those people, but I'll be right down there by that river this time next year in case you boys would like a little visit." Papa sat his big sorrel gelding, his eyes sparkling like sparks off his forge, a grin as wide and honest as a snow-filled plain.

"Sure you don't want to take Traveler back with you, Papa? You could go with us to Ft. Apache, stay a few days, then take Traveler on home."

"Naw, this old horse I'm riding is not as fast as Traveler, but that suits me just fine."

Coot turned his pony, and I followed him on up Pacheta Creek. We stopped at the top of the knoll and looked back to wave at Papa. He was heading east, all we could see were his shoulders and wide-brimmed hat going over the rise, his gray hair swirling like a desert rattler.

19

White Mountain is mostly high ground. Mountain peaks, pines, firs, with a goodly amount of cedar and juniper. The grass was dependable, plenty of water, the hunting good within half-a-day's ride. Two Sticks told us how lucky we were to be here rather than on the San Carlos to the south where there was much disease. The People were often near starvation. The agent was even more ruthless than the one at Ft. Apache.

Come September, Two Sticks talked incessantly about busting out of the reservation. His dreams taunted him, of being penned like a mountain lion he saw one time in a cage in Tucson. Two Sticks took on the habits of a caged animal, striding fast, stopping, turning, hurrying back to his lair. We'd go wherever he wanted. Iron Chain, Sly Fox, Coot, and I mounted up, Two Sticks turned his pony, headed down Pacheta Creek. Over the past months, he had talked a lot about his younger sister, that she was ill. We figured he wanted to pay her a visit.

Coot asked, "Many Fast Feet Two Sticks, sir, how will we find your sister? You said it had been many years since you had visited her on the San Carlos."

"Do not worry. Many Fast Feet Two Sticks find sister. I not forget."

I asked, "Well sir, how do you know that she is ill and dying? Do you know the cause of her dying?"

"The south wind tells me much. A warrior from there tells me." Lengthy conversations that pass on useless information was not one of Two Sticks' character problems.

We followed the Pacheta down to the Black River and our hunting headquarters. The line shack stood there, lonesome as an orphan.

Coot sidled over. "Now don't tear up, Kicking Bear. You're an Apache now, and warriors don't cry at the sight of a line shack."

Two Sticks led us down the Black River a few miles until its flow turned due west. There we left it, continuing south. The trail broke from Ponderosa pines to scrub oak and cedars, which, in its turn, led us into stark desert. Coot and I had lived our days in desert country, but this was a different desert, dry and lifeless as last year's cornstalk, ashen, all a'grind, a'glare, not a blade of green, yellow and brown as the earth.

True to his word, Two Sticks found his sister's village, and strolled up to her hut with no fear of being found out by the agent or his men. We four boys hung back in the salt cedars. Two Sticks turned to us and made an angry motion for us to come to him. He called out to the hut. An old shriveled woman emerged. She told Two Sticks that his sister was dying of shiver sickness. He ducked his head and stepped inside the hut. In a bit he came out, motioned for Iron Chain to come. They talked for a minute then Iron Chain returned.

"My father say his sister, Brook That Talks, is very sick with fever. He say for us to go find water, cool water."

We found water and pine-tar-coated jars to carry it in. Coot gathered the jars and entered the hut over Iron Chain's objections.

Coot came out, turned to me. "Malaria—needs quinidine. The old woman says the agent has the stuff, but refuses to give it to these people. Says he doesn't have much of it and what he has he's saving it for himself and the soldiers. Two Sticks wants you to build a big fire, and while you're gathering wood, put your head on how you're going to steal some quinidine out of the agent's issue house. Get with it."

He ducked his head as he went back in the hut. Iron Chain, Sly Fox, and I spread out looking for firewood. All the nearby firewood had been burned up years ago. We found precious few branches, but several women were willing to give us some of theirs.

Coot came out again. "I told Two Sticks that it's necessary to get our hands on that quinidine. He says the agent is known for his love of horses, and has a big black Arabian that he's real fond of. If he thinks that horse is in danger, or likely be stolen, he'll have every soldier on the reservation in hot pursuit. Narlow, here's what I think will work—check me out on this. Iron Chain, Sly Fox, and I will find the corral where the agent keeps his Arabian. We'll slip a hackamore on him and I'll ride him out and around to the agent's house and whoop it up. The agent will come running out, see his prize animal being ridden in circles by an unarmed crazed Apache. I'll tease the agent along, then take off toward the hills to the north. The whole damn army can chase me, but it's important that the agent be with them. That will leave the Issue House deserted and . . ."

My mind began to wander as I was mulling over how much Coot had matured. We were lifelong *amigos*, but I somewhere along the way he had gone on ahead. My mind was stuck on two words that I remember from Papa's big dictionary. Those words seemed to describe me and my confusion on taking action—*discomfit* and *discombobulate*. They meant the same thing as far as I could figure, yet here I was stuck on deciding which described me better. What if I wasn't up to the task Coot had planned out?

Coot's voice pushed its way back into my consciousness, " . . . and when the agent comes out of the house and takes off after me, Narlow, you sneak in the back way. Stay out of sight when you get in there in case somebody shows up. When Sly Fox sees the agent take off after me, he'll wait a minute then fire off three shots in rapid succession, signaling you to go to work. Two Sticks says that all agents have at least one room that is padlocked where they keep extra rifles and ammunition, whiskey, and every other thing they don't want the Indians getting their hands on, including quinidine. Shoot the lock off, find the quinidine, get the hell out of there. Steal some cartridges and a jug of whiskey so the quinidine won't be the only thing missing."

"Jeez-amighty, Coot, I wouldn't know quinidine from a ladle of salt. How will I know—"

"Tighten up, Narlow. Ignore everything else in that goddamn storeroom except quinidine. When you find it, you'll know it. Think it will work?"

"Sure it will, but I'll ride that Arabian and *you* go find the quinidine."

"You'll find it. Let's *go*."

The four of us rode toward the agent's house. On the way I had time to think about a stage in life that I thought I had already passed—going from a boy to a man, like the test we went through last year. Hadn't we passed the *Hombres del Campo* test? But now I had my doubts. Here was Coot taking charge of three of his friends to solve a problem that could easily prove deadly. Coot didn't ask for the job, didn't ask permission, he just grabbed it by the throat. He was truly a man. Coot rose to the occasion while my mind was still fumbling around deciding whether I was discomfited or discombobulated. I was way too young to have the dwindles, but maybe I got 'em already.

We found the agent's issue house at the base of a hill under a cottonwood grove, brush growing up behind it. Coot motioned for me to leave my horse, to

147

make my way to the brush. He tied his horse and mine together, left them there, turned and jumped up behind Iron Chain, and they made their way around to the corrals. Pretty quick, Coot came roaring out of the corral on the back of the agent's big black Arabian, the horse's mane and tail flying like a plume of black fire. Coot circled behind the house, grinned down at me as he passed, letting out a blood-curdling cry. He dug his heels into the horse's flank, circled around in front of the house with an endless hooping war cry.

The agent banged out the front door, cussing the crazy bastard who was riding his prize so carelessly. He took off afoot chasing his horse, revolver drawn. Every few strides, he'd stop raise his revolver, try to get a bead on Coot. I jumped through the back window, and hid behind the agent's desk. Peeking through, I could see Coot letting the agent get within a few feet of him, backing the Arabian, keeping the horse's head between him and the agent's revolver. The agent stumbled and fell. Coot turned the Arabian, whipping him into a run while staying low on his broad neck. The agent ran back to the corral.

"Sergeant, get your men mounted up and run down that damn crazy red bastard! Get a move on *goddamnit*."

A soldier had one foot in the stirrup. The agent jerked him down, mounted up, and raced off after his Arabian.

Sly Fox fired off his rifle three times. I found the padlocked door, shot off the lock, and started going through the shelves looking for something I had no idea what. There were boxes of cartridges, rows of rifles, shotguns, jars of pickled pig's feet, jugs of Kentucky mash, Mexican *mezcal*. On the top shelf a large wooden box with a red cross on it was full of iodine, bandages, smelling salts, a scapula, one side of a doctor's stethoscope. I rummaged around. There—a small white paper box wrapped with twine. It was full of white crystals, looking more like quinidine than anything else. *It better be.* I put the wooden box back on the high shelf, found an empty feed sack, filled it with two bottles of Kentucky bourbon and two boxes of 44-40 cartridges. I left through the rear window, and headed back up the hill to our horses, head pounding. *Please let the white crystals be quinidine.*

Two Sticks came out when I rode up to his sister's hut. I slid down and opened the white box. We smiled at each other not knowing if it meant quinidine, or maybe smelling salts, or cowlick.

"Narlow, take Running Duck's horse and sack. Ride to south, find a place to hide. I will send for you when Running Duck returns."

I found a rock outcropping on a small knoll about a half-mile south. In a bit, mounted Blue Coats went from one wickiup to the next, calling everyone out, then going in to make certain no one remained inside. When a trooper got to Brook That Talks' hut, he shouted out. Two Sticks and several women came out. The trooper went inside then came back out, pointing inside at Brook That Talks. Two Sticks spoke to him for a minute. The soldier got back on his horse and took off swinging the loose reins at the hind end of his mount.

After an hour, Coot and Iron Chain came in from the north riding double. Sly Fox rode in from the east. The Arabian was no where in sight. Two Sticks came out and talked to them, then pointed in my direction. I stood. Two Sticks waved me in. Coot came out as I trotted my pony in, leading his horse.

"Got scared and went and hid, huh?" he asked, grinning.

"No, I just took your advice and did exactly what Two Sticks told me do *the first time*. I don't wear sheep as well as you."

"Did you find the quinidine?"

I reached into the sack and tossed the box down to Coot. "I don't know if I found quinidine or a box of white sand. Now what?"

"I don't know, but if we don't try something that little lady in there won't be with us in the morning."

He sniffed the powder, dabbed his paw in, licked his finger, then looked up at me. "What do you think we do with this stuff? Breathe it, or take a spoonful of it and wash it down with water? What do you think?"

"Shoot, your guess is as good as mine. But if I was doing the doctoring, I think I'd mix up a batch of it with water, stir it up real good, and make her drink it."

"Let's try it. Find a bowl and some cool water and fix up a dose like you think it oughta be. You're almost a full-fledged medicineman now, so do what your gut tells you to do. Let me know when it's ready, but don't come in here. We're just guessing it's malaria—shoot, we don't even know if the stuff is catching. No sense in both of us getting whatever she's got."

When I had the concoction mixed up to my liking, I called out. Coot stuck out his hand and I handed it over.

After awhile Coot came out. "Two Sticks thinks you should all leave now. Go back to the south and hide yourselves. Kicking Bear, when do you think our patient should have another dose?"

"I have not one clue, but since I'm the doctor, I want to say that she should have another dose around midnight. I always subscribe all my patients with a dose every six hours."

Coot chuckled. "You don't *sub*scribe anything, you *pre*scribe."

I grinned. "I was just checking you."

Iron Chain asked, "What does Two Sticks think will happen when the agent finds that Kicking Bear broke into the storeroom?"

Coot said, "We talked about that. Of course, he doesn't know, but we have the agent's Arabian stashed where he can't find him if he looked for a month. He's going to be mad about the break-in, but not as *mad* as he'll be *glad* to get his horse back. We need to figure out how to arrange that."

At midnight I crept back down to the hut to deliver our patient's next dose.

"How's she doing, Coot? Any change?"

"Yeah, I think there is, and the women who have been nursing her say there is a definite improvement. All we can do is keep nursing her. Have you figured out what to do with that Arabian?"

"I'm the medicineman here, you're the military strategist. See you just before first light."

I went back to our hiding spot. Iron Chain was keeping guard while Sly Fox slept.

"Iron Chain, where is the agent's Arabian horse staked out?" I asked.

"Running Duck and I hid him where Running Duck says agent will never find him."

"Where is that?"

"In the agent's corral. We smeared white and gray clay over him, and cut off his long mane. Then Running Duck shaved off his long tail hair. He is very ugly. We will sneak in the corral every day to make sure the clay is still there."

"Should have known it. There's not place on this reservation to hide an animal like that, so Running Duck hid him right under the agent's nose."

We kept nursing Brook That Talks every six hours for the next two days. Then all hell broke loose.

"The word is out that the agent knows someone broke into the storehouse," Coot said. "And that stealing the Arabian was just a decoy to get him out of there."

"He must be real brilliant," I said.

"Well, this job doesn't call for much brains, just brawn and a cold-blooded attitude toward the people you're supposed to feed and protect. Have you thought up any sneaky way of using that Arabian to get us out of this fix? Come on, Narlow, think and connive like your mama."

"That's funny, Coot, because that is exactly what I'm doing. But, I haven't come up with a thing. But, I'm working on it."

After delivering Brook That Talks' morning dose, we heard a bell clanging, and everyone came out of their huts.

Sly Fox said, "The agent is calling everyone in the reservation to come in to be counted—probably searched. What do we do, Kicking Bear?"

"Jeez-amighty, I don't know. Let's go to Two Sticks and Running Duck and talk it over. Maybe we can think of something."

We left our ponies at the outcropping and ran back to Brook That Talks' hut. When we got there the little wrinkled lady was sitting outside.

"Where is Many Fast Feet Two Sticks and Running Duck?" I asked.

Coot called out, "We're in here. The agent would recognize me as the bastard that stole his Arabian, and Two Sticks isn't supposed to be here. When the agent or his soldiers come snooping around, this little lady will tell them in Spanish, '*Muy peligroso. La senora tiene mal aire.*' *Mal aire* is known in any language and they'll get the hell out of here pronto. Got any ideas how we're going to get out of this mess without these people paying a hefty price?"

"No, I haven't thought of anything. That's why we came down here to talk it over. How's our patient doing?"

"Not so good. She seems to be in a coma. She was doing so well, but now, I just don't know. Two Sticks is convinced she will die today. You boys better go back to your hiding place. What do you think about upping her quinidine dose?"

"Who knows? I sure don't, but I'll bring back another dose in just a bit."

When I got back to the hut with the quinidine, Coot was standing outside.

"No use. The lady just left us. Any ideas about what to do now?"

"We could use the agent's Arabian as ransom, but I don't know how to pull that off." I called in to Two Sticks, "Sorry about your sister, sir."

"Thank you, Kicking Bear. I have many sisters. Many brothers. Brook That Talks, my favorite—Many Fast Feet Two Sticks her favorite. Brook That Talks go to Happy Place. Make me happy. You go hide, come when sun is gone, bring Iron Chain, Sly Fox. We talk."

We stayed hidden in the rocks and watched the soldiers mill around harassing the villagers. They were afraid of *mal aire*, so they kept away from the wickiup. At dusk, the three of us returned. Two Sticks and Coot told us they had buried Brook That Talks in the dirt floor of her hut.

Coot gave us the details of his plan that was to begin exactly as the sun rose over the hill in front of the agent's issue house. "I think this plan is a good one and it'll work." He turned to me. "What do you think, Kicking Bear? Got anything to add?"

"No, looks like you have a good plan, and I bet the agent falls for it, too. He wants his Arabian back pretty bad, plus, he's scared to death of *mal aire* to boot. It'll work."

Coot lined me up alongside Iron Chain and Sly Fox. "Now, let me warn you boys that if I hear even one giggle out of any of you, I'll beat you to within an inch of your lives, and that goes double for you, Kicking Bear."

"Giggle about what?" I asked.

"You'll see in the morning."

Before first light, Iron Chain and Sly Fox slipped into the corral, led the mud-smeared, gray and white Arabian off to the west, then circled around behind the hill east of the agent's house. I rode my pony, leading Coot's with a travois rigged behind it, and headed for Brook That Talks' hut. In the dim light, Two Sticks and a woman in a hooded cape sat at their small fire, warming grain for their morning meal.

I joined them. "Where's Running Duck?"

The woman across the fire lifted her skirt. "Hi handsome."

"Coot. Why, hotdamn, *look at you.*"

"You can smile all day long, but you best not snicker even once. This outfit is Two Sticks' idea, and I admit it's a good one. I'm the only one the agent got a good look at when you stole the quinidine. I'll be riding your travois, taking Brook That Talks' place for awhile. She's buried under her own house, and the agent will never be the wiser. Two Sticks has a speech for the agent that will throw him off and get us out of here. It's time to go. By the time you get me strapped down on that travois, get over to the agent's house, the sun will be about up. Sunrise is important to our plan."

We strapped Coot to the travois, making certain his dress was plenty visible. The agent's fear of malaria would keep him at a respectable distance, so he wouldn't get a close look at Coot. We mounted up and started for the issue house.

Two Sticks' strong voice broke the early morning silence. "Mister agent. Mister agent. I bring you horse. The Arabian, I bring to you."

The agent came out on the porch still pulling up his britches, adjusting his suspenders. "I don't see no Arabian. Where's my horse, goddamn your red hide?"

"You see. We take Arabian with us two days, follow trail two days to Gila River. Where trail cross Gila you follow river upstream to hidden rock corral. Arabian safe there."

"How do I know you have my Arabian?" the agent asked as he came off the porch, heading our way.

Two Sticks pointed at the figure lying on the travois. "*Stay back*. This woman my sister. She bad sick. She *mal aria*. She die two days."

The agent backed off. "*Malaria?*"

"*Mal aria*," Two Sticks assured him, then pointed to the rising sun without looking back and said, "There. You Arabian."

The agent squinted into the sun. A gray and white horse stood with a tall boy holding its reins. The agent stepped over a few feet, then another several feet for a better look, trying to get the bright sun out of his view.

"That ain't no Arabian," the agent said. "That's an old gray bag of bones I've seen lately in our corral. What are you trying to pull, injun? Answer me, or I'll have you shot."

Two Sticks stepped toward the agent. The man stepped back, pulling a big revolver from his britches.

Two Sticks stopped, then threw a duffel at the agent's feet. "There long black hair from Arabian mane. From long flow tail. You see."

The agent opened the bag and pulled out handfuls of long, black hair. The hair could come from no other horse in these parts. "This looks like hair from my Arabian all right, but that ain't no Arabian up on that hill."

Two Sticks raised his arm high. Another Apache boy came into view with a bucket on either side. He threw one bucket of water on the animal, then the other. The boy disappeared for a minute, then returned with two more buckets. The animal held fast while the two boys washed the gray and white clay away, and quickly the animal became a fine black horse on the hill, minus only the long black hair of the mane and tail that lay at the agent's feet.

The agent looked up the hill, then bent over the bag of hair again. He squatted, examining the hair. He turned to Two Sticks. "Okay, so whadda'ya want? If that's my Arabian, whadda'ya want, injun?"

"I take sister Brook That Talks far to rising sun. She sick. You medicine no help. She die. Die where she came from our mother. Quiney no help her." He tossed the box to the agent.

"*You!*" the agent yelled.

"We break in issue house. Take quiney. Take whiskey. Take cartridges. People you reservation not guilty. *We guilty*. We take sister on travois and take nothing more that belong to agent. Only Arabian, whiskey, cartridges. We follow trail to rising sun two days. We leave Arabian where trail cross Gila. Leave Arabian in rock corral. You no follow this day. You wait tomorrow. You come slow. We see you or soldiers, we stop. Leave Arabian on trail. Throat cut. Our word is good. Arabian will wait for you at the Gila. Or on the trail in blood. You choose." Before the agent could respond Two Sticks turned, leaped on his pony. "Mister agent, these people not guilty—not steal quiney. *We* steal. You not punish these people. You punish people, wind tell Many Fast Feet Two Sticks, come back, steal Arabian. Ride him hard. He die. You choose." Two Sticks turned his horse and led me and Coot's travois up the hill to the east.

We came on the Gila late the second day, followed it upstream a half-mile. Two Sticks led us out of the water and behind a boulder outcropping. There, as he told the agent, was the rock corral. We left the Arabian and Two Sticks led us back into the shallow Gila, turning downstream. Two Sticks would lead us west to the San Carlos River, circle the reservation, follow the Salt River to our home.

20

One Year Later, April 1877

"Narlow, in a couple of days, we need to be heading to the Black River to meet your papa. But let me ask you something—how long do you plan on staying on here? Given any thought about going home?"

"Not really. Why?"

"Well, you're not making much progress at becoming a medicineman. Spend more time with me, Iron Chain, and Sly Fox than you do with Na-Tu-Che-Puy. Have you given up being a medicineman, or has he given up on you?"

"Some of both. Just last night, we were sitting across our fire, and he told me that he didn't think I had the determination to become a medicineman. I was glad he brought it up because it gave us a chance to talk about it. I reminded him that I never did think I had Power. He smiled, reminded me that he had witnessed my ability to warn of danger when we almost ran into that band of *comancheros*. I smiled back at him, reminded him that was nearly a year ago, and I've had no more mushroom visits since then."

"Well," Coot said, "you know I'm no quitter, and I admit that I'm having a good time, but this reservation is getting to be pretty tight quarters. I still want to see this country while it's still wild enough to hold my interest. Remember your papa warned us that this won't last much longer. I'm not pressing you to leave, want you to remember that."

"I suppose it's about time we move on. I'll talk to Na-Tu-Che-Puy. He's never given me any indication that I had to have his permission to leave, but I owe him."

That evening, Na-Tu said, "Kicking Bear, I had a vision I want to tell you about. Maybe you can explain it to me. In my vision it is very dark, the elders are sitting on fine elk skins before a great fire. There is much dancing, feasting, storytelling. Running Duck makes a speech, but I could not hear his words. Then Running Duck turns to Two Sticks, who calls you to speak to the elders. You stand before the elders, and you speak. Again I cannot hear your words. The women behind the elders begin to wail and cry, the children fall at your feet, at the feet of Running Duck.

"The children cry out, "*Dah bich'a'dighah. Dah bich'a'dighah.* They cry out many times. Then the great fire before the elders is dark, only smoke. When the sun comes, the children are lying on the ground where you and Running Duck stood, but you are no longer there. The children and the elders and all the People stand, a mist and smoke comes, then all the People are gone. What do you think my vision means, Kicking Bear?"

I knew the meaning of his vision, at least part of it. The speeches made by me and Running Duck, the children crying, begging us not to leave was clear. Na-Tu-Che-Puy sat smoking, looking at me. The old man's eyes glistened in the fire-light. Papa's image swept over me. I was never good at prevaricating, and telling Papa or Na-Tu-Che-Puy a lie never entered my mind. I figured the man sitting on a fine elk skin in front of his campfire could handle the truth as well as my papa.

"Great Father, you have taught me much. I know things that few Pale Eyes comprehend, and I thank you for it. Your wisdom is strong and it has nourished my soul, but—"

"But it is time for you and Running Duck to go to your home at the Pass."

"Yes, my father. We have learned much of the Apache and their ways. But it is time we learned the ways of our own people. Running Duck and I were boys when we came here. We thought we were men, but we were boys. You and Many Fast Feet Two Sticks taught us to be men. It is time, Father."

"I know. Tomorrow night there will be a feast, there will be dancing, great speeches. You are my son and the son of Can See Far. You are our only son. You will come to visit us?"

"Yes, Father, I will come to visit my father and mother."

Coot's speech was short as was his way, but there was barely a dry eye in camp that night when he sat down. Many Fast Feet Two Sticks was as staunch as a frozen oak, but his pride peeked through. Leaving these people was proving to be a mighty task. I gazed at Two Sticks, recalling the legend of this man running horses to death as he sprinted over treacherous terrain, his rifle slung over his shoulder, bounding from one boulder to another with the aid of his two running sticks.

I groped for words. I stumbled around, finally just said that I had already said my goodbyes to Na-Tu-Che-Puy and Can See Far, turned, and sat. The elders called Many Fast Feet Two Sticks before them.

He turned to Coot. "Running Duck, the elders want to hear story when you granddaddies save Apache mother, Little Flower, from Pale Eye scalpers. You stand, tell story."

Coot stood before the elders. As usual, he told them that while he knew the long-ago story, that Kicking Bear told the story better. The elders and the people had heard that story, and witnessed that same routine countless times before, but they enjoyed the way Coot excused himself, calling on his friend to tell it.

Two Sticks stood, his great arms crossed. "Kicking Bear, stand before the elders. Kicking Bear, you tell story about Little Flower in you tongue. Many Fast Feet Two Sticks tell elders."

The elders gazed up, waiting for me to begin the same story I had told so many times before. My eyes misted over. Coot was sitting, smiling up at me. He knew how I felt, knowing I needed a little boost, so he gave me one of his girlie winks.

"*Great Apache People.* I am honored to tell you the story of how our grandfathers saved an Apache princesses from shame, from certain death. The Pale Eyes who captured this Apache mother were evil. They hunted the Apache for scalps. They sold the scalps to the governor in Chihuahua for many *pesos.* Our grandfathers were *mesteneros*—horse traders. Twice a year they pushed a herd to market back East, to return to their *Valle de Mesilla rancho*, to gather, bust, and tame another bunch of broncs. The mustangs they delivered were the best they could find. No cripples. No bad feet. No outlaw ponies.

"On this particular day as they journeyed from the city the Pale Eyes call 'St. Louis' toward their home, grinding fatigue had set in some hundreds of miles back. They were lonesome as a nightbird for a fresh face to talk to across their evening campfire. Though the two men were spent, their concern was for their mounts, as they were in desperate need of water. The year was dry. The heavy black clouds at their backs proved to be more threat than promise, and a hidden spring at the edge of the caprock that had never failed them in the past, turned up bone-dry. Every horse step lifted another caliche mist from the desert floor. The little water remaining in their canteens was reserved for their horses. Not enough to give them a needed drink, but enough to occasionally stop to clean their nostrils of the chalk dust that choked them. A little thing, but as you wise elders know so well, little things count, add up in the unforgiving desert."

Two Sticks repeated my words, the elders sat solemnly nodding.

"The sun set as they eased down to the *Valle de Pecos*. By midnight they knew they were close to the *Rio Pecos* by the way the horses were acting up. They smelled water. They found new mettle, wanted to run, but the men kept them at a ground eating trot. They spied a campfire about a mile off, and talked about joining the travelers. Running Duck's grandfather, Skinner Boldt, and my grandfather, Shelby Montgomery, got close enough to hear the joking voices, the laughter of many men. Caution was in order. They rode downstream to slake their horse's thirst, then rode back up until they could once again hear the men. Shelby held the horses, while Skinner fought his way through the tangled salt cedars and bramble to get a close look-see. By the time Skinner got within looking distance, the men's voices turned angry. There were six of them, lounging by the fire, liquored-up, arguing, bragging. Arguing about what they were going to do to, *and with*, the Apache woman that sat across the fire. She was pretty, young. Tufts of hair hung from the men's saddles—*scalpers*. Mexico's 'War of Extermination' against the Apache paid handsome rewards for scalps—one-hundred pesos for a male, fifty for a woman, twenty-five pesos for a child. A little boy's or girl's scalp, no difference, the scalper would get his pesos for the small, dry twisted skin-tuft of dark hair.

"The men argued. 'Who would be first with the woman?'"

I waited for Two Sticks to catch up with his translation, waited for the inevitable murmur around the fire as the translation sunk in.

"One of the scalpers laid claim to being the band's leader. He figured that

157

high position gave him first turn on the woman. The others objected, agreeing that cutting the cards was the fair way to make that important determination. The Apache woman was wet, shivering, and in unforgiving, no-quarter company.

"Skinner heard all he needed and hurried back to Shelby and the horses. There were only two of them, but they determined that two sober men just might equal six drunkards caught by surprise. They kept their horses at a walk to within twenty steps of the campfire, then spurred their horses hard, fast into camp, hollering, shooting, kicking up a ruckus. The timing of their rush could not have been more favorable, as the drunks were huddled down on their hands and knees on a blanket near the fire to get a close look at the cards. Skinner and Shelby were on the scalp hunters before they even suspected they had company. Four of the six were shot dead, one was crushed by Shelby's horse, the sixth took off running. Skinner roped and tied him, and dragged him back into camp. The fun and whiskey's glow was now wasted on the last remaining scalp hunter."

A loud cheer went up.

"Our grandfathers learned from the Apache woman that the long drought had forced her people far east of their tribal home in search of food. Her name was Little Flower, the daughter of the Chiricahua Apache war chief, Smoking Wolf. Her husband, Eagle That Is Swift, had been killed by a raiding band of Comanches just four days before. She had witnessed her husband's death, muffling her nursing infant as they hid in the shadows. One of the Comanches crept up behind her husband, slid his lance through his heart, took his scalp. She would know her husband's killer – he was very tall, with a slumped shoulder. Smoking Wolf assured his daughter that her husband's death would be avenged. There would be no escape for the killer. Little Flower was not so certain, fearing the threatening clouds and blowing wind would hide the Comanche's trail. That night she left her baby inside her mother's lodge, then took two of her husband's best horses, and rode after the Comanches, pushing her mount hard, knowing how to get the most out of a horse. Both horses were ruined catching up with the Comanche band two nights later.

"The Comanches were dancing to the beat of heavy drums and a flutist. She watched them, spied her husband's assailant, and fell in with the circling dancers. Soon, she found herself opposite her husband's killer. She reached for his knife, lashed out, slashing the man's throat with such fury his head was almost severed. She fled on a rangy, nervous black stallion she had staked out earlier. She headed west, knowing the Comanches would be in pursuit. The pitch-dark moonless night was on her side. She made no effort to hide her trail as precious time, she had not to spare. She rode hard toward the heavy clouds and lightening to the west.

"Near sunset the next day, she was back at the *Rio Pecos*. The black had served her well, now its knees buckling, wanting to lay down. As she coaxed the horse out of the river on the far slippery bank, he struggled, floundered, fell back on her lower leg, crushing it. The Comanches could not be far behind her now. Before she could drag herself to a hiding place, the six scalp hunters found her. She held fast to a water-soaked log, trying to get away from the men in the swift current. They chased her downriver, taunting her. When the men tired of the fun of the chase, one of them threw a loop around her neck, dragged her upstream, the heavy flow forcing her to the bottom, bruising her on the rocks of the riverbed."

A loud murmur passed through the people as Two Sticks repeated my words.

"She feared the men would be on her when they first dragged her into their camp. But nature was on her side, if only for a short time. Before she left to pursue her husband's killer, she had wrapped her chest and heavy breasts with wide strips of cloth to give her some relief on the long, jostling trail. When the pressure became too great, her hands found her breasts under the bindings, milking herself as she rode on. The milk of four days had soaked the bindings, had turned rancid, staining her blouse.

"One of the scalpers told the others that his daddy warned him that his prune would fall off, that he would sure enough die if he bedded a nursing red squaw. That fear kept them at bay for awhile. But the scalpers' inherent lust overcame them. Their conversation drifted to reasoning why they would lose their manhood and die, just from mounting a nursing squaw. They soon shirked off any reluctance to bed this pretty woman. It had been a long time for them. They'd take their chances with the prospect of dying. In their line of work, death was always close at hand.

"Shelby Montgomery and Skinner Boldt did not know what to do with their captive. They weren't lawmen but they figured they sorta had him under arrest. But, who could they turn their captive over to? He had broken no law, as this was the year 1833, and they were in Mexican territory. But they sure were not going to let him loose to do more scalping.

"They talked about shooting him. Skinner smiled at the scalper and said, 'Naw, shootin's too quick for this gentleman, and dang it, these salt cedars ain't tall enough to hang him anyway. Say, Shelby, what say we treat him to a horizontal hanging? Saw it done one time, and I'm right eager to try it out on him.'

"All of sudden the scalper's *bravado* began to melt like an icicle tossed on mesquite coals, and he commenced to grovel. 'You skunks sure have a hard time hiding your stripes,' Shelby offered.

"Skinner explained to Little Flower in Spanish that Shelby had christened the scalper with the Mexican name for skunk '*zorrillo.*' She smiled her agreement."

Many of the elders had a spattering of Spanish and saw the humor in his name. There were whispers and giggles around the fire, but when Two Sticks translated skunk to Apache, *golizhi,* the people roared with laughter.

"One thing was certain—our grandfathers would take Little Flower home to her baby. Shelby washed her lower leg and set it in a splint while Skinner doused the scalper's cottonwood fire, and built a small, warming fire of dead mesquite limbs. The dry wood made no smoke and there was a fair breeze out of the east to carry the smell away from the Comanches. Our grandfathers had no clean clothes to offer her, but Shelby dug around in his saddlebags, found his cleanest dirty britches and a sweat-stained shirt. He offered them to her. She went to the river, bathed herself, and returned to the fire dressed in clothes that were strange to her, baggy, a yard long in the legs. Shelby and Skinner smiled their approval, and set her at ease.

"Well, the two horse traders got their wish. They had new faces across their campfire—one pleasant, pleasing, pretty to look at, the other with hate in his eyes, a permanent scowl etched across his venomous face. Skinner would not let the scalper near the fire, had him hug a tree where he tied him with his back to them so they wouldn't have to look at him.

"They took turns standing watch, chunking rocks at the scalper to make certain he didn't doze off. He ceased his whining and complaining when fist-sized rocks were chunked his way. Before first light, they kicked the scalper out of his stupor, made him take off his boots. They set him on a horse facing backwards without the benefit of a saddle.

"'I cain't ride this horse ridin' back'rds with my hands tied behind my back. Let me have one of them saddles.'

"Skinner whacked him on the knee with his rifle. They tied his hands behind his back, tied his legs under the horse's belly so he couldn't slip off and make a run for it.

"Shelby hurrahed the scalper, 'You know, *zorrillo,* there's something prophetic about you sitting on your steed facing his ass-end. That's a view you're accustomed to, ain't it, skunk?'

"'What about my boots? Ye just gonna leave 'em lie there?'

"'Yep, that's what we had in mind,' Shelby said. 'Besides skunk, you won't be needing your boots to spur your horse. Maybe being barefoot will discourage you from wandering off, should we be careless about keeping an eye on our new pet skunk.'"

When Two Sticks repeated this to the People, they howled with laughter.

"'Ye got no call to call me no damn skunk. And ye got no call to treat me so ill. You shouldn'a kilt my friends neither. Kilt 'em outright, ye did. Didn't give 'em no chanc't a'tall. Ye didn't show'd 'em no mercy. All'a y'all ain't the law. We're in Met-si-kin territory, and killin' and scalpin' them red devils is plumb legal. Hell, it's encouraged. They pays us cash money for them bastard's scalps.'

"Shelby sidled his horse over to the scalper, gave the scalper's dangling bare foot a swift hard kick with his stirrup. 'Best shut your yammer, *senor zorrillo*. Skinner Boldt and me believe you and your kind have broken one of God's holy commandments. And you know what, skunk? We're going to let Little Flower's papa be the sole judge and jury. Besides, if you don't hold a civil tongue, ol' Skinner will have your tongue ripped out and dangling from that pig-sticker you see there on his belt. Be well certain that Skinner Boldt would like nothing better than to usher you to the very gates of Hell.'

"Skinner gathered up all the scalps and tied the gruesome treasures around the scalper's neck. 'Show your trinkets to this little lady's daddy, skunk. I'll wager he'll find a way to repay you for your trouble.'

"They had plenty of horses to ride that the dead scalpers furnished, however reluctantly. They rode hard, the scalper jostling along, learning fast how to hang on riding backwards. They switched off regularly to keep the horses fresh as they crossed the bone-dry *Llanos Sin Agua*.

"Little Flower assured them that her father would be out searching for her, that he would not give up until he found her. She would tell her father what happened and he would want to smoke tobacco with them.

"Late the afternoon of the fourth day, they topped off the summit of the pass in the *Sierra de los Organos*. Shelby spied a band of eighteen Chiricahua Apaches off to the west about five miles, bobbing dots on the mesas far below, heading their way. Skinner could barely make them out, but he had learned long ago to trust Shelby's gray eyes. When the approaching band rode to within two miles of their hiding place, Little Flower recognized the horseman in front as her father. The scalp hunter cursed, pleaded to be set free so he could make a run for it and have a chance.

"Skinner snarled at the scalper, '*You bastard*. Of course we're going to give you a chance—a chance just like you were going to give that Apache chief's daughter.'

"The Chiricahua band came on, Skinner and Shelby pushed their horses up to show themselves against the horizon. Smoking Wolf raised his lance in salute. That brought on more screaming, begging from the *desperado* scalp hunter. He begged Shelby to shoot him. Shelby drew his revolver, shoved the muzzle in the scalper's mouth, cocked it, watching him choke on the cold steel, shutting his eyes hard, waiting to join his scalp-hunting *amigos*.

"Shelby grinned, uncocked the revolver. 'Now ain't that just like a skunk? We bring this skunk all this way, feed him good, keep him warm at night, then we go to the trouble of pointing out eighteen perfectly good male Apache scalps for the skunk to take, and all he wants to talk about is getting our pet skunk shot. That don't make no sense at all to a man. Scalper, you're thinking just like a derned old skunk, I do believe.'"

The people roared their glee.

"Smoking Wolf rode up, a magnificent deep-chested man, the rich bronze color of the setting sun shining on red granite. He looked the three men over then gazed at his daughter with a stern eye, reached over, touched the shirt that Shelby had given her. He glanced at the rough britches she wore. She motioned with her eyes toward Shelby.

"Smoking Wolf leaped from his horse, lifted his daughter from her mount, carried her to a rock ledge, set her on his blanket, listening to her recount her experiences. As she told him about the six scalp hunters, she pointed up to the one sitting his horse backwards—the one with dozens of cold-black scalps draped around his neck. The man cried out, kicked his horse with his bare feet, but Shelby held tight to the reins.

"Smoking Wolf nodded to a warrior, who cut the rope under the horse's belly, dragged the screaming man to the ground. The younger braves in the band were on him in an instant. Smoking Wolf called them off. The scalper would die soon enough, not today. The older warriors smiled as Smoking Wolf reminded them that the women waiting in their lodges would relish the teasing chase and the scalp hunter's death from the countless blows of the women's clubs and lances.

"They made camp behind a rock outcropping that offered protection from the howling wind, sitting close to the campfire to warm themselves. The younger braves made certain that the scalper was secure, warm as well. They strung him up between two live oaks, a rope secured to one wrist, another rope tied to the ankle of the opposing leg. They hoisted him off the ground, giving the scalper a most awkward, decidedly uncomfortable appearance. The braves made a small fire under him and fed it with green, mountain mahogany branches. The heavy smoke had a pleasing, sweet fragrance, but the scalper screamed his discomfort from the choking smoke and blistering heat. The braves shushed him and had their own way of warning him that they would not tolerate his screams. Every time he screamed, they poked him with a stick from the fire. There would be time and encouragement for screaming when they got him to their lodges.

"Little Flower smiled at Skinner and Shelby when her father rolled a *cigarro* in a dry oak leaf. He passed the smoke to them.

"As the two parties prepared to go their separate ways the next morning, Smoking Wolf approached our grandfathers, placed his hands on their shoulders. 'Hear me, brothers of the Chiricahua Apache and all Apache. For as long as the wind blows across this mountain, as long as the Pale Eyes calls every black bird by the name crow, no Apache will harm these brave men or those that follow hereafter through the ages.'

"And that, great people of the Apache nation, is the story of how our grandfathers saved the Apache princess."

21

Coot and I left the reservation long before anyone stirred, not wanting another goodbye. We rode down the trail to the confluence of the Black River and Pacheta Creek following the fresh tracks of a horse and a pack mule. Papa had beaten us here, even though we had figured we were two days early. He was sitting on a stump smoking his briar as we rode around the boulder at the bend in the trail.

Before we were within a hundred-yards of camp, Papa yelled out, "Kicking Bear, what are you doing riding Traveler? And Running Duck, what are you doing riding that old nag of yours, dragging your old cussed mule behind you? Going on a long trip, are you?"

"Yes, sir, Papa – we're going *home.*"

Coot stood in his stirrups. "It's Narlow and Coot from now on, Uncle Abe. We're ready for the soft life of a goat herder and a dirt-clod farmer."

Five days later we camped near a spring south of Hillsboro, just seventy miles from home.

Papa said, "Well boys, you'll be home tomorrow night. Guess you're eager to see your mamas. By the way, they're both fine."

"Aw, Papa, dern it. I'm sorry I didn't ask about her again—same as last year. It's just that we're so dag-gum happy to see you that we just forgot to ask about them."

Coot said, "I imagine the first thing out of my mama's mouth will be, 'Well, Coot, you've had the better part of two years sitting on your backside. Starting tomorrow before sun, I expect you out there cleaning those irrigation ditches on the end of a long-handled shovel.'"

"You boys shouldn't be so callous when it comes to your mamas. They deserve their children's respect and love. Your mamas are both good women, their lives haven't been easy, and remember, they've both lost some of your brothers and sisters. Losses like that have a way of hardening folks rough as a cob—especially women. And besides, boys, there's nothing much worse for a man than feeling bad about his mother."

Coot said, "Uncle Abe, I want you to know that I don't feel bad about Mama. I know she's had it rough and all, I just wish she didn't like my brother Richard so much more than me. Richard never lifted a finger around that farm to help out."

"I know, son, sometimes mothers and fathers are not very thoughtful about things like that. I suppose it's hard not to have a favorite. I don't know about those things. After Narlow's sister passed, Narlow's the only child I have, besides you, of course."

We talked about what to do about clothes for me and Coot. Our breech clothes wouldn't remind our mamas of a college classroom. Coot reckoned we could get IB to lend us some of his daddy's old britches.

Papa laughed. "And what are we going to do about that long hair you boys have growing down to your shoulders? Your mamas would shoot you on sight if you showed up like that."

"Papa, I guess when we get down around Brazito, maybe you should go on home. Coot and I'll cut each other's hair. Then we'll pay a visit on IB and get ourselves presentable."

Before the eastern sky showed a hint of pink, Papa was stirring around, packing up to head for home.

"Papa, don't you want to ride Traveler? I know you've missed him."

"No, son, your mama thinks he went to Austin with you, and I suppose that's the story we better stick with for the present. Unless you want to explain the last year and a half to her."

"No, thanks, Papa. We'll stick with that story."

"What are you going to tell her when she asks about your schooling? You can't just go on lying about it."

"I confess I worried about that myself, but mama never even asks me what I think or how I feel on my own fool birthday. I don't suppose she'll ask me one blessed thing about the university."

Papa mounted up. "What about you, Coot? What are you planning to tell your mama?"

"Well, Uncle Abe, I haven't given it a minute's thought. I'll think of something. She'll be mad as a hornet when I tell her where I've been, but madder at you for deceiving her. I'll handle it when the opportunity presents itself."

I cut Coot's hair with my long knife. When I finished, he looked a little chopped up. It didn't bother him a bit, he just smiled. "Besides it's my turn now, and you're fixin' to look just like me."

"You'll get your revenge, but I want to save my hair for one more day. I have a plan, and this long hair is an important part of that plan."

"You're thinking mean like your mama again. What are you plotting in that devious head of yours?"

"You'll see. I wouldn't leave you out of this for anything. Let's go find IB. Probably scare hell out of him, us looking like a couple of renegade warriors."

We first caught sight of IB walking along an irrigation ditch, a shovel thrown over his shoulder, heading to see if he could coax some water out of the river to water Shelly Brom's three-acre garden. He was still off about a half-mile.
Coot rested the butt of his rifle on his thigh. "Narlow, pull your rifle out and rest it on your thigh like mine. Let's see if IB's imagination is as good as used to be."

"Your mean streak is showing, Coot—but I'm liking your idea."

We crossed the *Rio* and started down the irrigation ditch toward our old friend. When we rode within a quarter of mile of him, his head jerked up as he caught sight of us. We were too far away for him to get a good look at us, so he kept coming, and we kept riding. IB craned his head and neck this way and that, trying to get a fix on the riders heading his way. He stepped over to the ditch bank, dobbled a bit of dirt on a low spot in ditch bank, then resumed his march toward us.

"Coot, ol' IB is just about to have the crap scared out of him. You have turned mean, Running Duck. *Real* mean."

"Not as mean as your mama, Kicking Bear, and I have a notion not as mean as what you have planned for that long hair of yours."

IB's head and neck were bouncing, craning around, but he kept coming, though his pace had slowed considerable. He stopped, bent over, his hands on his knees, trying to get a fix on what was headed his way. He jumped back, threw the shovel in the air, turned, and started sprinting for home, screaming, "*Injuns*. Injuns. Glory be. They're after me. Land O Goshen! Injuns are coming, Shelly Brom. *Injuns are coming."

Coot kicked his pony into a lope to catch him, IB screaming all the way. I started laughing so hard that I fell off Traveler. Coot stopped and came back grinning down at me on the dirt. "Come on. We gotta catch that idiot before he has the entire valley up in arms."

When we were within shouting distance, Coot yelled, "IB, it's me—Coot. It's us. Coot Boldt and Narlow Montgomery."

If IB heard him, it sure didn't slacken his pace for home.

I yelled out after him, "IB, it's your friends—Coot and Narlow. It's okay, *amigo.*"

He kept running as fast as his scrawny legs could carry him. I pushed Traveler past him and jumped down.

He turned and started running back toward Coot, who was right on him. He turned again, took off running across a fresh-plowed field. I ran after him, tackled him, IB screaming, kicking, and punching the whole time.

"IB, it's me, Narlow. Narlow Montgomery. It's okay, IB—it's Narlow and Coot." I was on top of him, his shoulders pinned.

He stopped kicking as Coot rode up. IB pushed me back to get a better look at me, looked up at Coot, who was grinning a grin that could only belong to Coot Boldt.

IB looked back at me. "Narlow? Is thet really *you*, Narlow?" He looked up at Coot. "Coot? Is thet really *you*, Coot?"

"It's us, IB, your ol' *amigos*, Coot and Narlow."

I started to stand, but IB held me. "You ain't my friend, Narlow Mont-gom-ery. Narlow's papa would skin him alive if'n he caught him with long hair like thet."

Coot got down. "IB, I'm really sorry we pulled that trick on you. It was Narlow's idea, and you know how mean he can be sometimes."

Coot took IB's hand, and pulled him to his feet. "Here, let me dust you off."

"Wh-ut in the world are you fellers dressed up like a couple of injun boys fer?"

That was not the last of IB's questions we could not answer to his satisfaction. We finally prevailed on him that if he would loan us some clothes, we'd come back soon and tell him all about it. The three of us sneaked into the Crane's barn and IB led us to an old dust-covered trunk. It contained all of his daddy's old clothes and things his mama didn't have the heart to throw away. Coot and I each borrowed a pair of britches and a shirt. We gave IB a ride back down to the *Rio* so he could get on with his irrigating.

It was getting late in the day. We followed the river down to a grove of cottonwood trees where we had played and camped so often as young boys, the same place where IB and Shelly Brom had their run-in with Rye Green and Seth Byrne when we were all fourteen. Three years ago. How could that be?

"Okay, Narlow, let's have it. Why didn't you want me to give you a haircut this morning? What do you have in mind? I know it's something that includes your mama in your scheme, so let's have it."

"You'll see, my friend. Let's shoot us a rabbit or a couple of ducks. I'm tired and ready to lay my bones on the ground."

"The sun is not even down yet, and you're talking about going to bed. What's wrong? Feeling poorly?"

"No, I'm not feeling poorly, fact is, I never felt better in my life as I do this very minute. It's just that we have to get a real early start in the morning."

"What do we have to get up early for? We're within two miles of your folk's dugout."

"You'll see."

Before first light, I was up and went to work with the white and black clay I had brought from the reservation for my welcome home. When ready, I chunked a rock at Coot. "*Hey*. You going with me or are you going to wait for the sun to warm your bones?"

He sat up, rubbed his eyes. "What in the hell have you got smeared all over your face? Looks like you have black and white paint smeared all over your face."

"You're close. It's not paint, it's some of Na-Tu-Che-Puy's clay. How do I look?"

"What does my evil-minded *amigo* have in mind?"

"Come on. It'll soon be time for Mama to be gathering eggs in her hen house."

"You're gonna pay, Narlow Montgomery—you're gonna pay."

We rode within a quarter-mile of my folk's dugout, and left our horses tied to a mesquite. When we got within 200-yards of my folk's place, Butch started barking, raising a fuss.

"Dern, I forgot about Butch. He'll have the entire valley awake if he doesn't stop that barking."

"The breeze is out of the east. Let's go around to the east of your dugout and maybe Butch will get a whiff of you."

Butch kept up his barking as we backed away and made our way around. Sure enough, Butch seemed to stop a yelp in mid-yap, and his bark turned to playful screams of glee. He ran up to us. After I hugged on him for a spell and he sniffed me and Coot to his satisfaction, I said, "Now Butch, I know you've missed me, but I'm going to have to leave you with Coot for just a little bit, okay? Coot, give me a few minutes, then bring Butch along with you. Find yourself something to hide behind between the dugout and the hen house."

Coot grinned, shook his head.

I slipped through the hen house door. The hens started cackling their uneasy cackle. I got in behind the row of hen coops, feeling around under each hen. The third hen was on an empty nest. I picked her up real gentle-like, eased her out of her nest, and set her on the rafter above me. She fussed for a minute, then settled down. I tried out the rear end on the nest to make sure my head would fit in the small opening. Now all there was to do was wait. Which was not long.

Mama must have more Comanche blood in her than I thought. I had no warning of her approach until the hen house door creaked open. She stepped through the opening, carrying a lantern and her egg basket. I eased my head in the back of the nest.

Mama was never the gentle sort. If a hen put up the slightest argument about giving up her nest of eggs, Mama would grab her by the neck, fling the poor thing over her shoulder. More than one hen found its way into our pot for arguing too frequently with her. She gathered the eggs in the first nest, then the second, then in the dim light, her hand came into my nest, groping around for the eggs that were not there. The back of her hand brushed my face. The lantern came up with the basket slung on her arm at the elbow. Her head came into view, gray hair falling down her face. She brushed it back, her sleepy eyes peering into the nest. Her gaze came up and our eyes met not ten inches apart, my face a jagged line of white and black gleam.

"*Ahhhhhh, Ahhhh.* Oh, God help me. Oh, God. *Ahhhhh.*" She jumped back, fell in a heap, jumped up, tripped over a bucket, and hit the far wall.

She got to her feet. "Son-of-a-goddamn-bitch. *Ahhhhhhh.*" She bolted through the hen house door screaming for Papa. "*Abe. Get up.* There's a goddamn savage in the hen house. He's after me, Abe! *Save me, Abe.* Get your shotgun. Oh, Abe, he's'a ugly bastard son-of-a-bitch. Shoot that bastard before he stabs and rapes me."

I fought the urge to laugh out loud, slipped through the door, darted around the side of the hen house, and ran toward our horses. Coot ran up behind me, Butch still begging for attention. We jumped on our horses. "Come on, Butch. Let's go."

We didn't stop until we saw the river coming up in the improving light, dark cottonwood trees looming up from the river bottom.

Coot said laughing, "Narlow, you are going to get it for certain. You know that don't you?"

"How do you figure?"

"Well, you *are* your mama's son, you know. You may be all decked out with long hair and painted up like a lightning bolt, but when you show up today, she's liable to put two and two together, then all hell will break loose. Hell, I'd rather see that show than the one I just witnessed. You didn't see it, but she did a somersault over her cauldron out there in the yard. Fell down, her lantern dumped in the cauldron, she jumped back up screaming, ran into the dugout screaming her lungs out, 'Son-of-a-shit-kicking-son-of-a-bitch.' You've told me that your mama could out-swear a mule skinner, but I had never heard her until just now. That woman can cuss!"

I laughed. "Yeah, she's a cusser that's a certain, but there's no way she would ever know it was me in that hen house."

"Maybe not, but I know someone who will?"

"Who?"

"Your papa, that's who?"

I stopped. "Uh-oh. I never thought about that. He'll know it was me sure enough. Or *you.* Yeah, if he asks, we'll tell him it was you playing that trick on Mama."

Coot shook his head. "No, *you* can tell your papa it was me in that hen house, but if he asks me about it, I'll tell him the truth—the *whole* truth. I'd sooner tangle with Two Sticks than your papa when he's mad. And nothing makes him madder than a liar."

"You're right. Right as cool rain. Guess I'm in for it, huh?"

"Oh, I don't know. Your papa has the biggest tickle-box I ever saw strapped on a man. He's liable to think that was real funny, might even say it serves your mama right, the way she treats you and all."

We rode down to the river and took a bath in the muddy water. Coot took out his long knife, and had his revenge for the haircut I gave him yesterday. We were both pretty chopped up, but our haircuts would have to do. We changed into IB's daddy's shirts and britches. The feel of the rough britches on our legs felt strange after so long with nothing but a breech cloth to hide our privates. We remained barefoot, as we had no boots.

"Well Coot, what do you say? Time to go home."

"Yeah, I suppose. The prospects of going home make me wonder if I had good sense leaving Two Sticks. There's nothing for me here but the end of a long-handled shovel. Reckon I was born with one of those damn things in my hand, at least it seems that way sometimes. What about you? Ready to go home to face your mama?"

"I've been thinking about that very thing. I think what I'll do is *not say one word* to her. I'll just wait and see how long it takes before she says, 'Welcome home, son—good to have you back, Narlow.' Got any idea how old I'd be if I waited for those words?"

"No I don't, but it'd be a hell of lot better than to hear her ask, 'That was you in my hen house this morning wasn't it?'"

I went home, all the while hoping that Papa would be there to greet me. Somehow I knew he would be off with Fernando Valdez. Papa would want, or hope, that Mama and her son would have a nice long talk after so long a time.

Seems some things never change. Mama was out making soap in the cauldron she had tripped over earlier that morning, her back to me. Over the years, that woman must have made a million bars of soap in that pot, selling them to a peddler who came by every now and again. Lye leached from ashes from Papa's forge, rendered lard from animal fat, and water—a little salt to solidify it, let it cool and cut it into bars. Simple recipe, but I had to admit it was pretty good stuff to wash off the grime and goat stench of the workday.

I rode Traveler through the yard, reminded myself to hold my tongue to see how long it would take before she would say something. I stopped and got off. My yammer outran my thinker—I blurted out, "Mornin', Mother. Nice day isn't it?"

She didn't reply.

I heard myself ask, "Mama?" I could have bitten my tongue off. I hadn't called her Mama to her face since the night she hit me with a horse quirt. But when

I asked for her recognition by calling her Mama, her head turned to the side just enough for me to catch a knowing smile on her face. She had won.

She turned back to stirring her concoction. "*Shit.* Nice a day as the next, I reckon."

I mumbled and stumbled around. "Well, I guess I'll take Traveler back to the corral, brush him down real good, give him some grain." I stood there, unable to stand the ear-splitting quiet. "Yes, Mother, that's what I'll do. Yes, ma'am, right this very minute."

I felt like IB Crane's pure-identical twin brother, standing there with my tongue wagging, getting no response from my own mother after nearly two years. I rubbed Traveler down, gave him some grain, then rubbed him down some more, all the while kicking myself for being such a fool and for my lapse in calling her Mama. I about rubbed the fur off that handsome gray gelding before Papa and Fernando Valdez came in for their noon meal.

Papa rode in the corral, got off, and came over. "How was your greeting, son?"

"It's as nice a day as the next, Papa."

"That warm, huh?"

"Yes, sir, just about. Don't worry yourself—that's just the way it's always been, and always will be. But, you're more than plenty enough for me, Papa."

22

Canutillo, Texas
Summer 1877

Coot and I spent that summer at home—him chopping cotton, me, tending and milking goats. Papa spent most of his time taking turns on Coot and me, twisting our arms nearly off at the shoulder, trying to talk us into going off to school come fall.

"Papa, Coot and I want to see this country before it changes, and starts looking like New York City. If we don't do it now, it'll all pass us by, never to return."

"There's plenty of time to travel around, son, *after* you and Coot graduate from college. *Then* you can go back to the life you are so hell-bent on living."

Coot didn't come around much. I supposed Papa's grind on us kept him away. Then one day, Coot came by in his buckboard.

"Howdy, Uncle Abe. I'm going to El Paso for supplies. Anything I can tote back for you or the misses?"

"No, don't need a thing that I can think of. But if you're looking for a little company, Narlow and I'll climb up and make the trip with you. Narlow gets mighty stale out here on this dusty ol' goat ranch."

I welcomed the chance to go to town, but thought it mighty curious that Papa'd be willing to take off the better part of the workday to make a twenty-five-mile roundtrip to town if he didn't need anything.

We loaded Coot's supplies, then he turned the team toward home. Papa said, "Coot, turn down Santa Fe Street toward Old Mexico. I've heard of a new confectionery in town."

"What's a confectionery, Uncle Abe?"

"You'll see. Might even like it."

We gathered around the glass displays.

"You boys help yourself to anything you want," Papa said, grinning, poking Coot in the ribs, "as long as its horehound candy."

"Papa, you know I can't stand that stuff. I'd rather suck a skunk's teat."

"Horehound is a *man's* candy," Coot said to the clerk. "I'll have a sack of horehound, please sir."

Papa said, "And I'll have the same. A man can never get enough horehound candy, isn't that right, Coot?"

"Yes, sir, Uncle Abe. I bet if a man sucked on a horehound every day of his life, he'd live to be a hundred."

"No," I said, "if you sucked on that stuff everyday, your life would *seem* like a hundred."

They stood sucking on that horrible stuff, their expressions and grimaces almost gave me lockjaw, a candy that sucks more from you than you'd *ever* suck from it.

Papa elbowed Coot in the ribs. "Suppose we oughta get Narlow a sack of peppermint for the road back home?"

"Oh, I suppose so. If peppermint isn't too strong for him, that is."

We started back up the river road, and passed by Hart's Mill. That's about the time Coot and I found out why Papa was willing to take the day off for no good reason.

"Seeing Mr. Hart's mill and *hacienda* reminds me that I need to return a book he loaned me years back. Can't believe it's possible, but he died back in '74. I must return that book to his widow. It's a book written by a bright eastern man by the name of Thoreau. He styled his book, *Walden Pond*. In it, he writes two full pages all about trains and the mighty locomotives that pull their tremendous weight. To paraphrase him, he speaks of 'the scream of the locomotive's whistle being like that of a red-tail hawk.' He says that folks that live in their vicinity get to where the scream of that locomotive gets no more attention than a wagon creaking by. But, the effect of those locomotives' whistle is profound. Farmers back east set their clocks by that whistle. Hear it for miles, always punctual, it's called the 'railroad way,' bringing a certain order to the countryside. Trains will soon find their way to these parts. They'll bring commerce and money the likes of which we have never seen. There won't simply be farming and ranching, and blacksmiths and a hotel or two, and a score of saloons to quench the thirst. Men like me, uneducated, maybe even dull, will sit idly by, ill-equipped to grab a hold of the opportunities. There'll be easterners on those trains that'll take advantage of all that is lost to our untrained eyes. All we'll get out of it is telling time. There won't be a man among us that can tell time by sun or star."

"Aw shoot, Papa, you're about the smartest man in Texas and the territories. You and Judge Murdock, that is."

"Judge Murdock is an educated man. He's prepared for the red-tail whistle. I can read one of their books, but that doesn't make me educated."

Papa's arguments for education were tight. Coot and I were no match for his reasoning, but we fought like cornered mountain lions to stay out of his snare.

Papa and I spent our time alone on the north end of his 9,000-acre goat ranch that summer. After supper, we were sitting by the fire as the wind was blustering out of the north. I was dreamy, schemy, poking the fire. My poking at the fire caught a shower of swirling orange sparks on the wind. I watched the orange, giving me a moment to phrase my scheme tight as Papa's own arguments.

"Papa, here's the way I see life. You see, Papa—you see, God's already got it all planned out for us. It's all predestined, predetermined, and there's not a thing we can do about it."

173

"Well, son, you could argue that point, I suppose. That is if you don't have a real argument to promulgate. But it has been my observation that most folks make no attempt to control their fate, like so many dried-up autumn leaves in a dust devil, blowing hither and yon. Some men and women I have known choose to take a firm grip on life, direct their own circumstances. The choice is always ours. A leaf in an aimless circle of wind, or a strong, determined hand on the reins of life."

Papa sorta held his own defending himself against my argument, but by the next evening, I came up with something that would corner him. I recalled my conversation with Coot back up in James Canyon about how smart we were, that we could get in college without much formal schooling. That night, after we got the goats settled down, I gathered mesquite for a fire, puffed myself up.

"Papa, you know – you know, Coot and I are already smarter than the other boys, and we know our multiplication tables up to twenty times twenty. Shucks, IB Crane and the other boys can't even go higher than five times five." I was sorry before I finished the sentence. Jeez-amighty, what a lame thing to say. I know it showed on my face.

Papa's face soured, turned to face me. "Well, son, I do believe you'll make one fine lawyer. You've already learned one of the lawyer trade's favorite tricks – the use of the lowest common denominator. You're using IB Crane, a boy with both boots in the same stirrup, and you're content to use that poor lad to judge your own worth, to set the standard by which you will live out your days. A poor lad who's as ignorant as a fish. This country is for those that want to succeed, to be their best and not be judged by any other man, much less a mindless cretin. Best raise your sights, Narlow Montgomery. Best set higher standards for yourself. I can't do it for you."

He dragged a hot iron skillet off the mesquite coals with his boot, fighting for the right words, as he never dwelt too long on a subject. He tapped burnt tobacco from his briar, pointed the stem at me. "Son, don't ever look to others for your ruling principals. They are within you like a hidden, untapped artesian well. It will bubble up the knowledge within you, but to get at it, son, *you have to dig.*"

Hours after we stretched out on our bedrolls, I was still awake, and knew Papa was as well.

"Papa?" I whispered.

"Yes, son?"

"I know you're right about this, I just can't get my arms around going off to college, being stuck in a classroom for four solid years. It'd drive me crazy."

In a bit, he replied, "You'll do the right thing. Perhaps college can wait. We'll see. Just don't let life and your opportunities pass you by. I've been right about a few things, mostly wrong I admit, but in either case I've been at it longer than you and Coot. The west is just now in the throws of birthing. I read the other day that New Mexico's population is crowding 120,000. That's one man in every square mile of this territory. Soon enough it'll be two men, then ten, then a hundred men for every blessed square mile. Things will get crowded. You boys need to prepare yourselves for your life work. Like that old Chinaman said long ago, 'Do what you love and you will never have to work a day in your life.'"

Long about the end of summer, Papa had just about convinced us to go off to school—Coot for certain. He was feeling guilty about Uncle Doyl's gold, and tried repeatedly to give it back to Papa. It was getting close to the time we would be going off to school, *if* we were going. We were still grasping for any excuse to get out of it.

Then Chief Victorio and the Warm Springs Apaches broke out of the Mescalero Indian Reservation. Geronimo had broken out of San Carlos at the same time. Things indeed would never be the same for Coot and me, and the halls of higher learning were about to lose their two favorite sons, perhaps forever. The US Army was soon in hot pursuit of Victorio and Geronimo and their renegades, but the Army was wising up to the Apache. Over the years, the Army had chased the Apache for countless thousands of miles, crisscrossing the western states and territories dozens of times, and the Pale Eyes had been bested every time. The Army was never successful at starving even one Apache into submission as long as they were free. Only their damnable reservations could teach the People about hunger.

The Blue Coats were on the prowl for local recruits to serve as scouts. Local men who had the good fortune of growing up in the hot, dry desert southwest. Most of the cavalry were boys from the fertile, green states of Arkansas, Kentucky, Tennessee, Georgia. Almost to a man, these stouthearted men hated the bleak desert, and who could blame them? Those boys missed the green of home, mama's muscadine grape preserves, hackberry jam, their girls and families so far away. The desert has no accommodations for fence sitters, you love or hate it. The Apache loved and knew the desert, every dry *arroyo* that hid the abundant water that waited for those that knew where to dig – just three feet down in the gravel in what appeared to be just another dry *arroyo*. They knew the land, every watering hole in Texas and the New Mexico and Arizona territories. The border crossing into the northern Mexican states of Chihuahua and Sonora was a drifting line in the sand with only one meaning to the Apache – the Blue Coats would not pursue them to the south, and the Mexican *Federales* and *Rurales* would not chase them north of that same shifting line.

The Apache traveled light, even when burdened with old folks, women, and children. Even so encumbered, the Apache outdistanced the white man, hour after day after endless months, years that had now turned into indeterminable decades. His smaller ponies were tougher than the soldier's heavier mounts. He loved his ponies, but if chased, he would ride them to the ground, carve off what he could carry, and jump on the back of the closest one at hand. He carried no equipage, no grain for his pony, or bacon, beans, salt, coffee, or water for his gut or that of his family. He made-do off the land, often making for *caches* of rifles and ammunition. He knew the location of supplies stashed in a rock outcropping, hidden cave, or in the crook of a particular mesquite tree. The desert teaches patience and destroys with dispatch those who do not quickly learn its unforgiving lessons. The army had been slow learners when it came to the Apache, but the Pale Eyes were getting educated.

An Army sergeant was recruiting the Mesilla Valley for scouts late that August of 1877. He was looking for two scouts in particular, namely Coot "Running Duck" Boldt, and Narlow "Kicking Bear" Montgomery. We heard the sergeant was looking for us, so we showed up at his recruitment office on the square in Mesilla. The sign outside his office read, *Local Men Wanted to Hunt Down Renegade Indians – No Danger – Six Months Obligation for Top Pay.*

The sergeant signed up two local Mexican cowhands and turned to Coot and me. "What can I do for you boys? Lookin' to sign up, are ye?" he asked, giving us the once-over.

Coot said, "Well, that depends, sergeant. We heard you were looking for us."

"Lookin' fer ye? Say, you boys aren't Kicking Bear and Running Duck are ye?"

"Two in the same, sergeant," I answered. "How do you know our Apache names, sir?"

"From an old Indian scout I used to scout with, Many Fast Feet. Say, just to prove you're who you say you are, tell me, do you know the rest of that Apache's name."

Coot looked at me and we both turned to the sergeant, grinned. "Two Sticks."

The big burly sergeant grinned, too. "That be the man." He stuck his meat cleaver paw out and shook our hands. "Ol' Two Sticks says you boys can track an Apache where a coyote would loose the scent. Sure puffed you boys up as mighty good trackers. You as good as he says you are?"

Coot said, "Well, sergeant, that depends on whether you think two young bucks that were trained by Two Sticks is worth their salt. Reckon ol' Two Sticks knows a little about tracking?"

"I reckon he do, son, I just reckon he do."

Scouting for the Blue Coats was nothing we'd ever dreamed of doing, but who knew? We might save the lives of a few Apaches along the way. But, truth be known , it provided the perfect excuse we'd been looking for all these months. Our enlistment was for only six months, then we'd go off to school. That's what we promised Papa.

The sweat-stained sergeant boasted, "You boys follow me and help us out a little bit. You'll see I'm right. Six months is more than enough time to corral that murderin' renegade, Victorio. Shoot, you boys might be back home with your mamas before Christmas. Go on home now, kiss yo' mamas good-bye and be ready to move out at first light."

We were obliged to furnish our own horses, rifles, and bedrolls. Coot had Uncle Doyl's heavy Winchester 44-40, and Papa gave me his lighter but faster, flat-shooting 32-25. We didn't exactly kiss our mamas goodbye, but Papa did ride with us as far north as La Mesa to see us off. We trailed out the same trail our old hunting parties used, up toward the Black River. We were quiet as we rode along, there didn't seem a whole lot to say, although Papa did remind us that it had only been a year since Little Big Horn when Crazy Horse and Sitting Bull dispatched General Custer and his entire command to their Maker.

Papa didn't like what we were about, but he stuck out his hand and shook our hands. "You boys keep your wits about you. You hear, Coot? Keep a sharp eye out for Narlow. And, Narlow, you do the same for Coot. Stay close. Don't you *dare* let the army separate you. There's always a way – *find it*. Watch out for some fool lieutenant or that sergeant up there, who might be looking to make a name for himself at the expense of your blood. Victorio is no fool, as you're certain to discover. He's liable to kill more than a few of your company before you capture him."

Papa's hand was fidgeting with the Colt at his side, then he flipped aside the leather holding-thong on the hammer, lifted the heavy revolver, let it drop home in its brittle-hard holster. He repeated it several times. We sat, fidgeting. I started to speak, but for once I had the uncommon good sense to hold my tongue. What was going through Papa's mind? He was wrestling with a heavy burden.

He slapped the reins on the saddle. "Boys," his voice the tenor of a dust devil, "there's *nothing* Victorio won't do. Bet on it. I would think the Indian is out-numbered a couple of thousand-to-one—maybe better, and his only chance of surviving

177

the onslaught of the whites is surrender. But you boys keep one thing uppermost in your minds – Victorio and his band don't give a tinker's damn what odds are stacked up against them. Care less. But I'm here to remind you boys of something you already know – submission runs counter to the Apache soul, their spirit. They'll fight you down to their goddamn teeth, their toenails, their very assholes before they'll quit. So would you boys. *So would I.* It will take time, but God willing, *damn it,* we've got to find a way to live together. The ways of the Apache are yesterday's ways, that will be tromped lifeless in the sand by the whites. The white race is restless, but worse, it's *resistless.* The white man will not be denied. *Damn.*"

Papa sat Traveler for a minute, squirming in his saddle, fidgeting with his revolver, lifting it, dropping it, lifting it, dropping it. His chest heaving as he labored for breath, his other hand busy with the reins, slapping his saddle. He was facing the west wind, his slate-blue eyes glistening in the stiff breeze, looking at me, then Coot, then at the Army sergeant waiting at the top of the rise, the rising sun shining through Papa's hair that was swirling under his old hat like a gray diamondback. In all my born-days I had never seen Papa so upset. *Never* heard him use such language.

Without another word, he turned his horse, loped off to the south. Coot and I sat our horses and watched him disappear around the bend in the *Rio Grande.*

It always seemed to me that the three of us were very much alike, but Coot was always more pragmatic than me, while I had a bent for wondering, misting-up for crushing ferns underfoot, that sort of sensitive, romantic foolishness, while Papa continued to be out unshakable goldmine of reasoned wisdom.

We glanced at each other. "Narlow, that man doesn't like this one bit. Let's see that we don't disappoint him, do this job right. Might even make him proud."

23

Arizona Territory
Near Mexican Border

December 15, 1877
Dear Papa,

I have intended to write for many weeks, but we haven't seen a town or even the smallest village for some time. You probably laughed when you read that sentence, thinking I'm just guilty of off-putting. I'll finish this and send it on with the next courier who comes in with orders for our captain. We are bivouacked near a point where the line between Arizona and New Mexico Territories meet the northern border of Chihuahua, just east of the Chiricahua Apache Reservation. Even though it is only ten days until Christmas, the temperature at mid-day is always in the nineties. Lieutenant Bands has a thermometer, and he and the other staff members wager with one another as to the day's high temperature. He claims the high temperature here is the result of a combination of low humidity and low altitude, he believes to be only 2000 feet. I don't know so much about that, but I can vouch for the high temperature in these parts. Coot swears that he'd give half a month's pay for a gallon of cool water from your spring at the base of Anthony's Nose.

I don't have a lot to report. We just wanted you to know we are fit and in fine fiddle. We have traveled near night and day since we left El Paso. I do believe we've tramped over half of the territories, and maybe even a little of Georgia thrown in for good measure. In all those miles, tribulations, and hardships, we have only rounded up a dozen or so Apaches – old women and men and a few of their children. Our enlistment will be up at the end of February, or early March of next year, and we sure plan on mustering out of the Army. Coot, in particular, is not cut out for the life of the Blue Coat. He bristles every time a corporal or sergeant barks an order at him, or questions our tracking talents. Just the other day, I had to jump between him and a brash young corporal who was funning our Apache names.

We heard a rumor that Chief Victorio and Geronimo split up. There have been several reports of Geronimo being in Mexico, that he plans to slip back to this side. We have been patrolling the border and posting lookouts every mile along the border. Coot and I tried to convince the sergeant that posting a lookout every hundred yards, much less every mile, is a waste of time. If Geronimo wants to come out of Mexico, Geronimo will come out of Mexico.

I'll write soon, but if you don't hear from me again, you'll be seeing us no later than March.

Your son,

Narlow

P.S.: Coot says, Howdy, Uncle Abe. Oh, and please give my regards to Mother.

***

San Simon, Arizona Territory

March 26, 1878
Dear Papa,
Coot is nineteen years old today. Can you believe that? I've been calling him
"the old man" all day and will continue to do so until I catch up with him in
five days.
When I last wrote, I said that our enlistment would be up early this month
and we were going to head for home. When we reminded Sergeant Moses
that our enlistment was up, he said he was sorry but the cap'n had extended
all enlistments indefinitely. So for a while, we'll just sit tight and see what
happens.
We keep hearing a persistent rumor that we will be heading for San Carlos to
guard its southern border to keep the Apache from breaking out and heading
for Mexico. The Army has decided to round up the Apaches from all the res-
ervations, including Ojo Caliente, and house them at San Carlos. The Apache
scouts with us say that Chief Victorio wants to come in give himself up if
he and his people can stay at Ojo Caliente. They consider Ojo Caliente their
home, but Victorio will never go back to the hellhole of San Carlos. Can't say
that I blame him much on that count. Coot and I've witnessed San Carlos for
ourselves, and it's not pleasurable.
I was mistaken when I complained about the heat in my December letter
to you. I only thought it was hot! Now every day is over a hundred and the
nights often get down close to freezing – a seventy-degree swing in twelve
hours! I promise not to complain about the Pass's summer heat or its spring
sandstorms – ever again!
Your son,
Narlow
P.S.: Coot wants to scribble a note here to you.

Howdy, Uncle Abe ~
Keeping track of your son is full time employment. If I was
paid by the hour, I could retire by summer. We're staying safe and
sticking close. I don't believe Narlow told you that Sly Fox and Iron Chain
joined up with us in January, thinking that if we were so intent on gathering

the People, keeping them from being killed, that they'd come along and see that we do it right. Many Fast Feet Two Sticks sent word that he wanted to be remembered to his amigo, Papa Abe Montgomery. He sure thinks a lot of you, Uncle Abe, as do I and everyone I know. I never had Narlow's gift for gab nor have I ever had cause to write a letter before, so I'll just say goodbye and sign my name.

Coot

***

Ojo Caliente, New Mexico Territory

August 4, 1878
Dear Papa,
We have been camped downstream about a mile from Ojo Caliente, better part of two months. Victorio and his people showed up here in the spring and we thought for certain that the Army would come in force and take them to San Carlos, but they're stalling for some reason. We have no contact with Victorio's people. We have an unsaid agreement with them – they hunt to the west and north and we restrict our hunting to the east and south. Deer are plentiful on San Mateo Peak, antelope are thick as fleas on the plains to the south.
We've had other visitors aplenty, however. Men from the Interior Department's Indian Service have come and gone by the droves. Coot overheard Captain Brook complaining to his lieutenants that the Indian Service men were typical bureaucrats – they spend more time planning, prophesying, and protecting their derrieres than they do solving the government's problems. No one wants to make a decision that can be traced back to them and cost them their careers. No decision, no risk, no consequences. They would drive a man like you plumb crazy, Papa! The Army is growing increasingly weary of "baby sitting" Victorio even though he is under the Indian Service's charge and responsibility. The Service men offer different approaches to solving the problem, but nary a word set to pen and paper. Some want to force Victorio to San Carlos, others want to leave him here at Ojo Caliente, still others want to ship him off to Ft. Sill, Oklahoma.
A newspaperman by the name of Horace McLeesh from the Silver City Daily Press came through a week ago, accompanied by a large group of ranchers on a hunting expedition with some eastern dudes. Mr. McLeesh told Captain Brook that he had it on very good authority that General William Tecumseh

181

Sherman had threatened to turn Victorio loose if they did not make up their mind pretty damn (his words, Papa, not mine) quick! There's something to that story. Captain Brook announced this morning that he had orders directing him and his men to leave immediately for Ft. Sam Houston. We reminded the captain that we, along with the other scouts, had enlisted for six months, and that we are now approaching one full year. He made no reply to that reminder, but the good captain pulled out his orders, and read the following to us – You will instruct the scouts in your command, both white and Indian, that they will remain in place at your present encampment, and should Victorio and/ or a large contingency of his men suddenly bolt and leave, your scouts are hereby commanded to follow Victorio from a distance and not engage him or his warriors unless attacked. Two companies of 9th Cavalry troopers under the command of U.S. Army Captain F. T. Bennett are on their way to Ojo Caliente and should arrive on or before October 1, 1878.

Iron Chain and Sly Fox are threatening to go home to Ft. Apache, but Coot has them pretty well convinced that will mean trouble for their families. They'll listen to Running Duck and not leave Ojo Caliente.

I am giving Sergeant Moses this letter as he promised to post it for me when they arrive in El Paso in about a week. I told him that he wouldn't make it to El Paso for the better part of a month as this country is wetter than anything I've ever seen. Their heavy wagons will spend the 120-miles south to El Paso axle-deep in mud. We have plenty of ammunition and staples to see us through the next two months, so don't worry about us. Coot's still as ornery as ever, maybe worse, probably worse. He is worse.

I think of you every single day, and sure would like to be out camping with you and Fernando Valdez, tending your fine herd of goats.

Your proud son,

Narlow

P.S.: I'll try to send a letter back with the scouts who bring in the new troopers so maybe you'll hear from me sometime in October.

✳✳✳

Ojo Caliente, New Mexico Territory

October 10, 1878

Dear Papa,

Two days after the 9th Cavalry troops and Captain Bennett showed up, Victo-

rio and around one hundred of his warriors bolted out of Ojo Caliente.

When Captain Bennett arrived, he immediately called a meeting with Chief Victorio. We tried to get him to put that off to give him and Victorio an opportunity to know each other. But the captain is a strong-headed man, and called Victorio in. Captain Bennett told Victorio that he and his two companies of well-armed men with fresh horses were here to effect the transfer of the chief and his people to the San Carlos Reservation. Victorio explained that Ojo Caliente was their home, they were born here, and loved their home. He emphatically told the captain that neither he nor his warriors would go to San Carlos, peacefully or in chains. Captain Bennett told Victorio he must obey his orders.

Victorio shouted, "You can take our women and children in your wagons to San Carlos, but my men and I will not go!" While we were translating Victorio's words for the captain, the chief and a hundred of his men mounted up and bolted for the mountains. We tracked them for two days, but the weather was decidedly on the side of Victorio – autumn rains and storms covered their trail, and they vanished in the high country.

Coot and I were not raised to question the authority or the decisions of our elders, but it occurred to us that perhaps Captain Bennett might have waited a spell to give the last remaining Apache chief an ultimatum like that at their first introduction.

I must close now as the scouts are leaving in a bit, and Coot wants to scratch out a line or two.

I think of you everyday and trust God is looking out after my Papa,
Narlow

Howdy, Uncle Abe ~

You would have been proud of your son and me when Chief Victorio called on us to translate for him. I suppose he had heard of us being at Ft. Apace and knew he could depend on us to speak his words and the words of the captain without interpretation. We have witnessed many white translators interpreting from the seat of their pants, at times we are certain that they falsely translate to give a slight twist to favor their own ideas on the subject.

I hope Uncle Abe's goats are fatter than ticks on a lazy dog, that your horse always has the frost kicked out,
Coot

183

24

"Coot, what are we going to do about getting out of this Army? When we signed up to scout for them, we didn't know we were really signing on as regular troops. But we are, except we're only paid about half, and that doesn't count having to supply our own weapons, ammunition, and horses. How much do you suppose we're losing every month?"

Coot kicked the fire. "More than two broke twenty-year-old roustabouts can afford. If I hear one more sergeant, or one more lieutenant, tell me they're not authorized to let us go home and get the hell out of this outfit, you'll be paying me a visit at the guardhouse."

"There has to be something we can do to force them to let us out, maybe something legal-like. We have rights, don't we? Like every other citizen of this country. Don't we?"

Sly Fox laughed. "My friends, you have the same rights your Apache brothers enjoy – *doo at'e da.*"

Coot asked, "Why don't you write your papa and see what he can come up with? When's the last time you wrote him?"

"I don't know. A month or two ago, I guess."

"Yeah, right. A month or two, or a year or two. Let's go talk it over with Lt. Merritt. He's fair enough. Maybe he has some pull in the Army, or a suggestion for us."

"Boys," Lt. Merritt said, "if there was anything that I could do to help you, you know I'd do it. I came out here to relieve Captain Bennett after Victorio bolted. Do you have any idea what little power a lieutenant fresh out of West Point enjoys? About as much power as popcorn-induced wind through my Army issue blue britches, that's how much."

I asked, "Do you think a lawyer, or somebody with a little influence, could help us?"

"In Washington that's what it's all about—who's got the gold and who's got the power. That's why every blasted one of them are up there. The politicians, the bureaucrats, and yes, the military brass. If you can make enough noise, or get someone to rattle their cages, you'll get some action. Maybe even your mustering-out orders. But, don't get your hopes up too much. Remember that in February, Victorio came in and asked that they stay at Ojo Caliente, or anywhere besides San Carlos. I sent a message to General Hatch, and he relayed it onto Washington. It was arranged for Victorio to be sent to the Mescalero Reservation, and now you boys are bringing in rumors that Victorio suddenly has decided that he doesn't want to go. And that's *after* he has already said he would go anywhere but San Carlos. I put myself on the line for him. If he bolts out of here, refuses to go to Mescalero, then I'm through with him. I would wager the Army is fed up as well. If we have any trouble with him, then I'd say your chances of getting out of the Army in the next twelve months are slim. None."

As our luck would have it, Victorio did indeed bolt out of Ojo Caliente again in late April, and took to the high mountains. In early June, Victorio called out for Sly Fox, Iron Chain, Coot, and me. He wanted a parley with those he could trust. The lieutenant had tried to help Victorio, but he was new to the west, untried by the Apache. Chief Victorio said that if the Pale Eyes wanted them to go to the Mescalero, they would do so on two conditions—that the four of us travel with them to guarantee their safe passage, and to insure that nothing would happen to their families who were now at San Carlos. Victorio outright refused to surrender to Lt. Merritt, or to accept an Army escort to Mescalero. Lt. Merritt sent a request to grant Victorio's wishes to approve sending us as escorts to show good faith, and to provide Victorio some sense of security for his warriors. General Hatch sent a courier back authorizing the request.

I wrote Papa a letter, and asked Lt. Merritt to post it the first opportunity he had. We were taking his advice to get some help getting out of this Army. I told Papa that we were headed for Mescalero Indian Reservation, that he could write us in care of the small Mexican village of Tularosa, New Mexico Territory.

***

Mescalero Indian Reservation, June 1879

Our trip to Mescalero was just 130 miles, but the trail went right through the heart of some of the most desolate and difficult country on the continent, the Tularosa Basin. This was the same country we had traveled three years before, when we were gathering herbs and sacred clay with Na-Tu-Che-Puy and Can See Far. The sulfur spring was still flowing at the base of Sacred Mountain, the bones of a single dead horse lay close by, a desperate animal that should have kept on his way instead of succumbing to his thirst, likely foundering himself.

We arrived at Mescalero in late June, and appeared with Victorio before the agent. He agreed to take in Victorio and his men if they promised to take up nothing but a hoe and grow corn, and stop raiding and causing trouble. As the agent phrased it, *They would have to be good Indians.* Although the agent made no outright promise, he offered to encourage the Indian Service to allow their wives and children to join them from San Carlos. Victorio and his warriors were elated with that prospect, and agreed to the agent's terms. They were earnestly attempting to take up the lifestyle of corn tenders.

But three weeks later, the agent called Coot and me in his office. He showed us a recent issue of the Silver City *Daily Press*. The paper reported that Victorio and several of his warriors had been charged with murder and horse thieving. The agent figured that the news would soon reach Victorio. His figuring was right.

That night Victorio came to our camp and told us he'd heard the same story.

"Chief Victorio, the Pale Eyes' communication system should take a page out of the Apache book," Coot said. "The agent showed us the *Daily Press* with that same story just this afternoon."

"What will this agent do?" Victorio asked. He threw his arms in the air, pounded his chest. "These lies makes my men difficult to control."

I said, "Chief Victorio, we do not know what the agent will do. It is not his place to do anything about arresting you without authority, either from the Indian Service or the Army. We think you should sit tight, see what happens. Keep a watchful eye, and you have our word, we will immediately tell you anything we know or suspect."

Keep a watchful eye, Chief Victorio sure did. Late that summer, Victorio and some of his men were out tracking deer. They saw a large, white, hunting party coming in their direction. Victorio and his warriors hid themselves and their horses. They watched the Pale Eyes pass close by. One of Victorio's men recognized a judge and prosecuting attorney in the group, and near panic swept the reservation. Victorio and his people packed hurriedly, bolted once again, heading for the westward mountains.

"*Doo hak'I da da like go!*" Victorio shouted at us before he turned his horse and headed out. "Never again will Victorio believe the Pale Eyes. Never again will

Victorio live on the Pale Eye's reservation that make women out of men, slaves of our women and children."

That was September 4, 1879. Within a few short months Chief Victorio had more than 400 warriors. From now on, it would be war.

Coot and I, Sly Fox and Iron Chain, had nothing to do, or anyone to report to. The agent was sympathetic with our plight, but was quick to point out that he was not authorized to release us. "In fact, I'm not even authorized to issue food rations to you scouts."

In late September, Coot and I were summoned to the agent's office. He stood on his front porch, a letter in hand, smiling broadly. "You boys have probably been waiting a long time for this. It's postmarked July 31, here it is almost the end of September. From the dog-eared appearance of this envelope, I'd say it's been around The Horn a couple of times."

I could tell by the writing on the envelope that it was Papa's strong hand.

July 30, 1879

Dear Narlow and Coot,

I have hired Judge Murdock to represent you in your effort to gain a lawful release from your obligation with the US Army. Judge Murdock wants you to immediately make a list of every scout that is with you presently, and those you left behind in Ojo Caliente, who you consider to have reason to believe have been forced to stay in the service of the Army far in excess of the original enlistment that was guaranteed you.

Neither Judge Murdock nor I are suggesting that you do anything illegal, or that goes against your sense of duty, moral standards, or principles, however, we both strongly recommend that you and your friends immediately hand over to the agent in charge, anything in your possession that belongs to the US government, and that you pack your personal belongings, and head for home. Judge Murdock has already set the grinding wheels of justice in motion, and has wired the War Department of his intention to bring suit against them in order to gain your lawful release. The judge is well connected and has given me every assurance that he will be able to quickly perform as promised. He is on a first name basis with General William Tecumseh Sherman, Commander of the US Army, and he was a law school classmate of Philip Sheridan, Commander of the Division of Missouri that oversees the territories.

I'm enclosing a letter from Judge Murdock addressed in care of the agent of the

Mescalero Indian Reservation which explains all of this to the him, the Indian
Service, and the War Department.
Come on home, boys.
Papa
P.S.: Your mothers will be glad to have you back.

25

El Paso. October 1879

Judge Murdock was true to his word. The War Department wired confirmation that we had been honorably discharged from the Army, and that written orders would follow in the mails. We no more than had time to store our gear, when Papa was on us like a duck on a June bug. He had checked, and it was not too late to enroll in fall classes. I did my best to dodge the subject, but Coot was adamant.

"Uncle Abe, you always knew what was right for me. You were all I had after Uncle Doyl died, but now, I'm in command of my life. My only wish is that you take this $5,000 in gold. It was Uncle Doyl's, and it never really belonged to me. Because of that gold, I feel obligated to go to the university up in Boulder. But I don't want that – not now anyway. Uncle Abe, if you don't take this gold back, I'm going to set it down here by the road, and whoever wants it, can have it. I don't want the burden of the stuff."

Guilt and an active mind are bad combination and they'll gang up on a man's soul if he's not vigilant. In late December, Coot came back to Papa. "Uncle Abe, I guess I'll be taking that sack of gold off your hands again. I don't know what kind of luck I'll have up there in Colorado, but I've determined to give it a try."

Papa never said it, but my steadfast refusal to go off to college was a great disappointment. Papa tried again to get me to go on to Austin, or even Boulder with Coot, but I refused.

"Papa, I want to earn my keep, to be a man and put in a man's day."

"If there ever was a boy, and now a full grown man, that has earned his own way ever since you were a mere scruffy lad, it is certainly you, Narlow Montgomery. You have no call to prove anything to anyone."

"I know, Papa, I know. I suppose it's proving myself to me in my own way that's important right now. I have things to sort out in my mind, in my gut. Maybe even in my heart. I know I couldn't concentrate on my studies until I do."

26

January 1880

The night before Coot left for Boulder, I had supper with him and Mrs. Boldt. Coot and I talked all night, never did bed down. Before there was even a hint of pink in the eastern sky, Coot packed up his mule, I saddled his horse.

He mounted up, looked down at me, smiled. "Narlow, the thought keeps going through my mind that you have your pack mule staked out down by the *Rio*, and about the time the sun is chest high, I'll ride around a bend in the trail up past Dona Ana somewhere, and there you'll be, sitting your horse and ready to go to Boulder with me. Is that what you're planning?"

"No, but I admit that idea has teased my mind often enough. But no, professor, I have some schooling of my own to get through right here in a canvas-covered dugout, twelve miles north of El Paso. Maybe next year I'll be heading for Boulder or Austin, but it's just you this time. Rest assured, you won't ride around a bend in the trail and see me grinning back at you."

***

Brazito, New Mexico Territory, May 1880

The far north section of Papa's ranch sat east of Brazito. That northern stretch is the roughest, bleakest section, but prized by Papa's goats for the ample browse that abound in the deep *arroyos*. Near sunset, I rode down to the rocky canyon where Coot and I had found a wagonload of settlers that had just been killed by

189

the Apache. That was back in 1873, when we were just fourteen years old. When we rode up that morning, blood was still oozing out of those folks. We figured the warriors must have recognized us as the grandsons of Skinner Boldt and Shelby Montgomery, took off when it was obvious that we would soon be happening on the scene. We buried those folks on a knoll next to that boulder-strewn canyon, piled rocks high on their graves so the wolves and coyotes couldn't get at them. Over the years, every chance I had, I'd go by that gravesite, stack up the rocks, pull weeds just to pretty up the place. Coot and I had no idea where those folks were from, where they were headed, no way to let their kin know of their circumstance, that they'd not likely be seeing them anytime soon. Coot often funned me for keeping their graves tidy, but it seemed that was the least of their due.

I made camp, laid back to read my book, Coot heavy on my mind. I was still questioning my decision not to go off to school. The same senseless thought rolled around endlessly in my head: *I'm a grown man, a grown man without even his own dern hat rack.* I had an empty gourd in my gut, like I didn't belong anywhere. Not back with Two Sticks and Na-Tu-Che-Puy, not in college, not in my folk's dugout, not even on this red-rock mesa. I hated disappointing Papa, and tried to make up for it by working extra hard, often being gone for weeks at a time gathering strays, keeping them doctored so Papa and Fernando Valdez wouldn't have to work so hard. That was some of it, I suppose, Mama, the most of it. For weeks on end, she would give me nothing but the silent treatment. My gut wretched being around her, never said a word to me unless Papa goaded her into it.

The next morning I mounted up and left Brazito, and headed back up to the south end of *Sierra de los Organos.* I planned to work around Bishop's Cap until noon make a swing past it then head home. I hadn't eaten anything but jackrabbit and rattlesnake for a week, my store of coffee and bacon long gone. Besides, I had read the dog-eared book I brought along three times, weary of my company, especially come dark.

The sensation that haunted me was so remote, I couldn't get a handle on it. At first I sloughed it off as being homesick and lonesome, believing the two were inseparable soul mates, all the while knowing that was not the case. If homesick, I sure wasn't sick for my thin pad on the earthen floor of our dugout, or my new hayloft bed quarters. Maybe a home of my own. I considered homesteading the eighty acres north of Dona I'd heard about, build me an *adobe hacienda* like Rodolfo Bustamonte's, just smaller at first. What was I thinking? I could see me in my new home, the sun going down over the *Rio* and *Cerra Roblado*, showing pink on the fresh raw, straw-laden bricks, *pintos* simmering on the open firepit, but it all added up to eighty acres of lonesome.

After considerable grinding, I rejected the notion of homesick and lonesome being one in the same. I was not homesick, just plumb lonesome, hopelessly *numb* lonesome. Lonesome for another face across my evening fire, lonesome for the clasp of another man's hand, lonesome to see a pretty girl's smile though I could not recall that delight since Coot and I left the Frontera school house well over ten years ago. Oh, sometimes I'd go to the Pass with Papa for supplies, twice a year maybe, and catch sight of a fair lass with her mother, but never to talk to or catch her eye. I came to view my condition as severe aloneness, a malady far worse than either homesick or lonesome. My search for goats around Bishop's Cap didn't turn up a thing but more lonesome, so I headed home.

I was aware of smelling burning oak, but there was precious little oak in these parts. The dank odor persisted, occasionally mixed with a faint brush of burning leather. The sensation brought on a thought I had not had for over two years—my mushroom. I stopped, stood in the stirrups, looked around, trying to get a fix on the source of the smoke I imagined I was smelling. The last time I was on this mountain and smelled burning oak and leather was when I told Papa that Many Fast Feet Two Sticks was close by. *This'll pass*, I told myself, and rode on.

But in an instant, I reined in. *Coot.* Coot was close, but where—*why?* Coot's first semester in Boulder was not up for another month. He wouldn't be coming back so early, in fact, when he wrote me in late March, he said he was staying over in Boulder for the summer. He closed his letter, *The only reason I'd come home for the summer would be to see you, but you know I wouldn't cross a dry creek bed on your account.*

Coot's presence faded, and I turned my horse, hit the trail for home. I didn't get far. Oak smoke again. I pulled up and dismounted, loosened the cinch, hunkered down, looked across the valley below me. I didn't see a thing stirring, only a brush fire fifteen miles north, likely a squatter clearing *bosque* land for the summer crop he hoped to make. That was surely the source of the smoke. But I knew better. That gray smoke was drifting lazy away to the north.

Coot was coming down the river road. I pointed at the Brazito bend in the river, two miles upstream. "He's right down *there*," I said aloud. I smiled to myself. "Better watch it. Papa says talking to yourself is a bad sign, comes on folks when they get old, even young folks, if they find themselves alone too much."

I tightened the cinch, mounted, and headed down an *arroyo* off the mesa to the river road. Coming out at the river's edge, I looked upstream. About a half-mile up, a man in a buckboard, lumbering along, heading my way. Coot. But it couldn't be Coot. Coot would never travel in a buckboard. And, that buckboard was being pulled by two brown mules with a sorrel trailing behind. What was that? Looked like somebody sitting on the wagon seat next to him. A small man, maybe a boy. No, by golly, a woman! And that sure as the dickens was Coot Boldt driving that team of mules. Before Coot came on up, I knew all there was to know.

Coot stopped the team, haggard, but grinning. "What are you doing out here, shithead? You the welcoming committee? Your mushroom announce me?"

I nodded.

He turned to the woman sitting on the bench at his side. "Geraldine, this is my very best friend. He's the clown I told you about—Guillermo Narlow Montgomery."

I doffed my hat and nodded.

She stood on the floorboard of the buckboard, stretched with her comely arms over her curly blonde head, leaning back to show off her ample bosom, sighed, then glared down at me. "Can this idiot talk?"

"Oh, he can talk all right—talk a rock out of a fence. Narlow, this is Geraldine."

"Glad to make your acquaintance, Miss Geraldine," I said, again doffing my hat.

"*Mrs.* Geraldine Milsap-Boldt, I'll have you know."

"I . . . I . . ." I had never heard of a wife keeping her own last name. Again I attempted to form the words, *I'm right pleased to make your acquaintance,* but could only stammer, "I . . . I . . ."

"Well, maybe this idiot can't talk, but he stutters just fine." With that, Coot's bride doubled over laughing.

"*Shad-dap,*" Coot barked, and slapped the reins on the mule's rumps.

Geraldine came close to doing a backward somersault over the buckboard's bench. I had never heard Coot speak ill to any lady—girl or woman.

He called back to me, "I can see you don't require an explanation. I'll have plenty of that to do when I introduce this *lady* to Mama. I'll be over in a day or so."

I went on home and told Papa about Coot being married. When my friend came by the next day, Papa congratulated him. "Well, son, I understand you're a married man. That's grand, and I'm proud for you."

Coot reached in his saddlebag. "Yep, you're looking at a married man, spliced according to the law." He offered Uncle Doyl's sack of gold to Papa. "Uncle Abe, this bag of gold has been nothing but an irritation and source of great misery to me. I suppose there's no use asking you to take it back."

"No," Papa said, laughing, "you and I've about worn out that old leather sack passing it back and forth between us. You have a family now, and you'll be needing a place of your own. I recommend you put your uncle Doyl's gold to work for you, buy yourself your own place. Five-thousand-dollars will go a long way in getting yourself established."

That's exactly what Coot did. The next day Coot and his mother drove up in the buckboard. Coot jumped to the ground, helped his mother down, then turned to us. "Uncle Abe, I told Mama what you said about buying a place of my own, and Mama said—"

She brushed him aside. "I asked him if he thought he was too good for his mother's place. He said my place fitted him just fine. So, I'm selling him my place for his $5,000 in gold. And quit calling him your uncle. Abe's no relative of mine."

Papa said, "Well, that's fine—just fine. It worked out well for both of—"

"Yes, Abe, it worked out just fine. Just fine except for the poor soul that Coot stole that gold from."

"Now, Mrs. Boldt, I can tell you for a fact that Coot came by that gold honestly and—"

"I've already got one boy in the state penitentiary, and I sure don't need another one. If that gold is so all-fired honest, then tell me where he got it."

"I don't believe that is my place to tell you that, Mrs. Boldt."

"Didn't reckon you'd tell me. Coot won't neither. Far as I'm concerned, he stole it. The sooner we get to the courthouse, file this deed, the better off we'll all be. Except for the feller Coot stole that gold from." Mrs. Boldt turned back to the buckboard, lifted her heavy dress. "Come on, boy. Help your poor mother back up there. We got a deed to file."

27

Six months after Coot came home with his "bride and biscuit," as he called his ready-made family, I married a girl who was twenty-five years old, almost four years my senior. Sophie Lewinski, the only child of Horace Lewinski, who lost his wife shortly afterward. Mr. Lewinski was a good man, in possession of an honest reputation, a thriving business, and a heavy Polish accent.

Mr. Lewinski threw a grand wedding reception, invited everybody on both sides of the *Rio Grande*. At that occasion, Mr. Lewinski took me aside. "Narlow, I'm proud to have you for my son. You are an honest man—just like your papa, Abe Montgomery."

"Thank you, sir. I hope to be just like Papa one day."

"And, Narlow, it does you no good to have anger for your mama. It is bad. Bad for your heart, my son. Try to understand."

"I have no anger for my mother, sir. I am not even disappointed that she was not present today. But I don't take kindly to anyone slighting you and Sophie. For that, I offer my sincere and humble apology. I can only say that you and Sophie should not take offense to her absence. My mother wouldn't have been here if your name was Abe Lincoln, Benito Juarez, Booker T. Washington, Moses, or Jesus Christ."

My Sophie was a shy, timid, frail woman, but a real lady with auburn hair. I suppose her shy and timid ways attracted me to her more than anything, gave me something to protect, and guard. But Sophie's complete lack of self-confidence and self-esteem soon weighed heavy on me. She needed a strong man to overshadow her frailties, to feed her timid soul. I tried hard to be that man.

Papa's proud slate-blue eyes showed even brighter when he came by almost every week. But somehow, Sophie didn't seem to share his adoration, never even invited him to stay for supper. Horace Lewinski died two months later, leaving Sophie a little cash, considerable land, and several El Paso building lots he had taken as payment from people who owed him and could not pay. Most of the parcels were down near the river where it flooded most every year, but some of Sophie's inheritance had a lot of promise. We took up residence in Mr. Lewinski's two-story stone house on Utah St., high on a mesa overlooking El Paso and Juarez. The stately home came equipped with a houseful of furniture, icebox, plates and flatware, fine china silverware, even a fulltime housekeeper, Miss Wanda. We sold Mr. Lewinski's hardware business, and I opened an office on Mills Street, dabbled in real estate and second-lien mortgages. Pretty quick I had a steady handle on both.

I took Mr. Lewinski's passing harder than his daughter. She never shed a tear, though I know she adored him. I could not suppress the thought, *She doesn't miss him because she married another father.*

Geraldine never did have that child she claimed, never even had morning sickness to Coot's knowledge. Geraldine was a looker all right, flaxen-haired, bright green eyes, creamy skin, buxom, but her looks stopped at the water's edge. That gal had a straight razor for a tongue, with a mind that did not have a notion how to wag with any finesse. There was never any doubt that Mrs. Geraldine Millsap-Boldt firmly believed that she had married "beneath her station." She continuously referred to him as a dirt-clod farmer, was not bashful in the least about telling total strangers and friends alike. She detested Coot. So why would she feign pregnancy?

Usually when we invited Geraldine and Coot over for supper, Coot would come alone. But one particular evening, we had the pleasure of Lady Millsap-Boldt's company as well. She came through the front door, swift as a scorpion, waving her stinger in the warm summer breeze, looking for a place to plant it.

We sat down at the dining room table, Sophie offered the blessing, there were three *"Amens,"* and before we opened our eyes, Geraldine was out for the kill.

"Everyone in town knows that I married beneath my station."

She paused, shot me a sideways smirking glance. "But then *all* women do. Don't you agree, Sophie?"

Sophie's gaze dropped to her lap. She turned to me for help. As I passed the green beans to Coot, I tried to change the subject, but the scorpion-lady would not go unheeded.

"Sophie, it is impolite for the hostesses to ignore her guest's question. I asked you—"

Coot smiled that certain smile over at me as he returned the beans. The thought crossed my mind that he might slap the skin clean off Geraldine's face. He held back, but his words had force, their slap, hard, taunting.

"Look, *lady*, you very well may have married beneath your *station*, but when I was on top of *your* station, pruning it several times a day, well into the night up there in Colorado when I should have been studying, you couldn't get enough of this dirt-clod farmer and his prune. How many times have I heard you whimper, '*Oh please, Coot, just one more time*'."

Geraldine jumped to her feet, her mouth agape, pointed her finger at him across the table, started to protest.

Coot stood, stuck a big, stubby finger on the end of her nose. "*Shad-dap.*"

***

A week later, Coot banged into my office, interrupted my nap. He scared me so, my boots slipped off my desk, hit the floor.

"I hate to pull you away from all high-finance business negotiations, but could I please ask you to take me back to the farm? The axle broke on my buckboard, filled to the brim with supplies, dern near dragged itself in the *Rio* before I could get it stopped. Big George will fetch the buckboard, have it fixed in a day or so." Big George was a black man who ran a livery and could make an anvil sing. He was our friend from the first day he came to the Pass from Tennessee, always chided us about being so similar. "You boys are like two snow peas in a pod, sprinkled with confectionary sugar."

I asked Coot, "Why don't you stay over? Stay at our place." I smiled. "Unless you're just too eager to get back to your darling, Geraldine."

"Can't do that. Promised IB and Shelly Brom that I'd go by their place, pick them up and a month's worth of vegetables they have for Geraldine, a gift for her. Shelly grew them herself and I don't want to disappoint her. Get a move-on, and you'll be back in time for your supper."

Shelly almost overloaded my buggy, filled it to the rafters, if buggies had rafters.

Coot looked over her baskets of sweet corn, summer squash, tomatoes, onions, and all manner of delights. "Shelly, you've got the greenest thumb in the Territory. This is mighty kind of you to want to give all this to Geraldine. I'm sure she'll be real thankful."

Shelly twisted her hands in a knot in front of her feed-sack dress, blushed, signed that it was nothing, just some old vegetables.

I drove the buggy in the dooryard up to the Boldt's kitchen door. Coot went in to get Geraldine, tell her that Shelly and IB were here with a gift, homegrown vegetables. I heard her response, but couldn't make out exactly what she was saying. Shelly's head cocked to one side. Her keen ears hadn't missed a word.

Then, of a sudden, Geraldine's voice raised to a crescendo that a blind man could hear halfway back to town. "Mr. Boldt, I saw that *friend* of yours drive up in

196

his buggy, you by his side, both of you grinning like you had good sense. *Oh, yes,* I saw you! I also saw that wretched girl and her idiot twin brother, both hanging on in the back seat. I cannot bear to even *look at her* much less have their kind in my home. Her brother's laughable, if he wasn't so damn *pathetic.* They're white-trash. Your friend's white-trash. *You're* white-trash, and half of El Paso's white-trash, the other half is a bunch of greasy Mexicans. I detest—"

I heard a hollow crash, like a number-two washtub bouncing off a porcelain bathtub, witnessed my white-trash-friend bust through the kitchen door to join his white-trash *amigos.* The color of his usual bronze face was that of a red-hot branding iron. I feared he just might explode. Shelly Brom and IB turned to walk back home.

Coot said, "I had to get away from her before I broke her damn fool neck. " He fumed, made a motion to go back in the house.

I stepped in front of him, grabbed him by the shoulders. "Coot, don't! You can handle her later." I turned him around. "Look. When all this commotion started, Shelly grabbed IB by the arm, and they started walking. We need to—"

"But, that damn woman said—"

"I know. But right now, we need to take care of our friends. Let's get them back home, you do what you can to smooth things out on the way. Come on."

He stood looking first at Shelly and IB, then the kitchen door, his dark eyes darting back and forth.

"Come on, Coot. I'll bring you back and you can deal with her later. But, right now . . ." I jerked my head toward our friends on the road back to their clapboard shack.

We caught up with Shelly and IB, talked them into climbing back in the buggy. I clicked my mare into a trot, Coot climbed over the seat, sat between Shelly and IB, put his arms around them, started apologizing, making excuses for his wife's belligerence.

When we got back to the Crane place, Coot jumped out, helped Shelly down, shook IB's hand. IB said, "Aw, Coot, don' ya be worry'n yorsef none on our'n count. Everything's gonna be jest fine. Jest wait. You'll see."

Coot hugged Shelly, she brushed her hair back, smiled. "Shelly, there's nothing I can say that can ever take back Geraldine's words. All I can do is say I'm sorry. That's kinda weak, but I suppose that's all I can do. Narlow will take your beautiful gifts to town, won't you, Narlow? There's a new orphanage that just opened on Fourth Street, and I know they'll be real proud to have your beautiful vegetables.

Tell you what—I'll be around tomorrow. Maybe you'd serve me up a big dish of homegrown vegetables and rabbit stew. That's my favorite."

✳✳✳

Never knew what happened after I delivered Coot back to his house, didn't care to know, as my ears are far too tender. But soon after, Geraldine left him, moved to town, bought a house right across Utah Street from Sophie and me. That house was the closest thing to a mansion that El Paso had to offer, besides the old Magoffin *hacienda*. Geraldine's place featured eight bedrooms, indoor plumbing, the works. She was from a family with money back east, Connecticut or New York, so she claimed. That was probably so, as she bought the mansion for cash money and for show, and had Sophie and me as neighbors in spite of her inability to tolerate us. There was talk that she would divorce Coot and move back east. Coot was always a lucky cuss, but all things have their limits.

A short time later, Geraldine Millsap-Boldt stormed into my office, slammed the door, swirled her skirt around in a flourish. "You can tell your only friend in this god-forsaken, wind-blown, two-bit, Mexican-ridden dump of a town that there will be no divorce for Mr. Boldt. *No sir.* There has *never* been a divorce in the Millsap family. *Never.* No divorce. Not *now*, not *tomorrow* or *next year*. *Never.* And I am *not* tucking my tail and returning to my family. I am staying *right here* so I can make that bastard's life as miserable as possible, and you can tell him I said so, you frothing dingdong!"

I stood, smiling.

"Did I talk too fast for you, Narlow Montgomery? Do you want me to repeat it? Can you replicate what I said just now to your pumpkin-rolling friend without stuttering?"

I sat down, smiling, leaned back, put my boots on my desk. She reached out and brushed them off with the same flourish as her swirling skirt.

I sat up to keep my balance, leaned back, smiling, put my boots back on my desk.

She stood fuming, her green eyes ablaze, hands on her hips, slipper tapping on the hardwood floor, glaring down at me. I let her fume.

"*Well?* Don't sit there looking dumb as a box of rocks. *Well?*"

"Well, what, Geraldine honey?"

"Will you tell Mr. Boldt what I just told you?"

"What's that?"

With that she whirled around, screamed, "Don't call me honey!" went through the door, slammed it with such force that the thick windowpane bolted out of its frame and splattered on the boardwalk, her skirt caught in the doorjamb. She pulled on it, but to no avail. She opened the door, jerked her skirt loose, tearing the hem completely off, then slammed the door again. I had just had that pane gold-leafed with my name and all my credits. Cost me $7.45 cash money.

A crowd gathered. Since my office was just two doors down from the *Times* office, a reporter sauntered by. The gentleman, Jake Connor, asked me what the commotion was all about.

"Oh nothing, Jake," I said. "Just old lady Geraldine Millsap-Boldt, screaming her undying love for my lifelong friend, Coot Boldt. I reckon she'll get over him one of these days, when she gives up getting him back. Then, I reckon she'll catch a train back East to take care of her poor mama—they're destitute you know. *Absolutely penniless.*"

Jake whipped out pen and paper, ready for an assignment. "Mr. Montgomery, are you going to file charges against her and make her replace your door window and all that fancy gold-leaf lettering?"

"Gee, Jake, I hate to think that things have come to that. But, shucks, I reckon I'll have to. Here we are trying to run the riffraff out of town, put a stop to men shooting it out on our streets, why, we can't have our womenfolk threatening the very men that are trying so hard to make a safe and decent town out of El Paso."

"Can I quote you on that, Mr. Montgomery? Can I repeat what you said about her family being destitute and all?"

"*Whoa now.* I'll have to think on that, Jake. You know how thin-skinned Coot can be. This incident just might be enough to run him clean out of town with embarrassment. But, I guess we'll just have to chance that, now won't we, Jake?"

28

"Sophie, I'll be back before nightfall. Meeting Coot to take our Christmas presents out to Papa like we always do."

She was still dressed in her house robe, hair up in curlers, though it was well past 9. She reached up in the kitchen pantry. "Here, take this to your papa. A jar of Miss Tilly's homemade fig preserves. He always likes them so much."

I had ordered a Stetson for Papa, the newest thing available. It was delivered from Dallas in a big box, cost me fifteen-dollars with the freight, but I was eager to see his eyes light up when he opened it.

It was good to be out on horseback, something I promised myself to do more often. It gave me time to think, reflect, sort things out, though I found myself fighting *not* to think of some things more than what I really wanted to mull over.

Mama was one, but there wasn't anything to do about that. Sophie was another, but after being married for thirteen months, I was pretty-well resigned to thinking there wasn't much to be done about that either. Why wouldn't she want to make those fig preserves herself? Why buy them from Miss Tilly? Before we were married, she enjoyed giving and receiving presents. Now she waved off the idea, says it was a waste of time. Why didn't she ever invite Papa to our home for supper, for his birthday, Thanksgiving, Christmas? When I mentioned that to her, her stock answer was, "Not this time, Narlow, perhaps next year."

Over and over, my mind held on our wedding night. We'd spent the night at El Paso's newest, the Pierce Hotel. Sophie's voice haunted me. *"No, Narlow, not tonight. Just hold me. Let's put that off until we know each better."* My tepid response, "Sure—sure, Sophie. Sure. Good night."

My mind raced back to when I was sixteen, Papa telling me that I'd be married and have little ones running underfoot. *"Shoot, Papa, I won't be having any children. I don't know anything about all of that stuff."* Papa's voice, *"Oh, you'll figure it out, and if not, that lucky little gal will put form to it for you."* I was pretty certain I had it figured out, but had no willing partner to try out my unproven theories.

A month after our vows, I rested my hand on her hip as we lay in bed, turned her on her back, eased a leg over her, and—*"Oh, Narlow, please! I cannot bear it. It hurts so much. Please, no!"*

I hit the saddle horn, muttered, "*Hurts so much?* How in the world would she know? My nightshirt was still down to my ankles, much less entering her."

My mind wouldn't release me from a matter that I'd failed to mention to Coot. Actually, it wasn't all that much, just a little altercation at the Acme Saloon last month. He'd been on me about my drinking, gambling with the local shystering riff-raff, stumbling home just before daybreak most every morning. Yeah, I was a bit in my cups that night when these two strangers swaggered through the batwing doors of that tawdry tavern, got to big-shoting, huffing and shouting, ordered drinks all around, pushed themselves in on our game of five-card stud. We no more than had the cards dealt when one of them accused my *amigo*, "Cue Ball" Stanley, of cheating, a man who'd'a given his life for his good name. Cue Ball stood. The man cocked and leveled his Colt Peacemaker at Cue Ball's watch fob. I bumped the table hard in the man's midsection. He turned his revolver on me. I struck him a mighty blow across the bridge of his nose with my four-pound Schofield 44-40, causing a most severe bloody mess. His partner pinioned me from behind. Swung me around. Knocking my revolver from my hand, but his grip slacked. I grabbed up a chair and beat his ass to the floor. Stomped on his skull till he quieted himself. The nose-bloodied man came across the table at me, me still holding the leg of the busted chair. With no time to take an honest swing, I stuffed the floor-end of the chair leg in his mouth, tickling his tonsils as it made a canorous clatter about his teeth, just as his wadded, sledgehammer fist hit me upside the ear, spewing blood. Three men spread like dying crows on the sawdust-strewn floor of the Acme, where three men once stood, all spitting or bleeding. The exhilaration caused me to get on my all-fours, heaved, then the first thing that befell me was the vision of Papa's unutterable contempt of his son's drunken fist'a'cuffing and puking in a public saloon—followed closely by the image of Coot kicking my derriere for denigrating the Montgomery name. I stumbled to the bar, pulled a chew of bills from my purse for the damages, told Phil the barkeep that I reckon I wouldn't be back for a spell. Sophie never even inquired about my blood-crusted, swollen ear or missing coat sleeve.

When I rode up to Papa's and Mama's dugout, I knew Papa was not nearby. I always sensed that without knowing. Things were different when he was around. Somehow, his essence glowed things.

Mama was in the yard tending her cauldron. Seems she spent her entire life tending that black pot. She didn't bother to turn around or say diddly. Never did.

I sat my horse. "Good morning, Mother. Is Papa around?"

"Do I look like I know where that bastard is?"

"Called him that to his face lately?"

Damn bitch. I winced—first time I'd ever thought ill of my own mother, even to myself.

"What'da got in that big box? Looks like it might'a cost money. You big-rich these days?"

I made no reply, refusing to take the bait for an argument, me still looking at her backside. She knew I had that box up here with me, tied on with twine behind the cantle. Likely saw me coming a mile off.

I turned my horse, yelled over my shoulder, "Merry Christmas, *Mother,*" and headed around the corrals, trying to get a fix on where Papa might be off to.

"He ain't around here. Off with that Met-si-kin son-of-a-bitch, Fernando Valdez. Been gone more'n'a week."

"Called Fernando Valdez that lately? To his face, I mean." *Goddamn bitch. What I'd give to pinch her to the ground, cover up her pile of bile.*

From the level of the water in the horse trough, it was obvious they'd been gone a spell, ponies milling around, nudging the empty trough. I pulled the wire running up the side of the windmill to the vane, the wooden mill turned into the westerly breeze, the fan creaked to life, water belched out the trough pipe.

Mama started screaming, yammering about me wasting water, wearing out her windmill, mind my own goddamn business, get the hell off her place.

God, I wanted to scream back at her. Tell her to shove it up her I ass. But I let her yammer, filled the trough, shut off the windmill, and started up North Arroyo. I figured Papa and Fernando would be up around Brazito or Bishop's Cap, if not, I'd find them at Anthony's Nose. All high country. They'd find me.

Why was I letting Mama get under my skin? I had her right where I wanted ever since I was eighteen, but the day Sophie and I married—yeah, maybe that was it—Sophie's refusal of my advances had pushed Mama back to the foreground, got my dander up again. Let her gorge at my gut.

Fresh tracks came in from the west, turned north where I was headed. It was Coot. After a mile, his tracks headed back east toward Anthony's Nose. I stopped, considered following him, but decided to go on.

Before Sophie and I married, I had Mama shoved back in a dark place of my soul. No, I hadn't resolved her in my mind, but neither was I consumed by her evil-dark ways. But now . . . now when I thought of her, I envisioned the thousand-centuries-baked red clay chambers of the underworld, of hades, sulfur stench, copper-glazed scorpions in the chamber that should house her heart. Heart—humph! What heart?

I found no sign of Papa and Fernando Valdez at Brazito or Bishop's Cap, so I headed south for The Nose past Webb Gap. The trail crossed the wide plain of the pass between the Organ Mountains and Anthony's Nose, gouged by deep canyons and arroyos where browse was plentiful, a favorite for Papa's goats. I rode off the deep sand at the base of the peak, and there were Coot and Fernando Valdez, milling around in circles, studying the ground around a dependable spring. This place called *Campo Azul* was one of Papa's favorite base camps, plenty of water with springs up the side of the Nose so their presence didn't keep wildlife from water. Named for the dark-blue horizontal volcanic spear that had lifted a solid rock shelf at the spring. The spear shape began just west of the spring and tapered out to a point three hundred yards to the east where endless sand was busy covering it over time.

Fernando smiled, doffed his *sombrero*, a habit he'd begun when Sophie and I married, something he didn't do even for papa, for god's sake! He probably thought he owed it to me since I was a man now, but I hated it.

"*Hola, Senor Valdez. Que pasa, amigo? Adonde esta Papa Abe?*" I doffed my own hat, pointed it at him.

He chuckled, crammed his *sombrero* down tight. "*Quien sabe, senor, pero* maybe no so good."

Coot walked up. "Fernando tells me that he and Uncle Abe separated three days ago. Uncle Abe working this side of the mountain, Fernando working the east side and most of *Puertos de los Alamitos*, tracking a mountain lion with a cub. He heard a single rifle shot, figured it was Uncle Abe calling him over. Fernando searched, but couldn't find either Uncle Abe or his horse. Nothing. Only the spot by the spring where the dirt and sand had been recently disturbed, horse prints all around."

He turned to Fernando. "That about right, Fernando Valdez?"

"*Si, Senor.* I did those things. I could not find *Senor* Montgomery or his horse. I look all day. Then, over there by that blue rock ledge on the other side of the spring, I find this dirt stirred around. Many horse tracks, one track is *Senor* Montgomery's gelding, *Manana.* I look all over, climb that steep rock slab, climb to the top of the mountain, look all around. *Senor* Montgomery, he teach me to look, to see good. I see no things, *senores. Nada.* I follow those horse tracks many miles to the south toward El Paso, *pero* they stop where the rain come down. No more tracks."

He stepped forward, handed me a spent casing. "All I find is this brass. I find it on top of rock over the blue spear—I believe it is a 44-40, maybe so shot from a rifle."

I gazed at that grand old man, a man I'd loved since I was a pup. He hadn't changed all that much, coal-black hair just gray in his broad, cropped beard. No, Fernando Valdez was not my papa, but if anything had ever happened to Papa when I was a boy, I always knew where I'd go.

We scattered out, searched for awhile, then came back to the spring at the edge of the steep blue lava slab, a fifty-degree incline, pockmarked with goose egg-size holes.

Coot said, "Getting too dark to see anything. Might as well make camp. Narlow, what about Sophie?"

"Oh, she'll be all right without me. Probably welcome the relief."

He laughed. "What do you mean? Been married just over a year. You're still newlyweds and—"

"In word only. Sophie's still as fresh and untouched as an uncut spring flower."

"What do you mean? You saying you didn't—you haven't—"

"Didn't. Haven't. Embarrassing—isn't it?"

Coot and Fernando stood quietly, their lower jaws resting on their chests.

"I suppose I should have mentioned it before now, but the longer it went, the harder it was to bring up. Damn certain humiliating. I figured on asking Papa about that. But, shoot, Coot, you're a married man. Do you have any—"

Coot's head jerked up. "Hey, don't look at me. I'm as inexperienced as you are. All I know on the subject of holy matrimony is Geraldine bedding me the first day I met her. She led me up the fire escape of her dormitory building, threw me on her bed, pulled off my boots, and had her way with me with her feet in the air. That, my old friend, is the sum total of my carnal knowledge or a damn thing else about women."

He shrugged. Fernando found busy-work. I untied Papa's present, set it on the gravel, then the smaller package tied behind my saddle. "Fernando Valdez, *amigo todo mi vida*, here is a little something special for your Christmas. *Feliz Navidad, amigo!*"

He set back on his heels, eyes glistening as he peered up at me, placed his *sombrero* on the gravel beside him, opened the package carefully so as not to break the twine or tear the wrapping paper. He wrapped the twine around his fingers, stuffed the twist in his vest pocket, folded the brown paper, and set it aside.

"Oh, *senor. Midi! Que bonita el sarape! Y como es? Aye, Senor* Narlow*! Un funda por mi pistola. Gracias, Senor* Narlow. *Muchas gracias!*"

"I hope that holster is long enough for your old Peacemaker."

He stood, strapped the holster around his middle, crammed his old revolver in place. Like a glove. He threw the *sarape* over his head, adjusted it to his liking, a heavy woolen rectangle with a slit for his head, adorned front and back with game-cocks facing each other—one bright green, the other rooster red. Fernando didn't have to utter a word to express his love for that heavy hunk of wool.

Fernando gave me a tight *abrazo*. We gazed into each other's eyes. I recalled back to my early tadpole days, seeing those same clear, bottomless, dark-emerald eyes. He had been on this ranch since the day Papa learned he was going to be a father. He needed help if he was going to properly provide for his family in this unforgiving country. Fernando Valdez walked past the dugout that night, Papa invited him in for supper. He never left.

***

"Damn it, Coot. All we have here is some disturbed sand and gravel by the spring. Could have been caused by any number of things or animals. We have three sets of horse tracks. Fernando recognized one of them to be one of Papa's horses, *Manana*. Probably the next day, another set of tracks. Two are the same, along with another horse, but not *Manana*."

Coot dumped the coffee grounds out of his cup, cleaned it with his bandana, set it with Fernando Valdez's gear, and pointed over at him squatting on his heels at the edge of the rock slope, peering at something between his tattered *huaraches*.

"*Senores, mire.*"

Coot asked, "What'd you have there, Fernando?"

He scraped his gnarled fingernail in a crack in the blue lava rock, studied what he dug out, tasted it.

"*Sangre.* Not very old the blood."

We spread out along the steep blue slope, began crawling up its face on all-fours, and came to a ledge about twenty-feet up.

Coot was far to the right. "Narlow, Fernando. What do you make of this?"

Coot was on his hands and knees, peering back into the darkness of the north-facing crevice, waiting for his eyes to adjust to the dark.

"Look past those rocks—bones. Top of a skull is partially visible on the far side of that rock to the left."

"Human skeleton?"

"Looks that way."

We inched ahead on our bellies to the skeleton, a narrow opening visible further back. Coot scooted the bones away to his right, the clatter bringing on the unmistakable buzz of a rattler greeted our ears—eight feet to the right of Coot's elbow. A Diamondback.

We lay motionless, letting the guardian of the bones settle himself.

Coot whispered, "Look at the size of that bastard, will you? Couldn't cover him with a peach basket."

Fernando Valdez quieted us, his finger to his lips. "*Que es? Escuche!*"

A groan. From inside the opening.

"That's Papa! He's back there." I inched past Coot, reached in my trouser pocket for a kitchen match, struck it. Its pitiful light showed nothing but the palm of my hand in the vast darkness. "Papa! Can you hear me, Papa? It's Narlow."

I crawled through the opening of the cave, crusted with dry molten spikes. Just inside, I bumped into Papa's boots. Again, he moaned.

I struck another match. All I could see in the brief flare was Papa wrapped in his *sarape*.

"It's Papa. He's alive, but the ceiling of the cave's too low to squat or lift him. Grab my boots and pull. I'll hold onto him."

He yelped like a sleeping dog when we dragged him over the rough opening, but we kept pulling, got him out past the skeleton on the ledge. Papa's *sarape* had pulled away, exposing his bloodied chest and shoulders, his body trembling, skin ice cold.

Coot said, "Let's ease him off this rock ledge, get him back down to camp, get him warmed up."

Fernando ran down the steep slope like he was chasing a nanny, had our fire kicked back to life before we had Papa covered with Fernando's new *sarape* and bedding.

Papa lay on his back, still trembling.

Coot asked, "What's that he's clutching in his hands? Looks like a leather pouch." We peeled back his covers. It did indeed appear to be a leather pouch, but Papa had a death grip on it with both hands.

After Papa warmed up, he came around a little, still woozy but awake enough to sip water. Fernando broke up pieces of jerky in a tin cup with a little water, put it next to the fire, stuck his finger in the cup to test the heat, handed it to me. Papa sipped it, smiled.

Coot chuckled. "Glad to see us, Uncle Abe?"

He smiled, blinked his not-so-sparkling-slate-gray eyes, gulped the jerky brew, then dozed off. While he was out, we cleaned the wound on his chest as well as the one on the back of his shoulder.

Coot said, "Some son-of-a-bitch shot him in the back. Neat, round hole in his shoulder, gaping exit wound on his chest. What do you make of this, Narlow?"

"Looks like he was shot at close range by a rifle—probably the 44-40 casing Fernando found on top of the ledge. Glad he wasn't shot by anything heavier, like a 45-70, or his shoulder would have been torn off. Look, he's coming back around."

Papa struggled to sit up. We leaned him against our saddles. He sipped more of Fernando's jerky broth.

"Papa, you have infection started in your exit wound, but we think you need rest, water, and food before we address that problem. Do you feel like telling us what happened, or do you even know?"

He leaned forward, arched, stretched his back, then sat back against the saddles. "*Whew!* Yes—yes, I recall everything from start to finish. From the time I found myself face down in this arroyo, hearing two men talking, heard the clatter of their horses as they left, hiding myself in that cave. If it hadn't been for that cave, I'd be a goner.

"I heard the rifle shot and felt the thud in my back at the same instant. No doubt the shot came from no further than thirty-or-so yards. I recall leaning on my left stirrup to dismount, fill my canteen. If it hadn't been for that, he'd'a shot me dead center in the gullet. I was stunned, but conscious. I'm pretty sure the one who shot me was on horseback, the other seemed to be afoot. He walked up to me, didn't touch or roll me over, just said, 'Aw, shit, Homer! You done kilt the wrong man.' The shooter shouted out, 'Don't blame this all on me, Mo. You're the one that tolt me to shoot him.' In a bit, he said, 'And jist exactly what makes you so all-fired certain that we done shot the wrong man?' He answered, mentioned a man's name, strange, yet familiar name. I don't recall it now. Mo said, 'Because he said the man coming down from Denver was a young man, around twenty-years-old. This'un's got to be close to sixty. We best go tell him what happened here, see what he wants to do about it.'

"They rode off, heard Mo call out, 'Homer, fetch up that horse. Don't want him standing around, advertising this dead man's whereabouts.' I figured they'd be back, bringing their money-man back with them, so when I was certain they were gone, I gathered myself up, wrapped my sarape tight around my chest so I wouldn't be leaving a trail of blood to wherever I could find to hole-up. I had my revolver and figured that's all I'd need to protect myself from those two neophytes should they decide to return."

Coot said, "Well, Uncle Abe, you dern certain took care of that. We searched for hours, gave it up until this morning, then Fernando squatted down over there, found a tiny speck of red in a crack at the base of that blue rocky slope, scratched it up, tasted, assured us it was *sangre*."

Papa's gaze turned to Fernando, gave him a wink, then winced. "I think I need to lay back down, getting woozy again."

We pulled the saddle away and got him comfortable, told him he could finish his story after he rested, but he insisted on going on, motioned to the tin cup at his side, said to Fernando, "*Poquito mas, mi amigo.*"

He drank down the brew. "*Ah.* Mighty tasty, Fernando, just like the old days, *eh*? I climbed that blue slope, figuring to gain the high ground. Soon enough, I came upon that shelf with the skull and skeleton, a doorman most men dare not pass, and eased myself past the bones." Papa laughed. "Did that rattler shake his calling card at you boys when you came looking for me?"

"Yes, sir," Coot said. "Biggest bastard I ever saw. Oh, excuse my foul tongue, Uncle Abe. Then what happened?"

"That night, I came back down here. Had a torrent of thirst. Had to have water, but when I got back in the cave, I was spent. Lost too much blood, knew I couldn't go for any more water, plus I was still concerned that my would-be assassins might be coming back for a visit, bring their boss to view their handiwork.

"The next day, around noon, I heard horses. Not two, but three. Same two men arguing about who shot who and under whose orders. Another man spoke up, the money-man, I suppose, told them to shut up, asked them what happened to the body, told them they probably only wounded the man, screamed at them to search for the man, or his body, and not come back until they found it.

"I heard one of those geniuses crawling up that rocky slope, heard his boots scuffing on the rocky ledge, got clear up to where I could see his outline. I cocked my revolver, took a bead on him, watched him crawl another step or two, got clear on top of that skeleton before he was aware of it, let out a whimpering yelp that disturbed that monstrous rattler that shook his castanets at him. Heard him kicking and cussing all the way back down that rocky slope, got up and took off running, screaming the strange name of the money-man, reporting that there was a twelve-foot rattler up there, swore there couldn't be a living soul up there on that shelf."

Papa laughed. "I don't know so much about that rattler's measurement, but I confess he's about as big as I've ever laid these tired old eyes on."

Papa had more jerky stew and a gallon of water, rested some.

"Uncle Abe, I know you're not looking forward to mounting a horse and riding twenty-two miles back home, but where that bullet came out is mighty ugly, needs medical attention. It's infected, turning yellow and green. When we get you close to home, I'll ride on into El Paso and fetch Doc Green and be back to your place by the time Narlow and Fernando get you—"

"No, Coot, can't let you to do that. Narlow's mama won't hold still for having that fine physician on the place. The way she carried on when I brought him out there to take a look at an infected boil on her backside was an utter disgrace. Called him all manner of names, a pervert wanting to take a gander at an innocent woman's behind. Besides, I'd be ashamed to face the man."

"Papa, I think that I can . . ."

"You think you can do what, son?"

My mind raced back to my days with Na-Tu-Che-Puy. One night, a man brought in his brother who had been shot in the leg many days earlier. Na-Tu searched his medicine bag, brought out a stem of yarrow, broke it in half. Shoved it deep in the wound. Stuffed cottonwood punk in and around it. Took up an ember from Can See Far's cook fire, placed it on the punk, blew on it. It caught fire. Na-Tu pressed the flames to distinguish them. We had to hold the man down while Na-Tu continued to blow on the smoldering yarrow. He had to be certain that it burned its entire length. Not just the surface. Down deep in the tissue, the source of the infection.

"Papa, I still have the medicine bag that Na-Tu-Che-Puy gave me. Still carry it in my saddlebag out of habit, reverence for that sainted man. It contains yarrow, cottonwood punk, things that Na-Tu used to treat infection. I saw him treat the People with it on several occasions, many of those he treated had severe infection, gangrenous, puss and corruption far worse than your wound. If you like, I could—"

"So what are you waiting for? Besides, we don't have much choice, now do we? Get to it, boy!"

Fernando Valdez fashioned a travois behind his pony for Papa's long, rough ride home. We kept to the sandy bottom of North Arroyo to ease Papa's ordeal, stopping often to rest him and Fernando's pony.

209

Coot got down on his haunches by Papa, handed him his canteen. "Here, Uncle Abe. Take a long pull on this canteen. Sorry we don't have any *mezcal*."

Papa reached up with his good hand, and grabbed a fistful of Coot's coat sleeve. "I've a good mind to get up off this travois and tan your hide. You know that, don't you, boy?"

Coot grinned. "How's that, Uncle Abe. Were we too rough on you last evening?"

"*I'll say*. Narlow told you to hold me when he was setting fire to my innards. What did you do? You sat on my chest! About choked me for air. And, I'll tell you this, and you best hear me—when we get to my place, you need to get in Traveler's water trough and tend to your privates."

Mama's welcome held no surprises, went on a ranting rage, the stench of the yellow bile of her irascible temperament whelmed over me. Cussed me, blamed me, glared at Coot, ignored Fernando Valdez . . . until Papa spoke.

"*Hush up*, woman. Get these men something to eat. *Be quick about it.*"

29

January 15, 1882

Coot and I went back out to check on our patient, see what he wanted to do about finding the money-man and his two hired killers, Homer and Mo. Papa was sitting on a stump in the middle of the corral, soaking in the sun, talking to Traveler, sporting a beat-up, but otherwise new Stetson.

Coot hollered out, "Hey, Uncle Abe. Looks like you've just about worn out that new hat that your no-count son gave you for Christmas."

Papa laughed. "Fernando Valdez found my present hanging on a mesquite halfway up Anthony's Nose. Little beat up, but brand-spanking-new as far as I'm concerned." He flashed me a smile. "One of a kind, the way I see it. Thank you for the thought, son. Mighty generous of you."

"How you feeling, Papa?"

He scooted around on his stump. "This warm sun feels mighty good on it, keeps me from getting too stiff and sore. Your mama keeps it rubbed down with axle grease, so I'm thinking I'll be fit as a fiddle soon. Your cure for my gunshot wound may not have felt too good while it was burning in that hole in my shoulder, but it worked miracles. Never did swell or fester. I saw you boys coming a ways off, wondered what you were up to—besides checking on me. Bet you're eager to get after those ignorant men who shot me. That about right?"

"Yes, sir. That's about it."

"Well, forget about it, boys. You've got more important kettles of fish to fry. Besides, Fernando Valdez and I've talked it over. We'll handle those gentlemen in due time, never fear."

"Uncle Abe, you said that you heard the money-man's name, but couldn't make it out, a strange, but somehow familiar name. Did you ever recall his name?"

Papa smiled, sighed. "Strange name all right. Similar to my granddaddy's given name—Zachariah. But, like I said, Fernando and I'll take care of those gents, so don't give it another never-mind."

"Papa, don't you think we should at least report those men's attempt on your life to the El Paso County Sheriff? Let the New Mexico Territory marshal know about it so he can be on the lookout?"

"Son, you know what that would accomplish? Suppose the sheriff or marshal should capture three *desperados*, bring them to see me, hear my accusations against them. What do you suppose would be the outcome of that four-way battle of I-said-they-said? Nothing. Absolutely *nothing*. Only now, the law knows of my anger toward those assassins. If something untoward should happen to them, on purpose or accident, who do you think those lawmen will visit first? Manacle *whose* wrists and ankles, and send *who* off to Huntsville or Leavenworth? What do you suppose would be the outcome?"

***

February 10, 1882
El Paso, Four Days Before Papa's Sixtieth Birthday

I threw my horse's reins over the hitch rail in front of the post office, stepped inside the cool, shaded building, an old, converted adobe, and greeted the postmistress.

"Mornin', Narlow," Miss Patricia Diaz said. "My, my, this place's about covered by with Montgomerys this morning." She laughed, winked. "Bunch'a no-counts, that's what I say about 'em."

"Well now, aren't you full of yourself, Lil' Miss Patricia? But besides *this* Montgomery, what other Montgomery are you talking about? The only other Montgomery in a hundred miles of El Paso is Papa Abe Montgomery."

She laughed. "One in the same. He came in here last week, asking whether I knew a certain feller. I told him I did, that he'd showed up a few of months ago. Wealthy, I have to think. Word got around that he was buying up every piece of vacant land, building, hotel, and laundry he could get his hands on. He's smart. El Paso's already can brag of upwards of a 1,000 citizens. When I mentioned all that to your papa, his eyes got big as teacups, turned to Fernando Valdez, smiled and winked. Then your papa asked me if I knew of a new lawyer in town, a Mr. Michael McNameriz. I told him that I did, that his office was just down the street. He thanked me kindly, then left."

She handed me my mail. "Then wonder of wonders. Your papa showed up again this morning, which I thought mighty strange. He usually comes in every two or three months for his mail. But this time, he was carrying one of those lawyer-looking files, a big envelope-looking thing. I believe they call it a brief. He asked me where he might find this Mr. Zacharackary, the same man he asked about the week before. I told him where he could be found, and without even a thank-you-ma'am, your papa turned on his heels, took off with Fernando Valdez hot on his heels. Not more'n three minutes ago."

"He was? Which way did he go? Who'd you say was the man he asked about?"

"A man by the name of Zacharackary. Samuel T. Zacharackary, to be post-of-fice-exact. Owns a lot of properties around this old dusty town—but I think I already told you that. He's just opened a church down on Second Street. Nice man. Then, danged if he didn't come in here just yesterday, invited me to . . ."

I ran back out, almost slipped in the pig slop, jumped on my horse, turned him south down Stanton Street, encouraging him along. I pulled him up short when we got down to Second, look west, didn't spot anything looking like a church, but when I turned back east, there it was—a brightly painted green building with a stee-ple, a white sign above the entrance: "A Peaceful Repose Awaits All Sinners Behind This Sacred Door. Church Of The Unclean Who Seek Redemption." I ran around another sty of pigs, up the stairs to the porch, and through the entrance. Papa stood at the far side wall, the business end of his double-barrel, 10-gauge shotgun stuck at the throat of a man I could only conclude was Samuel T. Zacharackary. Fernando Valdez stood next to Papa, his machete raised above his head, two *bandeleros* of cartridges slung across his chest. I didn't move, leaned against the doorframe, and listened, for there was not one blessed thing I could do to change the outcome of this interview.

"*Listen here, you.* Why'd you send those highwaymen after me, Homer and Mo? *Don't lie to me!* While I was laying in a pool of my own blood, I heard them say they'd shot the wrong man, said they needed to go tell some man or other with a strange name what happened. *You*, Mr. Samuel T. Zacharackary, are that man with the strange name, and *I'm* here to guarantee *you* they, for a fact, shot the wrong man!"

"Oh—oh, you must be Mr. Montgomery. Mr. Abe Montgomery, I believe."

The Right Reverend Samuel T. Zacharackary's eyes appeared as two bowls of orangy-red *menudo* left over from yesterday's breakfast hangover, his head resting on the end of a categorically cocked twin-barrel shotgun.

"Well, answer me, you shiftless skunk, before I send you to meet your Maker! Separate your evil head from your fat ass. Fool with me, *just once,* and I shall send this gentleman standing before you, *Senor* Fernando Valdez, across that wooden bridge down the street into Mexico. He'll be back in less than fifteen-minutes with his eight brothers, *Los Asesinos.* They'll make short work of a skunk like you, relish every second of chopping you up into 10,000 pieces to feed the pigs out front of this house of godless ill-repute."

"Well, Mr. Montgomery, I—I wish you would put that weapon—"

Papa crammed the shotgun deeper in his craw.

"Yes, Mr. Montgomery, uh, please, let me explain. I—I came here from Denver where I—where I had a similar establishment. I mean I had a church, and other business endeavors. Then two months ago, I receive a post from a young man from that fair city demanding money. I suppose you might call it hush-money, $5,000 worth of ransom. If I refused, he would go to the local newspaper and disclose the nature of my, uh, business dealings in Denver. Well, what was I to do? I agreed to—"

"What kind of business dealings? Pimping? Whorehouse?"

"Well, uh—yes, something on that order. I agreed to pay him, told him that I would send a man with the money, and would meet him south of Las Cruces, New Mexico Territory on the river road, detailing that he should ride his mount up a certain dry *arroyo* that was marked by a white pointer-sign, turning toward the mountain, to the east. I have not heard from him since, but obviously Homer and

Mo believed you to be the man from Denver. An honest mistake, I assure you, a mistake that—that can be rectified by that same $5,000, payable to you. To you, *of course*. If you will allow me, I shall take pen-in-hand and make out a draft in your name *this very instant*. I assure you that I have more than sufficient funds in the El Paso Bank to cover that amount. That way, we can forget this entire matter and go our separate ways. How does that sound to you, Mr. Montgomery? And, uh, of course, you as well, *Senor* Valdez?"

"Where are those two worthless lizards you hired to do me in? Homer and Mo. Where are they this very minute?"

"Oh, I can assure you that when we learned your identity, they left town on the very next train. They heard about you in the Occidental Saloon, about you and the menfolk in your noted family, about you fighting at Shiloh, in the Indian Wars, scouting for the Blue Coats. The Montgomerys are legendary, and you should be honorably proud—"

"Listen here, you. Folks in this town know I'm hard to rile, never curse or use the Lord's name in vain, but we didn't come in here to listen to one of your sermons, or listen to your choir sing my family's praises. We came in here to explain to you what we've decided to do with your sorry ass. Whether to scattered your brains all over the inside this bordello, or chop you into a gazillion pieces to feed the pigs milling around outside, to 'hide the body,' so to speak."

He turned to Fernando. "What do you think we should do with this snake, Fernando Valdez?"

Fernando rushed the reverend, got up in his face, spit, rubbed his face with his gnarled fist, raised his machete high above, and with great zeal, brought the blade crashing down swift as a viper next to his head, close to kissing his right ear, crashing through the clapboard wall.

The reverend melted to the floor. Out cold. Cold as the underbelly of one of the alligators recently introduced to El Paso's Public Square.

Papa picked up a large spittoon sitting against the wall, peered into the partially filled vessel, peed in it, handed it to Fernando Valdez, who did likewise, then splashed the still-prostrate reverend in the face with the yellow and brown contents of the spittoon. He came up spitting and cursing, using the Lord's name in vain—the same Lord he claimed to be saving souls for in his Temple of Repose.

"On your feet! *Up against that wall.*" Papa jammed his side-by-side up against the reverend's Adams apple, and the interview commenced once again. "Now, listen up, Skunk. Here's what you're going to do—*today*." Papa shoved a single sheet of legal-size paper under the reverend's nose. "Read this, *out loud*. Loud enough so the pigeons in the loft can hear every syllable."

The reverend retrieved his reading glasses from his vest, adjusted them, began to read:

"I, Samuel T. Zacharackary, having been previously funded with $100,000 of Mr. Abe Montgomery's and *Senor* Fernando Valdez's hard-earned money, do hereby promise to repay that princely sum in the following manner: I will, this very day, deliver $5,000 in cash money, to the newly founded El Paso Orphanage on St. Vrain Street, El Paso, Texas, for which I will receive a written receipt, and deliver same to the aforesaid Mr. Montgomery and *Senor* Valdez, via US Postal Service, General Delivery, El Paso, Texas. Furthermore, I agree to deliver one-hundred dollars on the Friday of each week to the same orphanage, and deliver their handwritten receipt to the aforementioned gentlemen as provided above. I will continue to deliver that same amount to the orphanage until the entire $100,000 balance is repaid in full at three percent per annum."

Papa shoved the note under Zacharackary's, nose. "See that?"

"But, Mr. Montgomery, surely sir, you must recall that I did not borrow $100,000 from you and at that annual rate, it would take me over thirty years to repay that amount and this cannot be a legal docu "

"Twenty-eight years is the number. Not legal, huh? Who's your lawyer? What's his name?"

"Well, I—I don't have a lawyer, as such. I deal in real estate often and do not require the services of a lawyer."

"Got a fool for a client, huh?" Papa jabbed the reverend in the gut. "And, yes you sure as hell *did* borrow that money, borrowed it in an *arroyo* forty-odd-miles north of here, *on my own damn land*. I'll grant that you're something of a mathematical genius, but as to the question of this note's legality, I'll wager that my lawyer is better than yours. Read on, Reverend Zacharackary."

"Where was I? Oh, yes. I further agree to place all of my real estate holdings as collateral for this indebtedness, and to place all future acquisitions as collateral, to be filed of record in the El Paso County Clerk's Office, to be held there until the entire principal and interest of this demand note is paid in full.

Signed and Witnessed in the presence of those Witnesses who affix their signatures below, this 10th day of February, 1882.

Samuel T. Zacharackary

Witness: _____

Papa jammed the shotgun hard up the man's throat, got up in his face, smiled. "Did I miss anything? Do you understand me, *Senor* Tobacco Juice?"

"Yes, sir! Perfectly. I—I understand *perfectly*, and will commence *immediately* to make amends as soon as that shotgun is removed from my neck."

"Good. You wait right here while I go out on the street and find us two upstanding citizens to witness your skunk-scratch. In the meantime, *Senor* Fernando Valdez and his machete and 45-70 will keep you company. Wash your face and hands so they don't spoil my finely crafted demand note."

Papa walked past me at the door, and stopped. "Oh, good morning, son. Been here long?"

30

March 26, 1882
Coot's 23ʳᵈ Birthday

It was Coot's custom to drop by my office on his birthday. Mine was on the thirty-first, so we always celebrated both of them on his day. We'd walk across the wooden bridge to El Paso, Chihuahua, have a toddy and lunch at *Café Central*.

"I dropped by your folk's place on the way to town. If I don't go by to see Uncle Abe on my birthday, he gives me grief the rest of the year. We jawed awhile, your mama tending her cauldron as usual. Narlow, I swear your papa's going to have to buy her a new black pot before long. I don't recall ever going by there that she wasn't feeding mesquite limbs to her fire, stirring whatever she's got in that pot with her long-handled cedar ladle. The woman's a study."

I laughed. "How's Papa feeling? I'll never rid myself of Reverend Zacharackary's image when Papa and Fernando Valdez cornered him. You missed something special."

"Your papa's healing just fine, stout as ever. I wouldn't want those two wolverines after my ass. Anyway, Uncle Abe wants us to pay him a visit, says he and Fernando Valdez have something special for our birthdays. Wants us to stay over a few days, camp again up near Anthony's Nose at *Campo Azul*. He grinned wide when he said that we were in for a mighty big surprise."

As we rode up Utah Street to my house, Coot asked, "Think Sophie will throw a fit for you being gone for a few days?" He winced, sorry for the question. I didn't reply.

Sophie's response to my announcement that I'd be gone two or three days was a *se le vie* if I ever witnessed it. "Of course, Narlow, have a grand outing. I've been wanting to invite some of my lady-friends over for an overnight encounter. We've been studying night and day dreams, and their effect on marital bliss. This will provide us with an opportunity to delve deeply into the subject."

On the ride to Papa's place, I chuckled aloud when I thought about her last sentence. Would I ever ever delve deeply into Sophie's "subject?"

We rode up, Coot pointed to Mama, grinned, as she stood with her back to us, stirring whatever she was mixing or warting in that cauldron with her cedar ladle. We sat our horses, waiting for our welcome we knew would never come.

Papa gave a whistle from his shed past the corrals. He was tending the billows at his forge, great showers of orange sparks, red flames showering up in the late afternoon sky.

Every time I saw Papa at his forge, I was reminded of the Apache's belief that a man working iron is a witch, possessed of the Spirit of Iron, *Pesh-Chidin*. He was pounding out iron shoes for his big mules.

"Papa, you're getting around like a man who wasn't shot less than three months ago."

"Afternoon, boys. Glad to rest these tired old eyes on the likes of you. Light yourselves down, take a load off. Tomorrow's a day you've waited for your entire lives. Oh, I know, you didn't know you were waiting for a blessed thing, but..."

He gazed off at Mama at her black pot, laughed. "Well, maybe you've been waiting a spell for the missus to show her face, say howdy when you ride up." He shrugged, gave the handle on the billows a pull, then stepped out into the open evening air. "Like I was saying, tomorrow's going to be a special day for you boys. Fernando Valdez and I will see to it. He's gone off to *Campo Azul*, dragging in firewood, logs to sit ourselves down, discuss a matter or two." He winked. "Might even take a pull or three on a jug of *mezcal* he's totting."

He sniffed the air, looked at the dark clouds building over the Organ Mountains. "Hope you boys brought along some warm bedding. I believe we're in for a storm. Maybe an inch or two of snow while we're up there."

Coot grinned. "Kinda late for snow, isn't it, Uncle Abe?"

"I recall it snowed a foot the first of May the year you boys were born—foaled, as Uncle Doyl would say."

We followed his gaze up to the Nose of the peak to the northeast. "You boys recall me clutching a leather pouch when you dragged me out of that cave at *Campo Azul*?" We assured him that we remembered.

"That's our surprise—mine and Fernando's. We'll get an early start in the morning."

***

Fernando Valdez was always a happy man, difficult to rile, but stand back if his mood clabbered. From the time we stepped out of our saddles at the same place Papa was shot, Fernando had a broad smile on his craggy face, a grin as wide as a wagon track.

"What's so funny, Fernando?" Coot asked.

Fernando's grin vanished, a scowl replacing it for a moment, then back to his grin. "I am just—how you say? *Happy*, yes, happy, very happy to see *Senor* Coot Boldt. *Es todo, Senor, es todo.*"

Coot laughed. "I don't believe a word you're saying. You've spent so much time on this mountain with these nannies, you're getting to favor an old billy goat."

It started to snow just after noon, and by 4 the ground was covered with three inches of white fluff.

Coot said, "Uncle Abe, your weather gauge needs adjusting. You said it *might* snow an inch or two, and I don't see any let-up in that cloud bank."

We strung a rope across our camp area and covered it with Papa's oilcloth.

Long about early evening, we threw a couple of mesquite logs on Fernando's fire, sat around sipping *mezcal* from his jug, jawing and hurrahing each other. Fernando took a *cigarro* from inside his vest, rolled it around in his mouth, licked it, held it out in front of him, put a burning twig to the end of it, twirled the *cigarro* until it smoldered, then flamed. He snuffed the flame, then sat puffing, great swirls of gray, ropy smoke circling his *sombrero*. It was their ritual, and true to all great ceremonies, Papa stuffed tobacco in his briar, tamped it to his satisfaction, held another flaming twig above the bowl, squinting down his nose and pipe stem at the flame burning downward as he sucked it to life. The two of them had nursed a tobacco patch in a *bosque* close to the *Rio*, surrounded by cottonwoods and *tornillos*. Friends and passerbys alike new of it, helped themselves, but only after watering the thirsty plants, pulling weeds, tidying up.

Papa smiled all around, pointed over his shoulder with his pipe stem. "Son, do you ever recall the times when we'd sneak off and camp out in the nostril of Anthony's Nose up there where my little gold mine was? Remember, you were just a little shaver on our first trip. We'd camp, play all manner of games in that cave. Play war games, read about famous wars back 4,000 years. We'd make stick soldiers, a sawhorse, everything imaginable out of sticks and twine. That, and feed sacks stuffed with straw that served as our generals and those of our contrived enemies. We played like little kids do. Fernando Valdez was in on it. You probably thought we were nuts, playing with you like that. Remember those days?"

I laughed. "Sure I do, Papa, but I never thought you were crazy. I liked it. I remember—"

"Son, that's the first happy look I've seen on your face in over a year. I've shivered at the sight of you, like . . . like something lonesome passes through your soul to mine. That smile looks good on you. Work on it. You're far too young to be sporting that careworn look on your face. Maybe you'll rekindle that gladsome way about you of your youth, the jocund lad I knew. Narlow, don't—"

"Like I was going to say—"

"You've developed an intolerable habit of interrupting me, something you would never do just a couple of years ago. As I was in the process of saying, don't let the yesterdays of your recent youth push past you and grab the promises of all your tomorrows. Narlow, I hope you think on that." He smiled. "Now as you were saying before I interrupted you . . ."

"Forgive me, Papa. Sometimes I don't listen, hate it when I'm disrespectful to you. But I can still recall, remember one time up there in that cave, you were Xenophon, and I was Cyrus, the would-be king. We led our army of cutthroats over 1,500 miles, I went chasing off Cyrus' brother, and you had to lead that ragtag army home through snowdrifts, fought hunger all the way back. Boy, Papa, that was sure fun for me, a ragtag myself, otherwise I would have spent my entire youth dodging Mama, chasing nannies, and cleaning out Coot's Mama's water ditches."

Coot grinned, shoved a burning limb back in the fire. "For all the ditch-cleaning you ever did on that farm, you couldn't water a thirsty watermelon vine."

Papa reached behind him, threw a leather pouch in my lap. "Remember that, Narlow? I recall you boys trying to pull it out of my grasp when you first pulled me out of that cave up there. Just after you covered me with Fernando's *sarape*. Maybe the contents of that pouch will put another smile on your face." He grinned. "Well, aren't you curious what's inside? Open it up, boy."

219

I untied the leather thongs that held the top of the pouch tight. The pouch was cracked, worn. I pulled back the top of the pouch, peered inside . . . gold.

I handed it to Coot. "*Woooeee*, Uncle Abe. What do we have here?"

"Looks like gold to me. Pecan and pea-size nuggets mixed in with in a sandy sea of yellow dust."

I grinned up at Papa. "That's what you found in that cave? Reckon it's pure stuff?"

"I'd say it will essay out as the genuine item. Old, yes, but recall that all gold is old. God's not making any more of the stuff."

"Papa, what do you suppose that sack is worth? What's gold worth these days anyway?"

"Same thing it's been worth since back in the 1820s. The government set the value at twenty-dollars-sixty-seven-cents an ounce. When I heft that pouch, I'd judge it to be a hint over ten-pounds. One-hundred-sixty ounces. Almost $3,000 in gold in that pouch. That's a lot of greenbacks no matter how you count it."

We all sat there, passing the pouch around, first one, then the other, enjoying the feel of ten pounds of gold.

Papa said, "I had to push that pouch aside when I first entered that cave." He chuckled. "That is, *after* I inched passed that skeleton and his bedding companion."

Coot asked, "Who do you suppose stashed that pouch in the cave? Robbers? Gold miners?"

"I have my suspicions, even a story I'll relate in awhile. If you boys took a good look at that skeleton and skull that's guarding the entrance of the cave, you'd only come to one conclusion. It's not the bones of a full-grown man or woman. Arm and leg bones are too short, the teeth in the skull shows nearly a full set of ivories, a little worn, but still in place, like those of a young person. Probably killed there, the man who did the killing left him there thinking dern few men dare to get that close to a skeleton, much less crawl on his belly around one.

"As to the identity of the possessor of those bones, that's anyone's guess, but I'd wager he was the traveling companion of a German man who walked through here in the late Seventeenth Century. When Coot's daddy and I were just little shavers, our menfolk told us a tale that their ancestors first heard when they came to this country They purchased their ranch and home from Felix Madrid back in 1819. All the lava and sandhill country west of La Mesa, San Benito, Santo Tomas. That country had been owned by the Madrid family since before 1650, close to the old *Camino Real* trail from Mexico City, on up north to Santa Fe. But the recent coming of the Atchison-Topeka Railroad put an end to that hard road. Anyway, *Senor* Madrid told our granddaddies that his grandfather, four-times removed, a German-born man by the name of Bernard Gruber came to his place on top of that lava mesa in 1670, accompanied only by an Indian boy. Slave most likely, leading a single stout burro. Seems Mr. Gruber had been arrested and jailed by Santa Fe mission priests, charged with heresy and witchcraft and theft of the church's gold. The German and the Indian boy escaped, made it down the *Camino Real* to a place now known as *Aleman* in his honor, little place just fifty miles north of here. Got themselves attacked by Apaches. Word got back to Santa Fe that the man and boy had been killed. End of story for the missionary priests, but they weren't dead, as *Senor* Madrid's ancestors could attest.

"Mr. Gruber was in a hurry to be on his way, but he was in sore need of rest, get himself and his burro back in condition to travel. Everyday, he thought he was strong enough to go on, and every day, he and his Indian slave boy packed the burro, but every day they unpacked the animal, too weak to go on. The Madrid family told of the German man packing his burro with nine leather pouches, unpacking them and laying them on the ground in a row. Every night, he and the slave boy lay down beside them, covered themselves with their *sarapes*, and slept.

"The routine repeated until early one morning, the Madrid family found a large gold nugget in a tin plate at their front door. They watched the man, boy, and loaded burro trudging off across the valley floor toward the rising sun, headed for the mountain pass south of the range named by Juan de Onate, "*Sierra de los Organos*," just north of a promontory called, *Nariz de Santo Antonio*."

I glanced up at the peak above, showing itself swirling in the snow with the moon beyond as a hallowed cathedral. "Saint Anthony's Nose."

"So, Uncle Abe, you think there's a good possibility that it was Bernard Gruber who hid that pouch of gold in the cave up there?"

"Well, I wasn't ready to say that with any certainty, then Fernando and I took a closer look at the cave the other day. We left the cave and its contents untouched." He tossed a candle to Coot. "Why don't you boys go take a look for yourselves."

We crawled up the slippery rock slope, crawled by the skeleton, lit the candle to make certain that the cave's guardian was coiled in his nest, then inched through the opening of the cave. Coot held the candle while I looked and felt around.

"*Coot*. Look! Another leather pouch. One, two, three . . . Coot, there's *eight* of them!"

We gazed at the stack, laughed at the wonder we caught in each other's eyes in the candlelight.

"Come on, Narlow, let's gather them up and get back to the fire."

When we walked up, carrying four heavy leather pouches apiece, Papa and Fernando were grinning like cats caught in a cream barrel. "Happy birthday, boys! Fernando's and my present to the two of you. Don't know of any two more deserving boys on God's good earth. Sit yourselves down and let's take a look."

"But, Uncle Abe, I can't take any part of this gold. Didn't do a blessed thing to deserve it. Give it to Narlow, he's your son. Besides, you gave me Uncle Doyl's gold when I was sixteen years old. Remember that?"

"Sure I do, boy. But that was between you and your Uncle Doyl. Hadn't a thing to do with me or Fernando Valdez. You didn't squander a dime of it, bought your mother's farm, making a show place out of it, make your daddy mighty proud. Besides, it's not your place to refuse a gift like this anyway."

"But, Uncle—"

"Coot, my son, before your daddy died, long, *long* before that sad day, he and I made an agreement, a solemn pact. If something happened to your daddy or me, the other would look after the other's son, take him as his own. I took you for my own, treated you as such. I hope when you reflect on those years, that you'll agree that I kept my promise to your daddy."

"Of course you did, Uncle Abe, but—"

"Papa, what Coot's trying to say is we don't know *what* to say. We know you won't let us refuse it. It's not your way, nor is it the way of Fernando Valdez. But—but, why don't you and him take at least half of all this stuff. Coot and I don't need it all. Worth . . . by your calculations, it's worth nearly $30,000. That's a fortune!"

"You're mighty right about that. More money than any five men could ever expect to earn in a lifetime."

Coot said, "Uncle Abe, don't we have an obligation to try to find the rightful owner of this gold. Like running an advertisement in the paper—something like that?"

"Well, we could, but you'd be swamped with men from all over the country trying to lay claim to it. Wouldn't do a bit of good, just stir up a bunch of unwarranted trouble for yourselves. Far as I'm concerned, it's been there for three centuries, might belong to either Bernard Gruber's heirs or maybe the *padres* of Santa Fe. Who am I to say? Who are they, or *anybody* to lay claim to it? I asked the lawyer about it,

222

recommends we just let sleeping dogs snooze, don't take it to the bank stirring up curiosity, besides, it's safer right where it is than Fort Knox."

Here Coot and I sat with two men in possession of a fortune in gold, smoking hand-rolled cigarros, stuffing a handmade briar with rough tobacco they'd grown in a sandy bosque. I gazed at them in complete wonderment, as if knowing them for the first time.

Fernando Valdes filled our cups, sat, threw another mesquite limb on the fire. "*Senores, mi amigos*, what are you going to do with all those golds? *Mucho dinero, eh?*"

Coot and I glanced at each other across the fire, unable to express our surprise, helpless to go against Papa's and Fernando's wish.

"Boys, we understand your reluctance, but Fernando and I have talked it over, thought long and hard on the subject. We're firm. We don't want it, have no use for the stuff."

Coot's gaze shot up. "You don't have any use for *nine sacks of gold*? A fortune enough for as many men?"

Papa sighed, began explaining that they didn't know what to do with it, how they'd gotten along without for all these years, and . . .

My mind was racing—two older men, sitting around a campfire burning mesquite limbs that one of them spent an entire day gathering. Papa was all I had as a boy, all I had except Fernando, a man who had no boy of his own, taking me for his own, bouncing me on his knee, squeezing me, loving me, taking delight in his *amigo's* treasure. Papa'd been wearing the same britches and boots for as long as I could remember. Fernando'd been patching the same *sombrero* for years, wearing the same *huaraches* so long they'd grown a part of him. He grubbed at a strata of coal in the far hills, loaded it on his burro, and presented it to Papa for fuel for his forge to make his own horse and mule shoes, hardware for his gear. Papa'd sewn countless soles on his old boots. Fernando was a man who saved three-feet of twine from a gift, carefully folded a four-foot-square of cheap brown paper for tomorrow's use. And they asked, *What would we do with it?* Say they had no use for this gold. I just didn't underst . . .

Papa turned to Fernando. "*Mi amigo*, suppose I was to sell my entire herd of goats, gave you half the proceeds, say $1,000, and half of these pouches of gold. What would you do tomorrow morning, and all the rest of your tomorrows that God grants you?"

Fernando stirred the fire, gazed up at the drifting snow. "*Aye, Senor* Abe. *Yo no se.* Maybe so . . ." He chuckled, his dark eyes widened. "All our years together, you read me your books, all those great speeches and wars, all the history of the world. You teach me to write what the books say . . . you say you write what you read, you rememberize it. I write those words. You were right. I feel those words . . . feel those words crawl up my arm like . . . like little mouses . . . feel them go in my head." He patted his chest. "Feel some of those words go here. You and me, we talk about what you read, what we write, what we rememberize while we sit at our fire . . . a fire like this one."

He sat quietly, so long I thought he'd had his say. Papa waited.

"*Pero, Senor* Abe, you ask me what I do you sell you goats, give me all that money, all those golds. *Ha!* Maybe so I find the man you sell your goats, buy them back, take you to help me with *mis chivas.*" They laughed. "You bring you books to Sonora, read those words, we write them down, keep them for all our time. Maybe so we start a school at my village. Maybe so I find a cave somewhere, bury the golds there. *Quien sabe, amigo.*"

Papa smiled, turned to Coot and me, let Fernando Valdez's words soak.

"You see, boys, you're sharing a fire, your supper, Fernando's jug of *mezcal*, with two men who are living their lives the best they know how. We're faithful to ourselves, to each other. We'd lay down our very lives for each other. Something we both know in our hearts, yet never discussed. Fernando has no place to go, no family except for the three of us here. I can't leave your mother. She's my wife, your mother, and I'll not break our vows. Fact of the matter is, boys, I'm like Fernando Valdez. I have no other place to go. A priest by the name of Father Vessels married your mother and me. He said something that's stuck with me all these years—he was impressing upon us the necessity to enjoy life as God gave it to us, to laugh, dance, to sing, to work hard, but not in excess. Another thing that old *padre* said that's stuck with me to this day, 'What you don't have, you don't need.'"

Papa stood, pushed up against the tarpaulin to relieve it from the weight of the wet snow. "If a man set out to spend every cent of this gold, this pestilence, he'd find himself now possessed, *jailed* by a fine house, golden carriages, fine clothes, all the trappings of the rich. But, he'll soon learn that he cannot leave all that wealth unattended. Why, shoot, someone's liable to steal his jailers!"

He laughed. "And, yes, it's true, Fernando and I do sleep with ants, flies, lice, and scorpions, but you know what, boys? This country's first President slept with bed bugs, as did every President since then. Queen Victoria slept last night with their cousins. The richest people around the world, living in their chalets, their finely

224

appointed hotels and Park Avenue apartments, all share the same bedfellows—bed bugs."

Papa squatted, threw a stone in the fire, watched the sparks rise, orange, snapping as they rose in the wet snow. He chuckled. "*Humph!* You boys ever try to wear two pair of boots at once? Don't need that stuff, that gold. Simply stated, we're not equipped to handle it."

Fernando filled our cups with the remnants of his jug, stood, saluted Papa with his cup held high. "*Senor* Abe Montgomery *y* Fernando Valdez, for the rest of our days, we sleep with *hormigas, moscos, piojos, escorpiones.* Maybe so *una vibora.* When we roll over in our flimsy blankets, maybe so we will listen to them shake their *castanetas* like that big one up there at the cave."

31

El Paso, January 1883

Coot stayed on at his farm, came to town a couple of times a month for supplies. Occasionally, he'd have supper with Sophie and me, but mostly, just stop by for coffee or a whiskey. Coot and I were drinking coffee in my office one morning when Clem "Back Slap" Wallace came in, a friendly old gent. He ranched a big place forty miles west of El Paso on the US/Mexico border known as the Camel Mountain Ranch, so named for a big black lava mountain that straddled the border, looked very much like a lazy camel lying down out there in the sand.

"Narlow," Clem said, "I want you to keep your ears peeled for some Yankee-dude that's crazy enough to buy my spread. Ranch, cattle, house, barns, the whole shebang. Know anybody that's got a few *pesos* in his pocket looking for a prime, well-watered, desert ranch?"

Coot asked, "What are you asking for it, Clem?"

He scooted his chair around, glared up at Coot. "Why you askin', Coot? You want to take up ranching? Can't lose enough money farming, eh? Thinkin' about doubling up on your losses with a big desert ranch, are you?"

"That depends on how much it will cost me to get into the double-starving business."

"I want $20,000 for the whole shebang. Cash money. None of this dollar down and a dollar a month for the rest of my life."

Coot and I knew his place to be a high-desert ranch with good water and grass and browse in the hills and arroyos. Clem's cattle were always in good shape and brought top dollar.

"That's a fair enough price, Clem," Coot said, "but it's too rich for my blood."

"Clem, what about if Coot and I partnered up?" I asked. "What if we could scrape together $10,000 today and gave you the other $10,000 in six months?"

"Nope, $20,000 *cash* on the barrel-head. That's final."

I said, "Tell you what, Clem, it would take you and me a year, maybe two, to find some Yankee-dude to buy your place. So the time element is not going to cost you one red cent. You know Coot and me—we always do what we say we'll do."

The old gent glared at me. "Have you gone plumb deaf, boy? Or, do you just like to hear your tongue twaddle?"

"You sure have him pegged, Clem," Coot said. "He does like to wag his tongue. But let me ask you something. What if we give you the $10,000 *right now* like Narlow offered, another $10,000 in six months, and an *additional* $10,000 at the end of the first year?"

Clem stood, his gnarly fists planted on my desk. "Why hell, boy, that's $30,000. That's $10,000 more'n I want for the damned old place. You reckon you boys could handle that? Then I can go on off to Los Angeles, get me a woman, buy myself a place overlooking that big ol' blue bay, sit myself down on the porch with my woman, a jug, and do absolutely nothing? You boys can do that, you reckon?"

"Coot, maybe we should think this over. Remember, Sophie and I just got married, and I probably should—"

"You got *married*, you didn't quit living."

He turned to Clem. "You'll have to give us twenty-four hours to come up with the balance, but we can give you $6,000 today. We'll have your other $4,000 tomorrow, and if we don't perform to your satisfaction, you keep our $6,000. Deal?"

"Deal."

"Narlow, write out a check out of our joint account, payable to Mr. Clem Wallace. We'll walk him over to the El Paso Bank and see that he doesn't have a problem getting his cash."

It didn't make much sense to me to pay $10,000 more for something than what the man wanted, but I shrugged, and we shook hands on it.

✳✳✳

We headed for Papa's place, intent on explaining our sudden need for a dab of that gold stashed in that cave at the base of Anthony's Nose near *Campo Azul*.

Papa grinned when we told him about our plan. "Well, it sure didn't take you boys long to find a use for that stuff that you were so hell-bent on refusing. But you needn't come asking Fernando's or my permission for buying that ranch or a bag of horehound candy." He chuckled. "Remember that, Coot? Narlow never did develop a hankering for that delicacy."

Next stop, the cave at *Campo Azul*.

I asked, "How much of that gold will we need to take back to cover the $4,000 we owe Clem? A little over a full pouch?"

"Yeah, but we might as well take two full bags in case something else comes up that we need ready access to it."

Clem came by early the next morning, looking for his cash money. I pulled out a deed form and filled in the blanks, and suggested that Michael McNameriz be named trustee to hold the deed until we performed as promised. He had just been elected county judge, fine, upstanding, curly-headed citizen.

Clem stroked his chin. "*Hmm*. Well, Narlow, I don't know nothing about no trustee holdin' my deed, but I reckon it sounds like a real pregnant idea."

We gave Clem $4,000 in gold, he signed over his deed and a bill of sale for his stock.

"Boys, I'm gonna get me a jug and head for the train station and buy me a ticket to Los Angeles."

Coot said, "Well, dang, Clem, aren't you going back out there to gather up your things? You can stay on as long as you like."

"No, son, I *don't* like. Don't like it worth a damn. What I do like is the thought of that pretty little gal, that jug of fine bourbon whiskey, and the view of that crashing blue water in the Los Angeles bay from the top of that high hill, all just a'waitin' for handsome me."

We put Clem on the westbound train. I turned to my new ranch partner. "Where in hell do you suppose we'll get $10,000 in six short months? Can I ask you that, *partner*? We can't be going back to our stash to bail us out of every raw deal we make. It'll soon be gone, and that's not something either of us want to face. Coot, have you gone daft?"

"Stick with me, Narlow. I'll have you passing wind through silk underdrawers in no time. That place is worth twice as much as we're paying for it."

"Yeah, if Clem doesn't call our note in six months." The realization of our commitment sunk deep in my gut, the thought of our $10,000 taking wing. We already swore a pact that we'd never use a dime of that gold to bail us out of a blessed thing we got ourselves into.

"Narlow, let me tell you what will happen in the next six months. There are over 300 head on that ranch. Mostly mamma cows. They'll be dropping their calves pretty quick now, they'll be just about be weaned when that $10,000 is due. Some of those mammas are getting a little long in the tooth. We'll sell off 200 of those older mammas, some of the yearlings and then we'll—"

"*Whoa.* Hold up there, Coot. What the hell are you talking about? We can't sell what we don't own."

"Who says we don't own every damn cow and jackrabbit on that place? Hell, we've got a bill of sale to prove it!"

"We're going to pay Clem off from the sale of his own damn cows?"

Coot crossed his arms, glared for a minute, stuck his finger on the end of my nose. "Narlow, let me remind you of something. It's Clem, *not us,* that's in such a rush to get to Los Angeles, that jug, and that pretty little gal. Who the hell are we to deprive an old man his lifelong desire? Besides, who else would buy the place?"

We packed enough gear and groceries to last us a week, led our horses up the gangplank, and loaded them into a cattle car. The new Southern Pacific line ran just north of the Camel Ranch, and the train would cover the forty-miles in just two hours. Clem had a bunch of cowhands, and Coot wanted to see if any of them were worth their keep.

We rode through the overhead entrance to Clem's, "Need More Ranch." The only thing in sight was Clem's old blue-tick hound, who came out from under the front porch, stretched, scratched his ear with vigor, licked his ass, then flopped back in his shade. Not a cowhand in sight. We rode around the ranch in a big five-mile sweep. The cows and grass were in good shape, all the water tanks were full. A few pasture fences were down, but generally we congratulated ourselves on our purchase and new partnership. We decided that the first thing we'd do was pipe the water from a free-flowing spring to every dry area of the Camel.

When we returned to the ranch house we still had not seen a soul. We sat on the front porch scratching Clem's blue tick, when right at sunset a lone Mexican *vaquero* came riding in from the north. He appeared to be around fifty years old.

We introduced ourselves, and he said his name was Jeraldo Valenzuela. Coot explained to Jeraldo that we were the new owners of the Camel Ranch, that *Senor* Clem Wallace had caught a train for Los Angeles.

Jeraldo laughed. "*Aye*, for many years I work for *Senor* Wallace. I come to *Senor* Wallace when I was eighteen years old, all of those years he talk about selling his *rancho* and going to California. To sit on a hill and look at the big blue water. I am glad he sell. Happy you buy Camel Ranch—*muy buen rancho*. Never did *Senor* Wallace have too many cows to eat too much the grass. You buy very good *rancho*, senores—*muy buen rancho*."

I asked, "Jeraldo, where are the other *vaqueros?*"

He laughed, pointed over his shoulder. "Oh, they go to Mexico. To Palomas, just across the border west of here. They go there every time *Senor* Wallace he go to El Paso. The *vaqueros*, they get very drunk. They go with the foreman of this *rancho*, *Senor* Otis Sanders. They come back when *Senor* Wallace comes back from El Paso, and he send me to Palomas to bring them back every time. Take many days before they can work. *Muy borracho, senores. Muy borracho.*"

Coot said, "Jeraldo, you must know this *rancho* better than any man. Do you know other *vaqueros* who will work for you on this *rancho?*"

His head jerked back, eyes wide as saucers. "Work for me, *senor?* Why do you ask me that question?"

"Because, Jeraldo, you are the new foreman of the Camel Ranch, you will need many *vaqueros* to help you."

"But what of *Senor* Otis Sanders and his *vaqueros, senor?*"

"*Senor* Sanders and his men don't work for the Camel any more, Jeraldo."

"Oh, *Senor* Boldt, Otis Sanders very bad man when he is mad. When he is drunk he is very bad man—*muy mal hombre*. I work for him—it is better that way—it is okay, *senor.*"

"Well, Jeraldo, it is not okay with me and *Senor* Montgomery. We live in El Paso, and that's forty miles from this *rancho*. We'll be needing a man we can depend on to tend our cattle, this *rancho*. We can't depend on Otis Sanders and his bunch. Tomorrow, *manana*, you go find ten or twelve *vaqueros* that you can depend on."

He rolled his eyes, shrugged. "*Pero senor es imposible. Senor* Otis Sanders, he has twenty men—sometimes he has twenty-five, thirty men. We cannot do all the work with only ten or twelve men. Besides, *Senor* Sanders will not let me have his job."

"Otis Sanders doesn't have a vote here, Jeraldo. Only three men vote on the

Camel Ranch – me, Senor Montgomery, and you, Jeraldo Valenzuela. Your job tomorrow is to get some *vaqueros* you can depend on. We'll pay them top wages, and you, my friend, can depend on that. Our job is to tend to *Senor* Otis Sanders and see that he doesn't give you any trouble."

The next morning, I was sitting on the porch drinking coffee. Coot came out, walked to the barn, saddled up, and came out of the barn leading another horse. "Come on."

"Where we going?"

"We're going to Palomas. Get shut of Otis Sanders and his men. I don't want them back here harassing Jeraldo when he gets back with his *vaqueros*."

We crossed a line in the sand, the border where the *Rio Grande* doesn't flow, and found *Senor* Otis Sanders and his gang in the first dingy, dark, smoke-filled, puke-hole-*cantina* we came to. A red-headed man sat with his boots cocked up on a table, his chair leaning against the wall on its back legs. We figured the *gringo* was Otis Sanders. Several men were lying on the floor, on the bar, on the several pool tables.

We made our way to the bar and Coot asked the bartender, "Where can we find Otis Sanders?"

The bartender pointed over at the red-headed *gringo* sitting at the table.

Coot walked over to him. "Otis Sanders?"

The man ignored Coot.

"*Otis Sanders?*"

He looked up, his eyes matching his red hair, and mustache-yellow marks of throw-up caked on his shirt. "Yeah, who's asking?"

"The new owners of Camel Ranch are asking."

"Your ass, shit hole."

Coot swept his boot under Otis's chair. He went sprawling. Every man in the *cantina* took on airs of instant sobriety. On their feet, groggy, bristling, ready for a fight. Otis tried to pull his sidearm as he stood, but Coot's own revolver was out, the end of the barrel pointing at close proximity to the end of Otis' snout.

"Now, boys, just rest easy!" Coot shouted. "You need to know that this man at my side is Narlow Montgomery. Wouldn't surprise me if you haven't heard of him. He's quarter Apache, quarter Comanche, the other half is purebred mean-ass side-winder. Been known to dance with thousand-pound grizzlies, drill holes in boulders with his eyes, so you best watch yourselves. I recommend you not rile him.

"Now, as I was about to explain before Mr. Sanders began swearing, Mr.

Montgomery and I are the new owners of the Camel Ranch. Bought it two days ago from Clem Wallace. We rode all the way over here to save you boys the trouble of going back to our ranch. You see, boys, we have our own *vaqueros*, and won't be needing your services. We don't want any trouble. As long as you stay off our ranch, there won't be any. *However*, let me warn you, you step *one foot* on that ranch again, Mr. Montgomery will drill your shirts full of holes, shoot you deader'n a pile of porcupines if he catches you in daylight. If he catches you at night, it'll go far worse for you. He'll tie you to a fence post, skin you like a polecat. If you require proof of his skill as a cat skinner, just step forward, be my guest. He's always looking for practice. He's a mild-mannered sorta feller, but looks are deceiving, believe-you-me."

Coot cocked his head over to the side as if making room for the devil on his shoulder, grinned, then motioned with his revolver for the redheaded man to get up.

Otis got on all fours, then stumbled to his feet. "Mister, you can't just kick us off that ranch. You gotta give us a chance to go back and get our gear. Besides, how do we know you own the Camel? Where's old man Wallace?"

"Well, as to the location of Mr. Clem Wallace, I'd judge right about now he's halfway to Los Angeles. As to our proving our ownership of the Camel, that may be a little harder to prove to your satisfaction. But we're not here to prove a damn thing to you or anybody else. As far as your crap back there in the bunkhouse goes, that worn-out shit stacked up and sold to the highest bidder wouldn't bring two-bits. But if we have your solemn word that you'll stay the hell off our property, we'll give you each a twenty-dollar gold piece, and throw your horses and saddles in to boot.

"What'll it be, gents? Twenty dollars and your mounts and gear, or face up to Narlow Montgomery. I want your answer, and I want it *right now.*"

The men stood looking around, first at each other, then at Otis Sanders, then Coot, then me. I opened my vest, exposed my Schofield in its cross-holster, tried to snarl. They held their tongue.

"Good. Then we understand each other," Coot said. He walked to the door, turned as he holstered his revolver. "Narlow Montgomery, watch your temper now. No cause to maim or kill any of these boys. Pay them their twenty-dollar gold pieces so we can get on back to the ranch."

Coot was already back on the American side of the border before I caught up with him. "Coot, you're going to get me killed pulling that kind of crap. You know that don't you?"

"Don't know any such thing. You obviously scared hell out of them. But I confess that I damn near snickered when you showed them that old cannon you carry."

We stayed on with Jeraldo Valenzuela for ten days, working alongside him and his *vaqueros*. His men were hard-working, and soon learned exactly what we wanted, what we expected in the way of care for our animals.

Every passing day had me worrying about Sophie, me, gnashing about my extended absence, so much longer than the day or two that I expected. I shrugged it off, telling myself that I would dedicate exactly twice of my wasted time worrying about Sophie as she exhausted on me.

32

El Paso
February, 1883

Coot banged through our kitchen screen door off the alley, plopped himself down at the table. "Morn'n, Sophie."

"Good morning to you! Would you like some coffee? Narlow made some earlier, but I'm afraid it's burned by now. Would you care to make another pot? I'm embarrassed to admit that I still simply cannot boil coffee without making a complete mess of the kitchen. And, alas, this is Miss Wanda's day off."

"Thanks, don't need any. Where's Narlow? We've got important business with Rodolfo Bustamonte in Sierra Blanca. He's waiting for us."

I came in from the living room. "Oh, it's you. Didn't hear you knock when you came in. Married folks need their privacy."

Sophie blushed. Coot laughed.

"What's this about meeting Rodolfo in Sierra Blanca? What's he got on his mind?"

"Don't know. He just sent word asking that we pay him a visit at the Sierra Blanca jerkwater. Something about the Southern Pacific needing water."

"What's that got to do with us?"

"Don't know. Get your hat. I've already saddled your sorrel. We can catch the noon eastbound."

"Coot, things are moving along too fast for my taste. We need to settle back, let things settle, sift down, see how we do with the Camel. Rodolfo most likely has something up his sleeve to help us get rich. I say we're already well on our way in that regard, and I have more on my plate at my office to handle without taking on something else. And I have Sophie to worry about, and—"

"Oh, Narlow, dearest, don't worry about me. I'll be just fine. You men run along now. I have my Lady's Club to occupy my time."

✳✳✳

Rodolfo met our train at the jerkwater stop. No train station, just a dirt loading dock on the siding, and a jerkwater tower—dry. Sierra Blanca jerkwater—two inhabitants, if you don't count jackrabbits and horn toads, all bone-dry and thirsty.

"Gentlemen, I want to explain the problem my friends at the S.P. and the G. H. Rail companies are experiencing here. Their lines extend from the east, west to El Paso and beyond to California. Their water west, from halfway to El Paso and east past Van Horn, has dried up. When they brought their rail through this country, they were assured good water in unlimited supplies, and at first, that was the case. Now, what little water their wells produce is brackish, smells of sulfur. Their steam locomotives must have clean water—a *tremendous* amount of water."

I kicked a rock, grinned. "Rodolfo, you're sure right about those locomotives sucking up a lot of water, wells have gone sour because of the drought, but what's that got to do with us?"

He smiled. "Oh, my friends, what does that have to do with you? I was so impressed with the water system you improved on your Camel Mountain Ranch. A wonderful ranch with some of the best graze available in the southwest. No matter how severe this drought turns out to be, or those in the future, your ranch will never go without a dependable source of water. You found fresh spring water near the top of that red mountain, and successfully watered the entire 60,000-acres without the aid of a single pump or windmill. All gravity flow. You strung pipe to every remote section, much to the delight of your fat and sassy Longhorn cattle. You know water, and my friends with the railroad need that knowledge. They'll pay handsomely for your services."

Coot turned to the south. "Tell your friends to drill a well on the slopes of that pile of rocks over there—Eagle Mountain. Solve their problem in no time at all."

"They've tried that, but were unable to find water. They drilled over fifty dry holes at a tremendous expense. I believe you have the means to solve that problem." He smiled. "Unorthodox means, perhaps, but means and methods that will circumvent their problem."

Coot grinned. "You mean witching for water?"

"Precisely. I informed them of the process, but they just scoffed at that silly notion. I asked them if they would like me to pursue their problem with you gentlemen. They were immediately agreeable. I am in a position to offer you, on SP's behalf, a twenty-thousand-dollar fee if you can install a jerkwater station halfway between El Paso and where we stand, and another at Van Horn, and fill them with adequate and reliable water. They will promptly pay all costs. The fee is yours when your project is completed. However, the project must be completed by the end of May."

I whistled. "Twenty-thousand simoleons, huh? Rodolfo, that's an awful lot of money for four months work. Hardly seems legal."

He laughed. "That's the way it is with big corporations these days. But you must consider that they have millions invested in this line, and without reliable water, their entire enterprise is at risk. Your fee is a paltry amount for solving their immediate problem."

I turned to Coot. "Less than four months. Think we can get that done?"

"Not if we stand around out here watching you scratch your ass in the heat, moaning about being paid too much."

∗∗∗

We hired Old Man Lawrence, and had him scurrying over Eagle Mountain before the next evening. "Wondrous Wand" Lawrence was the best in the witcher trade, and we placed so much confidence in him that we ordered 150-miles of three-inch pipe and had it offloaded in stacks along the railroad's right-of-way. Our blacksmith-friend, Big George, put us onto an ancient ditch-digger machine in Sweetwater.

I thought Coot had lost his senses when he showed up the following week in a raging sandstorm, the ditch digger on a flatcar. The digger appeared as a twenty-foot high, double-masted ocean-going vessel, plowing through the waterless waves of west Texas sand.

"Narlow, take a gander at this. The old man who sold this contraption to me is a certifiable genius. He made certain additions to this thing, including the installation of an auxiliary steam engine to propel it, *and* a steering mechanism. Pretty slick, huh?"

The thing was monstrous, filling the entire length of a rail flatcar. A gangway circled the entire contraption, fifteen-feet in the air without guardrails. Eighteen-inch drive sprockets lined each side, two-inch-wide chains led from one to the other, all manner of pulleys and belts propelled this gadget and that widget. It towered over any locomotive I'd ever seen.

We fired both boilers, waited for them to build up steam. Coot grinned when she was ready to go, steered it off the flatcar onto the loading dock. It creaked and groaned, moving with the gate of a dying elephant, lumbering along on its six, eight-foot-diameter iron wheels with paws for traction, swaying from side to side, sighing, belching, teetering, stretching up in the sand-filled air. When it got on level ground, Coot turned it paralleling the rail track, stood on a foot-pedal, pulled down a lever, and the giant wheel of the digger began clawing at the earth with its circular row of buckets, dumping their loads on a side-facing conveyor belt, inching, grinding, clawing, heaving when it hit a boulder, shook till it dislodged whatever was deterring its progress, then lumbered on, never wavering from its assigned task, throwing great mounds of dirt to the side as it made its way along the track, digging a ditch two-feet wide, six-feet deep.

Coot jumped off the ditcher, beat the dust off his britches with his Stetson, smiled. "Pretty wide hole for a three-inch pipe, but too wide is better than too thin. Let's go see how Wondrous Wand's doing. See if he's found any promise of water."

We found the old white-haired gent on the east-facing slopes of Eagle Mountain. "Now, gol-dang it, fellers, I was just about to give up the ghost on this pile of no-count boulders, but about that time, my willer stick commenced to begin to jump and dive in my hands, 'bout to knock me to the ground. I got a'holt of myself, walked back to where I started the run to be certain of it, and shor' 'nough, that willer limb got the heeby-jeevies onct all over'n again. Right over yonree, next to that sorry looking piss-elm tree. Poke yor hole rat next to it. There's water down there, lots of it, five-thousand gallons an hour. Sweet, pure water. I'd say right at two-hundred feet. Gor-an-tee!"

He belched, lifted a leg, eased one off. "You boys'll have to put a big windmill on that hole. Get yorselves at least a twenty-foot mill. Maybe bigger. 'Nd, you'll be needin' a holding tank next to it. A big'un. Say 50,000 gallons or so. Bein' on this mountain, thet'll build up a bunch of pressure, push that water a thousand miles in both directions. Water under pressure is mighty hard to deny. See you, boys." He turned and started down the mountain.

Coot hollered out, "Hey, Wondrous Wand, what do we owe you?"

He shouted, waved over his shoulder. "More'n you kin afford. I'll send you a bill. But rat now, I need to get to town. Stop by the Gem Saloon, sit on my slat-skinny ass for a week, soak up some suds. Quit this shit. Too damn old for this crap no-how."

We were in business.

33

We set up our headquarters at the base of Eagle Mountain, equipped with a chuck wagon and two Chinese cooks, a brother and sister combination, Bo and Liling Wang. Best dern cooks on either side of the Pacific. They, along with their older brother and parents, had come to the US for work offered by the railroads to build their roads east from California, and decided to stay on. While Bo and Liling tended to our culinary needs, the other three members of the Wang family were working on a rail crew taking a spur south of Sierra Blanca to the Mexican border.

Coot hired a crew of ten men, starved dryland farmers caught in the drought. They were eager for work, anxious about their women and little ones, willing to work seven days a week, sun-to-sun, can-to-cain't. One of their number was in possession of a .22-rifle and a pocketful of ammunition. Before dawn, we could rely on him to bring in any number of cottontails, maybe a javelin or two, possum, and an occasional mule deer. One of the crew said it was impossible to kill a deer with such a small rifle, but laughed, agreed saying it "shor' tastes like deer." Fresh meat was always a welcome addition to the fare. Those well-fed men laid pipe faster than five mules could drag the pipe to them.

Our two young Chinese siblings serve as cooks and fetchers, also more than eager to work, anxious about their younger brother and elderly parents working on a rail line south to the Chihuahua border as their mother was not well.

We bought groceries by the carload, cooked to perfection, served in style and grace by Bo and Liling. Our pipe crew thought they'd died and gone off to the Happy Land of the Dryland Farmer.

I couldn't shake the thought of Sophie, a lady with a weak constitution, unhealthy, susceptible to about everything imaginable, real or imagined, heavy on the latter. I caught the late afternoon train back to El Paso every two days, spent a couple of nights at home, picked up supplies in town, and headed back to Sierra Blanca for another two days. Wanda, our housekeeper, took care of the house, *everything* at the house, so Sophie had no chores to do, fact is, *nothing* to do, real or imagined, except her Lady's Club. A condition that seemed to suite her, while it rubbed my ass raw as a fresh-peeled onion.

The day after we started laying pipe, one of the workers suggested that we string the pipe along the edge of the ditch, screw them together, then lower a quarter-mile section in like the oil field workers do. He went on to say that it was not uncommon for them to do that in mile-long sections, but their pipe had much thicker walls and could handle the stain.

Coot said, "That sounds like a damn good idea. Get that sweaty job done up in the cooler air, not down in that sultry, dirty ditch. Probably double our progress." He smiled. "Sir, what's your name?"

"Julio Limon, *senor*."

Coot chuckled. "July Lemon, huh?" The man grinned.

"Well, tell you what we're going to do, Julio. We're going to name Julio Limon the head swamper of this outfit. You're the boss man. Let's go to work. What do you say you get these men a'poppin'?"

***

In three weeks' time, Julio Limon had that pipeline dug and buried to within five-miles of the main railroad track, averaging over two miles a day.

Often times, late at night when the wind was right, I could hear the rumbling of a train, almost hear the clatter of dominoes as its steel wheels passed over unforgiving rails, its whistle as Thoreau described it, was, 'the scream of the locomotive's whistle being like that of a red-tail hawk.' When it passed the dry Sierra Blanca jerkwater, I recalled Papa telling Coot and me, "Boys, the train is coming, and soon there won't be one farmer or goat herder in a hundred that could tell time by the noon sun, or the position of the Big Dipper, relying solely on that whistle. They'd all learned train time." He scolded us to go off to the university, warning us that only those who prepared themselves could keep up with folks from back east who'd come by the trainload to take what we were not capable of defending or possessing.

***

At our noon break, a buggy came roaring out of the desert from the north, in the direction of the rail we were headed for. The driver didn't slow his rig until he almost overran our camp, sharing a generous sprinkling of sand on our meal. He stepped down.

Coot said, "In a hurry, mister?"

"Who's in charge here?" our smartly attired guest inquired. He stepped out of the buggy, dusted his pinstripe suit, wiped the tops of his lace shoes on the back of his pants leg.

"Who's asking?" my lifelong shabbily dressed friend asked.

"Mr. Nathaniel G. Gosselin is asking, *that's who*. Railroad detective for the Southern Pacific Rail Road, *that's who*. Who might be in charge of this motley outfit? Bunch of no-count greasy Met-si-kins, a handful of ne'r-do-well white-trash boys, and looky there, will you? A goddamn black buck-nigger, eating at the same table with white folks."

Coot glanced my way, waved his hand at his side, telling me to settle down. "Well, you might say that I'm in command here, or you can address your business to that man seated over there under that tent. The one with the Porfirio Diaz *be-gote*, wearing the big black Stetson. Might want to doff your hat when you make his acquaintance, assuming, that is, that you wish to conduct your business with Mr. Narlow Montgomery. You see, he's an ornery cuss, quick to slap leather, usually shoots first, talks later. *Much* later." Coot's smile was quiet. "If at all."

Our guest turned to the crew who had not even looked up, still wolfing down their meal.

"I'm Mr. Gosselin, railroad detective for the SP Railroad, and I'm here to ask a simple question, an inquiry that had better be answered *truthfully*, and *without delay*. That question is, do you have any Chinese workers on this crew? *Any at all?*"

The crew continued their wolfing.

I eased around in my chair to see if Bo and Liling were anywhere to be seen, but they seemed to have vanished. I didn't know what they obviously knew, but I thought I best intervene before things got nasty between our smartly attired guest and my shabbily dressed *amigo*.

I stepped out from under the canopy, wiped my mouth with the linen cloth the siblings had provided for that use. Ignoring his earlier statement, I said, "I'm Narlow Montgomery. What can I do for you?"

"You heard what I said about my asking if any Chinese coolies are working for you here. *Well?*"

"You say, Chinese coolies. What's that? I've heard of cooties, you know those pesky little bugs. Loose slang for body louse, but I don't believe I'm familiar with those coolie critters you mentioned. What do they look like?"

He started to stammer, looked me over, his gaze turned to Coot, my friend, dirty, grimy, sand-blasted, dressed for work manhandling a steam-powered ditcher, wearing the silliest grin I ever witnessed. I turned aside to keep from guffawing right there in our guest's face.

"Uh . . . uh, what does what look like? A cootie? I have no idea. I am speaking of coolies. Chinese goddamn *coolies*. Surely, you must have heard—"

"Oh, you're talking about those Chinese bedbug things I've heard-tell of. Naw, we don't have any of them around here. Say, mister, you being a detective and all—do you carry a gun? A revolver under your coat? I do."

I pulled back my jacket so he could get a good look at the hunk of iron I always wore in my shoulder holster-rig, squared around to him. "That's a Schofield 44-40, put a hole in a man's gut you can slide a pie plate through. Man you've been talking to in such an ungentlemanly manner, has a .45 Army Colt stuck in his belt at his back. You need to know that I've got a bee up my ass in the form of an uncooperative woman, putting me in a sour mood, a don't-give-a-damn frame of mind. You say you're a railroad detective, likely carrying a firearm yourself. Show me your gun, Mr. . . . what is it, Mr. Gosling, isn't it?"

"Yes—er, no."

"Which is it, Mr. Gosling? That's not your name or, yes, you do have a gun?"

He peered around as though one of our crew might come to his rescue. "I have . . . I have a .32 revolver on my person."

I laughed. "Mr. Gosling, let's get back to your business at hand. Exactly what were you in such hot pursuit of? Were you chasing someone when you skidded your rig into our campsite, throwing dust all over the place, ruining my plate of rabbit stew? Or were you just out for a Tuesday morning ride in the desert chasing cooties?"

"I . . . I wanted to know if you have any Chinese workers in your employ."

"Not that it's any of your goddamn business, but, no, we don't—no coolies, cooties, or Yaqui warriors, as you can see. Just ordinary, often hard to abide, dryland dirt farmers, and Mr. Coot Boldt and me. You may have heard of him—famous Apache tracker. Me, I'm just a mean-ass Apache medicineman—do things like sticking needles in dolls that look like a certain man . . . like the likes of you. But why are you so interest in the Chinese variety? I've only met one or two of them, seemed like real nice folks to me."

He leaned back in his high-top laced shoes, jammed his thumbs in his vest pockets, cocked his head to the side. "Because the Chinese Exclusion Act is in effect, and I, *personally*, aim to rid this country of the vermin. It is my mission to inform the entire southwest of that law, and run every damn one of those yellow, slant-eyed, pan-faced bastards out of the country."

I raised my hand to give him what-for, but Coot stepped up. "Mr. Gosling, have you—"

"Gosselin! *Not* Gosling!"

"Oh, beg your pardon. Mr. Gosling, but have you checked with your superiors regarding the work we're doing for your railroad? Are you aware that your locomotives don't have enough water to get them from Van Horn to fifty-miles west of here to El Paso? And, are you aware that their trains are presently carrying their own water with them, weight that could otherwise be used for billable freight? Have you checked on that, Mr. Gosling? Do you think your superiors would look kindly on anyone slowing our progress, impeding our effort to provide their expensive locomotives with water for their boilers?"

"Well, no, I . . . I must say I have not. But that has no bearing on—"

"Mr. Gosling, you've outstayed your welcome. Get back in that buggy, turn it back to the north where you came from, and get your ass out of our sight before I unleash the likes of a known *desperado* in the form of Narlow Montgomery on your popgun-totting ass!"

34

After the detective beat his hasty retreat, Bo and Liling suddenly reappeared from the brush.

Coot asked, "What's all this talk about the Chinese Exclusion Act? You must know something about it or you wouldn't have run off and hidden. What do you know? What are you afraid of?"

Bo wiped his brow with one of his linen napkins. "We don't know much about it. Our people are confused, some believing we will all be sent back to China, others believing that we will not be done so, just no more Chinese will be accepted into your country. We know of some who have paid large bribes so they will not be returned to China. We just do not know."

I said, "Coot, Rodolfo's due back out here tomorrow, needs to report back to the rail companies on our progress. I'd bet he's familiar with that Exclusion Law, and if not, he can find out for us. In the meantime, let's keep a sharp eye out for Mr. Gosling, or some of other henchmen, keep Bo and Liling close around their cook tent. Rodolfo's also bringing along a special guest to help you with that ditcher. It's wearing on you."

***

Rodolfo stepped off the early train, IB Crane close behind.

Coot hollered out, "Hey, IB, glad to see you. Come all this way to lend us a hand?"

"Shor' done thet, Coot. Narlow says I can hep ya with yor ditcher. Says you can be my relief driver."

Coot shot me a glance, chuckled, filled Rodolfo in on what the train detective said yesterday. "So that's the story, Rodolfo. We've never heard of this Chinese Exclusion Act, and Bo and Liling say their people are confused about it. Ever heard about it?"

Rodolfo turned to the two best cooks and fetchers in Texas. "I can assure you that neither you nor your people who are presently working or residing in America today, have a thing to worry yourselves over. It's your family and friends back in your home country who are to be troubled. The Act precludes any further Chinese migration into the US. No more may enter legally. That is all. You may be *certain* of that fact. It does *not* address those Chinese who are already here. No one will be deported as long as they remain law-abiding citizens. *No one.*"

***

IB worked out pretty well on the ditcher. Of course, the first time he took the controls, he dug the first quarter-mile dern near straight, then got to wandering across the desert in the wrong direction. When we caught up with him, his head was in his lap, sawing logs. Coot threw a dirt clod at him to jolt him out of his slumber, a repose so intense that it took IB a full minute to realize what had happened and pushed the steam-engine control lever out of gear. He got the message of how dangerous that thirty-ton ditcher is when Coot explained what that revolving wheel with all those buckets dumping their load on the conveyor belt would do to his innards, told him we didn't have time to take his bloody remains to town for a proper burial, have to burn him up and strew his dust over the desert floor.

35

Sierra Blanca Jerkwater
April 20, 1883

On the fifteenth, we wired Rodolfo that we would be finished with our project any day now, and would like for him to come check it out for the rail companies. Not wishing to take advantage of our friendship, we wanted him to be in a firsthand position to assure them that the work was completed in a workmanlike manner, that the water was flowing as promised, and that their jerkwater towers would shortly be overflowing.

Rodolfo gazed around, pointing at the jerkwater tower, water lapping over its edge. "My, my, gentlemen. Your commission is complete. Water spilling over the jerkwater fifty-miles to the west of here, the same at Van Horn, just as promised. Not to mention that you are over six weeks ahead of your scheduled commitment. I shall immediately have your fee wired to your El Paso Bank account. Congratulations, my friends."

Coot said, "Thanks, Rodolfo. We performed as you knew we would. We kept our promise to both you and the railroads, so maybe you can help us out on a little problem that we seem to be inheriting, as you're likely to have the answers. As usual of late, Narlow's reluctant to stick our noses in someone's else's business, but I say we'll see that they get back to China safe and sound."

I said, "Rodolfo, or problem concerns our Chinese employees, Bo and Liling, mainly their aged parents. Their mother is approaching eighty, but to look at her, you'd swear she's no where near sixty. The railroad doctor at *Ojo Caliente*, a little settlement down near the *Rio Grande*, has diagnosed the lady with something they can't even pronounce, says she has less than six months to live."

"I'm sorry to hear that. Sometimes people from other parts of the world are susceptible to diseases that give us no concern. How may I be of service to you and that dear lady?"

"She and her husband were brought here last week by their youngest son with the idea of putting them on a train to Los Angeles where they can buy passage on an ocean-going vessel. The old couple has every dime they've been able to scrimp and save over the seven years they've been in America. One-thousand-one-hundred-dollars-twelve-cents. That includes Bo's and Liling's earnings as well. Coot and I are of a mind to pitch in some of the fee that you're depositing for us to help them along. Do you have any idea how much the fare would be for the two elder Wangs to board an ocean-going ship from Los Angeles?"

"I can find out precisely the amount, but I can tell you that they would be ill-advised to consider leaving for China from the port at Los Angeles. The train does not even go near that small village of possibly two-hundred people, mainly *pobres* from Mexico. Ships do drop anchor off the shore, their meager cargo offloaded onto small rowing vessels, and brought to shore. No passenger service is available that I am aware of, and I certainly would not entrust those folks to any captain that agreed to take them to China . . . or anywhere else, for that matter."

"So, where do they have—"

"San Francisco. Several hundred miles up the coast, and that fair city is also served by rail. That's where this very line began, and their ocean-going shipping network is unexcelled. I have an associate who owned a mail freighting company, sailed the seas for thirty-years, but he sold his vast enterprise for a fortune just last year. I still hear from him from time to time. I believe he still lives in San Francisco."

Coot said, "So, if they can get safely to San Francisco, your friend might be able to arrange passage for them to China. Is that right?"

"My dear friend, your use of the term 'safely' is the key to that statement. Does this elderly couple speak English? Spanish?"

"Not a word in either language. We've eaten with them, laughed with them, pointed, made gestures, but if none of the siblings are around, hardly anything is communicated."

"*Hmm.* That's too bad. There are thieves, pickpockets, and conmen all over the globe. There will undoubtedly be conmen on those sailing ships, and you can be assured there will be more than a few on their long train ride. Thieves gravitate to traveling folks, especially the elderly, the poor, and those who are ignorant of the language and our customs. From what I have heard from very reliable sources, I can almost assure you that they will not arrive in San Francisco with their hard-earned $1,100.12, much less their homeland. Almost guarantee it."

My glance in Coot's direction told me all I needed to know. "Aw, shit, Rodolfo. Sorry for the foul tongue, also sorry I asked."

36

"Narlow, darling, please believe me. I will be perfectly all right during your absence. San Francisco will be good for you. You're tired, need rest, a vacation is in order for you. Besides, Miss Wanda is here to take care of my every need. The Lady's Club annual meeting is set for the fourth of the month." She glanced at the hall calendar. "Oh, my goodness! That's *next week*, and I have an important part in the program, a part for which I have not prepared sufficiently. Oh, whatever shall I do? *Goodness me*. I must get Miss Wanda to take me down to the clubhouse to retrieve my papers. Oh, how utterly embarrassing!"

With that, she was calling for Miss Wanda to hitch-up the buggy.

I started to pour myself a stiff one. The Lady's Club was four blocks from here and she was having Miss Wanda hitch up the buggy. I took a pull on the bottle, put it back in the cupboard, mounted up and went down to the Gem Saloon. I overstayed my welcome, got in a cussing match with the new banker in town, slapped him around a little, and was rather unceremoniously asked to leave the premises by the barkeep, Fred Cates, and old running-mate of mine and Coot.

"Sure, Fred, I'll run along." I took two steps, turned, and flattened El Paso's newest moneychanger on the sawdust-strewn floor of one of the town's oldest gin mills.

***

Coot came out of the train station ticket office, turned and walked toward me. I was peering up at a pointer sign that read: "San Francisco—1,295 Smooth Carefree Miles."

Coot asked, "Here's your ticket. Was Sophie all right with you traipsing off to San Francisco?"

I grabbed the ticket, stuffed it in my pocket, and headed for the Pullman.

He caught up with me. "Narlow, I heard about you pounding on that new banker in town. You're getting quite a reputation for yourself. Mean hard-ass, know that?"

I boarded the car, found our compartment, dropped my valise on the floor, and went back out on the gangway, looking for Bo and Liling and their elderly parents. We found the four of them seated on the back steps of the train station.

I said, "*Bo, Liling!* What the hell are you doing sitting back here with your parents? Do you have their luggage? Are they ready to go? Do they have their money?"

Coot said, "Don't worry, folks. Narlow's just uneasy. His new bride's upset that he's leaving again so soon. Blushing bride, you know."

They smiled, nodded.

We ushered the Wangs to their Pullman sleeping quarters, taking Bo and Liling with us to see that their parents understood everything that needed an explanation, warned them again to stay in their quarters and not leave without one of us escorting them. To lock their door, and open it for no one. My instructions were stern, but I didn't want any misunderstanding as to my intent. "We will inform the porter that we will pull down your beds every night. Do not open your door for anyone claiming to be a porter. We will escort you to the dining car when it is time to take your meals. Do not leave your quarters for any purpose. Keep your money on you at all times. Mr. Wang, you keep one-half of the money, Mrs. Wang, you keep the other half secured in your clothes." Bo translated, the Wangs smiled.

Satisfied the Wangs understood the seriousness of our rules, Coot and I retired to the smoking and beverage car.

I said, "This trip's going to be longer than we bargained for. Know that?"

"Aw, you worry too much. The Wangs will be just fine. You'll see. And go easy on those old folks. Not like you to be so abrasive like that."

Coot was edgy, something on his mind. In a minute, he said, "Narlow, let me ask you something. Whatever happened to that friend of mine who was so full of action and promise? A man who now appears to not want a damn thing but to remain as you are at this very minute for all time. Your inertia is not static, but it's damn certain plodding on a straight line to destruction. *Utter* destruction, unless you change course. If you don't change it, I will."

"Don't try it."

Coot's hands shot up. "Don't try it, he says, like he's talking to a complete stranger. Narlow, do you ever listen to yourself? Ever hear how hollow words have become over the past many months? You threaten every yahoo you meet, then yesterday, you knocked that young banker senseless. Now, it's me you're threaten-

245

ing. Next it'll be Uncle Abe. You're verging on being a disgrace to the Montgomery name. Taking a dump on our grandfather's good names, our daddies as well. My daddy and your papa! El Paso's already got its share of murdering scallywags, and you don't need to be adding to their number. Maybe this long trip to San Francisco will give you time to think things through, get your head on straight and out of your ass, come to grips with your problem with Sophie. Not much you can do about her, but there's plenty you can do about yourself. Like paying a visit on Miss Ana, pay your respects for the loss of her stupid husband, for squaring off with that kid who just rode in from Pecos, looking to making a name for himself. Just drop by, take the little lady a little bouquet of posies, offer your sincere condolences, tell her that you'll be checking on her from time to time. After a while, she'll encourage your visits, might even be susceptible to an occasional little kissy."

***

It was supper time when we crossed into the Arizona Territory at Stein's Pass. Coot found me in the smoking car, sipping another whiskey. We gathered up the Wangs, got them seated in the dining car, watched them eat with the chopsticks that suddenly appeared from their coat sleeves, laughed at our inability to communicate a blessed word, observed their awe at the passing landscape that changed with every turn of the locomotive's eight-foot drivers.

Mr. Wang produced a pencil and paper, slid it across the table to me, motioning for me to write something, *what* I had no clue. They both spoke with their hands, pointing back and forth between us, their intense gazes coming to rest on the paper.

"Oh, you mean our names!" They smiled, nodded with vigor.

I pushed my bar glass aside, spoke as I wrote, first pointing to Coot. "This is Coot Boldt. We've been friends since we were very little boys, born in 1859 within five days of one another. Our fathers were also close friends." I pointed the pencil at me. "I am Narlow Montgomery."

Their bright black eyes swept across the paper in front of them, attempting to cipher my hen scratch, sounding out our names, glanced up, laughed. They talked between themselves, then he pushed the paper back to me, both of them encouraging me to write, again, *what* I hadn't a clue. They made a steeple with their hands, like maybe a symbol for a house.

"Oh, you mean, where do we live? You want our mailing addresses. Is that right?" They glanced at each other, shrugged.

Again, I wrote and spoke as if they understood my every word. "I live at 1901

246

North Utah Street, El Paso, Texas, and Mr. Boldt lives on a farm northwest of El Paso near La Union, New Mexico Territory. We both get our mail at the El Paso post office. Just write General Delivery on the envelope. We'll get it."

Mr. Wang folded the paper very carefully, placed it in an inside pocket of his frock. We escorted the Wangs back to their sleeper, folded their beds down for them, wished them good night, made motions for them not to open their door for anyone.

"Narlow, let's have a nightcap in the smoker, relax before going to bed."

"Lead the way."

We ordered our drinks. I gazed out the window, wondering what the living hell I could do about Sophie. *Nothing.* Can't make love to her. Can't divorce her. Can't kill her. I took off my hat and beat it against the table. "Shit!"

"Narlow, this thing's getting the better of you. You're troubled. If you don't mind my saying so, you're—"

"I do mind."

"You're like being around a keg of dynamite with a lit fuse, ready to go off any second. Out there when that idiot train detective, Mr. Gosling, first showed up, I thought for a minute when you showed him your Schofield that you were set to shoot that bastard. That's not like you. Not at all like the man I know."

"Truth be known, you read me right about my intentions about that dumbass pecker-headed goose. He riled me, I admit. Talking down our crew, calling them white-trash, greasy Mexicans, big black buck nigger, the way he described the Chinese—yellow, pan-faced, slant-eyed bastards. If it had just been you and me out there eating rabbit stew, I'd'a dropped him, dragged him behind a mesquite and be shut of him. For *certain.* But too many innocents on the scene. Too many goddamn witnesses."

"I know. Saw it in your eyes. What are you going to do about your problem with Sophie? You were just fine the day you and she tied the knot, then it's been all downhill since then. Maybe you should take her to Dallas, see one of those head-shrinks I hear about. Maybe they—"

"Yeah, I suppose. I admit that I'm at a loss as to what to do, what to say, how to act around her. Looking back on it, I don't even know why I married her. I see now that I never really loved her. Hell, I don't even like that damn woman. Felt sorry for her, wanted a woman to love. Thought I found one. Didn't happen. Before we were married, we were close, talked a lot, shared our dreams, that sort of thing. Then, on our wedding night at the Pierce Hotel, I fumbled the key, got the door unlocked, we stepped through the opening, and it was as if our fairyland, pixie-dust-world vanished into the night air with those few steps. Nothing was the same. *Nothing.* The woman I thought I'd married did not step through that opening with me. A complete stranger. A frightened teenage girl. Could hardly speak. After an hour or so, we undressed, got in bed. I put my hand . . . just my *goddamn hand* on her *goddamn hip*. She spoke as if reading a prepared speech: 'Oh, not tonight, Narlow. Please, just hold me. *Please.* Please, Narlow, not tonight. *Please.*' I rolled over, bewildered, meekly whispered, 'Okay, Sophie. Sure, Sophie. Goodnight, Sophie.' Should'a dragged her ass out of that bed and slapped the shit out of her.

"Same every night since. One night when I thought we were making progress, I gently eased my leg over her, got on her, resting my weight on my elbows. She gagged for air, almost convulsed, saying that it hurt. *Hurt?* Hell, she still had on her goddamn nightgown, my nightshirt draped down to my ankles. Came nowhere *near* entering her. How would she know it hurt? After that, I started sleeping on the davenport in my upstairs office. That night, I tapped on the bedroom door, said, 'Goodnight, Sophie." She didn't question where I was going to sleep, what I was up to, *nothing*, just mumbled, 'Goodnight, Narlow. Thank you.'

I slammed my fist on the table, spilled our drinks. "Goddamn it, Coot, did you hear what I just said? I tapped on my own *goddamn bedroom door*! Tapped like little prince charming, instead of pounding through that door and having my way with her. And why the hell not? She's my goddamn wife isn't she? Ever since she said it hurt, I catch myself wondering if she might have experienced sex before, wondering how many 'Toms' she'd had, how many of them were laughing at me for marrying a woman wearing the white gown of virginity, wondering—"

"Narlow, you're eating yourself alive with that—"

"Damn it, don't you think I know that? Think I can't taste the bitter, bilious copper of my soul when I think those thoughts, the brassy-lead on my tongue as I mouth them? It's like how I felt when I used to think and talk about Mama all the time, what an unfathomable bitch she was to me, calling me a son-of-a-bitch, never a kind word. *Never!* Goddamn, I hate that bitch! Hate her more than I have the words to tell. I'd like to see her soul burn in—"

"Narlow, *Narlow.* You're tired, completely spent. San Francisco will be a breath of fresh air. We'll kick up our heels a bit, spend a wad of the railroad's money, have some laughs."

We ordered another round, listened to the train click-clack on into the dark night. Ordered another round, heard the bumping rumble at the far rear-end of the long line of cars, began to slow, each car humping into the one ahead. The brakes squealed, we lurched to a stop.

The porter went through the door and platform to the next car, came back in a moment. "There'll be a short delay. A crew is pulling trees off the roadway. Won't be long, folks. Relax, enjoy yourselves."

I banged my fist on the table. "Great god almighty! Coot, what the hell . . ."

Coot said, "You know, Narlow, this thing between you and Sophie keeps up, you're going to start looking around for a gal to have a relationship with. Sophie would probably welcome it, relieve her of the pressure."

"I could never do that." I slugged down my whiskey. "What kind of relationship?"

"Well, for starters, Miss Ana. Nothing serious at first. Or, you'll find a young lady, maybe even Miss Ana, some sweet little widow with a kid or two, not looking to remarry, just lonesome, consuming lonesomeness, lonesome for male companionship. That sort of thing. One night, she'll put her head on your chest, snuggle a little, like I said, maybe a little kissy or two. Then things will heat up between you and that pretty young gal, and—"

"You don't know me very well if you think that will ever happen."

37

May 6, 1883 Heading North In The Golden State

Coot strutted around our sleeper, snapped his galluses. "Well, chalk up another one on my side of the old tally-board. Right again. Where's all those boogie bears you were so certain we'd have to chase away from the Wangs? Four more hours and we'll be in San Francisco. Be there by mid-afternoon. If we hadn't had that twenty-hour delay at the washed-out bridge crossing the Colorado River, we'd'a been in San Francisco yesterday. Now, we're cutting it kinda thin before the Wang's ship is set to sail. All that worrying over the Wangs you've done was for naught. Come on, let's get some air."

Just as we were stepping out in the hall, Mr. Wang was coming out of his sleeper, turned and scurried off down the passageway.

Coot called out, "Mr. Wang! Where do you think you're going? Where's your wife?"

He turned to us, his eyes wide, pointed over his shoulder, and took off running.

We chased after him. He went through the car door, crossed the platform to the next car. When he opened the door, the reason for his fright and haste was waiting at the far end of the car—the shark-skin-suited-railroad-detective man, Mr. Gosselin holding Mrs. Wang by the arm, the finger of his other hand was busy jabbing her in the face, screaming at her to be quiet.

I rushed past Mr. Wang.

Coot yelled, "Narlow, wait! Let me—"

I hollered, "Gosling! Let go of that lady's arm?"

He turned to me, went for his revolver. I knocked it away. Reached over Mrs. Wang, grabbed him by his coat lapel, pushed to get him off balance, whirled him around, grabbed him by the seat of the pants, and hustled him through the door to the platform between the cars. He struggled to free himself, grabbed the brake wheel. I came down hard on his fist with my Schofield, kicked him off the platform, saw him bounce twice in the bar ditch before his tumbling form disappeared behind the car of the fast-moving train.

The Wangs tried to explain exactly what had happened, but their jabber had little information to impart. Best we could figure, they felt safe after so many days and hours on the train, wanted to look around, so they left their sleeper. They were soon accosted by the train detective, he flashed a gold badge at them, frightened them. He asked for money. They didn't understand. He pulled out his purse, showed them a wad of bills, stuck out his hand, motioning for them to hand it over. They shrugged, motioning that they had no money on them, but had cash in their sleeper. He spun Mr. Wang around, pushed him toward the other end of the car, motioned for him to *go!* Again showed him the wad of bills, grabbed Mrs. Wang and drew his hand like a dagger across her neck.

I started in on them. "*Goddamn it to hell.* Didn't we tell you to stay in your quarters? Warn you that there were evil men on this train. Didn't we tell you that—"

"Narlow! *That's enough.* You're scaring hell out of them. Let's go to the dining car. Feed my bear and get these folks some hot tea and a diner roll."

***

We hustled the Wangs off the train at the San Francisco train station, hired a porter to find their luggage, found a jitney-man who'd take us to the wharf for a dollar. When we got there, the driver asked the name of our ship.

"The *Madre Auxiliadora*. Great World Freight Company."

"Ah, Cap'n O'Toole's ship. A fine sailing vessel, equipped with steam-driven, side-mounted paddlewheels. Excellent cap'n."

We turned south along the wharf, found the *Madre Auxiliadora* tied up in her berth, recently painted a coral and light-blue combination. A beautiful sight. The Wangs peered up, their eyes sparkling. She wept.

The sign in bold lettering above the entrance to the gangway, read: 'Home Berth of the *Madre Auxiliadora*. Finest sailing ship under the banner of the Pacific Mail Steamship Company—Bound for Yokohama and Hong Kong, Sydney and Auckland, New York and Panama. Steerage available on first-come-first-served basis. Limited First Class Accommodations. All voyagers must provide bona fide references.'

A big man approached. From the gold, silver, and blue cap he wore cocked to one side, he had to be Cap'n O'Toole. "Ah, and what have we here? Ye must be me sailing companions, ain't ye? A man from the telegraph office brung me a wire just three days ago, announcin' your need for passage clear across the ocean blue to Hong Kong. Well, now, that's a bit of territory I'm familiar with. I've sailed these seas all me fifty-three years, so's that something I know from the bottom of me heart."

Coot said, "That's welcome news, Cap'n. But tell me, what do we owe you for passage for these folks? I believe Mr. Rodolfo Bustamante wired you to reserve their quarters."

"Indeed he did, me lad. Indeed he did. I reserved the cabin right next to me own for these folks, Mr. and Mrs. Wang, I'm told. But don' ye be worrying your-selves none 'bout what ye be owing the likes of me. You see, your friend sent me a wire-draft just yestiday. Their passage is paid in full, it is." He winked. "And a bit'a lagniappe for me. And don't ye be worrying none about these fine folks. No harm will come to them, ye got me word on it. The word of Cap'n Riley O'Toole backs up that solemn vow."

He studied the sky, his bright-blue eyes twinkling the truth of the man. "Good sailin' weath'a tomorree. Be pullin' anchor and castin' off by 3 of'a mornin', we be. Now. Be saying your goodbyes now, and I'll be showin' these fine folks to their private cabin."

Mr. Wang spoke to the Cap'n in Chinese. He turned to us. "Mr. Wang wants you to know that you will always be in their prayers, wants you to know the meaning of their names. The mister's given name be, Hai, which means, The Sea. 'N the missus is Chinguang, means morning glory. Right pretty names, I'd say."

We bowed to them, Coot smiled. "Hai—The Sea. Chinguang—Morning Glory. A man whose eyes are as bright as the sea. A beautiful lady, more beautiful than a sea of morning glories."

I swear they understood him. Their eyes glistened as he spoke their names.

A man came by barking a cry for his wares—a photograph to remember the occasion. The Cap'n explained it to the Wangs. She gleamed.

The man explained that his photographs were far superior to the humdrum tintypes, tan from the outset. His was the daguerreotype photograph, a silver process on metal. "Bright and shiny forever," he guaranteed. Coot could tell Mrs. Wang was intrigued, wanted nothing more than to have a photograph of her heroes. The Wangs lined up, Coot on one end, me on the other.

She hugged and kissed us both, then spoke to her husband. By the motion of her hands, she wanted him to produce something. She took the single piece of paper he offered, the one that I had written our names and address on. She placed it in the document holder with the daguerreotype, pressed it to her breast, held it tight while she said what needed to be said in her language. Funny—I understood her every word. She bowed, blew a kiss, turned, and followed her husband and Cap'n Riley O'Toole up the gangplank.

"Coot, I wonder how long that dear lady has to live. Will she ever pull out that piece of paper and think of those two men? One the son of a farmer, the other, the son of a goat herder."

"You've always wondered too much, Narlow, but I like the smile your wondering washed over your face. Looks good on you." He slapped me on the back. "Come on, let's find us the swankiest hotel in San Francisco, blow a wad of that $20,000 that Rodolfo Bustamante pushed off on us. I'm hungry, and damn certain thirsty."

38

San Francisco

Our jitney driver was still parked at the curb, waiting for a hire. Coot said, "Take us to the financial district. The most expensive hotel in San Francisco, if you please, my good man."

When we crossed the cable car line on California Street, Coot hollered out, "Hold on right about here! This will do just fine."

We gazed up and down both streets, the tall buildings, the hustle and bustle of a truly metropolitan city, our first. Coot plopped down in the middle of the cable car tracks, peering up California Street past a cable car that was approaching. We looked past the car, the tracks disappearing in the mist over a far hill. Still sitting between the tracks, he asked a passing lady-pedestrian what we were looking at. She walked around us, giving us a wide berth, pulled her parasol down over her eyes, her bustle bustling on by. Coot called out after her, "Thank you kindly, ma'am."

A more accommodating man walked by, and answered Coot's query. "That far hill there in the fog that you are inquiring about, sir, is none other than Nob Hill. Perhaps you have heard of it. One of our most delightfully rich areas, one for which we hold much pride. Enjoy your stay, gentlemen. I bid you a fond adieu."

"My god, Narlow, will you just look at that? Do you believe we're in San Francisco? Look at those tall buildings, will you? I have a feeling that this city's going to be good for you." He jumped to his feet, kicked the rail. "Let's catch the next cable car heading west up Nob Hill, get a closer look. Get up there and do a little hob-knobbing with the Nob crowd."

We boarded the next westbound car, stood, like everyone else, soon realizing the overhead bars were not just decorations. They proved mighty handy in keeping us inside the swaying cable car.

Coot hailed the driver. "Excuse me, sir, but could you direct two old country boys to the most exclusive, most expensive hotel on California Street? Maybe something on Nob Hill. Just drop us off where you think we need to be."

He stopped in front of a lavishly decorated hotel, the sign above the gold plated entrance read, "Hotelier César."

Coot grinned, pushed back. "By golly, Mr. Montgomery, I do believe we've found the perfect place for you and Mr. Boldt to hang their bolos." He laughed. "If we had bolos to hang."

A bellman met us at the bottom of the stairs, polished stone, pillars of polished red and cream marble rising on either side up to the lavish entrance. "Welcome to the César, gentlemen. May I take your bags?"

Coot glanced down at his valise. "This old thing? Not as heavy as a woman's purse. But, sure, you can tote it if you care to."

We strolled across the marble floors, the same cream and red wavy color, Coot signed us in at the counter. The attendant said, "Welcome to the César. Have we had the pleasure of you gentlemen's company before?"

I said, "No, sir. Our first time out of Texas and the New Mexico Territory. I've read that fancy hotels such as yours offers what they call a suite of rooms. Say two bedrooms, separated maybe by a parlor. Have something along those lines?"

"Indeed, sir. Indeed we do. A quite large parlor, as you term it. Quite large indeed, so spacious that one of our fulltime guests, an Italian gentleman, refers to it as a *salotto*. He conducts all of his business affairs there. *And* all of our accommodations include their own private bath area. A bathtub, a lavatory, and a water closet." He said lavatory like it possessed a dozen syllables, probably containing a scientific experiment.

Coot asked, "Excuse me, sir, but what's a water closet?"

"Well, sir, it's a . . . a . . ."

I said, "Coot, it's a crapper, a shithouse, an indoor two-holer."

The man chuckled. "Yes something on that order. But, sir, you shan't be embarrassed. Many of first-time guests are surprised with that accommodation as well." He smiled, reached across the desk. "Here are the keys to your suite. You will want to know that our checkout time is noon, and our nightly rate is—"

Coot slammed his open hand down on the desk, took the keys. "We don't give a tinker's damn what your rate is. We'll pay you with cash money. Thank you for your time."

"Yes, of course. The bellman will escort you to your suite, carry your bags, and—"

Coot smiled. "Thank you kindly, but we can find our room on our own, but he can tote our heavy luggage up those stairs for us, leave them where we can find them. And speaking of finding something, where can we find your bar?"

The saloon's greeter welcomed us, appeared to be Spanish by his appearance and manner. On the way to our table, I asked him we could order something to eat while sitting here. He stopped, turned to face us. "At the César, sustenance is *not* served at the bar." He said the word, César, as if it slipped off the sharp side of a straight-edge razor.

Coot sliced it back. "The César, huh? Okay, bring us the finest sour mash bourbon whiskey you have in the house, ice on the side." He smiled. "Make certain that it's César ice."

After several whiskeys and five-pounds of inside-ice, we paid the tab, decided to go to our suite and stretch out for awhile before supper.

I fell face down on my bed, didn't move but I dreamed one nonsensical, endless dream after another . . .

"Narlow. Hey Narlow. *Wake up*."

I bolted up. "Glad you woke me. Damndest dreams I ever experienced. What time is it anyway?"

"Nine p.m. You've been sawing logs for three hours. I was afraid you were going to sleep the clock around."

"I was having the damndest dream. I was back in the bar with a beautiful, auburn-haired lady on my lap, both puffing Papa's old briar, having a grand old time. Auburn hair like Sophie's, but this was definitely *not* Sophie. My revelry was interrupted when who do you suppose was standing at the door? Na-Tu-Che-Puy. Leaning against the doorframe, shaking his head, while Can See Far was combing his pounded-pewter braid. Na-Tu was frowning, unhappy about something. I motioned with Papa's pipe, thinking that was what he found so offensive. He shook his head. I held up my whiskey glass. Again, he shook his head. His gaze turned to the beautiful lady in my lap, shook his head, picked up a wine glass, broke it against the doorframe, and threw it at the lady, and . . . and that's when you woke me up, my bull elk call whistling in my ear. Sure was real, almost like a vision with Na-Tu in it and all. But that auburn-haired woman was the most gorgeous creature I've ever seen. God, she was beautiful. What do you suppose that was all about?"

"Who knows. I went back downstairs to take a peek at the dining area. Their rules don't bend. Gotta wear a dinner jacket. But don't worry, the *maitre d'* assured me that he has loners. Come on, I'm hungry."

We were seated near the middle of the circular restaurant, place was crowded, not an empty table or chair in the place. Coot ordered an expensive French wine, the waiter brought it, poured a bit in Coot's glass, and stepped back. Coot said, "Looks good, but I'd like a full glass if you don't mind, please sir."

"Coot, I think he wants you to sample it—taste it. See if it meets with your learned approval."

Coot tossed it down, nodded to the server. "*Ahh*, now *that's* some damn good grape juice."

That bottle was so tasty that we ordered another.

Coot gazed all around. "Will you just look at all of this? Red velvet carpeting, red velvet chair coverings, every table with flowers, enough flowers to flower-up a hundred funerals."

His gaze continued, stopped, he leaned forward, whispered, "Narlow, there's a lady seated behind you at a table against the far wall. Most beautify creature I have ever laid eyes on in all my born-days. *Absolutely gorgeous woman*. With all the right curves and bulges, all in the right place."

Not wanting to seem to be gawking, I eased my chair around nonchalantly, saw the woman, jerked back. "*Coot, that's her!*"

"That's her *who*? And not so damn loud. You've got the volume of a foghorn out in the middle of the bay."

"That's the woman that was sitting on my lap in my vision when Na-Tu appeared. *That's her!*"

"*Uh-oh*. I do believe she overheard you. She just stood up, peered over here . . . headed this way. You're liable to get us thrown out of here on our ears. You better think of something, my friend—*quick*."

We stood as she approached in a long flowing white gown, low-cut, a delightfully-draped playground that could not tolerate much more exposure. She laughed. "Bonjour, messieurs! I'm sorry, but I could not help but overhear what you said just now. Do I know you? By chance, did you return from Paris just recently? Or, did you see me on the train from New York last week? Perhaps you caught my show tonight at the San Francisco Opera House." She held out her hand. "Forgive me for being so forward. I am WP Goodyear. Perhaps you've heard of me. I'm an actress and songstress." She smiled. "World renown, I hasten to add." Miss Goodyear was a willow of a lady, sinuous yet buxom, downright sensuous.

I took her hand. "So pleased to make your acquaintance, my lady. I'm Narlow Montgomery, and this is Coot Boldt. Please forgive me. Mistaken identity, but your name is Goodyear. What a coincidence. We have a letter of introduction from a mutual friend of Mr. George William Goodyear. That couldn't be—"

"*Yes*, that's my father! Now *this* is a coincidence. Oh, please, you must join me and my friends. They're all actors, poets, an assortment of artists and eggheads, but they're interesting, so much fun. You'll love them, and I know they'll adore you. Won't you join us?"

I glanced at Coot who stood grinning, admiring this lady. I said, "Tell you what, Miss WP. If you will allow us to buy your friends a bottle of wine, the best in the house, *your choice*, we will most certainly join you. Will you allow us that privilege?" I smiled, dropped my head, raised my eyebrows. "Please?"

She laughed. "Who can refuse those bright, hazel, puppy dog eyes? Of course you can. Come, now. I'll have the waiter bring along your drinks."

She turned to the side, offered her hand. "*S'il vous plaît.*"

She introduced us to her lady-friends, sat Coot next to another knockout lass, a blue-eyed blond. Built like the proverbial. We made a night of it. They told us all about themselves. When WP mentioned that her father was an inventor, Coot said, "Inventor, huh? I always considered myself something of an inventor. Farm equipment, that sorta thing. What kind of things has your father invented? Industrial, shipping?"

She laughed. "Hardly. Father's distant cousin was Charles Goodyear who died before the Civil War. Destitute, $200,000 in debt. You may know that he invented the vulcanization process that somehow or other converts raw rubber to something more useful. Father took an old idea, changed, improved, made rubber more pliable, and has successfully marketed his products worldwide. A soft, wide disc for the ladies, prophylactics for the men.

She hesitated, the ladies at the table giggled. WP licked her red full lips, glanced at me, her pale-hazel flashed with a hint of emerald. "In France, they call them, *caoutchoucs*. Rubbers, here in the States. And Father's have little thingies on the ends, 'ticklers,' he calls them, why I have not a single clue."

Coot laughed, pointed around the table. "What are all you hussies giggling about?"

But the conversation made me uneasy. I sat, nervous, not knowing what to do with my hands, first sitting on them, then found them under my chin, elbows resting on the white laced table cloth. My gaze slid from the ceiling down the red-velvet walls to WP, whose own gaze was sailing delicately at me. She reached out and patted my hand, still holding my chin. I smiled, nodded at her beautiful face.

I felt my shoulders relax and began yammering away. Coot and I were an instant hit with WP and her friends, all a bit strange, but they welcomed us, laughed till they cried at our antics, stories from our past. Our lives with the Apaches, me studying to be a medicineman, Coot's ability to track a man or animal across rocky territory was legendary among the Apaches. When I told them about our years chasing Chief Victorio and Geronimo, one of the ladies, Sheila, huffed, jumped up.

"Indian fighters! You should be ashamed! I loathe—*loathe* the white men who put those poor people in those horrid reservations." I tried to explain that we were out there trying to get the runaways back on the reservations before the Blue Coats killed every one of them, but I found myself finishing my explanation to her backside as she hustled for the door.

WP laughed. "Sheila should be more like me, more reflective, for you see, I am a self-reliant woman. The little needle always knows the north, the little bird remembers his note, and this wise Seer within me never errs. I never taught it what it teaches me; I only follow, when I act aright." Coot and I glanced at each other. Then she added. "Oh heavens! I did not intend to get so philosophical, it's just in my being."

WP asked about my heritage. I told her that I was what is commonly referred to as a half-breed, something not to be advertised—half-white, quarter-Apache, quarter-Comanche.

"What's wrong with that?" a lady with a strong French accent asked.

Coot said they'd lived too long in Europe, not enough in America if they didn't understand, "what's wrong with that."

He got the subject on a more casual side, told the story about IB Crane and his twin sister's scorpion, One Legged Lilly. It was a house-burner. When one of their male friends joined the party, they insisted that Coot retell the story. The man's name was Francois, a golden boy in vermillion, velveteen tights with the face and haughty demeanor of a roadrunner chasing a lizard. The ladies sat quietly, their chins in their hands when we spoke of our childhood, living a full half-day's ride from each other, Coot living on a farm, tending to it almost by himself since his daddy died; me, tending goats, milking 1,500 nannies.

More wine, then more. Things loosened up. WP leaned close, whispered, "*Mon coeur,* I'm curious to know—is it true what they say about men with big hands, thick wrists, and long feet? Big, thick, long . . ." I mumbled around, sloughed it off, told her they were the result of milking nannies as a boy. She giggled. "Long feet from milking nannies? Really?"

I changed the subject, asked WP about her name, how she came to have it. She laughed, said her father pinned the name, Willy Peabody, on her as her given name—Willy, in honor of his father, Peabody, her mother's maiden name. Her mother wasn't around, as she died giving birth to their only child. Her father finally allowed her to adopt the initials, WP, which proved to be the brand in her career.

"My initials are my trademark, like this beauty mark on my cheek. They adore it in France and Spain."

"*Ha!*" I said. "I've got a birthmark on my hip–all red and fuzzy–Coot can tell you it's shaped like a mushroom, laughed when he first saw it when we were boys, told Papa, 'Yep, Uncle Abe, sure looks like a mushroom, and you know what they feed mushrooms.' An old Apache medicineman was convinced it was the source of what he called my Power."

WP smiled as she traced her finger around her beauty mark. "I can only imagine, but I'll show you mine if you'll show me yours–sometime–real soon." Her lady-friends giggled.

More wine. WP turned to the waiter and called him over, rattled off in French. I asked what she had said to him. "Well, Mr. Narlow Montgomery, if you really must know . . . we've all sat here drinking wine by the *carafe*, and if we don't have a bit of sustenance, they'll have to carry us out of this divine establishment, noted for its *haute cuisine*. I ordered *hor d'oeuvres—escargot* over beef, prepared *roseate*. Men of the west are noted for preferring their beef cooked until it's indigestible, but you'll find this delectable." She smiled, licked her lips. "Juicy and red on the inside." Coot nudged his boot against me under the table.

Coot told of our annual trips to the Black River, hunting elk, making jerky from their meat, about Many Fast Feet Two Sticks, and the long knives that he gave us. When he started telling about Papa and Uncle Doyl stranding us with no horses or mules, I interrupted him.

"*Wait.* That reminds me of when we had been out skinny-dipping just before our menfolk left us there to fend for ourselves. We'd been out there skinny-dipping for over an hour, throwing boulders in the Black River, the water going up in a gusher. We got on a ledge we called Pricilla's Perch, laid down, let the sun dry us, then took off running back to camp, *buck-ass n'ked.* I was always a bunch faster than the character sitting here with us, but looking back over my shoulder, watching Coot try to run while holding his balls, I got to laughing so hard, I fell down, rolling, trying to get my breath."

WP laughed, asked, "N'ked. Is that Spanish? Don't believe I'm familiar with the word."

I thought a minute, grinned. "N'ked? Oh, I mean nekkid–I reckon you'd say, naked. But in any case, we had nothing on but our birthday suits."

Coot and I bantered back and forth for another hour about our escapades.

While Coot was relating another story, WP leaned over to me. "You have such a delightful way of speaking. Have such a . . . such a *capriccioso* manner. You're playful, full of fun, light and gay. I like you, Narlow Montgomery. As you would say, a *bunch*."

Playful? Me? Fun? Yeah, I used to fit that description, but that was long ago, before . . .

She inquired about what we did, how we built our fortunes. By that time it was past 3, the eight of us had consumed $150 worth of the César's finest cellar. I got to big-shotin' it pretty bad. Told them we owned several cattle ranches, bought and sold the only class hotel in El Paso for a fortune, but that we were too young to have amassed such a fortune on our own. That brought up the question of how it could be that we were in possession of such a fabulous amount of wealth. That got me blabbing about Papa's gold cache. My wine-soaked brain finally caught up with my jabbering mouth. It occurred to me that I might be telling something that would come back to haunt Coot and me, might even put Papa and Fernando in peril.

I glanced over at Coot, who was busy studying his boots. His menacing glare came up, eyes dark, deadly, his brow corrugated like the pipe we'd laid to Sierra Blanca's jerkwater.

WP's friends began peeling off one at a time, leaving Coot and his well-endowed blonde bomb wine-sipping companion, and WP and me to finish off the last of the wine.

She said, "I'm so glad all my friends have left us. I tire of them, they're so dissolute at times, while you are so refreshing. A bit staid and old-fashioned, but excellent, reputable company, I dare say. You have the air of a British cleric."

Coot guffawed.

She invited us to lunch at her father's estate, that she wanted to be the one to properly introduce us to her father.

"Nothing special," she assured us, just a few of her close friends. "He's such a dream of a father. Never once did he refuse any of my outlandish requests, showered me with extravagant gifts. So many that I've given most of them away."

Coot's dreamboat-cohort said, "Yeah, like this white-gold and diamond bracelet that WP give me. Must'a cost a fortune, it did."

Coot grinned, winked at me.

WP went on. "Father has built an enormous home overlooking the bay from a sheer cliff. Built his chalet next to a home known as the, Cliff House. Ask anyone. They can easily direct you right to it."

Coot and the blonde bombshell took their leave.

WP said, "Narlow, you are such a wonderful man. You and Coot have lived such interesting, exciting lives. You could tell that all my friends are so envious of you. I hope we spend more time together while you're here so you can tell me more. All about yourself. Start with your parents. You've spoken so admirably of your father—call him Papa, I believe, but you've never said a word about your mother. What's she like?"

"WP, that's a long story, not a very happy tale. Her own brother says she's the meanest woman alive, too dern much Comanche blood. She's no dummy, but someone who doesn't know her might think she's a bit slow, but that would be a mistake."

"Like what?"

"Oh, like she refers to me, her only son, as a son-of-a-bitch. I've been able to put her behind me until recently, now she's coming back in my head. Pretty hard to forgive someone who stole your childhood." Na-Tu screamed in my ear: *You must never speak of this again, or it will possess you.*

"Your mother stole your childhood—*hmmm*, interesting. Do you dwell on your mother, your childhood?"

"I admit doing that until I was around eighteen, about ate me alive. But I got it behind me and just went on with life. Seems it all came back on me when I moved to town, and for the first time in my life, I lived under a roof. I think living in town, not out in the sun all day, may have somehow brought all those memories back. That likely sounds peculiar to you, but the thought has crossed my mind."

She clasped my hands. "Oh, Narlow, my new friend. Just now, when you spoke of your mother, your face, your entire essence, fell, drooped dolorously. Is she a trouble in your life?"

I fumbled for an answer.

WP squeezed my hands. "Enough of your—

"WP, all you need to know about my mother is that I've never seen her smile. But I know for certain, that if she did, I'd not have the courage to look upon her face. Her smile would be like ice from hell."

We were quiet for a while. "You have to know that my friend Coot is more man than me. When we were just scruffy boys, I asked him if he thought God requires that I like my mother. His answer was short, his way—he said, 'No, you don't have to like her, but you have to love her.' That pretty well settled the issue for me."

WP smiled. "Smart man, that Coot fellow. Now . . . you said you moved to town? Why did you do that? To marry, settle down in town with your new bride?"

"No—I mean, *yes*." I smiled. "Yes, I . . . I'm married . . . not exactly." Shrugged, felt a silly grin cross my face, began searching the ceiling. "Sorta."

"Sorta? You're married, *sorta*. What does, 'exactly-sorta' mean?"

Once again, the wine and my big mouth overloaded my cart. "I married a young woman four years my senior. Why? I haven't a clue. We've never had anything to do with each other. Never even . . . well, we've never . . ."

"You mean, you've never . . ."

"That's right. *Never* in sixteen months of marriage. Haven't even come close."

"Why do you suppose? It's not you, is . . ."

I laughed, pushed back in my chair. "No, it's sure as the dickens not me!" I felt my shoulders pull up, then drop. "No, it's not me. I'm *ready*, so ready I'm about to pop." *God, I wanted this woman!*

She frowned. "Oh, Narlow, that is not good! Doesn't your wife know that? That if she doesn't perform her wifely duties, that you will go elsewhere like any red-blooded man would do. Doesn't she know the peril her refusal places on her household, her marriage?"

I winced. "I shouldn't be talking to a complete stranger about such matters. Please forgive—"

"Oh, *per contra*, my dear man, *per contra*. We're far from being complete strangers. I've never felt closer to anyone in my entire life than you, man or woman. And you are *definitely* a man. A gorgeous man. And, you, Mr. Narlow Montgomery, feel the very same about me . . . don't you?"

Browning's lines etched their way across my forehead: *Then how grace a rose? I know a way! Leave it, rather. Must you gather? Smell, kiss, wear it . . . at last, throw it away!* My gut told me that if I ever kissed this rose, she'd not be thrown away.

I spun the stem of my wine glass in my fingers, took a sip, sighed. "Yes, I do, Miss WP Goodyear. I feel the very same way about you. Sadly, maybe, but I do."

"*Sadly?* Why would you say that? *It's not sad.* No reason for sadness between you and me—about *anything*." She reached across the table, took my hand. "Narlow, don't you know that? Don't you feel it in your heart? Besides, we don't have that much time left. You say you must be leaving within a few days, and we shan't waste a moment of it being sad. I have too many plans for you, and sadness is not in that mix." She smiled, tasted the wine with her tongue, licked the edge of her glass. "I assure you."

In a moment, she said, "Narlow, I know you'll think this strange since we just met, but you must know that I love you."

"You *what?* How can—"

"Love comes easily if you allow it. I love you. Is that so hard to imagine?"

"Well, I . . ."

"Let's hear you say those three innocent words. Listen to me . . . I love you."

I smiled. "And I love you."

"No, that's not what I want to hear. Say the three words without any introduction. Try it."

"Well, I . . ."

"Say it."

"I love you."

"*See?* That wasn't so hard, now was it?"

"Well, it's just that . . . well, I've never said that before."

"Never said it? Never mouthed the words, I love you? Not even to your wife? Your mother?"

I smiled, my mouth contorting a bit. "WP, I never thought about it before. For *certain* never said that to my mother, but come to think of it, I don't recall ever saying those three little words to Sophie either."

"Why do you suppose that is? You're a smart man. A loving man. A man built to please a woman. You speak so kindly of your father. Did he not tell you that it is normal for a man to tell his spouse that he loves her? Did you ever hear him say that he loved your mother?"

"No, never did. Certainly *did not*, but you'd have to know my mother to understand how that could be. But, I know he did—he *had* to love her to put up with her. She's not a loveable woman. I suppose she's the most hateful person, man or woman, that I've ever known."

"I plan on working on that issue, my dear, adorable, loveable man. We'll work on that together, shall we? I am in the habit of thinking—not, I hope, out of partial experience, but confirmed by what I notice in many lives—that to every serious mind, Providence sends from time to time five or six or seven teachers who are of the first importance to Him in the lessons they have to impart. Narlow, I believe God sent you to me, sent you as one of those five or six or seven teachers, one of first importance to me. And, you know what else? I believe God sent you to me as one of those five or six or seven teachers in *your* life so that I may impart my view and knowledge to you. Does that make any sense to you?"

I thought a moment, mulling over the words, *five or six or seven teachers*, thinking I'd heard that phrase somewhere. "Makes perfect sense to me, Miss WP Goodyear. Perfect sense to me—five or six or seven times."

39

The Pass Bumpkins arrived unfashionably early at Mr. Goodyear's home. When the jitney driver dropped us off at the gate, a tall, stately, white-haired man was walking toward us. Coot grinned. "Suppose this is Mr. George Goodyear?"

The man opened the stately, royal-blue, cast-iron gate, stuck out his long, gnarled hand. "Welcome, gentlemen. I am George Goodyear. Our mutual friend, Rodolfo Bustamante has told me all about you. Rodolfo and I were classmates at the University of Paris. One of my fondest friends and business associates. Brilliant man, I'm certain you will agree."

During lunch, I counted tables, guessed at the number of guests at a typical table, came to the conclusion that the "few close friends" that WP mentioned would be in attendance, numbered over 200. Back at the Pass, I didn't even know that many people. WP and I, Coot and the wine-sipping blonde, sat with one of the guests and his wife. A portly man, the president of the Wells Fargo Bank. Very interesting man, who spouted statistics like a lizard catching flies. He claimed that San Francisco was the proud home of over 250,000 souls, ranked ninth in America, spurted out the various percentages of several races of people in that number, the growing number of hotels, global shipping concerns, multi-national insurance companies, and others.

Banker-man said, "Mr. Boldt, I understand that you gentlemen are from El Paso, Texas. I've heard of it, recall that its sobriquet is Sin City, is it not? How big is your fair city?"

Coot squirmed, grinned. "Well, sir, El Paso's suddenly found itself with rail lines coming in from all points of the compass. I reckon . . . *I mean*, I imagine it'll be a boomtown before long. But, sir, I don't believe you'd call a little dusty border town with maybe a 1,000 people a city, 4,000 in the entire county."

"*Hmmm*. I suppose not."

After most of the luncheon guests had taken their leave, WP and I were chatting with her father. She said, "Narlow, I have a splendid idea. Why don't you stay over for the evening? Father has a dozen bedrooms, and you can have one of them that overlooks the bay."

I felt uncomfortable with the suggestion, but since the invitation was issued in the presence of her father, I accepted. Coot left with his wine-sipping companion, shot me a wink as he stepped up in the jitney.

Mr. Goodyear showed me to my quarters, suggested I nap for awhile. I attempted that, but had other things on my mind.

WP met me on the veranda an hour before sundown, wearing what I can only describe as a silver-blue, tight-fitting, one piece outfit, draped *way down* in the front, with a zipper running down its back, her shapely legs also incased in the shiny fabric. *Mercy!* I'd never seen a lady wearing anything but a full dress that went clear to the floor. *Get thee behind me, Satan!*

I grinned. "WP, please don't misunderstand me, but . . . but may I ask what's that you're wearing?"

"Oh, it's just something the ladies have adopted on the east coast." Her eyes flashed. "That is, when their fathers aren't around. It's a fad that had its start in Norway. Boston ladies wear this over their bathing suits, quickly zip it off when they're ready to bathe in the frigid Atlantic. Father suggested it might be a bit revealing—its *décolleté* nature harbors most of his complaint. Do you like it? Not too revealing?"

"*Décolleté?* I'm afraid I'm not familiar with that term."

"Low neckline, you silly man."

"So, you have your swimsuit on under it, huh? Prepared to take a dip in that icy water?"

She swirled around on the lawn. "Now, did I say a word about swimming? I have not a single thing on or under this playsuit."

Concerned I'd step on my tongue, I made no reply.

We made our way down the long, wooden stairway to the beach. The wind picked up, waves crashing on the rocks, a huge spray of mist covered us, wetting WP's playsuit that pressed and clung to her skin. We wended our way on through the slippery rocks and came to a sandy beach. We walked along, WP teasing me, trying to get me to hold her hand. She laughed, told me not to take it so seriously. "Holding hands is not kissing, a long way from caressing, even further from fondling my breasts, laying me in the sand, making love to me all night."

Oh my god!

"I suppose we could have our second lesson in the fine art of saying, 'I love you.' Would you like that?"

She ran ahead, splashing in the water as the waves swept back into the dark ocean, screaming into the wind, "I love you, Narlow Montgomery. I love you, *I love you!*" There was a chill in the air, but she gave it not a care, lay down on her back, began waving her arms and legs in the wet sand, then jumped up, pointed to the impression she'd made in the sand. "Look, Narlow. Have you ever seen an angel laying on a wet beach." I made no reply, but indeed I just witnessed one.

Again, she ran ahead, laughing, turned in a wide circle, came running straight back at me, again screaming, "I love you, Narlow Montgomery," leaped in the air. I caught her in my arms, swung her around, told her she was crazy.

"Crazy? Well, maybe so, you handsome man. Or maybe I'm just happy. And, maybe . . . who knows? *maybe* I really am falling in love with you. Does that frighten you, Narlow?"

"Oh, that can't be it. We've just met and—"

She pulled my face down, stood on her tiptoes, kissed me, deep and long. She pulled at the back of my head, kissing, sticking her tongue in my mouth, sucking at my tongue, pulling it in her mouth. She pulled away, her hair flying in the wind like raven wings, pulled me down, guiding my hands to her breasts. Pulling at my britches, popping the buttons at the front of them. Reaching in—

"WP, what's that? Hear that?"

"What? I didn't hear anything."

I jumped to my feet. "WP! Someone's calling your name. There it is again. Hear it? Sounds like your father, calling out to see if you are all right. *Must* be your father—heard him calling for Willy Peabody."

"Oh, don't worry about him. He's too old to come down that rickety stairway. Come back down here, my dearest. We've just begun."

"No. Your father's worried about you—"

"You're afraid! What are you afraid—"

"I'm *not* afraid. Let's at least call up to him so he'll know you're—"

"Oh, all right. I often think my filial responsibilities to that man will never end. Come on."

We trotted back to the rocks, looked up at her father standing at the top of the stairway who stood braced against his cane and the railing, gazing across the bay, his white hair blowing in the stiff breeze. WP waved up to him. He saw us and returned the salute.

266

"*There.* Satisfied now? Come with me, my darling." She started back to the sandy beach.

I shrugged, followed along. "WP, aren't you freezing? You're wet and this wind—"

"*Cold?* Surely you jest. My heart is beating like a flutter-fly. Much too young to have hot flashes, but I swear I've got them. Never been so on fire."

She pulled me down on top of her, pushed her hands inside my trousers, pulled at my rear, kissing me. Her mouth and lips were large, the most luscious thing I ever devoured. We both tugged at the zipper at the back of her playsuit, groping at each other. *God, don't let me lose it before I get her playsuit off.*

"Oh, Narlow my darling. I love you. Tell me you love me."

"Love you?"

"Yes, I want to hear you say you love me."

"I . . . well, like I said last night, I never—"

"Surely that cannot be. Never told a woman you love her?"

"WP, like I said last night, I've never told *anyone* that I love them. Not even my wife."

"We'll talk about it later, but right now I want you. Want you *now.* Here. *Right now!* Here, pull my playsuit from my legs. Hurry, my darling. I must have you this very moment."

A sand crab scratched at my elbow, throwing sand in my face. I peered down, and there he was—Na-Tu's image, chanting, "*Dii jii ye, dii jii ye*"—From today on." Papa's words, *Your mother is my wife and I'll not break our vows.* He would not forsake Mama, never desert me.

I jumped up, got myself back in my britches. "WP, I can't! Please forgive me. I want you so bad I can taste it, but I just can't. God, how I want you! But I can't."

She wiped the wet sand from her hands, brushed her auburn hair back. "It's all right, Narlow. I understand. Perhaps I've been a bit hasty. And you know what they say—'through patience, chalk becomes a ruby stone, a diamond from a lump of coal.' But, next time, my sweet, you must not be the winter of my heartbreak. I could not bear it."

***

I slept fitfully that night at the Goodyear mansion, half expecting WP to slip under the covers with me at any moment. My god what if her father caught us? Before dawn, I was up, found a note slipped under the door—from WP, telling me she had an early rehearsal before today's matinee performance. She'd return before noon, we would enjoy an early luncheon, then off to the theater.

Before full light, I stepped out on my private terrace, leaned against the railing, breathing in the cool air off the bay. *I'm becoming a swirling rose petal, whirled around at the pleasure of the wind.* I didn't used to be—at least never thought it.

I decided to stroll the 400-yards north to the point where WP and I had had our frolic on the beach below. The grass was wet, everything soaked, fresh, so unlike my Chihuahua Desert. So wet the trees rained when it blew. The firs and gnarled trees along the precipice were bent by the wind as were all things mastered by the constant stiff breeze from the sea. It seemed odd, but the bay was clear, not a hint of fog. To the north lay meadows, countless vales filled with haycocks and fens.

I turned on my heel, slumped to the grass, rolled over on my belly, elbows spread wide, my chin resting on clenched fists, my eyes cooled by the wet. I often did that as a boy while studying the moon. And, there it was—shining blue in a circle of soft white, reminiscent of the ring around the sun, but this circle of white was ready for its dive into the Pacific, seabirds already out on their early rounds, larks, thrushes, long-tailed linnets darting about, buoys clanging their mournful boredom, lanterns blinking yellow on sailing ships anchored at bay in the shadowed blue-gray. Men in fishing skiffs, tacking into the offshore wind seeking their daily catch. Everything about the ocean was alive, white with silent light, growing on me, had given me new life, to relearn life, to accept it, bouquets, accolades, pitfalls, warts, and boils—to take it all in, deal with it as I will. Like the ocean, I must take it all, soft sand at my feet, waves that topple me, dash me against the rocks—I must take it all, salt and all.

After a bit, I stood, drenched, wetter than if I'd slept at the bottom of the *Rio Grande*. I continued my stroll. As I approached the precipice, I heard an eerie, buzzing sound, maybe the caterwaul of bobcats, reminiscent of my warning bull elk whistle that I hadn't experienced in years. I gazed all around. The whistle became distinct. It was just warning me away from the cliff.

I turned. No, it was from over there. A quarter-mile away, two large dogs running around a white horse barn. Stout dogs, largest I'd ever seen. Far heavier than the biggest wolf. They'd winded me. I turned back to the house. Too far to make it before they got here. They came on, their rear legs churning like locomotive drivers, front legs stretched far out in front, their wide bodies the exact same width from their shoulders to their hips. I was a goner. Their approach lacked any semblance of a pleasant, "Morning, Sunshine." This was it! Ten feet away, they stopped. Sat. I sat cross-legged in the grass. They lay down. Fawn-colored, had to be 175-pounds or more. Their heads, large as a yearling's, their muzzles, black, same as their short, sharp ears. Their massive legs and paws stretched out in front, appeared a matched set of regal sphinxes, their dark-hazel eyes unblinking. The wind fanned their handsome faces, hair swirling, reflecting the early sun like the mirror of wings. I agreed with them. The three of us would stay right there.

A man pushing a cart loaded with horse droppings strolled by, a boy around four tagging along behind. The man stopped, his jaw dropped. "*Senor*, you don't know about those dogs? *Senor* Goodyear, he did not warn you?"

"No, my friend, but as you see, they have given me all the warning that I require."

"They are guard dogs. At night, they roam freely inside the fence that encloses *Senor* Goodyear's estate. No one comes inside the fence. The dogs have killed intruders, torn them to shreds, these dogs. You are very brave."

"*Por favor, amigo*, don't tell them that I am unafraid, as I'm to the point of peeing in my pants."

The little boy giggled.

I asked, "What's your name, young man?"

"Juan Andres Rodriguez," he said, with uplifted chin.

The man stepped up to me. "And I am Juan Andres Rodriguez de Delgado. I am the proud hostler of *Senor* Goodyear's fine horses."

"*Senor* Rodriguez, please forgive me for not standing to shake your hand and properly introducing myself." I glanced at the dogs. "They seem to prefer that I keep my seat, but truly sir, I am pleased to make your acquaintance and that of your son. I am Narlow Montgomery."

"I do not believe they will bother you, *Senor* Montgomery." He chuckled. "Look at them, laying there with their tongues lolled out. This is very strange. *Mi mama*, she would say you have witched them, *senor*."

"Maybe that is true, but if it's all the same to you, and since you're here, I'll just get up real gentle-like, and let you and little Juan Andres see me back to the safety of my veranda."

The little boy came over, sat cross-legged in my lap, mirroring me, his double chin resting on his chubby fists, at ease with life and himself. His dark eyes came around to me. He smiled.

Senor Rodriguez took his hand. "Come, my son. We must see *Senor* Goodyear's guest back to the great house."

***

On the carriage ride to the theater, WP laughed. "Juan Andres tells me that you had the pleasure of meeting father's guard dogs. I know it wasn't funny, but I can just imagine you sitting out there on the lawn with those two utter giants staring at you."

"Highlight of a man's day."

"You mustn't make light of it. I should have warned you. It was horribly careless of me. They're mastiffs, highly trained animals. They do not maim, they kill."

"Difficult to believe that your father would unleash them on a mere trespasser. He's such a mild-mannered—"

"You don't know the dark side of George Goodyear, I assure you. For you see, he was orphaned in the back streets of New York City, not a nice place. But, in his defense, he was driven to the extreme of the mastiffs. Two years ago, pirates broke through the fence, ransacked the servant's quarters, and kidnapped five little girls, held them for ransom. My father paid the ransom as agreed. The next morning, the bodies of those five girls were found floating in the bay, their heads chopped off, tethered to their bodies with rope, half eaten by sharks. Father placed an advertisement in every newspaper along the coast, a warning that no further negotiations would take place with pirates, that guard dogs would roam his estate, and should any trespasser escape their trained fangs, they would have an opportunity to try their luck with a noose. They must have believed him."

She smiled. "Juan Andres believes you are a witch, that the dogs are afraid of you. I think they respect you, admire your confidence. I'm curious—if you had been warned, would you have gone out there on the lawn overlooking the bay?"

I thought on that for a bit. "WP, I *was* warned in the form of a bull elk whistle. But if I told you all that, we'd be late for your performance."

"Well, you must tell me all about it. Juan Andres also told me that when you stood out there in the grass to go back to your veranda, that the dogs crawled up to you on their bellies like frightened puppies, you held the back of your hand for them to smell, they began licking your fingers. When the three of you walked away, Juan Andres said he turned to make certain the dogs were behaving. They had turned on their backs, their tongues lolled out, rubbing their backs on the wet grass, appeared to be playing, something neither of us had ever seen them do."

"Ha! That old medicineman would have enjoyed that scene. I can hear him say, 'Kicking Bear, you say you do not possess Power, yet the bull elk whistle warns you of the grave danger of the dogs. If you do not have Power, how do you explain that?' That old man was hard to dodge—his wisdom was relentless."

"Well, my dearest pet—Kicking Bear, is it? when you elucidate regarding your

270

bull elk whistle, I'd like to hear your explanation of the dogs' behavior as well as the Power your medicineman believes you possess."

Coot was waiting at the entrance of the theatre house. He doffed his hat, swooped majestically as the carriage came to a stop.

I said, "Coot, I've warned her that we've never seen an actual play, just a bunch of rowdies and bawdy girls on a Saturday night at the Gem Saloon."

WP took his hand to help her from the carriage. "You two will love it, so please relax. Mine is the staring role as I play Lady Macbeth. I adore it. I believe you will be impressed with my singing voice, for father has invested a fortune in it. All of Paris swears my voice possesses a rather cello-like resonance, not the high shrill of the violin as possessed by other female artists. You must promise me that you'll come backstage after the play. I want all of my dear friends to meet my handsome man."

We were escorted to our seats—front-row-center—all was well, and we enjoyed ourselves. And then . . .

Lady Macbeth is proclaiming to Macbeth the need for a *real* man to go through with their nefarious scheme of murdering the king.

Sayeth she,

"They have made themselves, and that their fitness now

"Does unmake you. I have given suck, and know

"How tender 'tis to love the babe that milks me;

"I would, while it was smiling in my face,

"Have pluck'd my nipple from his boneless gums,

"And dash'd the brains out, had I so sworn as you

"Have done to this."

With eyes wide, Macbeth asks, "If we should fail?"

"We fail!

WP screamed the next line, and rolled the "r,"

"But *scrrrew* your courage to the sticking place . . ."

With that, Coot howled, laughed so uproariously the play stopped, the actors glaring squarely down at us, every set of eyes in the theater, scrutinizing us in a most unfriendly manner, the fox-fur-clad lady beside Coot yanked her neck pet and body away from him with a mighty, "*Humph*!"

After the play and three curtain calls, I said, "Come on. You're going backstage with me to meet WP's friends. Remember—"

"Aw, she won't want to see me after . . ."

"Remember what Papa always advised, 'Eat your crow while it's still warm.'"

WP spied us in the crowd, and broke away from the throng of well-wishers, strolled up to Coot, took his hands in hers, smiled. "I must say that I don't know how I will ever be able to voice that line again without fighting an urge to do just exactly as you did this afternoon."

He said, "WP, please—"

She waved him off, kissed him on the cheek.

40

WP's life was one party after another. After her every performance, there was always a party. Saturday evening, her father hosted an extravaganza in his daughter's honor. Seemed half of San Francisco was at the St. Regis ballroom.

Coot and I wore the new outfits we purchased that morning, spatterdashes and all. The gals were all catcalls. It embarrassed Coot, but me, *I loved it.*

I hadn't seen much of my roommate of late. He spent most of his days with Mr. Goodyear, talking inventions and patents. The rest of his time was busy with his wine-sipping blonde.

The wine flowed, the whiskey, gin, and the vodka oozed, and champagne ran like water cascading off an ice sculpture of a platypus duck in the middle of the dance floor. Somewhat comical, but the hit of the evening.

WP and I danced every waltz and every new dance that was the rage of New York, clear across the land to San Francisco. I didn't know the step for any of them. Seems the rage had swept past dusty ol' El Paso.

Before midnight, older couples began drifting out the door. Fact is the only man in the building with white hair was George Goodyear, spry as a housecat after a fresh mouse.

WP and I went out on the terrace to cool off. She was ravishing, dressed in an elegant, low-cut, white gown adorned with what I assumed were sequins. I was wrong—diamonds. The soft breeze caught her auburn hair in the moonlight, the light from the ballroom sifting through the thin curtains at the door. WP was . . . enchanting.

She stood gazing out over the city. I thought about resisting the temptation to take her in my arms, but brushed that idea aside. My arms wrapped around her, rested my chin on her head, asked her what she was thinking.

She swayed. "Oh, I'd never tell you that. Besides, I'm not crowding you, remember?"

I chuckled. "Yeah, I remember."

"Love me, Narlow?"

"Yes, I love you. I love you. I love you."

"I believe you." She giggled. "*And*, I love you!"

We began swaying to the music. I held her tight, squeezing her, thinking how badly I wanted her, *needed* her. I pressed against her, pressing her against the granite railing of the terrace, pushing, rubbing against her backside. *God, I wanted her!*

"*Narlooow*. You shouldn't do that. I'm warning you, my dear man."

I kept at it. She pulled my hands up to her breasts, turned in my arms, encircling each other. I tasted those luscious lips again. We held tight, she began sucking on my thumb, on my tongue, her back arched. We began pulling at each other. I led her out of the light from the ballroom, back against the terrace wall. I lifted her dress, pulled at her pantaloons, her only nether garments. She scooted out of them. My fingers found her warm. I moaned, "*Oooooo, god*, WP, you're delicious." She pressed against my fingers, begged me to take her to my room. I kept at it, my fingers groping in her pudenda, she arched, pulled back, went down on her knees, fumbled my britches open.

"Oh, WP. *Oh my god*, no . . ."

A figure walked past the thin flowery curtains to the terrace. "*WP*. Someone's coming!"

I pulled her to her feet, she pressed her dress down, snapped up her pantaloons as we turned and walked to the far end of the terrace.

"Willy Peabody. Is that you, my dear?"

She sighed, her eyes rolled. "Yes, Father. It's me and Narlow. We'll be there in a moment."

"Good, my child. Suddenly, I'm not feeling any too spunky. A little dizzy. I would appreciate it if you would see me home."

41

I made no contact with WP the next day. Far as I know, she'd didn't try to find me. For the first time in my life I was scared to a trembling, mumbling mum-mute. I'd faced a cornered mountain lion protecting her cubs; a rabid wolf that chased me up a tornillo tree, kept me there for two days and nights until Papa found me and put the wolf down; survived a fall into a rattlesnake-infested ravine with a broken ankle, never had reason to be frightened of a thing in my life. But this was different. A *woman*. A delicious delight, hot for me, intent as a badger after a mouse. I was no match. I'd never let Papa hear me say this as he always cautioned me not to say that something was not fair. But, if this didn't qualify, then I don't know . . . plus, my resolve had melted like a snowball rolling through the gates of hell. Remorse set in like black fog when I recalled telling her repeatedly that I loved her. All I could think of was how much I wanted her—in bed—all night long.

Coot thought it hilarious my hiding from the most gorgeously bedecked creature in California, especially in the most beautiful city on the continent, unable to show my face on the street, the bar, or the dining room. He spent most of day with Mr. Goodyear, came back to the hotel late in the afternoon chasing his wine-sipping companion around his room.

Later that evening, a soft rapping came at the door of my room to the hall. Afraid to open it, I crept to the parlor hall door, peeked around to see who was pecking at my bedroom door. WP . . . her nose not more than four-inches from my own.

"Hello, my darling."

I was speechless.

"Are you going to make me stand out here in the hall all evening, or are you going to invite me in? I'll behave—promise."

She strolled in, sat on the divan, patted the cushion beside her, motioned for me to come sit. "What am I going to do with you, Narlow Montgomery? I've frightened you, haven't I? I have—haven't I, dear one?"

I laughed. "I'd be lying if I said you haven't given me a run for my money."

"Narlow, let me ask you a question. If it's too painful to answer, just say so. The other day when we kissed, then last evening . . . is that the first time you have ever kissed a woman? When you were a boy, did you ever kiss a girl?"

"Sure I did. Lots of times."

"How many times, with how many girls? How many women?"

"Well—uh, let me see . . . I uh . . . I guess I don't recall right now."

"How many times did you ever kiss your wife? Sophie, isn't it?"

I stalled, smiled, laughed. "Once. At our wedding ceremony."

She leaned forward, laughing. "I knew it! I just *knew it*. Damn, I wish I was in Monte Carlo. I'd have broken the bank."

I joined her amusement. She gathered up my hands. "Now, Narlow, exactly how many naked women have you laid those beautiful hazel eyes on?"

My blank stare told all. We roared with laughter.

"Well then, I don't suppose there's any reason to revisit the number of women you've told that you love them." Her hazel eyes brightened, the glint of emerald flashed. "At last count, I'm the only one—in a class of my own."

We sat looking at each other, smiling, me wondering what was on her mind, she smiling, then grinning. She *knew exactly* what was on *our* minds.

"Narlow, listen to me. I'm not asking you to leave Sophie, or anything of the sort. You must know that I could have any man I desired in San Francisco, New York, or Paris. But, I don't want them. I want *you*, and I will *never* make any demands on you regarding your marital status, never demand that you divorce your wife for me. I promise you that. I *promise*. All I want is *you*. I want to love you, have you love me, hold me, press me to the sheets, pull my feet in the air, make love to me all night long, to make love to you all that same long delicious night. Is that so wrong, so bad? To want someone to love? Is it, Narlow?"

God how I wanted her, then Na-Tu-Che-Puy's voice came to me – "*Dii jii ye* – From today on." His story about geese mating for life . . .

WP leaned her head on my shoulder. "Don't answer right now. Think on it for a little while. Then answer. Just know that though I've had plenty of opportunities, I have never gone to bed with anyone in my life. I promise you." She giggled. "Yes, I've kissed a few, but you're not the only virgin in this room."

I smelled her hair, the hint of her intoxicating perfume, felt her full breasts pressing on my chest, gazed at her legs crossed at her ankles. Her body and legs were as trim and taut as trace chains. I was sitting with the most beautiful woman that

I'd ever seen, possibly the entire world. I had observed how respectful she was with coachmen, waiters, her father's servants, her friends, fellow actors. She had been reared with riches, yet she didn't seem to yearn for them. Her father was rich, yet she pursued a career of her own when most women would simply let life slide by like fog lifting off the bay. She knew what she wanted, and prepared to go after it. I had to admit it—I was lost in her essence. She was someone I could trust.

I chuckled.

"What's so funny?"

"Nothing, not funny at all. I was just thinking. Here I am, a grown man, just kissed only the second woman I've ever even *touched*, and the weirdest thing is . . . I've never made love to a woman in my life. I've told you that I love you. You say that I'm handsome. I've heard that said before, so I suppose looks is not my problem. I was raised by the meanest damn woman in captivity, yet I've always wanted a woman to love. Guess I was searching for the love of a woman to replace what I never had with my mother, a woman who robbed me of my childhood. I've read that children, especially boys, who are reared by a mean-hearted woman, a woman who withheld her love, or worse, had none to offer, those boys grow to men who go through life in a lost world. It's strange, I readily admit, but while all that time I wanted a woman *to love,* I do not recall ever yearning for a woman to *love me.* Perhaps I was never prepared to engage in a two-way relationship, I don't know. But, something's damn certain bassackards about that scenario. But, you know what, WP? It's me that's strange. Why would you want such a strange, screwed-up man like me?"

"I don't know, Narlow. Sometimes I'm not certain I know myself as well as others believe I do. Maybe none of us are that familiar with our real selves. All I know for certain is that I want you. I love you with all my heart, want you to be the first with me, want to be the first for you. God, how I want that, especially knowing that you return my love."

After a moment, she asked, "Should I leave? I will if you want me to. Never bother you again. Promise."

"No, WP, I don't want you to leave, and you know it. And, I'm sorry about today, I just needed to . . ."

I was through talking, through beating myself up, through fighting both her and myself, tired of worrying about Sophie, a goose's mating habits. I picked her up, carried her through my bedroom door, hooked my boot behind it, and pulled it shut.

42

The following morning, WP came by the César in her father's four-wheel, gilt-spoked, gold leaf-etched, Phaeton carriage, pulled by four matched black Arabians, every metal surface of their harnesses gleamed gold, the driver perched high and forward. I motioned to the driver that he need not trouble to step down on my account—I'd open the carriage door myself. The stately gent doffed his top hat revealing an avalanche of snow-white hair that fell to his dove-colored, scissor-tail coat. Mr. Goodyear was proud of the geldings, proud of his carriage, equipped it himself with both a glass windshield and thin isinglass shields inside the glass and on all window openings, making the interior of this beautiful conveyance as cozy as his daughter was breathtaking. Mr. Goodyear was also quite proud of his version of isinglass, saying that while it was a bit more brittle than what was generally available on the market, it did not discolor and possessed less waviness, almost as clear as glass, a marked improvement.

The forward-facing seat was more bed than chair, the back so far to the rear making it impossible to sit upright with your feet and legs stretched out in front of you. The accordion roof was pulled open, fog swirling around like silver ghosts hiding in every crevice.

I scooted in. "God, being in this carriage is like the breath of a field of flowers, just like your body, lithe as roses in a carpeted meadow."

"You devil of a man. Talk like that will get us back in bed."

I laughed. "Where are we off to, my beautiful love?"

She pulled her gray shawl close to ward off the chill of the heavy fog. "Wherever Michael—he's the driver—wherever he takes us. He's been with father for nearly fifty-years. I told Michael nowhere in particular, but I did want him to take us down Nob Hill, then around to the far side, then up the Nob to where the cable car runs. From there, I asked him to take us down to the bay. It's a beautiful drive. Something very special."

She snuggled close. In a moment, she asked, "No regrets about last night, I trust?"

"No. *None.*"

"Neither do I. Oh, Narlow, I'm so thrilled my first was with you. You're so gentle, so loving. Last night could be with none other."

I pulled her close. "I admit thinking that perhaps I should have plenty of regrets, but I don't. Not a one. God, you're incredible, WP. I never dreamed it could be like that. My god, WP, you're luscious. I could just eat you alive like the crunch of a ripe pear."

She smiled. "*That*, my dear man, can be arranged."

"I don't mean just that. I mean *you*. You're a delight, so different from anyone I could ever imagine. No wonder I love you." I fell back against the seat, smiled. "You say we can go our separate way, that this is a mere dalliance, and that may very well be true, but, I'm *struck*, WP, struck to the core."

She purred, snuggled close. "My dear, you're no huckleberry, you are my true champion, but I must admit you are a complete enigma to me, a paradox of biblical proportions. So colloquial, yet so intuitive, worldly in a strange way. I want to celebrate your coming to me, to plan our lives together, to travel, see the world together, stay six months at father's Mediterranean villa, stay so long that I'll be the dread of your existence. Doesn't that sound lovely?"

"I'd be lying if I said otherwise, but I can't be gone that long. And, besides, don't forget, I'm—"

"Can't Coot take care of your business matters? From what you've said, Sophie would welcome your absence."

"Well, you're right about Sophie, and yes, Coot can take care of things for me—he'd be the first to say that me being gone and with you would be the best thing for me."

"Oh? Why's that?"

"I've been so screwed up over Sophie, he's afraid I'll kill some fool, and Papa's beside himself with grief over what I've done of late."

"Then we have a lot to plan. A lot to think about."

The drive up the far side of Nob Hill to California Street was shrouded in fog, ancient trees, old homes, four-stories tall, cragged, beaten by the weather, 200-years of damp fog draped over them.

"Narlow, tell me about this bull elk that whistles when you're in danger. Has it always protected you?"

"Oh, I suppose. Warned me before Mama hit me with that horse quirt, but I ignored it. Learned not to do that again."

"A bull elk whistle, huh?" She giggled, nudged me. "Do you ever whistle, Narlow?"

Near the top of Nob Hill, the carriage broke through the fog into the crystal-bright air. WP's auburn hair turned golden-russet, mirrored like a raven's wing, her gray worsted shawl framed her face, sparkling silver diamonds from the mist in the sunshine's lace.

"God, WP! What I'd give for a picture of you right now. You're *unbelievably* gorgeous." I thumped my head, patted my chest. "But, I've got you captured away in my noggin, stolen away in my heart. I'll never forget this moment."

"It's such a delight to hear you express your love! Indeed, so heartwarming."

The carriage plowed through another fog patch, denser, if that's possible, then slowed as we approached the cable car tracks on California Street. The driver clucked the team across the busy avenue into a barricade of fog.

A man lifted a shout to my left, "Watch out!"

We both leaned forward. I turned to him.

WP flew out of my arms. I grabbed at her. Rolled off the seat, fell to the floor. Her lower legs and ankles pinned beneath me, her body fell back on me. I arched my back, fumbled with her feet and ankles, finally got them out from under me.

She was bleeding. I couldn't figure out what happened. The carriage horses were screaming like animals do when they're mortally wounded, dying. I rolled WP off of me. She was unconscious, blood gushing from her face, dripping from her nose. I sat up, pulled her to me, and stood, looked forward through the shattered glass and split isinglass. One of the horses was under a cable car. *Where did that car come from?* The horse was trembling, the other lead horse was laying on its side, kicking in the traces, frothing at the mouth. A headless man lay under the cable car, his head on the near side of the tracks, blood pooling under a great shock of white hair, motionless—Michael, the driver. The rear horses tried to bolt, to run, escape, but were constrained by their harnesses.

Two policemen ran up, first checked on the cable car passengers, some still clinging to the overhead rails, others strewn around on the ground. Cries of anguish. Cries of pain. Cries of befuddlement. One of the policemen came up to the side of the carriage, stepped up. "Everyone all right in there?"

"*No sir*! This lady is bleeding badly. Severe cuts on her neck, face, and nose. She's unconscious, though I've tried to bring her around."

I looked at the windshield where WP's head had hit it, the isinglass sheeting, torn and split, blood streaking down both sides. The heavy glass had shattered, daggers pointing in all directions, blood streaking down the inside.

The policeman leaned his head in the carriage. "Here comes an ambulance. Mister, I recognize your lady. That's Miss WP Goodyear. I've seen every play she's ever shown in San Francisco. I'll see that she's immediately taken to Christ Church Hospital."

The hospital staff wheeled WP into the operating room, asked that I wait in the hall, assured me that Dr. Nuninski was on his way. The operation would likely take several hours. I sent word to Coot who came immediately. After I told him all I knew, he left to tell George Goodyear about the accident. When I saw the old gentleman walking down the corridor toward me, he appeared to have aged ten years since yesterday. In late afternoon, Dr. Nuninski appeared.

He shook hands with Mr. Goodyear. "Gentlemen, Miss Goodyear is doing as well as could be expected. We were finally able to stop the bleeding. Her face and neck were lacerated, some rather deep. I took great care in stitching her wounds, however, since it necessitated over 300 stitches, scarring will be inevitable. There is nothing that I can do about her nose. The end of it appears to have been snipped off. Having nothing to compare it to, I would judge that she lost slightly less than half-an-inch of her nose. Her upper lip on the left side took several stitches. It appears that the lip injury was caused by the same sharp edge that snipped her nose. Either the windshield glass, or the isinglass. I suspect the later as the officer who accompanied her in the ambulance mentioned that there was a great deal of blood on both sides of the isinglass. Take hope—"

Mr. Goodyear sighed. "Oh, my God. My own isinglass did that to my beautiful daughter."

Dr. Nuninski went on. "We're not certain of that, Mr. Goodyear, just supposition. But, take hope in that both the nose, and especially the mouth, heal exceptionally well, far better than other parts of the body. I have a colleague in New York, a surgeon by the name of George Monks, who is in the final throws of perfecting his technique of heterogeneous free-bone grafting to reconstruct saddle nose defects. Perhaps he can be of assistance in reconstructing Miss Goodyear's nose. And, there's always Paris. I've read that their surgeons are making great strides in plastic surgery. Let's pray that either Dr. Monks, or a Paris surgeon, are able to do their wonders on her nose. And, gentlemen, today's cosmetics hide a multitude of Nature's flaws. No reason to believe she will not come through this in fine fiddle. But, hear me, gentlemen—infection is our only concern at the moment. No telling what her bleeding face came in contact with on the glass and isinglass, and of course, your coat, Mr.

Montgomery, when you lifted her out of the carriage. She will receive our constant vigil in that regard. You may be assured that we will do all that is humanly possible. Pray, gentlemen, *pray* that we are able to keep infection at bay."

The three of us sat in the hall, discussing how we maintain our vigil over WP. At first, her father insisted that he would stay close at her side until he could take his daughter home with him. Coot convinced him that the strain of that commitment would likely put him to bed as well. He should maintain his strength until WP was able to go home, be in condition to help nurse and care for her.

At 8 that evening, a nurse came out to tell me that I could see her for a few minutes. I went in, knelt by her bed, reached out and took her hand. Her face was completely bandaged so I wasn't certain whether she was awake.

In a moment she whispered, "Narlow? Is that you?"

"Yes, WP, it's me. I'll stay with you, if you like."

"I would like that . . . like that very much. I told Dr. Nuninski that I wanted you to be able to sit with me—that is, if you want to. He said that he would arrange that for me, but that you would have . . . have to be scrubbed down, wear one of those silly gowns . . . for fear of infection."

"I'll stand on my head buckass n'ked if they'll allow me to stay with you."

"Don't make me laugh. I'm supposed to . . . to remain perfectly still. The stitch . . . the stiches, you know."

"Oh, yes. Sorry."

"Narlow, I don't want us to end this way, and . . . well, with you thinking it was just a lot of candles on a small cake, but—"

"Please don't say that, WP, it hasn't been that—"

"If it hasn't been trivial . . . trivial to you, what has it been to you?"

"Why, WP, you'll be up and around in no time . . . no time at all. And when you're healthy and strong, let's spend that six months at your father's Mediterranean villa you were talking about. Shoot, Coot can take care of things for an entire year if you want—"

"Narlow, I asked what our time together has meant to you."

I squeezed her hand, but before I could respond, she drifted off. The nurse came in, led me back into the bowels of the operating area, showed me a sink and some rank, medicinal-smelling, yellow-caked soap, told me to wash everything about me, especially my hands, face, and hair. Told me to take my pick from the stack of gowns to don when I was squeaky clean.

Throughout the night, a nurse came into WP's room every half-hour, sometimes just to check on her, on other occasions to give her a shot of something or other. If she was in pain, she showed no signs of it.

Coot brought Mr. Goodyear to WP's bedside at 10 the next morning. He put his head next to hers, whispered to her for an hour, then Coot took him away.

Around 5 that afternoon, I guess I had dozed off, heard WP whisper my name. I bolted up. "Yes, WP, I'm here. How are you feeling?"

Her hand came up, waved her finger, telling me not so good. In a minute, she said, "Narlow, I was dreaming just now. You went away, to El Paso, I imagine, but you came back to me, handsome as ever. After some period of time, I don't know how long, maybe a year—longer—you disappeared again. The next summer, you came back to me—father's villa on the Mediterranean, told me that you had divorced Sophie, that you wanted nothing in this life but—but me. It was so lovely— not just a dream. You won't leave me, will you . . . will you, Narlow?" Before I could reply, she patted my hand.

She rested somewhat easier that night, though she was struggling with something, like she was arguing with herself. At one point she cried out, "Oh, I see. So, *that's* how it happened!"

The next morning, she was adamant that I return to my room, clean up, lie down, see if I could sleep.

At noon, I came full awake. I'd dozed off far longer than I had planned. I dressed and rushed back. As I came down the corridor, a policeman was coming out of WP's room, turned and walked down to the service area, bolted down the stairs. He looked familiar, but how many San Francisco policeman had I seen since we first helped the Wangs off to—Wait a minute. That was the same policeman who directed the ambulance crew to take WP to the hospital before the injured cable car riders. He rode with WP and me to the hospital. Suppose he just dropped by to check on his favorite actress?

WP acted as though she were asleep. I knew better—the officer left only moments before I came through her door.

She moved her arms, stretching them. "Narlow, are you there?"

"Yes, WP, I'm here, all cleaned up, fresh as mint julep."

"Narlow, I've been thinking about the accident. I'm uncertain. What do you remember? I only recall being bolted forward into father's isinglass curtain and the windshield, falling back, more like jerked back. Do you recall any of that?"

The policeman, her questions—like a script. "Gee, WP, it all happened so fast that I'm still vague on the particulars. I recall a man shouting, 'Watch out!' We leaned forward, I turned to my left to see what he was yelling about. I turned back to you, rolled on the floor as you hit the windshield. You fell back on top of me, but your lower legs and ankles were under me. I arched my back, got them out from under me, rolled you over, saw all the blood on your face, got my feet under me, and stood with you in my arms. I heard the horse's screams, one of the horses was under the cable car, the other . . . I don't recall where the other lead horse was, but the rear two were trying to bolt from their traces. Your driver, Michael, was also laying under the cable car. Blood all over the place. Several car passengers were scattered about on the ground, everyone screaming. Policemen came running up. Two, maybe three of them, I don't recall. They checked on the cable-car passengers, then one of the policemen came over and asked if we were all right. He recognized you as he is a fan of your work, said that he would direct the ambulance driver to immediately take you here to the hospital. That's all I can remember at the moment."

She was quiet for a spell. "When you rolled onto the floor, did you grab at me, pull me back down on you?"

"I'm not certain. I recall grabbing at you, but I don't believe I pulled you back. Why do you ask?"

"The officer you spoke of paid me a visit just before you came back, and—"

"Yes, I saw him. Did he come to check on you, or did you send for him?" Why didn't she ask me about the accident before talking to the policeman? I held my tongue.

"Oh, he just dropped by. Think nothing of it." Again she was quiet.

She asked, "Narlow, has Dr. Nuninski told you about my injuries, what's in store for me, what I can expect?"

"Only what he told me, your father, and Coot just after your operation. I've seen him here in your room when he drops by to check on you, read your charts, but not to talk—"

"*What* did he say? *What* did he tell you after the operation. *Exactly* what did he say?"

I squirmed in my chair, felt the skin on my face pull back. "He said that it required 300 stitches on your face and nose, and some on your neck, that there were surgeons who could—"

"*What* did he say about my nose?"

"He said that it had been snipped off on the end, that he had a colleague in New York who was perfecting a technique . . . I don't recall the specifics, but he—"

"What did Dr. Nuninski say about my damn nose? You're *dodging me*, Narlow, and I don't like that a damn bit."

"WP, I'm not dodging you. I'm trying to relate what the doctor told us. He said that the end of your nose had been snipped off. That's all I recall him saying about—"

"Did he mention exactly how my nose happened to be 'snipped off,' as you so flippantly described it?"

"That was Dr. Nuninski's word, not mine. He said that it appeared that your head went through the isinglass, hit the glass windshield, that you may have cut your nose when you came back through the ising—"

"Narlow, what is going to happen to you and me? What about our commitment to each other?"

"Well, uh . . . WP, please forgive me, but I . . . uh . . . I don't recall that we made a commitment. We agree that we just—"

"I want you to live up to your word, *you son-of-a-bitch*. I want you to get on the next damn train, get your ass back to El Paso, and *immediately* file for divorce from that weakling woman, a thing you call Sophie. Her name fits her—the personification of weakness. I hate her and never even met the creature. But you're going to rid yourself of that woman, just like you *promised me* before you bedded me in your hotel room. For once in your goddamn miserable life—*just once*, stand up and act like a man. Not a fumbling bumpkin that's afraid of every woman that he meets.

You're no man at all, whining that your mommy stole your childhood, that kind of crap. And what about all that bull-elk-whistling shit that always warned you of danger. *Ha!* Where was your bull elk when we crashed into that cable car? You're a fraud! Passing yourself off as a seer—my ass! Don't you realize that I *gave myself* to you? I was a virgin. I allowed you to enter my body, my person. I vouchsafed my virginity to you, while you claimed to have never been with a woman before. Now that's a laugh. You're far too experienced to have never been with a woman. You took advantage of me. You should be ashamed, and after I gave you my all, *my first*."

"WP, I don't blame you for being distraught over your accident, but I never— *not once* did I say or even *suggest* that I would—"

"Get out, you mountebankerous bastard! *Get out, you son-of-a-bitch. Get out*, before I . . ."

She began tearing at her bandages.

A nurse rushed in, asked what all the screaming was about, restrained WP from doing harm to her face, held her arms until she settled down. The nurse turned to me, motioned for me to step out in the hall.

I stood trembling in the empty hall, kicking my ass for telling WP so much about me, a woman whom I really did not know, but a woman who appeared to now be revealing her true self. Inside two minutes, the nurse joined me in the waiting area. "Mr. Montgomery?"

"Yes, ma'am?"

"I'm sorry, but Miss Goodyear ask me to inform you that she does not want to see you again. Asks that you leave this hospital."

"Yes, ma'am, I'll leave in just a few minutes. Give me a bit to gather my wits about me."

"Thank you, Mr. Montgomery. It's people like you that make my task a lot easier. I've watched you with Miss Goodyear. You're kind, considerate, sat in that chair beside her bed all these hours and days, fretting yourself over her. If you'd but listen, you'd know she's constantly onstage, quoting this line then that from Shakespeare and Emerson or whomever. I don't know what your problem is with her, but I know her, known her all of her life, helped birth her right here in this very hospital. Was here when her own mother passed away just a few hours later."

She made a motion to return to WP's room, turned to me, stuck her finger on the end of my nose. "Sir, I'm going to speak to you as though you were my own son. You are a smart young man, but you need to start thinking with what God gave you above your necktie, and cease thinking with what He bestowed upon you below your belt, for *it* has *absolutely* no conscience. As I said, do yourself a favor and do as she requests—*go*. Go from this place! Go back where you came from!"

After the nurse left me, I slid down in the chair. Granted, I hadn't known WP all that long, but something in my gut told me that Miss Willy Peabody Goodyear was not through with me—not by a country mile—and I might as well let her take her best shot.

The nurse referred to Emerson—I bolted up. That was it! My mind raced back to the first evening at the César, WP's reference to "the little needle always knows the north," and all that stuff about "five or six or seven teachers"—all memorized, word for word lifted right out of Ralph Waldo Emerson, mouthed by her as if they were her own thoughts. Who the hell was this woman? *What* was she?

WP came storming out in the hall, slipped on the slick, painted floor, pulling at her bandages, ripping at them, tearing them off her face. "Look! *Look*, you bastard! *Look* what you did to me. I'm ruined. I'll never act again. Never. *Never*, you hear me, *never!*" She continued tugging at the bandages around her neck. "First, you took advantage of my innocence, ruined me for another man, now you've ruined my career."

"WP, stop! You're hurting no one but yourself. The doctor warns about infection and–"

She got up in my face. "Pretty, huh? See what you did? Well, answer me, you . . . *you son-of-a-bitch!*"

"WP, you can rant and rave all you want, but I didn't do that to you, the damn isinglass did that. How can you blame me for that?" Her face was swollen double, a peeled onion, pink, the stitches covered her neck and face well up into her scalp line, her nose was swollen to an unrecognizable glob, the end of her once beautiful nose was trimmed off like it had been subjected to a pickle slicer . . . a red, round, scabbing glob of a flat stub.

"You know damn well how I can blame you. That policeman that visited me verified what I already suspected, what I vaguely recall. Yes, I went through the isinglass, and yes, I hit the glass windshield with my head, but you–*you* pulled me back through all that broken glass, shards of glass coming at all directions, and *you* pulled me through that isinglass, and that's when my damn nose was sliced almost completely off. Cut my upper lip almost off as well. The officer said there was blood on the *inside* of the glass, and *both sides* of the isinglass. Proof–*proof,* you son-of-a-bitch, that my nose was not cut until you yanked me back through the isinglass. You've even tried to blame my father, but that–"

"Your *father?* I haven't said a word about blaming your father."

"Oh, now you're call my father a liar, is that it?"

Two nurses and an orderly rushed in, pulled at WP, insisting that she get back in her room, that if she did not, the hospital could not be responsible for infection that would likely occur. She brushed them aside.

"You have besmirched my pristine reputation while making calumnious promises in your sanctimonious libertine manner, flitting around the countryside courting this dalliance then that, without a care for those you crush beneath your boots. You–*you worthless son-of-a-bitch!*"

The nurse was right–WP was quoting Shakespeare, maybe not her favorite, Lady Macbeth, maybe Hamlet. But for certain, I'd only seen those words one other time in my life–in my book of Shakespeare. *Who the hell was this woman?*

The nurse said, "Mr. Montgomery, I must insist that you leave these premises. If you do not, I shall send for the police. As I said before, *go.* Go from this place–this woman!"

Before the nurses could get WP through her door, she screamed, "I meant what I said about you divorcing that goddamn wife of yours! *I'm holding you to it.* Get your ass on that train back to El Paso, and be *damn quick about it.*"

I walked the twenty-four blocks back to the César, needed the time to think, to get a grasp on all the unanswered questions and issues that swamped my brain.

What waited for me slipped under my door answered all my questions—a yellow envelope—a telegram. I tore it open, glanced down at the bottom to see who it was from—Rodolfo Bustamante.

Narlow Montgomery, c/o The César, San Francisco, California

I regret to inform you that Dr. Leighton Green has checked Sophie into the El Paso Hospital. STOP. Return immediately. STOP.

Rodolfo Bustamante

"My God! What can it be now?" I plopped down on my bed to think a minute.

Only one thing to do. Coot wasn't in his room. I sat at his desk and scribbled a note to him, told him the wire would tell him all I knew, that I was headed to the train station and catching the next train to El Paso. Signed off by telling him that things between WP and I were a mess, that she blamed me for her injuries, claimed that I promised to divorce Sophie, marry her, and asked him to visit WP and do what he could to set order to this chaos. No way could he say or do anything that would make things worse, and who knew—maybe he could make her see the errors in her thinking.

43

May 19, 1883

The train ride back to El Paso was lonesome, long, too much thinking time. I spent its entirety in the bar, soaking up what I hoped would ease me into a stuporous escape. *Damn it,* I didn't want to make that trip to San Francisco. It was Coot's preposterous idea to escort the Wangs all the way from El Paso to their steamer docked in the San Francisco Bay. Me falling for WP's perceived brilliance—"the little needle always knows the north," and all that "five or six or seven teachers" crap. *You read that, damn it to hell, years ago, but you had your mind on your prune, you . . . you.* Her claim of virginity, that I stole it from her. All that big-thick-long crap. WP *a virgin? You dumb ass!* That nurse was right—a prune is ill-equipped for thinking, and as she said, damn certain not in possession of a conscience. WP's claim that I promised to divorce Sophie, marry her. Me telling her that I loved her—*my god*—you frothing imbecilic neutered moron! Over and over, beating myself to death over my indiscretion. *You were so hot, so disgustingly lustful for that auburn-haired, big-titted, gorgeous woman, you about lost it in your britches. You were like a damn billy goat around a young nanny coming into season, his pencil-dick squirting piss in his ears and all over himself to make himself appealing to her and her sisters.* And, Sophie! What the hell could be wrong with her now? And, why *now?*

My thoughts turned to the time I was tending goats at Bishop's Cap, lonesome as a whippoorwill. *I'm married, have a wife—well sort of a wife, a house, but not a home, certainly not one I want to return to. If I'd never left, I'd never known the delight of a woman . . . I wonder if it would have been different for WP and me if that wreck with the cable car had not occurred . . . would we eventually marry? There's always a chance . . .*

I stood, grabbed up my valise, and stepped off the train at the San Simon jerkwater just west of Stein's Pass. I'll wait for the next westbound train to San Francisco. WP and I can patch things up. Yeah, that's it! She was just delirious with fright, not knowing what will happen to her, her career. You have to understand why she would be upset, say what she said. I'll wire Coot to put everything in Sophie's name. Yeah . . . I don't want it, build my own fortune in California. Know damn well Sophie'll be better off without me.

The conductor came by, explained there would be a short delay, something about a brake problem on the last car. In a minute, he jumped back up on the step, yelled out, "Hey, mister. Just a rock stuck in that brake shoe. Best step back up here if you're going with us. Won't be another train 'til late tomorrow."

I turned away from him—I'd made up my mind. I'm going back to San Francisco. That's where I really belong. Nothing to go home to.

The conductor swung his lantern, the train lurched forward. I sprinted after it. What the hell are you thinking about? There's nothing for you in California—absolutely nothing. No telling what else that WP-of-a-Calypso-dragonfly woman is hiding. You'll just end up as her goddamn gigolo, nothing more than a step'n-fetch-it. Get your ass back on that train, go on home, face your problems like a man. You're acting like that golden boy in vermillion velveteen tights—no man at all!

When the train pulled into the El Paso train depot, I hailed a jitney to the hospital. I ran up the steps of the hospital, stopped at the nurse's station.

"Yes, Mrs. Montgomery is in Room 132. I believe Dr. Green is with her now."

I ran down the painted lime-green corridor, not knowing what awaited me on the other side of that lime-green door. I pushed it open, Doc Green sitting at Sophie's side, listening to her stomach with his stethoscope. She appeared unconscious.

"Oh, there you are, my boy. Didn't take you long to get all the way back from San Francisco, now did it?"

"What's wrong with Sophie? Will she be all right? What happened, Doc?"

"Ease up, Narlow. I haven't pulled her completely out of this mess, but I'm beginning to have high hopes that she'll make it all right. Thank God your house-keeper, Miss Wanda, returned home when she did, had the uncommon good sense to bring along the drinking glass and poisons lying next to Sophie, carried her down that treacherous concrete stairway of yours to the street, hailed a passing buggy, and got her here quick. If Miss Wanda hadn't done all those things, well . . . your Sophie wouldn't be with us today."

He opened the nightstand, brought out a pasteboard box containing a small box with a tin lid and several bottles. "What I'll never understand is why you'd ever have this crap in the same house with Sophie. I've spent the past several days waiting for your explanation."

"What is it, Doc"

He held up the pasteboard box. "Rat poison in this small box, plus bottled solutions used in photography. All poisonous as hell."

"She took that stuff?"

"Yes, some of it, but not all of it. When your housekeeper found her, there was white crystal residue in this water glass—probably mixed the rat poison in water, drank it down with some of the photography developing solutions."

He replaced the box in the nightstand, sighed, turned back to me. "Narlow, why in hell would you allow this stuff to be in your house? It's dangerous, *damn* dangerous! And you've lost the best housekeeper in two states. You won't find Miss Wanda at your house when you get there. Swore she'd never go back, said Sophie's got her spooked."

"Damn it, Doc, I know rat poison's dangerous, but every household in El Paso always has it around. Rats are everywhere, you know that. And I have no idea where she got all those developing solutions."

He cocked his head to the side, gazed at me for a moment. "Narlow? Narlow, you don't know? Do you?" Cocked his head to the other side. "Do you?"

"Know what?"

"About Sophie. First when she was fifteen. Tried to hang herself as a child, the second attempt was when she had her first bout with rat poison and photography developing solutions, just six months before your wedding. *Damn it*, Narlow, I thought you *knew*! Horace Lewinski didn't tell you? *Ever*?"

I sat on Sophie's bed. I couldn't believe my ears. "No, Doc, her father never mentioned a word about Sophie's troubles. Probably afraid I wouldn't marry her if I knew. Come to think of it, I remember that time sometime before we married. Every time I went by to see Sophie, her father said she wasn't feeling well, needed rest. I didn't see her for maybe two months, made me all the more eager to get married. *Hump*! Hell of a note to come home to this, especially after what happened in San Francisco."

"What happened in San Francisco?"

"Nothing, Doc. You wouldn't believe it anyway."

✳✳✳

I went home, almost had a smile on my face, knowing that *absolutely* nothing else could go wrong in my life, even in my life with two women and a bad-ass mother.

I stepped through the alley door, checked the icebox—empty except for a chunk of ice. I got a bottle of brandy out of the pantry, a glass, and a cheroot, intent on sitting on the veranda, consuming that entire bottle of high-dollar Spanish brandy, a fine stogie, maybe get me another one. Maybe one of each . . .

As I strolled through the dining room, I spied a telegram on the table sitting next to my library dictionary. I set the glass and brandy down, picked up the wire.

Dear Mrs. Montgomery,

I have big lips. STOP Narlow loves them and my big tits. STOP.

I yelled, "Oh, my God! *This just cannot be.*" I glanced at the bottom of the yellow paper to verify who I knew this was from, went back to the wire.

Our Narlow loves them. STOP Do you have luscious lips and big tits, Sophie? STOP Narlow told me about your bedtime problem. STOP Do you know what they say about men with big hands thick wrists and long feet like our Narlow? STOP You should try him sometime. STOP He is the best I have ever screwed for he is the master of the four-masted bed ship. STOP You should go sailing with him sometime. STOP I am an actress who has accumulated a vast repertoire in my body of oeuvre. STOP Never be jealous when he visits me again in San Francisco. STOP When I send him back to you he will leave you alone for a month, for I will send him back with his brains screwed out and his balls floating in your bathtub. STOP Do not let my name fool you as I am all woman. STOP I am certain that Narlow will tell you all about me. STOP Drop in and see me if you are ever in San Francisco. STOP

FROM Willy Peabody Goodyear. Everyone calls me, WP. STOP

I yelled, "*Good God Almighty!*" I ran down the concrete steps to the street, hailed a friend driving his buggy down Utah Street, ask him to hurry me to the El Paso Hospital.

Ten minutes later, my friend pulled his buggy over to the side of the road, I jumped out on the run, hurried up the hospital steps, turned around and shouted my thanks.

Doc Green was coming out the front door.

"Doc, I'm glad I got here before you left. I need to tell you something. I need to tell you that I—oh, hell, Doc, read this. It'll tell you all you need to know why Sophie took all that poison."

He put on his readers, read the wire.

"Doc, I found that on the dining room table. No doubt Sophie read it, found the poison, sat down on the divan with a glass of water, and took it. The particulars and veracity of that wire are not important, but I thought you should know the cause of Sophie's problem."

He handed the wire back to me. "That information helps, Narlow. Indeed it does. Let's keep this between you and me. Sophie's resting, probably not come around until tomorrow sometime. You might as well go on home and get some sleep." He smiled. "No offense, Narlow, but you look like you've been dragged through a briar patch by an angry mule."

For the first time in days, I smiled. "Thanks, Doc, but you're wrong. *Three* angry mules."

"Narlow, let's sit a minute. Over here on this park bench under the shade."

We sat under a heavy magnolia tree, its blossoms still folded tight. "Narlow, my young friend, I don't—Aw, dang-nab-it, Narlow, I gave my solemn word to Horace Lewinski the night Sophie tried to hang herself, *swore* that I would, under no circumstances, repeat what I'm going to tell you now. But Narlow, you *must* know. Old Horace's soul will just have to forgive me. You said the telegram from your lady-friend was the cause of Sophie's problem—that is only partially true, for you see, Narlow, before Horace brought his family to El Paso, while they were still living in Boston, your Sophie was raped. She—"

"Raped? *My god*. No wonder she . . .'"

"Yes, Narlow, raped. Raped repeatedly when she was thirteen by a trusted son-of-a-bitch neighbor man. Horace brought her here. To get her away from where Sophie suffered her tragedy. Where people knew all about it, who'd never let her live it down. Out here where no one would ever know, away from whispering old biddies. Where Sophie could get away from her past, to forget, to go on, to grow, to marry, have children of her own."

"That explains a lot, but how did she know anything about photography developing solutions, that they're poisonous?"

"Horace told me that one of Sophie's friends had an older sister who was acquainted with a well-connected Boston family—the Adames—Henry Adams, to be specific, descendants of two US presidents. His wife is a sophisticate nicknamed Clover, who, you guessed it, is a photographer—world renown photographer to hear Horace tell it. Miss Clover had warned the girls of the danger contained in those bottles."

✳✳✳

Coot stepped off the train the next morning. He said he quickly gave up on WP, called him every dirty name he ever heard, then some.

"Damn, Narlow, she's one pissed-off woman. Cusses with more velocity than Geraldine. I knew you didn't promise her that you'd divorce Sophie. Don't have it in you. Too much Uncle Abe. Reflecting on my brief interview with WP, I guess I shouldn't have led off by telling her she was as full of shit as a Christmas goose saying that you'd leave Sophie for the likes of dick-licking Willy P. Goodyear. She shouted for the nurse, and that nice lady and a big bastard-orderly escorted my young ass out to the street, told me not to come back, and slammed the door."

He grinned, shook his head. "By the way, how's Sophie?"

"She took rat poison and solutions used in developing photography, but Miss Wanda got her to the hospital soon after she took the stuff, Doc Green pumped her stomach, filled it with whatever that crap is they use to counterbalance the effects of poison."

"Any idea why she did it?"

I handed him the telegram.

"WP Goodyear. *That goddamn pernicious bitch*. Narlow, don't argue with me 'cause it won't do you a damn bit of good. I'm taking the next train back to

San Francisco. Straighten out that damn slut. Get shut of this shit, *right now*! She'll never—"

"Coot, you need to know what Doc Green told me yesterday about what happened to Sophie when she was a girl."

When I finished telling him, he bolted up. "*Goddamn it*, Narlow, that's all the more reason for me to go back to—"

"My friend, I just can't let you do that. I can't—"

"You sure as hell *can*. You can't handle this sorta crap. You handle things better on the spur of the moment than me, or anybody else I know. You act, decisively, with haste. Like you handled that bastard train dick that was conning the Wangs. Given time, I might have handled it as well, but you did *exactly* what needed doing at the moment. You threw that bastard off that train, and I'd wager you killed him. But, so what? The Wangs, and a bunch of other innocents were shut of his sorry ass, the very first time it bounced in that bar-ditch *at sixty-miles-an-hour*. Right now, if you went back to San Francisco, you'd kill that bitch."

He slapped his Stetson against his leg, chuckled. "Besides, I forgot to bring back my spatterdashes. Won't the gals in El Paso love me when I strut down Mills Avenue in those black and white spats strapped on my boots?"

44

El Paso June 5, 1883

Coot returned to the Pass, gone exactly as long as it takes a train to travel those 1,285-miles, catch a jitney to the hospital, have a two-minute conversation with its famous actress-patient, catch the same jitney back to the train station, go to his sleeper with a gallon jug of sour mash, and let the train take him back over those same many miles, a shade under eight days.

He never would tell me exactly what he said, just assured me that Sophie wouldn't be hearing from Miss Willy Peabody Goodyear, *ever again*.

I asked, "Did you take the time to look up your blonde friend? By the way, does she have a name?"

"Damned if I know."

＊

A month later, Doc Green arranged for the hospital ambulance to deliver Sophie back home, weak as a kitten, emaciated. All those weeks, I tried to talk to her, but she simply sulked, roll over with her head under her pillow.

Papa came by almost every day, and when I finally confessed my wrong-doings to Papa, he said, "Son, I've always stressed the truth with you. A liar's far worse than a thief. And the good and forgiving Lord knows that it's bad business to speak ill of another's spouse. You'll have to forgive me, but Sophie can't handle the truth. You need to side-step it in this instance, do a little dance around it. From what you've told me, she can't handle the truth about anything in life, especially as regards sex. Piling your guilt on her won't solve a thing, can't convince her either way, and the furthest thing from her mind is wanting any details, a confession, or your beg for forgiveness. Deep in her soul, she must know this is not completely your doing, that she's the one who forced you to this desperation. If you don't want another suicide attempt on your hands, you best rein-in your natural hand for the truth."

"But Papa, I broke our wedding vows, something I never even dreamed I'd ever do. You've spoken of your marriage to Mama, and after all she has done to defame you, you're still true to your vows, something I was not man enough—"

"Son, you cannot compare your vows to the ones your mother and I repeated in that church in the *barrios* of El Paso. Recall that I was present at your wedding, served as your best man. I can still hear you say, 'I, Narlow Montgomery, take you Sophie Lewinski, to be my wife, to have and to hold from this day forward, for better or for worse, for richer, for poorer, in sickness and in health, to love and to cherish; from this day forward until death do us part.' Remember that?"

"Yes sir, but I—"

"To have and to hold. From what you've said, you have not *had* her, never even held the woman in all these many months. But your vows, as well as Sophie's, were based on untruths . . . you didn't want Sophie to have and to hold, and neither did she. Your mother and I, hand in hand, made a solemn vow to our Maker that what He joined together, we would not desecrate. I have kept that vow, and I know for certain she kept her part of the accord with God . But, son, you and Sophie made no such vow, neither in your hearts or in the deep recesses of your minds and souls. Neither of you entered that holy pact honestly—you, looking for someone to love, to take care of, she, looking for someone to take care of her, a father, not a husband. When a man marries a woman, he shouldn't be looking for something to take care of. You 'take care of' a house cat, son, not a real woman. I cannot imagine God recognizing a vow of any sort based on an untruth at best, a lie at its worse. I doubt He considers you married. Now, you listen to me. The Bible says that a woman is to give herself, her body to her husband, not shun his every advance. That's exactly what Sophie—"

"Yes, but you—"

Papa stood, walked to the door, and turned, his boots heavy, scuffing the floor. "Son, there was a day when what I had to say meant something to you. That time has passed as you are now the sole possessor of the world's wisdom. To perdition, you alone, *on your own*, have assigned yourself."

He leaned against the doorframe, sighed. "I'll say this, then leave you to your own devices. Narlow my son, in anger, unkind words you've said, allowed your anger to consume you to the point of it becoming intolerable to be in your presence, an irascible cur. The French have a term that describes what's lacking in you presently . . . *amour proper* . . . a sense of one's own worth." He took a deep breath, again sighed. "It is written that he who has a single enemy will meet him everywhere. You're meeting yourself at every turn, the only enemy you have of any note on this earth." He stepped through the door, turned, and said, "My own son—impossible to abide."

"Aw gee, Papa. I hate hearing you say that. Maybe time will—"

"Time never runs back. Time does not wait while someone runs back with their precious little golden pail to pick up the little dustings of a misspent life or any part of it. You've got to grab up an iron bucket, go back, gather up your broken pieces, and put your own Humpty Dumpty back together again."

45

Camel Mountain Ranch March 30, 1884

Coot came out on the porch, leaned back, scratched against the corner-post, gazed out across the prairie to the north. "Damn, it's hot for March. We've killed upwards of 200 wolves and still they're killing and maiming our cows. Bastards have eaten their fill, gotten themselves back up in good shape, now they're killing and maiming for the hell of it."

I took a pull at my bottle, lit a cigar, threw the match in the dirt. "I suppose you're right about them coming out of Mexico. Dryer'n'a popcorn fart down there, and our place is the only ranch on this side of the border that still has cows."

Jeraldo's ten men couldn't handle the herd and beat off the wolves, so we hired a dozen more *vaqueros* out of Mexico, furnished them with repeaters, and sent them out hunting wolves. They were having some success as they were deadly on the business-end of a rifle. Coot and I kept them supplied with shells and groceries, hunted right along with them.

"Narlow! Run your horse up that hill. There's a pack coming from the south. I'll ride around them, try to run them past you."

In two minutes, I was standing behind a rock when the pack came up the *arroyo* to the north chasing our prize bull. I emptied the repeater, but by the time I reloaded they were long-gone.

Coot rode up. "Well, did we get any of them?"

"Yeah, *we* got six of them, think I wounded another of the bastards. You can see a heavy blood trail on the far side of that mesquite."

"Six of them, one dying, makes seven. Pretty good shooting."

The men we hired to kill-off these packs killed for the money. But the more I killed, the more I liked it. I'd be out scouting around long before Coot and the *vaqueros*, come back to the house well after dark, kept a bottle stashed in my saddle-bag. I hated the loss of our cows and yearlings, but hoped the damn wolves would keep streaming out of Mexico so I could keep blasting their asses.

When I stumbled through the ranch house door, Coot was at the table, lapping up red-eye gravy and grits and a slab of ham. "Sit down, Narlow, pour yourself a glass of whiskey—not your first of the day, I see. Want to talk to you."

"Yeah? What's on your mind besides my share of that ham?"

"Tomorrow's your birthday, lest you forget. And, you still have a wife to worry about, lest you forget. Why don't you catch the early train in the morning, go home, check on Sophie, clean up, come on back in a week or two?"

"Because, I don't want to go home, check on Sophie, blow the candles off a goddamn store-bought birthday cake that my own goddamn lazy-ass wife didn't bake. And I don't want to check on things. Have things to check on right here at the Camel. More wolves to kill."

"Getting to like killing, good at it, aren't you, partner?"

"Not any more than the next man whose cows are getting hamstrung just for the sport of a bunch of goddamn mangy wolves coming out of goddamn, shithole Mexico."

"Uncle Abe would be real proud of your use of the language of the muleskinner, drinking out of a bottle as you ride along half sloshed in midday. But, yeah, you sure as hell like killing. I've been keeping a tally on who's killing what. Do you realize that you've killed damn near as many wolves as twelve *vaqueros* and I have in the past two weeks? You act like you're witched. Hardly say a word to me or the men. They think you don't like them, and I don't blame them the way you cuss them when they miss a shot, even if the wolf is near a *quarter-goddamn-mile away*. They're doing their best, but that's not good enough for you. *Nothing's* good enough for you. Do you and me a big favor. Catch that train tomorrow. Need to be standing at the jerkwater at 5:30 tomorrow morning. Besides, there's another good reason for you to go to town—you're out of cigars and you're about out of whiskey—*again*."

✱✱✱

Doc Green's buggy was in the alley when I walked through the kitchen door. Nothing surprising about that. As much as that buggy stayed in our alley while the Doc tended to Sophie, I should charge the old bastard rent. He was washing up as I stepped through the kitchen door.

"Narlow, I have terrible news for you."

"Yeah, Doc, what is it this time?"

He wiped his hands on a cup towel, pushed his spectacles up. "Narlow, Sophie just died."

"*Died?* For God's sake, died of *what?* She seemed to be just fine when I left here just fourteen days ago." I slumped at the table. "What happened, Doc? More poison?"

"No, she came down with diphtheria. A dreaded disease, but one you can overcome if you've got the will. When I came in this house five days ago, she was in bed, blinds taped shut, bedroom dark as the bottom of a well. I tried to let some sunlight in, but she'd have none of it. Said the dark was comforting. She—"

"*Damn*, Doc! She just up and died, for chrissake?"

He shrugged, shoved his hands in his pockets. "Appears so, my friend. I think the poor child was tired of living, probably more exhausted from faking it than anything. She just laid in that bed in the dark and willed herself dead. That's all I know to say—other than don't be too hard on yourself."

***

The women of the Lady's Club cried enough tears at Sophie's funeral to fill a tub, while her husband shed not a single drop. I was numb, just sat with Papa in front of her casket at Concordia Cemetery, frowning, wondering, now what? What the hell else could go wrong?

Long after the grave was closed and covered and everyone had paid their condolences, Papa and I sat on the mortuary chairs, Coot sat on the dirt off to the side.

I sighed. "I'm ashamed of my thoughts, Papa. When I walked through our kitchen door, saw Doc Green washing his hands, turned to me and said that Sophie was gone, for a second, I was shocked . . . then, I felt . . . I'm sad to say it, but I felt relief. Happy for the first time in months, *years*. Terrible thing to be joyful over the death of someone you're married to, supposed to love, sad beyond belief that your mate is gone so young. So young. She never had a chance in life, and what little chance she had, I stepped on it, choking the life out of it. Even when Doc Green told me about what happened to her as a child, I did not do one damn thing to help her, love her, let her know that someone cared about her."

I leaned over, doodling with a stick in the sand, gnashing, twisting in grief for myself, stood, kicked a caliche rock. "*Damn, m*y life's upside down, my gut's on fire with a cold flame, don't sweat, *can't* sweat, shirtsleeves in a blizzard. Any day now, I expect the sun to come up over the West Portrillo Mountains. The sun's shining cold, raining warm, nothing's worth living." Plopped down in my chair. "I failed Sophie, didn't take care of her as I should. I'm not worth a quarter-pound of black powder to deliver me from this miserable nonsense to the hell I deserve."

Papa sat quietly with his hand on my knee. He patted it, didn't say a word for the longest time. "Son, who's to say what or who could have ever made Sophie happy? She never gave herself a chance, never allowed herself to love anyone . . . hard to love someone if they don't even like themselves. I saw it in her eyes the very first time . . . hard to say, son, but I saw it in her eyes the first time you brought her out in your buggy to meet me. Saw it every single time I came for a visit in your home. You may have been guilty of stepping on her chances at life, but Sophie's size-six slippers were there long before your thirteens ever came on the scene."

"I suppose."

Coot said, "Uncle Abe, I've been on him to go away for a spell, get some breathing room, sort things out, but you know your son better'n me—he won't budge."

Papa slapped me on the knee, stood, offered his hand to Coot to get to his feet. "Coot, my boy, Narlow's forgotten all I taught him about God's love. Your lifelong friend must learn to love himself all over again, to look back over his youth and manhood, to come to the realization that at one time, he loved himself, firmly believed that what God loved was good and worthy."

"Papa, I know—"

"No, Narlow, you don't know a dern thing anymore. It's easy for me to say that you failed with Sophie, but since I was aware of your problems and didn't do a thing about it, didn't utter a dad-gum word, maybe it's me who failed you. But I was helpless to intercede. Maybe Coot failed you. Maybe he should have spoken up. Perhaps you should have pressed your demands on Sophie, not by force of will, but by the unstoppable free force of tenderness and love. But, you see, son, sex is supposed to be *love* in a marriage, to *give* your all to your mate, not to get. You failed that, Sophie failed that. You didn't love each other. Probably didn't like what you saw in the other."

He tapped me the chest. "But I do know what's in there, that you have it in there and in your head to get yourself straightened out. Your soul requires redemption, son. Not God's redemption, mine, or Coot's, but your own. You need to buy your own freedom, clear your mind of debt, wipe your slate clean. You must get away by yourself, get yourself gone for months, maybe an entire year. Doesn't really matter where, just go. Coot and I'll take care of things around here."

He put on his hat, adjusted it using his shadow for a mirror. "And, son, while you're at it, get off the bottle. A corkscrew's not going to pull you out the hole you dug for yourself. Might want to leave those expensive cigars alone as well. Gotten to where you're puffing on those things one after another, suck in the smoke, let it curl out of your mouth, and back in your nostrils like you're possessed. You've got work to do, my son—a *lot* of work."

***

A month later, Coot asked me if I was of a mind to head back to San Francisco, see if there was anything that could be done to get back with WP.

299

I turned, glared at my lifelong partner. "You spend all your time in a goddamn opium den with your blonde wine-drinking partner? Hell no, I'm not going back to San Francisco to see that bitch. Or take a bay cruise. Or any other goddamn thing with that treacherous . . . treacherous . . ."

I gazed off across the *Rio* to *Sierra Juarez*, watched a wagon strain its way up the rocky slope. "But I suppose I might have done that if she hadn't shown her true colors. Coming up with that commitment shit. Me divorcing Sophie, running back to her—*for what?* Spend the rest of my goddamn life kissing her ass? Proverbs speaks of a dog returning to his vomit. I'm no saint, neither am I a dog."

For weeks, Coot stayed on me, saying I was becoming more bitter with each passing day. He had to separate me from two city dudes who just stepped off the west-bound train from Dallas. Greenest creatures I ever witnessed without feathers. One of them hollered out to me, "Hey, hayseed, what's the name of this godforsaken pile of windblown sand?"

At first I ignored him, but his asshole partner joined in, laughed. "Aw, Jimmy, leave that idiot alone. He's so damn dumb he doesn't know his own damn name, much less—"

The back of his head hit the boardwalk before he finished the sentence. I kicked him around, stomped on his head to make certain he'd remember tomorrow why every bone in his goddamn body ached. I had to chase his friend clear up to the Public Square before I caught up with him. So frightened he jumped over the barricade separating the public from the alligators, hid himself behind the rocks on the island in the center of the mote. Coot ran up and stopped me before it got out of hand. Cost me fifty-five-dollars in hospital charges to keep from going to jail.

The judge waved the charges of public fisticuffing in respect for the recent passing of my wife. "*However,* since you've failed to explain to my satisfaction your use of the term, 'fugweasling, nightcrawling, prune-sucker,' I fine you five-dollars for profanity in a public place."

We went out on the boardwalk, Coot wanted to get back to his farm, but wouldn't leave until I promised to go home and behave myself. I suppose the reason I changed my mind about going home was the result of chasing that Dallas dude down to the alligator pond . . . I'd built-up a powerful thirst in my craw. When I walked through the swinging doors of the Acme Saloon, the sun was still naval-high in the blighted western sky. Next thing I knew, the barkeep was scraping me off the sawdust-strewn floor, sun coming through the saloon's batwing doors, handed me my hat, asked that I not come back. "Sure, Henry, sure. I'll take my business across the street."

Two days later, Coot walked into my office, didn't help himself to his usual free cup of coffee, or plop himself down like he usually does. No, today, he was sporting a most unfriendly scowl on his usually handsome face. He always slapped his hat against his leg when he's got a mad-on, but today, his britches got a good blistering.

"Damn it, Narlow, I no more than go back to the farm and you head for the Acme. Henry said he found you on the saloon floor yesterday morning, drunker'n the worst sot in town."

"Aw Coot, I wasn't drunk, I was just—"

"Don't give me that crap. If you weren't drunk, why were you spread-eagle, face down on that saloon floor two hours after sunup?" He kicked my desk. "Weren't drunk, huh? I suppose somebody nailed your ear to the floor, huh?"

I expected him to come over the desk at me, so I stood.

"Narlow, I'm going to say this just *one more time*—you need to get off by yourself. Like Uncle Abe said, doesn't really matter where. *Go.* You're so bitter you can hardly speak, and when you do, the words come out with all the force of the half-an-ounce of air above your tonsils. You and I've talked about everything under the sun trying to get your ass straightened out. Uncle Abe agrees with me, says—"

"Why'd you bring Papa into this?"

"He's worried to death what he sees in your eyes, thinks you're close to killing the next yahoo that crosses you. You're setting yourself up for hell-bent destruction, turning into the town drunk. An *utter disgrace* to the Montgomery name. You would have *never* divorced Sophie. What's worse, you couldn't live under the same roof with her either. I've told you repeatedly over these years that you need to take up with some young widow-lady. Not to bed her necessarily—come to think of it, that's not such a bad idea. But you won't listen, say you know more about women than I do. But I know this—you need female companionship, something you've been real short on all your life. You're not going to like it, and I hate to say it, but the happiest I've seen you since we went off chasing Victorio, was the first few days you were with WP. Yeah, that turned sour, but it doesn't always have to be that way with a woman. There's a lot of good—"

"Bullshit, Coot Boldt! I've been stung and strung out by three goddamn self-ish, self-centered women, and there's one thing that I'm damn certain of—there'll *never* be a fourth. Women are all bitches and—"

He slapped his Stetson down on my desk, leaned over it. "*Damn* it, Narlow, you're bitter! Your anger has a chokehold on your throat. No damn fun anymore, a pain in the ass. Like standing in the hot sun with a pocketful of scorpions, a coiled rattler for a belt. We've partnered forever, but you keep this shit up and you'll kill some damn fool. Get yourself hanged, or shipped off to Huntsville. I'm not planning to stand around to watch it happen. *No sir.* I think you would have drown that dumbass in the alligator pond. *For what*, for god's sake? Calling El Paso a godforsaken pile of windblown sand? *Which it is!*

He walked out on the boardwalk, came back, leaned through the door. "Now—now you get your ass on your horse, or a train, or a raft, float the goddamn *Rio* to goddamn Fort Brown, but get yourself *gone.* And by god, you *stay gone* until you straighten yourself out. Uncle Abe and I'll take care of things around here. Try to get you a housekeeper. We've got plenty of money in our joint bank account, so I'll take care of whatever comes up till you get back."

He glared across Mills Street, turned, pointed at me. "Now, you listen to me—*real good.* I'll be back tomorrow. And if you're sitting behind that desk—sitting behind *that* desk, brooding like a goddamn wet hen with a canker up her ass, you have my *solemn word*—I'll kick your goddamn ass where you stand. Not slap you around a little. *Oh, hell no!* I'm talkin' real old-fashioned ass-kicking. You think it'll help things for you and me to bloody each other's nose, well, by god, you just be sitting behind that desk tomorrow morning. By god, podnah, we'll just see about that!"

***

He was right. Papa was right. Always were.

I stopped by Myers' Emporium, bought a ten-pound sack of pintos, three slabs of bacon, five-pounds of coffee, and a sack of corn. When Old Man Myers smiled, said it looked like I was off on a fishing trip, asked where I was headed, I told him it was none of his goddamn business. Nicest man in El Paso, and my sharp tongue had to dress him down. Started to go back in, apologize—*Aw, to hell with him!*

I went home, packed my duffle and bedroll, took a frying pan and coffee pot out of the cupboard, got my 44-40 rifle off the rack, packed up my mare. I knew where I needed to be, but in the same breath, I feared the place. I would stay there until I had a smile on my face, wagon-track wide, just like Uncle Doyl's. I'd stay even if I ran out of beans, bacon, and coffee. I'd make-do on the land, something I'd done all through my youth. Thought about grabbing a jug of *mezcal* out of the storage shed, blew that off as I'd been drinking too damn much the past number of months. So much that even fine Kentucky straight bourbon whiskey tasted like coal oil before it reached my mouth. Besides, Papa's admonishment that I get off the bottle still blistered. I mounted up, thought for a minute. Went back in the house, came back out, packed Papa's Bible in my saddlebag.

46

Anthony's Nose June 5, 1884

I camped at *Campo Azul* at the base of Anthony's Nose where Papa had been shot, twenty-yards from the remaining seven pouches of gold. My stolen smile curled my mouth thinking of Coot saying that the big Diamondback guarding the cave's entrance was too big to cover with a peach basket. Next morning, I picked up a cracked *metate* that Fernando Valdez had discarded years ago, decided to take it along, find me a flat rock to grind my coffee and corn, make *gorditas* for bread.

Papa's essence was all over *Campo Azul*, all over the mountain, his words, *My own son, impossible to abide,* ate at me. I had to get myself straight, if not for me, for him. Ha! Papa'd never laid a hand on me, but if he heard me say I wanted to straighten myself up for anyone besides myself, he'd soon lay more than his hand on me.

I filled my canteens, not knowing for certain that the spring that ran on the east side of the Nose was still running clear and cold. Several years had passed since I'd last seen it. I needed Papa's cave and goldmine, yet I feared it, dreaded stepping into its coolness. Why?

My mare was a gift from Papa just last spring, raised her "from a pup," as he would say, born three years ago on the first of June, named her, Aunt June. He trained her as no other man I ever knew could, put a light bit in her mouth, rode her all over this mountain so she'd know it, not spook, get someone hurt. I let her have her rein going up the steep slope of the mountain, giving me the leisure of daydreaming on the way up.

Yesterday's twenty-mile ride across Papa's high-desert ranch gave me time to think, all the while feeling the unforgiving dry land pulling, tugging at me. How could I miss something as harsh and cruel as this scorched desert?

Uncle Doyl was heavy on my mind. He'd get a kick knowing he was "heavy" on anyone's mind. He was always thought that folks didn't think much of him, his lazy ways. Papa loved him, Coot and I idolized him, a long-drip-of-water of a man.

My thoughts slid into Mama. Until Sophie and I married, I was able to get past Mama, not really forgetting or forgiving her way of "mothering," just let those old memories slide as there was nothing to be done about that. What Sophie had to do with Mama's recurrence into my daily life, I could not determine. It wasn't Sophie—or was it? Maybe the correlation of Mama's withholding love for her son, Sophie's inability to give herself to her husband, maybe that . . .

Damn it. Get Mama out of your mind. Set Sophie aside, get it in your head that there's nothing you could have ever done about her either. Papa was right—Sophie and I never loved each other. Goddamn it, Sophie, why didn't you tell me what happened to you? I was your husband, goddamn your miserable soul. I might have been able to help you. No, Narlow, you wouldn't, you cold-lipped son-of-a-bitch! You've gotten too damn mean, just like your goddamn mother, you son-of-a . . .

Coot's thinly veiled threat to find himself another friend and business partner pestered me. But our problem was skin deep, hadn't had time to do any permanent damage, and I was determined to see that it didn't. He was one-of-a-kind, and our friendship had to be salvaged.

Now, that was a fine how-do-you-do! I was determined to see that nothing permanent happened between Coot and me, but I wasn't hearing anything about my guilt for not helping Sophie. Yeah, I was guilty, but also didn't give a tinker's damn. Wonder what Papa meant by saying sex is supposed to be love in a marriage? Didn't even really try, you heartless bastard. Took your pillow, quietly closed the bedroom door, and slept across the hall. Wish I had it all to do over again. Wish I could wish it all . . .

There you go again *wishing.* Wishing on a faraway star like a . . .

I was talking to myself. Papa would caution that I should take care not to start answering myself. That put a crack of a smile on my face. Papa had an easy way about him.

It had never been my habit to confide in anyone, especially with any haste. I could only recall confiding in Papa, Fernando Valdez, and Coot, and even those occasions were seldom. Yeah, that's right, you've always been a tight-lipped bastard, but that didn't keep you from blabbing your entire life to WP! And damn it, why did you reveal your Achilles Heel to a complete stranger? *Damn.* I bet she had cause to change her pantaloons when I told her that my mama had stolen my childhood.

You goddamn baby. Man, she sure stuffed it up your ass when she taunted you at the hospital, "You're no man, whining that your mommy stole your childhood." How come I couldn't remember to do a damn thing if I didn't write it down. But I sure as hell recall, *precisely*, her biting words as if she had just mouthed them this very instant.

But, *God*, what a looker. Her looks made me yammer when I should have been running for my life. I recalled thinking that night sitting in the parlor at the César that her body was as trim and taught as trace trains. I should have broken those chains at that very moment. WP would be the better for it, Sophie would as well. Maybe I would have learned to help her. Had I not bedded WP, would she still have sent that telegram? Was I sap enough to still believe that woman had never been to bed with a man before? That she was a *virgin*? That I was *the first*? *Really*? You fugweasling dumb shit! You'd fall for anything. *Especially* if a woman said it. Women didn't lie. They were pure as the driven snow. Women didn't have sex to have babies—the stork brought them! Yeah, that thinking was why men got themselves in such predicaments. It was *always* over a woman. True. So why was I so desperate to have one in my life?

There'd already been three women in my life. *Three*. Mama, mean, Sophie, weak, maybe with good reason, then there's WP, a conniving bitch. Maybe that's all you deserve. Coot said that it doesn't always have to be that way with a woman. *Ha!* He's a fine one to be claiming he knew so much about getting along with a woman. I smiled wide—wonder what Geraldine would have to say about his claim. The smile felt strange. Maybe time will solve all of this and I can go on . . .

Aunt June rounded the last turn in the switchback trail up Anthony's Nose, and there it was—the dark, foreboding opening to Papa's cave. I reined Aunt June, thought about turning her, going on back down the trail for home, get me a jug. Yeah, I need to go back and get me a jug. I thought a minute, got off, turned to the west, stood gazing across the valley, then back at the ink-black opening of the cave. *What are you afraid of? Why are you so reluctant to enter this place? Papa always said that fear and ignorance share the same berth. What secret does your gut suspect lingers in that dark place? Oh, horse shit! Those days here with Papa were special. Come on, let's go!* Two steps toward the entrance and I froze, paralyzed from my knees down, my feet in concrete. They would not be forced. I recalled reading, *Fear is interest paid on a debt you may not owe.* What the hell'd that have to do with me? I wasn't afraid of a damn thing . . .

I stood slapping the reins against my leg, took off my hat, wiped my brow, looked up at the half moon straight above, wondering, *Why? What's got you ready to buckle and run?*

I jumped back in the saddle, gathered what remaining wits I possessed, rode Aunt June on under the cave's fifteen-feet high entrance, her hooves clattering on the rock floor of the capacious vault. It tapered down to five near the end where Papa's gold mine started. It was cool, inviting, not the gloom of my reluctance to enter. *Why had I been so pensive? What could be my fear of this place I knew so well as a boy?* A glance over the eastern shelf satisfied me that the spring was still flowing strong, an acacia growing green and stout nearby. I filled my hat with water from my canteens, let my mare drink her fill while I looked around. *God, I loved this place. Mysterious, its rough walls gathered around me like a warm blanket, so many fond memories. Why were you afraid to come in here? I know—you know your sanity awaits your reaching out. Just reach out your hand. Grasp it! Regain your manhood. If you were just man enough. Reach out, goddamn it! You sorry . . .*

Looking north across the wide pass to the Organ Mountains, the wildness of this place swept over me. The lofted, polished peaks of the rough mountain always reminded me of an ancient giant's knees, thrust up out of the valley floor, the clinging clouds backed up at his mouth, drifting over the top, blowing clear-white vapor from his nose.

Memories swirled around those rough, red-rock volcanic walls. I made camp, thinking, *You haven't learned a damn thing in all your years. You didn't come up here to revisit every damn problem you've had in your entire worthless life. Especially Sophie. No, not especially Sophie. Especially WP—Willy Goddamn Peabody Goodyear. I should have caught the next train out of San Francisco when she told me her name. No wonder she's so damn screwed up. With a name like . . .*

I stepped to the far end of the cave to where Papa's gold mine started. Over the years, he and I had pecked and chipped and dug that red rock back another ten-feet until the vein played out. Never did find much gold, just enough to get Papa through hard times with his goats, to send me to the university if I hadn't run off to the reservation.

Papa's voice came to me, said as he handed me a pickax as a mere lad, "Son, just chip along this line. See what that old red rock's hiding back there." First time I found a little yellow, I held it in my palm. "Looky here, Papa. Gold!" He took the faded bandana from around his neck, placed the bit of gold in its fold. "Tell you what, son, let's bury this under that big square red rock over there next to the wall.

It'll be safe here, always be right here for you should you ever need it." He ruffled my hair. "This will always be just your and my secret, okay, son?"

I found the rock, tilted it aside, and there it was—the red bandana, threadbare, still held my little treasure. I tried to recall when that was, how old I was at the time. "Must have been twenty-years ago since I last saw you." I smiled, folded it back in the bandana, stuck it in my vest pocket, patted it, decided to keep it close while I was there.

Papa's and my stick toys, all still scattered around, a sawhorse just inside the entrance, fitted with a broomstick, the pony's head fashioned from a straw-filled sock, sewn-on buttons for eyes, waited with Job's patience to whisk me away on a faraway adventure, deep in the darkness of the third century. Straw-filled toe sacks, their faces drawn with a chunk of charcoal from our fire, the generals of our armies. At times the sack-generals loaded our cannon, often served us as "one for us good guys, the other for the bad guys." The sacks still hung from the ceiling of the cave, just like Papa strung them up with wire to keep the packrats off. Papa thought of everything. When I asked him as a boy why he was so careful with his belongings, he said, "Son, take care of them, and they'll take care of you. If you don't, you have to stop what you're doing, spend the day going into the Pass, spend your hard-earned money on what you should have taken care of in the first place."

No doubt about it—his ways rubbed off on me. I never fail to bend over and pick up a penny or a *centavo* in the dirt, while other passer-bys just strolled on by. Never saw a bent nail that I wouldn't stoop for, put it in my pocket, straighten it out the moment I got close to a hammer. Squat right down there in the dust and heat of the day, find me a rock, put that crooked nail on it, and tap it straight. Suppose those time-consuming habits were the reason that I was in such a state of mind? Naw, if those habits were bad, Papa would have been in the nervous house years ago.

Tap it straight. That's what I need. Need to go gentle, quit beating yourself up. Just a steady tap, tap, tap . . . tap yourself straight.

Papa and I would sit on this very ledge at midday, guess whether a little row of three puff-clouds would hit the moon. We'd punch each other, pointing at the fast moving clouds, convinced they'd miss their target, then giggle when the moon collided with our puffs.

I spent the balance of the day and evening sitting in the shade of the entrance of the north-facing cave. Just sitting. Gazing to the north at the Organ Mountains just east of the village of Las Cruces. Big, rough range with some pines at altitude, a lot of cedars and mahogany, browse and grass and such in its deep canyons. The sun set over Mt. Riley, forty-miles to the west, dark blue far above, the sun like a big, juicy orange, then it disappeared, slipped into Mother Earth without a "so-long" in its heart for the lonely.

My first night in the cave was spent thinking about going home, that this place was only filled with childhood memories, that I'd have to fight off all the bad about Mama, that . . .

I drifted off, woke well before midnight, cried out, "Why, God? Why don't you answer my prayers? Show me the way out of this mess. I'm begging you, God. On bended knee, I'm begging you!"

Papa's voice came to me, from a time when I asked him why God never seemed to hear my prayers, why I should believe in Him if he only ignored me. Papa said, "My young son, you must learn that God answers our prayers in *His* time, not ours." If pressed, Papa would say, "Quiet yourself and hear the word of the Lord."

I sat at the cave's entrance as sleep would be impossible. Far below, fifteen-miles out to the northwest, Papa's and Fernando's campfire sat flickering in the distance, on the northeasterly slope of Bishop's Cap near *Pena Blanca*. Sleepless nights would give me cause to watch the progression of their campfire, that flickering glimmer in the deep distance, their wanderings with their goats, steady meandering up the canyons of the Organ Mountains where winter fat and Apache Plume flourished, along with all manner of browse for their hungry animals, never allowing them to overgraze any one spot, coaxing them along to another green, a bit of shade for God's creatures, another small spring, every single day. Papa always stayed close to Fernando and his herd during summer months, as the young kids were easy prey for wolves and mountain lions, and the blistering heat of summer quickly took its toll on one man alone.

I determined to read the Bible every morning, first thing, no offputting. *Put your coffee on to boil, then read.* In its pages, Papa had written on a piece of wrapping paper, lines that I'd read a dozen times since Papa gave his Bible to me when I caught that Austin-bound stagecoach—east-bound stage, seemed so long ago, a century or more, yet less than nine, so long. In the past, those few lines Papa had written didn't register much, but today, they struck, hard as flint. The scrap of paper was noted at the bottom in Papa's strong hand, *Rabbi Hillel, a contemporary of Jesus.* The rabbi wrote, *Watch your thoughts; they become your words. Watch your words; they become actions. Watch your actions; they become your habits. Watch your habits;*

they become your character. Watch your character for it will become your destiny. If I am not for myself, who will be for me? If I am only for myself, what am I? If not now, when?

How could that holy man have written that almost 1900-years ago? He sure hit me between my eyes with, "If not now, when?" Papa always charged me to be mindful of the great debt we owe those who took the trouble to write things down, for without their dedication and effort, our kind would yet be locked in the Dark Ages.

I finished my coffee and a pan-fried *gordita*, mounted up, rode north, deep into the Organs to the head of Long Canyon, shot a young mule buck, quartered him, and returned to the cave. I ate an entire backstrap, then cut the remainder of the carcass into strips, drying them on racks in the sun, curing them with smoke from my mesquite-fed fire. Papa, Coot, Fernando Valdez, Na-Tu, Two Sticks, and yes, Uncle Doyl, all gathered around, sitting by my fire, smiling, jawing. So many fond memories, each man different, all wise, so much wisdom wrapped at the entrance of this cave.

The thought crossed my mind that Papa and Fernando Valdez likely heard my shot, but they were hard men to trick, knowing somehow that it was me that fired his rifle, me up there in that cave, doing what I could to get myself straight, while driving myself to the edge...

***

After about a week had passed me by, I began keeping track of the passing days by scratching a mark on the wall just outside the entrance of the wall. After a few days, I got to wondering why it made a particle of difference how many days I'd been in that cave. But, I did it anyway. Faithfully. Like picking up *centavos* and bent nails, with much staunch, etching a mark as the sun rose.

I had promised myself that I'd not dwell on anything. Nothing. Not Sophie, not Mama, not WP, nothing , *nobody*. But ignoring Sophie's and my problem wouldn't solve a thing, unless I could figure out why I married her in the first place. But, I already knew why.

Na-Tu-Che-Puy kept standing at the entrance of the cave, peeking in at me, chanting, "*Dii jii ye, dii jii ye*"—From today on.

One night as we sat in front of his wickiup, he spoke of the animals that mate forever, the lowly goose among them. "They know death. The Pale Eye believe all animals are ignorant. If they are so, how can it be that when one of a mated pair of geese dies, the other will not leave its fallen body for a long time? Much time must pass before that dumb bird allows itself to find another. It is the same with Apache. They do not know the Pale Eye word for divorce. It does not exist. Only when one is unfaithful can they part. The man will be banned. If a woman, the end of her nose will be cut off."

Humph! What would WP think of *that?* Poor woman. What a tragedy for such a beauty. But, ofttimes it takes a major life-changing calamity to unveil a person's real self—if not to themselves, to others. The mishap releases a person from themselves, while in others, it jails them for all time. Her father's horse-drawn carriage ramming the side of that cable car was certainly not the best thing that could happen to Willy Peabody Goodyear. *No sir,* but in that hospital room and the hallway just outside, when she ripped her bandages off her face, began screaming, blaming, claiming that I had promised to rid myself of Sophie so I could marry her, she *literally* unveiled her true self. I dodged a bullet that day. Maybe it would release me from myself, not jail them as I suspect would be WP's choice.

I should have known better than to think I loved her. Why couldn't I admit I was just a man, that I loved her tits, her ass, her love nest. It was absurd to think she could ever share love with me, with *anyone,* for that matter. *But goddamn it to hell,* I was so damnable enamored with her. I ignored it, but *knew* it. Like when she—it was silly to think this, to have even noticed this—but when she turned to me, her face, her eyes, her being, never brought her heart. Silly, yes, but God knew it was true. *But, God* what a luscious, crisp pear...

Damn it! *Don't dwell on her.* O, shove it up your ass! I couldn't just set her aside until I got her straight in my head. I put her on a pedestal the moment I gazed into her pale-hazel eyes with that glint of emerald. But . . . *damn,* it just occurred to me . . . in all those long hours after the wreck, lying in the clean and comfort of that hospital bed, she never once— not *once* voiced concern about the family of that dead driver, her own father's aged employee of fifty-years, or felt sorrow for the injured cable-car passengers, much less the suffering of those two beautiful, black, screaming Arabians that had to be shot where they lay, kicking, suffering. Colors don't reveal themselves in deep shadows, but the harsh light of day reveals all. Yep, sure dodged a bullet. It happens sometimes, that when another's chickens come home to roost, the limb they choose is *your* shoulders, drooped as they be.

I stood, gazed around the cave, shouted, *"Enjuh!"* Again I smiled, recalling Many Fast Feet Two Sticks' word for "good," but he said it with such finality, like, "Enough!" He said that every time he had finished his honey and coffee, had his visit with Papa, and left our camp on the Black River. But whether it was good or enough,

I had a goodly amount of memories of all those goings-on in San Francisco. More than enough, like soaking a warm August day in the shade of a pear tree.

I looked around the cave—the play-sticks of my youth, the feed sacks filled with straw with faces crudely sketched on them with charcoal from our fire. Papa's voice came to me as we were playing at the entrance of the cave—*Narlow, Narlow, my son, what do you think God meant by this?* Gazing across the plain at the *Rio Grande* far to the west, imagining that mongrel hordes were splashing across the raging river. Pushing their war horses, hot with the fire of hades. Intent on spurring their mounts up the mountain to our secret cave. Take us hostages, steal our gold, make slaves of us. Our straw-filled sacks on either side of a log we had dragged there as our cannon, prepared for action, ready to die for our worthy cause.

Papa shouted, "*Sergeant.* You there! Man that cannon. Aim high, *real* high, for the enemy is not yet upon us and far in the distance." He ran to me, helped me lift our imaginary cannon, set stones under its wheels for elevation. I stood, commanded my feed-sack troops, "Fire! *Quick.* Reload. Fire!"

We'd fire a hundred imaginary ten-pounders at that approaching horde, then double over, laughing. Papa would grab me up, swing me around, hug me tight as we rolled in the dust and heavy gravel, me lying on Papa's chest, him murmuring, *O Narlow, my son, Narlow, my son.* Papa always smelled—well, honest. That was always a mystery to me, but truth breathed his essence, honest sweat lingered like honeysuckle. We'd lay down in the warm sun, laugh, giggle, munch mule deer jerky, dream of our next carnage, snooze. Our giggle boxes got themselves turned upside down when Papa recounted the Battle of New Orleans and Andrew Jackson ordered his cannoneers, "Elevate those guns a little lower!"

Fernando Valdez. It finally occurred to me that he was in on Papa's play-scheme. When I was oh, maybe nine, I spied Fernando climbing the mountain up to our cave. I shouted, "Papa, here comes Fernando Valdez!"

"*Where?*" Papa shouted as he came running out, peered over the ledge down at Fernando. Papa took up an imaginary boulder over his head, shouted, "*Alto.* Stop, or I will cast this boulder upon your thieving head! *Smash you to dust.*"

I looked at Papa, wonder in my eyes.

He said, "Sergeant, don't waste time trying to figure this out. We have an intruder with a thousand cutthroats intent on taking our gold mine. We must stop his advance, or his band will do us in, slice our throats. Come to the aid of your general!"

We showered scores of imaginary boulders down on *Comandante* Fernando

Valdez and his troops that day. With desperation shadowing his face and beard, he raised his hands in surrender, came on up, begging for mercy, "Please, *Sargento* Narlow, don't shoot me." He'd wink. "We can be friends."

We laughed, he hugged me, bounced me on his knee, asked if he had caught me by surprise. "Naw, I knew all about it! I was just funnin' you, Fernando Valdez." He stayed the night as he often did in those days. He had a thunderous, baritone singing voice, knew a thousand *corridas*, ballads that he taught me over scores of dreamy campfires up here in our cave-of-make-believe in those long-ago years, so long. Yes—I remember now—he whittled a flute from a yucca stalk for me, blew on it, got it to his liking, played a mystic tune, then handed it to me. I huffed, puffed, sucked, and blew, but could never weld two notes together, while he played endless music on that simple, yellowed instrument.

"How old was I when Papa first began bringing me to this cave?" I asked myself. "Must have been three or four." I smiled. "Better watch that talking to yourself."

I had smiled. I felt the muscles in my face when I did so. They felt strange, weak, like those facial muscles had not been used for an intolerably long time. Made my face tender. A good sore. I frowned just to see how it compared. It was easier. Easier to frown than smile...

That's not good, Narlow Montgomery! You used to be a happy man, a happy boy. Remember Coot recalling his little sister's coloring book that had a cow dancing on a rainbow? He said, that to him, I was that cow on that rainbow, dancing a jig. Guillermo Narlow Montgomery, you need to vow never to frown, ever again. If something requires a frown, walk away from it. Come back to it when you're stronger, when all of this is behind you.

Papa and I were the Lords of the Battlefield, the Gods of Fear in the hearts of our enemies, the god, Phobas. All our enemies were slaves, unable to distinguish right from wrong on their own, that had to be told their every thought. We were always outnumber by our foes, but we persevered, beat them into submission with courage, and the might of right.

But we showed respect to those we captured, for today's enemies are tomorrow's friends. We, The Lords of the Battlefield, would grant them full humanity, charging with us to defeat tomorrow's enemies. Papa taught me that the opposite of fear is love, as the ancients taught their men to fight for nothing but the man who stands at your shoulder. He is *everything*, and everything is contained in him.

312

Papa read that free men wrapped in liberty while at battle have an edge over their slave adversaries, for free men have choices. When free warriors found themselves without their leaders, they elected them, discussed their plans, strategies, voted on whether their notions for getting back home had merit, decided to go through with their ideas, or voted otherwise. On the other hand, when warrior-slaves were left leaderless, they broke and ran, hid, threw themselves over a cliff. They had no ability to think for themselves, to act independently, for others had always done their thinking for them. *Am I a man of merit, or a thoughtless slave?*

"*General Papa!* Gillions of two-legged lizards with the heads of cocks are bounding up the rocks to our castle, their swords drawn, ready for a hassle." We watched their swift approach, lizards the size of horses, jumping, flying from one boulder to the next, ever higher.

"*Quick, Captain!* To the castle walls! Those are no ordinary lizards, but those of the two-legged dragon-cockatrices, the foulest evil ever unleashed by the twelfth century. Their wings will soon overpower us, their wicked glare will turn us to stone. *To the walls!* We shall boil them in oil."

"*General*—the roosters! Should we unhood them?"

"Yes, Captain! Your tactics are legendary. The crow of the cock will slaughter them all!"

✳✳✳

Papa's voice echoed off the walls of the cave, murmuring his wisdom. "Son, studying the history of war is not limited to armed conflict in the literal sense, but the wars we all fight everyday, in our families, relationships with friend and foe alike, strangers, fighting to defend our property, yes, but also our way of life, our freedoms, liberties, how we define ourselves and defend our sense of purpose, our integrity, who we are, our beliefs."

Yes, I often heard Papa observing the great debt we owe writers and scholars, for had they not taken the time and considerable effort to write what they observed of the greats of both antiquity and the present, our history, we would, as John of Salisbury wrote, " . . . been doomed to utter darkness unless illumined by the lamp of letters . . ."

Selflessness was our most noble virtue. Like the Spartans of old, Papa would only fine any of my warriors who lost his helmet or spear, but ordered death to any soldier who lost his shield. For the shield was a weapon, a unique, particular weapon that protected every man in the line, his brothers. Spartan mothers were legendary, for honor was everything to women as well. Papa told the legend of a

Spartan mother who handed her son his shield as he prepared to march off to battle. "Come back with this, or on it."

Sophie's mother died shortly after giving birth to her daughter. Maybe if she'd lived, she could have made Sophie more comfortable with life, teach her to accept what had happened to her, give her the love and tools so there would never have been any thought in her innocent mind to even consider hanging herself when she was only fifteen, took poison only months before our marriage, tried it again when she read WP's wire—yet . . . yet somehow she was able to will her own death. She didn't have the will to live, only the will to die, like committing suicide in self-defense. *Utter stupidity, but wait! You are close to the same offense against God's will. Wake up!*

Why didn't Horace Lewinski warn me of Sophie's tender mental condition, about her terrible life experiences? *Damn it*, he was her father! Had to raise his only child on his own, trying to do the very best for her that he could. He knew that I'd take care of her, depended upon me to do right by her. I wished he had told me . . .

There I went again, wishing. I used to wish that I had a loving mother, got over that foolishness before I was eighteen. Now wished that Mr. Lewinski had forsaken his duty to his daughter and warned me of her mental problems, told me that she'd been raped, her suicide attempts. *Ever think he thought another man would shun his only daughter if they knew it all?* Manly men didn't sit around wishing like a child, wishing, *Star light, star bright.* They *acted*, took risks, faced life as it was, not wringing their hands thinking about how they wished it to be.

When Coot and I bought the Camel Mountain Ranch, I was reluctant. Coot had to explain to me that we'd make most of our first payment due Clem Wallace with the sale of the old mama cows—cows *we* owned. I'd lost my confidence, lost my compass, allowed Sophie to drain it away. I would *never* have bought the Camel Mountain Ranch if it weren't for Coot. A bird nest on the ground, and I would have passed on the opportunity. Then Rodolfo dumped a fortune in our laps, contracting to lay the railroad's waterline. What did I do? I feared it was too much money for such a short period of labor, said it was probably illegal. Afraid, wanting to hide. *Weakling.*

I used to be tough-minded with unstoppable willpower. Papa reminded me that when I was eight years old, I willed myself up a sheer rock cliff to rescue a newborn kid who had lost its mother. A feat accomplished in a blinding sandstorm, my eyes so crusted with grit that I couldn't see Papa's outstretched hand for the kid tucked under my arm. Eight years old. More man then than now. Why, for God's sake, *why*? How did I singlehandedly, without a thought, throw that train detective off that train? For abducting a defenseless woman under my charge? Or simply anger, killing because I could? Killing like those wolves out of Mexico. But, God, I was so weak around WP. I thought I would be able to have that one fling, then come back to El Paso and take up with Sophie where we left off. *Left off.* Hell of a note, but that just about says it all. Sleeping in the hall or on the living room divan. How can a carriage wreck be a Godsend? But it was, saved my ass. Saved my *very* weak ass! I know myself well enough to know that even if I hadn't gone off to San Francisco, that I would have eventually forsaken my vows to Sophie. If it hadn't been WP, it would have been some widow lady. I wish—Aw, shit, *The first star I see tonight.*

Hump! Papa's lived most of his adult life with Mama, a completely *incorrigible* thing who calls herself a woman. While I knew that given time, I would have run off with the first hussy who waved her fanny at me—and that was what I did—Willy God Damn Peabody Goodyear! Thank the merciful God she overplayed her hand, lied about my promise to divorce Sophie, marry her. Her lying immediately erased all feelings for her—a lying chunk of coal coated in diamond sequins. Her screaming lies repulsed me, the line between love, adoration, and hate is mighty slim. But WP saw I was weak while she was strong, that I would do her bidding.

But, glory—our warm touching warm. Will there ever be another?

It muzzled out the day, mirroring my own disposition. I sat at the entrance after the rain ceased, gazed down at Papa's and Fernando's campfire, now almost due west of my perch, its yellow flicker stronger now as they were much closer. Why are the men down in the flats, when the browse was along the edge of the mountain in its deep canyons? Then realized they'd not want to crowd me.

I sat, wondering, *What happened to the fourteen-year-old boy who dealt so decisively with those two bastards raping IB Crane? Who was that lad who took an ax to two grown men, broke an arm on one of them almost in two, shoved a burning yucca stalk up the other's ass for pleasuring himself at the expense of my weak friend. Who was that boy who handed Rye's revolver to Shelly Brom, told her to cock it, help me persuade Seth to lay across that log while I shoved that flaming yucca stalk up the cheeks of his butt? What happened to that boy? A boy who was a man long before he turned eighteen. Two boys scouting, tracking for the Blue Coats, chasing Victorio, the last Apache chief in the west. A boy who turned himself into a man by fighting mightily, valiantly to come to grips with a woman who was no mother at all, but a birthing devise.* I continually rejected Coot's admonition not to dwell on Mama, to

315

view her as she is, not what I wished her to be. I can still recall him saying, "Damn it, Narlow, quit wishing and start facing the truth." Finally, I did, and the truth released me. Now . . .

When did I become so high and mighty not to take Coot's advice to take up with some young widow-lady? But, no, *oh, hell no!* I was far too pompous for such goings-on. But then I took an overland train across half the country to bed the first woman who hinted at the opportunity.

I read that when Edmund Burke learned of Marie Antoinette's assault before her visit to the guillotine, he said, "I would have thought to have seen 10,000 swords leap from their scabbards at this outrage. But the age of chivalry is gone."

Chivalry my foot. Don't even think the term when hashing out your low-lily problems.

Papa taught me that the hardest thing to accomplish in this world was to be myself. He said that until I had sufficient self-knowledge, I would never be able to write a few simple sentences that described who I am, to say this is what I believe, and finally, this is how I intend to live my life. If only—there you go again—*I wish I may, I wish I might.*

When I leave this cave, and started down that mountain, I needed to be able to write those few simple sentences. Until that occurred, I would stay in this cave—*remain* in this cave, if it took all the time God gave me.

I must learn to bide my time, not rush things. Learn from the Spartan King Leonidas, who chose 300 warriors to defend the pass at Thermopylae, bided his time, chose those *particular* 300 out of hundreds of other 300s he could have chosen, selected that *select* 300, not for their bravery, their courage, for all Spartans shared those traits—but because of their mothers, their families, as those sons and husbands would not be coming back, faced certain death against the hordes. King Leonidas knew that when word spread of their defeat, their deaths to the *very last man*, that their mothers had to be brave, honor their fallen heroes by resolve, to demand that their countrymen join them for the future of their country. Surely, I could be as courageous as those mothers with my slight life problems in comparison. And swear, Narlow Montgomery, *swear* you will find your lioness huntress, a woman who will not buckle, who possesses the will and resolve to defend her family against all odds, all comers—with a fair and delicate hand, but grit in her gut.

You *will not* fall for the next flash of a feminine smile or the whimper of a weak kitten seeking your protection. You are strong and require nothing less in your mate. Weakness does not suit you, nor does it become you. You dispised it in Sophie, but with WP...

I slept fitfully, again churning over Mama, Sophie, WP—Papa's voice gnawing at me, recalling years ago when he said that he hoped that he had not failed me, went on to explain that the most holy of all things that God admonishes all fathers is to love his children's mother. When I questioned him about that, how that could be possible: *Son, I won't try to hide your mama's many faults, the things about her that I don't like, cannot accept, but, in truth, I still love that woman.*

I threw my blanket back, stepped outside to view the moon, stars, the Dipper—2 in the morning. Couldn't locate Papa's and Fernando's campfire, thinking they were doubtless fast asleep after so many endless days in the heat. The moon shown circled soft and white, like the moon over San Francisco's bay. WP . . .

Easing myself down on my pad, I promised myself that if my thoughts turned to any of those women—those problem women—that I'd get up *and stay up* until exhaustion overtook me.

I drifted off, my dreams turned into a vision—I fought it, but it was real, nothing left to imagination. The wind, cold, wet, blustery, directly out of the north, driving hard into the mouth of the cave, wind woofing into the vacancy of the hard-rock interior, woofing, woofing, lightning flashes, cobalt against the red walls, sparking lilac in its crevices like lightning on horned creatures. Aunt June stood as a park statue, stock-still, midnight blue, flashes pulsing her muzzle.

Na-Tu-Che-Puy and Many Fast Feet Two Sticks appeared at the cave's entrance, leading a corpse, a cadaver, slime-green as the sides of a neglected horse trough. Na-Tu raised his hand, blessed the four winds, introduced the carcass as Bernard Gruber. Na-Tu said, "Narlow Montgomery, when you at my wickiup, you spoke of you Papa's Good Book, a thing you call Hebrews, that it speaks of entertaining strangers, that some have entertained angels unawares. Treat this stranger with respect, for he has a message for you." The two old Apaches turned, swirled, shadowed into the murk of the winded liquid misery.

Bernard Gruber's spectral ankles were clasped to a heavy chain, links the size of horseshoes. At their trailing end, a church altar, battered, scuffed, splintered. He labored to my side, dragging the alter, sat his tattered-and-dusted-self down in the coarse gravel of the cave. Removed his knapsack from his back, a shredded satchel filled with items a wanderer might have on his person—tin cup and plate, salt, a pouch of pemmican. His flesh like overripe figs, moist, pulpy, edged-brown-green, sagging under its own weight like greasy offal. Beetles and gnats crawled over his knees, scorpions darted in and out of his hairy nostrils and ears, caverns that had not been swept or clipped since before time. Heart rose-colored stinkbugs swarmed his chest. He ate them, picking each in its own turn and time. Offered me a delicacy. Tasted bitter, unpleasantness that turned to stick cinnamon, like a honey-sprinkled bun Papa and I ate at The Pass one day.

About the corpse, peeking over his shoulder, a nauseous-green bubble filled with phantom heads—skulls of women, three of them. One was holding the other two heads by their long straw-green hair, Mama, cackling her hoarfrost, heartless chant, her evil nose pointing at the heads of Sophie and WP, her mantra eulogizing, *There were once three, now only one. Only one. Only one. Only one remains to taunt the son-of-a-bitch.*

I yanked my Schofield from under my pillow, fired wildly at the green bubble. Through the black-powder smoke, there appeared two dead heads falling to the black gravel, the other flew away as though from a goat-entrail-balloon, darting and swooshing out into the ink of black.

Bernard Gruber and I sat eating his treats, first me, then my guest, as he gazed at the sack-men hanging from the cave's ceiling, turned to me, spoke softly with no haste, and I understood his every German syllable. *I chose to take what was not mine from the padres in Santa Fe, wandered the desert with a small boy, my slave, he died, laid his body in front of a low cave, knowing his bones would protect what I had stolen, nine sacks of gold from the Church's coffers. I continued my journey, became lost, could not find my way back to the cave, wandered, vanquished, aimlessly, these three centuries past in this bleak desert without kith or kin of my Fatherland, pulling the church altar by this heavy chain at my ankles, grinding at my bones. That was my choice, as this is yours. Do right by yourself, first, or wander these dry depths the rest of your days.*

He stood, turned, sprinkling lime-green dust, fine as cat tail pollen as he floated to the cave's entrance, dropped something near the wall, a heavy clink on thin metal, a mighty gust caught him as he drifted into the dark, hurrying, as if afraid of losing Na-Tu and Two Sticks.

It was near noon when I dragged myself from my pad, Aunt June stamping at the end of my bedroll, groggy from too much sleep. The vision persisted, but I shook it off as so much foolhardy dreaming of a guilty man. I made my way to the cave's entrance, leaned against the red west wall, gazed toward the Sacramentos where I found Coot at his daddy's fishing cabin after Uncle Doyl passed. Such a long time ago, yet only ten years had crept by.

I turned to go back in the cave—*What was this?* A tin plate at the entrance, a large gold nugget sitting on it. I squatted down, picked up the lump, felt its heft. Papa's voice, telling a story first told centuries ago . . . I pulled my revolver, checked the cylinder—one spent cartridge. *But I never shoot this thing without immediately replacing . . .*

∗∗∗

I sat at the entrance of the cave, watched the rosy fingers of dawn fade to the sudden stark-white of the coolness of dawn on one side of the Nose—to the clear blue of noon—to the orange ball drop into the earth at sunset on the other side, wondering all that while, all those hours, if I yet possessed the self-discipline that Papa taught me. Just two weeks after I rode into this cave, the summer solstice marked the longest day of the year, the shortest shadow at noon, then every dawn and sunset since showed the sun's journey south toward the winter solstice. I recalled Papa telling me of the locomotive's red-tail hawk call, and man's reliance on a train whistle for punctuality of time—that soon there wouldn't be a man alive who could tell time by the sun or stars. How many years would pass before the solstices will come and go without man's notice, care, a single thought of their meaning? Not many . . .

Papa's constant admonition that I not dwell on my anger for Mama's unloving ways, and Ephesians warning, "Be ye angry, and sin not: let not the sun go down upon your wrath," haunted me. *How many hundreds of suns have set upon my wrath?* Coot warned me of that as well. Damn! If only—*Have the wish I wish tonight.*

Maybe I was dwelling too much into what I was reading in Papa's Bible, trying to make it fit me and my circumstances. That would be wrong. But would it? One blistery-cold night while Papa and I were sitting around our fire at Brazito, we were talking about that very thing. Papa said that in his youth, he was in Bexar, a town now known as San Antonio, and asked a *padre* about interpreting God's word, that often it made no sense to him. The old *padre* said, "Who am I but another man to tell you God's meaning? As long as you think freely and don't begin preaching your own interpretation, God will smile on your thoughts and grace them."

Corinthians 1:13 nudged me in the ribs. "When I was a child, I spake as a child, I understood as a child, I thought as a child: but when I became a man, I put away childish things."

I glanced around the cave, the feed sack generals dangling on wires from the roof, stick soldiers and horses leaning against its walls, a sawhorse at the ready at the entrance, all childish things of my youth. *I became a man, but only recently did I begin thinking and acting unmanly. I will—I must regain what I have lost!*

∗∗∗

The jerky that I'd smoked that first morning was long-gone. I hungered for meat. At first light, I rode north twenty miles to Rattlesnake Ridge at the southern end of the Organ Mountains, then west to the mouth of Devil's Canyon. It was boulder-strewn, rough going, tough on Aunt June, so I did not advance far. I led her into a shaded rock corral that Papa, Fernando Valdez, and I built fifteen years ago. At one time a spring flowed by, dried-up years back, forcing the three of us to dig a well down fifty-feet to water. I checked the heavy wire bail on the oaken bucket, flipped the release on the windlass, dropped the bucket down the dark shaft, heard it plop hollow on the water, let it fill, then cranked the bucket back up and set it in the corral for the mare. I walked another mile, found a likely spot deep in the dark shadows of a mahogany grove that gave me the cover I needed.

I leaned my head against the smooth boulder at my side, munched yesterday's *gordita*, dreamed of my days with Standing Elk as we hunted for antelope with Lukey No-No. Standing Elk cut off the corner of his red bandana, waved it on a yucca stalk, told us to hide ourselves, showing us how with a few tufts of grass, a bit of sand, disappearing with those few strokes of his bronze hands. The curious antelope came, Lukey No-No's long knife came up, slit the young animal's throat, it lay down, giving up its body so the People might live. Standing Elk's knife came out of the sand, and another antelope fell, yet another to the long knife that Many Fast Feet Two Sticks had given me at our camp on the Black River.

My dream gave way to a yawn. I sat up. A young mule deer spike stood peering at me, not more than twenty-yards away. He paid me no-never-mind, turned and hobbled up the canyon. Young, tender, yes, but limping. He'd be my supper, or that of a mountain lion. That old mama cat would just have to go find this spike's mama.

I dressed and quartered him, mounted Aunt June, went back to the cave, began cutting the meat of the carcass in strips, spending the balance of the day drying them on my mesquite-fed fire on small racks fashioned with green sticks. I sat close to the fire, tending it, reading Papa's Bible.

The scratch marks at the entrance of the cave told me that I'd been here fifty-three days. My smile was coming back. I'd read Papa's, *King James*, from, "In the beginning," to Revelation's ending edict, "And if any man shall take away from the words of the book of this prophecy, God shall take away his part of the book of life . . ."

Yesterday, I'd gone back to the start of the New Testament. My yucca-leaf-bookmark was at the reading of Chapter 6:3 of the Book of Matthew. My gaze lingered there. I read it again, twice. Read it aloud, listened to my voice. "But when thou doest alms, let not thy left hand know what thy right hand doeth."

I read on, Matthew 20: "For the kingdom of heaven is like unto a man that is an householder, which went out early in the morning to hire labourers into his vineyard. And when he had agreed with the labourers for a penny a day, he sent them into his vineyard. And he went out about the third hour, and saw others standing idle in the marketplace, And said unto them; Go ye also into the vineyard, and whatever is right I will give you. And they went their way."

I read through Verse 11 when the owner of the vineyard paid all the labourers the same penny, from the last he hired on the eleventh hour to first that he hired early that morning. They began to murmur against the goodman of the house. He reminded them that he had done them no wrong, had paid them as they had mutually agreed, asked them if it was not lawful for him to do what he would with what was his own? Is thine eye evil, because I am good?

Then 20:16: "So the last shall be first, and the first last: for many be called, but few chosen."

The concept of "fair" crossed my mind. Papa taught me that lesson early-on. "Son, there's no such thing as fair. The only fare is what you pay for a trolley ride."

Was I only to be called, or did I have the stuff to stand up to be chosen? Maybe I was guilty of reading into God's word what was not intended. But, Papa's conversation with the Bexar *padre* eased itself back in my mind.

My slumber that night was light, not full awake, nor deep sleep, smiling often, the verses taking hold, their meaning were directed to me, "... let not thy left hand know what thy right hand doeth."

Its meaning gnawed at me, I struggled, reached out, ever reaching out, but could not grasp it.

I recalled Na-Tu's words when I told him about Mama hitting me with the quirt. He peered in my eyes. "I see much anger, much guilt. You mama put anger in you heart, make you feel guilt. Those things do not belong to you. You must never speak of the time when you were milking the mama goat. If you choose to do so, it will come to possess you."

At dawn, I sat with the book between my knees, gazing down the valley and across the *Rio*, opened the book in the low light to Verse 6:3, again read it aloud. "But when thou doest alms, let not thy left hand know what thy right hand doeth."

That was it!

I jumped to my feet. By God in all His mercy, *that was it!* He might have pushed Mama off on me, but His grace also gave me Papa. What one took away, the other restored. Mama didn't steal my childhood, she had no mother in her to give or steal. All Papa's and my camping at the cave through all those years, our play-making at war, their real meanings, his reading and explaining the great books he always carried in his saddlebags, his love and affection and care for his son, all those two-month ventures to the Black River so Papa could get away from Mama were not that at all. They were intended to get *me* away from Mama's wrath, to the quiet and solitude of that magical place, to *this* place, to Papa's cave, his goldmine. A goldmine in every sense of the word, waiting for me to only reach out and grasp it. He allowed his sixteen-year-old son to ride off to the White Mountain Apache Reservation to live with Many Fast Feet and Na-Tu, to learn their ways, to learn and test what I had, the mettle of my heart and soul. All of Papa's kindness, his wisdom, his patience with his son, showing me through his every thought, action, and deed the way of a real man to love.

"Yes! *Thank God Almighty*. Papa replaced my childhood, *double*. He restored Mama's ill-treatment of me with grace and kindness. He made certain that nothing lacked while I was growing up. I lacked *nothing!*"

I grabbed up Papa's Bible, retrieved the piece of wrapping paper where he had made notes, sat down and wrote on the back of it my newfound self-knowledge, three simple sentences: who I am, what I believe, how I intend to live the rest of my days.

I had done it. My ear-to-ear smile felt good. I stepped back to the big red rock, reached in my vest pocket for Papa's bandana holding my bit of gold, and Bernard Gruber's golden nugget, folded them together with Papa's wrapping paper, put them all back under the red rock in Papa's mine.

I looked around the cave one more time, smiled, packed-up Aunt June, and started down the mountain.

47

El Paso
March 26, 1886

"*S*enor Montgomery, a man he is at the door. He say he wants to talk to you."

"*Quien es, Ines?*"

"*No se, Senor.*" She shrugged. "*Un hombre—muy viejo. Muy alto.*"

Papa stood. "Son, I need to be on my way—"

"Please keep your seat, Papa. You too, Coot. IB stay where you are. Won't take but a minute. Besides, we need to decide what we're going to do for this scoundrel's twenty-seventh birthday."

The front door framed a tall, gaunt, elderly man. A stranger, somehow familiar, wearing an expensive pinstriped suit, certainly not a local.

"Good morning, sir. What can I do for you? Won't you come in?"

"Good morning." He doffed his hat. "Mr. Montgomery, I presume."

"Yes, please come in."

He braced himself against the door frame, leaned with both hands on his walking cane, took a long breath. "It would be nice—nice to sit, after—after climbing those concrete stairs. Must be three stories down to the street."

"Come in and sit on the divan. It's real—"

"*No*—no, please. If you don't mind, I'll just sit there at your dining room table. Nice, tall, straight-back chairs." He chuckled. "If I sat in that low divan, I would never be able to haul these old bones up again."

He stepped over to the arm chair at the end of the table, turned, offered his hand. "Forgive me, sir. Allow me to introduce myself. I am Buford C. Goodyear." He sat, sighed.

Papa and Coot came in and introduced themselves. Coot shot me a glance, asked, "Did I hear you say your name is Goodyear?"

I shooshed IB when he asked who the old gent was.

The old gentleman's head turned, his pale-hazel eyes glistened in the single ray of sun shining through the east window, flashed a hint of emerald. "Yes, I did say my name is Goodyear. You gentlemen don't know me, but I, and my traveling companion, just stepped off the east-bound train. California's a long train ride. Difficult trip for an old geezer like me, a delight for my young companion."

Papa asked, "Mr. Goodyear, could I get you some water? You look mighty tired. Do you need to lay down?" Papa smiled. "We old timers need to stick close."

"Sir, you're just a pup." He chuckled. "No, I'll be all right. Just need a moment to I catch my breath. This altitude has the better of me. The conductor told me that your city is at near 3,800-feet. Far cry from the sea level of San Francisco."

Coot pulled out the chair at the far end of the table and sat, shooting me another glance.

IB said, "Thet old man shor is an old 'un, ain't he, Coot?"

The old man chuckled. "You're right about that, my dear man. My niece's father, Mr. George Goodyear passed away just last month. Ninety-two-years-old." Again he chuckled, hazel eyes dancing. "*Humph!* My brother was a mere youngster."

He sat, his gnarled hands fingering the gold knob at the top of his walking cane. He took a long breath, sighed. "I don't know where or how to begin to explain the purpose of my visit. Please give me a moment to gather my thoughts, decide how to approach the purpose of my calling on you."

His gaze swept around the room to the fireplace mantle. He studied Sophie's mother's flowery plates that were still displayed there, leaning against the wall. Need to pack those plates away, or give them to charity. Didn't even realize they were still there.

Mr. Goodyear glanced down to the far end of the table, studied Coot for a bit. "You say your name is Boldt. Must be that Coot fellow that George spoke of, said he enjoyed your company, chatting, discussing the patent process as I recall. Fellow inventor, are you?"

"Oh, no sir. Mr. Goodyear's the inventor. I just enjoyed talking to him. Smart man."

He braced on his cane, scooted back in the chair, pushed himself straight against the chair, dabbed at his tearing eyes with a silk hanky from his lapel pocket. "Your part of the world is rather dusty, isn't it? Of course, the soot from that dastard-ly locomotive didn't help."

He scooted his chair around to face us. "Where to begin? George Goodyear—he was my younger brother. Did I mention that? He was married to a beautiful woman, Grace, who died the morning after her child was born. Auburn hair, hazel eyes that sparked a bit of emerald in the sunlight. Rather like George's, come to think of it. He passed away last month, but I think I mentioned that before. A day or two after George's funeral, maybe it was a week later. I don't recall, probably not important. No, it was two days after my brother's funeral." He smiled, waved his hand. "*Ha!* As I was saying, shortly after George's funeral, a young couple showed up at my door. Their news came as a shock to me. They announced that they had been employed by George for the past two years as nanny and caregiver for a young boy. They told me his name, informed me that George had told them only recently that if anything untoward happened to him, that they should immediately contact me. So sooth, I had never heard of this lad. *And,* I was named executor of George's estate."

He banged his cane down on the table. "Now, I ask you. Why in God's holy name would that old fool appoint a ninety-four-year-old man the executor of *anything*, much less a million-dollar estate, *and* put in custodial care of a two-year-old boy? *I ask you.* Doesn't make a lick of sense, but neither did most of what my now-deceased brother ever had to say or do. He was a weird one, even when we were youngsters. Always mixing this with that." He banged his cane on the floor. "Damn near burned our parent's house to the ground, *at three o'clock in the morning,* when one of his experiments caught fire. Required the services of three fire companies to extinguish the flames. Cost Father over a thousand-dollars in repairs and refurbishment."

He fidgeted with his cane, brushed his lapel with his hanky, gazed back up at the flowered plates on the mantel. "I let the lawyers and accountants sort through George's various banking connections, his voluminous patents, all those sorts of money-matters. The will called for the greater amount of his holdings to be placed in trust for a local orphanage, and $100,000 in trust for his grandson. Have I told you about that lad? No, I don't suppose that I have. At any rate, I tended to his personal papers, and the *very* first thing I came across was a letter, folded, placed in a sealed envelope, with proper postage affixed. It was dated April 1, 1884. Why he never placed that letter in the mail is anyone's guess, but the man's name to which it was addressed spoke volumes.

"The purpose of that letter was to inform the intended recipient of the untimely death of George's only child, his daughter, Willy Peabody."

I stood. "*What?* WP's dead?" My mind swirled, I sat before I slumped. *I still loved her?*

IB asked, "What's a WP?"

"Indeed, sir. George's letter explained that WP's infection contracted at the hospital became increasingly severe, necessitating the amputation of her foot. Her right foot, as I recall. No, it was her left foot. *Yes*, that's it. I'm *certain* it was her left foot. Anyway, it seems she asked George to take her down the lawn in her wheelchair to a spot overlooking the bay to the west, high above the crashing waves on the sandy beach just to the north of the rocks. George said she often asked him to wheel her to that spot, pointing down to the wet sand, saying, 'Father, that is Narlow's and my spot.'"

Mr. Goodyear wiped his chin with his handkerchief, tucked it away.

"On WP's last day on this earth, March 31, 1884, George once again wheeled his daughter down the lush lawn to the cliff, quite near the precipice. She was weak, not only was she suffering from the loss of her foot and her ongoing bout with the infection, she had given birth to her son only a little more than a month previously. Willy Peabody was dressed in a white dress with a blue shawl about her shoulders. She asked George to wheel her closer to the precipice so she could look over the cliff at the wet sand. She asked for a hanky from her purse that George had set down behind the wheelchair when he first set the brake. He stepped back, got the hanky from her purse, and when he turned back to her, the wheelchair was empty. He gazed all around, stepped over to the precipice, afraid to look at what he knew he'd see—his only child, dressed in white with a blue shawl, sprawled on the wet sand of the beach."

Dear God! Both WP and Sophie took their own lives on my twenty-fifth birthday! One by willing it, the other by throwing herself off a cliff. To blame me? For vengeance? Escape? Spite?

I said, "Mr. Goodyear, I—"

He waved his hand. "The young lad that the couple brought to me is two years old. The name on his certificate of birth reads, Narlow Willy Peabody Montgomery, born February 14, 1884." *Papa's birthday!*

IB grinned. "Some of thet name's yor'n, Nar-low."

I froze. My face tightened. Felt my ears point forward, the muscles in my face pull my cheeks taut—taut as trace trains—like WP's slender body. *My God—I thought I was over her, but I still loved her.* That cannot be! I only loved her body, being in her presence, acting the big shot in a glamorous metropolitan city with a famous woman, the talk of the town. I glanced at Papa, at Coot, looking for support. They both were sitting quietly like matched bookends, their arms dropped down between their knees, their eyes wide.

"Mr. Montgomery, I realize this is all coming at you in a torrent, but how else can an old man explain it all?"

Papa asked, "Where is this lad now?"

"When I arrived in El Paso, I hired a man and buggy. I liked the man, said his name was LeRoy Glardon, smiled, said all his friends called him, 'Slim.' He appeared to be honest, dependable, tall as a tree, stout as a rail tie, said he knew you, Mr.

Montgomery, and your son, Narlow, said they were school chums, said he would be pleased to deliver me and my companion to your home. Refused my insistence to pay him for his services. Not knowing how this interview would conclude, I left little Narlow with Slim Glardon in the buggy down on the street."

I said, "Mr. Goodyear, that boy cannot be mine. Why, WP and I only—"

Again he waved me off. "I am not in a position to say whether he is your son or not, but I can tell you this. That boy was born nine months, *almost to the day*, after the carriage in which Willy Peabody Goodyear was riding collided with a cable car. George told me that you were also in that carriage, stayed with his daughter in the hospital for days-on-end, cared for her, looked after her night and day. Then suddenly you just disappeared, fell off the face of the earth, as far as George was able to determine." He reached in his coat pocket, produced a single sheet of embossed paper. "You'll see that you are named the father of that boy on this certificate of birth."

Coot smiled, slammed the palm of his hand down on the table. "I'll be pleased to go down and fetch that boy from ol' Slim."

My mind swirled, unable to get my arms around it all. This boy *could not be mine*. WP and I were only together that *one time*. Only that *one night*. This boy simply *could not* . . .

Papa came to my side as Coot led the little man in by his hand. The way he held himself, small as he was, he stood erect, the tilt of his head, just like Papa did, just like . . .

I went to him, got down on one knee, gazed into his hazel eyes, the sunray caught them, an emerald glint flashed. Papa smiled down at the boy, gave him a wink, the boy smiled, gestured his hands to be picked up. Papa leaned over and lifted him to his chest, gave him a tussle. The boy stuck his finger in Papa's nose, pulled on it.

"Well, if you aren't something. You better be nice to me, Little Narlow. Know why? We share the very same birthday." Papa handed the boy to me.

I gazed into his eyes, bright, filled with wonderment. They might not be exactly my eyes, but they were dern certain his mother's.

"Hey, young man, you're sure big for a two-year-old. Heavy as an anvil. Let me put you down, stand back a ways, take a good look at what we have here."

The boy stood with his arms at his side, his hands fell naturally, not flat against his sides, but turned to show the backside of his hands and wrists. Big hands for such a little boy, wide wrists. Pale-hazel eyes, a glint of emerald.

IB grinned down at the boy. "Thet lil' boy shor is a fam-iliar little cuss."

Papa and I stood in front of the doorway, the little boy between us.

I sensed it.

I *knew* it.

Coot smiled. "What do you think, Mr. Goodyear? See any resemblance? Those three look like the first, second, and third edition to you?"

"Like three peas in a pod."

Readers Guide

After the Civil War, the West was inhabited by all manner of men and women. Most were good folks looking to better their lot, men of means who had lost everything, some ignorant but willing, others conniving, murderous bottom-feeders such as Seth and Rye who violated IB Crane in 1873.

Coot Boldt and Narlow Montgomery were born in 1859, spent a goodly part of their growing up years with the Apaches on their Arizona Territory reservation. The boys were rough and ready, but well-educated by Narlow's Papa Abe. Under Papa's care, they read every book in his possession as well as the well-stocked library owned by Simeon Hart down at the Pass. They gave up their golden opportunity of a university education wanting instead to heed the call of the wild, to see the West before the whistle of the eastbound train erased it for all time.

Papa squatted, threw a mesquite limb in the fire, watched the sparks rise, orange, snapping as they rose in the wet snow. He chuckled. "Humph! You boys ever try to wear two pair of boots to a dance? Don't need that stuff, that gold. Simply stated, Fernando Valdez and I are not equipped to handle it."

Q. Narlow was surprised that Papa had left so many clues indicating he knew he was headed for the reservation and not the new university in Austin. Were you surprised at Narlow's decision to jump off that Austin-bound stagecoach, mount Traveler and head out for the Arizona Territory?

Coot returned home with a new "bride and a biscuit" in the oven. Narlow married Sophie shortly after.

Q. What do you suppose was going through Narlow's head when he married Sophie? Did Coot coming home a married man push Narlow to a similar fate? Escape from his parent's dugout, his mama's lashing tongue?

Sophie's tragic sexual experiences as a child led her to repeated suicide attempts.

Q. Why would a woman go through with marriage if she was so frightened of fulfilling her "wifely duties"? Have things, has society changed that much since they were married in 1883?

Q. Narlow's frustration with Sophie was certainly understandable, but was his haste to carry out his angst on the two slicks from Dallas understandable after eighteen months of marriage?

Narlow slipped back to allowing his mother to reenter his life and once again, become an anchor on his shoulder.

Q. Why would a man allow his mother to impact his life as a mature man?

Narlow was filled with self-doubt; was hesitant, reluctant to buy the Camel Mountain Ranch, then anxious about Coot and him solving the railroad's water problems for a tremendous amount of money, the result of his experiences and self-doubts about women—and himself.

Q. From your own life experiences, can you relate to Narlow's withdrawal?

Papa and Fernando Valdez explained to Coot and Narlow why they did not want to keep the contents of the nine leather pouches of gold.

Q. At Papa's and Fernando's age, background, work ethic, what possibility of happiness do you think those men could possibly have enjoyed if they threw aside their lifestyles and set out to spend the great wealth contained in those leather pouches?

Narlow retreats into Papa's cave, his goldmine.

Q. Why is it so often a place in our past where the dark secrets seem to rise to the surface?

As Narlow rode Aunt June near the entrance of Papa's cave, he became reluctant to go further, even entertained a fleeting notion of quitting that nonsense and going home, get him a jug.

Q. What do you suppose was the cause of unwillingness to return to that place that was such an influential, pleasant setting for his youth?

Papa strongly suggested that until his son could write out a few simple sentences as to who he was, what he was about, and how he would live his life, that he'd never get himself back on track. You'll recall that just before he packed up Aunt June, he retrieved the brown paper from Papa's Bible, knelt down and began writing.

Q. What do you suppose Narlow wrote on that small scrap of paper that had been tucked in his father's Bible all those years?

WP Goodyear's aged uncle brought two-year-old Narlow Willy Peabody Montgomery to El Paso in 1886, two years after his mother's death on the rocks of San Francisco Bay.

Q. Can you imagine the life that little tyke had in that era, how he must have impacted the life of his father?

www.ingramcontent.com/pod-product-compliance
Lightning Source LLC
Chambersburg PA
CBHW020427030726
47495CB00006B/1692